Ramses
the
Great

Ramses
the
Great

Introduction by
Charlotte Booth

General Editor: Jake Jackson

**FLAME TREE
PUBLISHING**

This is a FLAME TREE Book

FLAME TREE PUBLISHING
6 Melbray Mews
Fulham, London SW6 3NS
United Kingdom
www.flametreepublishing.com

First published 2024
Copyright © 2023 Flame Tree Publishing Ltd

24 26 28 27 25
1 3 5 7 9 8 6 4 2

ISBN: 978-1-80417-718-1
ebook ISBN: 978-1-80417-996-3

Cover image created by Flame Tree Studio based on elements of a statue of Ramses II
and the God Ptah, photo by Jakub Hałun (Creative Commons Attribution-Share Alike
International license).

All inside images courtesy of Shutterstock.com and the following: Viktoriia_P, Lumir
Strbacka, Liudmila Klymenko.

This book is compiled and edited, with a new introduction, from *Egypt Under Rameses
the Great* by E.A. Wallis Budge, Vol V of A History of Egypt, published by Kegan Paul,
Trench, Trubner & Co. Ltd., 1902; with some preceding history from *A History of Egypt:
from the Earliest Times to the Persian Conquest*, by James Henry Breasted, published by
Charles Scribner's Sons, 1909.

Designed and created in the UK | Printed and bound in China

Contents

Series Foreword... 8

Introduction to Ramses the Great........................... 10
    Pharaoh of the Bible... 11
    Ramses' Inheritance... 12
    The Royal Harem 14
    Battle of Kadesh 16
    Building Works...17
    Modern Discoveries 18
    The Future... 20

The New Kingdom Before Ramses II.....................22
    The New State: Society and Religion................................... 23
    The Consolidation of the Kingdom; The Rise of
        the Empire 38
    The Feud of the Thutmosids and the Reign of
        Queen Hatshepsut... 48
    The Consolidation of the Empire: Thutmose III................ 62
    The Empire... 91
    The Religious Revolution of Ikhnaton...............................115
    The Fall of Ikhnaton, and the Dissolution of
        the Empire 136

The Ramesside Era.......................................148

    The Nineteenth Dynasty 149
        Rameses I 149
        Seti I... 151
        Rameses II.. 158
            Rameses' Wars in Nubia, Libya and Syria............... 159
            The Battle of Kadesh...160
            Renewed Hostitlities and Final Peace Treaty 167

Rameses Marries a Kheta Princess............................169
The Works and Buildings of Rameses II.................170
Wives and Family of Rameses II.............................175
Tomb and Mummy of Rameses II 176
Mythical Exploits of Rameses II a.k.a Sesostris? 178
Menephthah...191

The Exodus of the Israelites from Egypt..........................199
Seti II...210
Amenmeses..212
Sa-Ptah...214

The Twentieth Dynasty...216
Set-nekht..216
Rameses III..218
Rameses IV..238
Rameses V 239
Rameses VI..240
Rameses VII 241
Rameses VIII..242
Rameses IX...243
Rameses X..249
Rameses XI...251
Rameses XII 253

Series Foreword

STRETCHING BACK to the oral traditions of thousands of years ago, tales of heroes and disaster, creation and conquest have been told by many different civilizations in many different ways. Their impact sits deep within our culture even though the detail in the tales themselves are a loose mix of historical record, transformed narrative and the distortions of hundreds of storytellers.

Today the language of mythology lives with us: our mood is jovial, our countenance is saturnine, we are narcissistic and our modern life is hermetically sealed from others. The nuances of myths and legends form part of our daily routines and help us navigate the world around us, with its half truths and biased reported facts.

The nature of a myth is that its story is already known by most of those who hear it, or read it. Every generation brings a new emphasis, but the fundamentals remain the same: a desire to understand and describe the events and relationships of the world. Many of the great stories are archetypes that help us find our own place, equipping us with tools for self-understanding, both individually and as part of a broader culture.

For Western societies it is Greek mythology that speaks to us most clearly. It greatly influenced the mythological heritage of the ancient Roman civilization and is the lens through which we still see the Celts, the Norse and many of the other great peoples and religions. The Greeks themselves learned much from their neighbours, the Egyptians, an older culture that became weak with age and incestuous leadership.

It is important to understand that what we perceive now as mythology had its own origins in perceptions of the divine and the rituals of the sacred. The earliest civilizations, in the crucible of the Middle East, in the Sumer of the third millennium BC, are the source to which many of the mythic archetypes can be traced. As humankind collected together in cities for the first time, developed writing and industrial-scale agriculture, started to irrigate the rivers and attempted to control rather than be at the mercy of its environment, humanity began to write down its tentative explanations of natural events, of floods and plagues, of disease.

Early stories tell of Gods (or god-like animals in the case of tribal societies such as African, Native American or Aboriginal cultures) who are crafty and use their wits to survive, and it is reasonable to suggest that these were the first rulers of the gathering peoples of the earth, later elevated to god-like status with the distance of time. Such tales became more political as cities vied with each other for supremacy, creating new Gods, new hierarchies for their pantheons. The older Gods took on primordial roles and became the preserve of creation and destruction, leaving the new gods to deal with more current, everyday affairs. Empires rose and fell, with Babylon assuming the mantle from Sumeria in the 1800s BC, then in turn to be swept away by the Assyrians of the 1200s BC; then the Assyrians and the Egyptians were subjugated by the Greeks, the Greeks by the Romans, and so on, leading to the spread and assimilation of common themes, ideas and stories throughout the world.

The survival of history is dependent on the telling of good tales, but each one must have the 'feeling' of truth, otherwise it will be ignored. Around the firesides, or embedded in a book or a computer, the myths and legends of the past are still the living materials of retold myth, not restricted to an exploration of origins. Now we have devices and global communications that give us unparalleled access to a diversity of traditions. We can find out about Indigenous American, Indian, Chinese and tribal African mythology in a way that was denied to our ancestors; we can find connections, match the archaeology, religion and the mythologies of the world to build a comprehensive image of the human adventure.

The great leaders of history and heroes of literature have also adopted the mantle of mythic experience, because the stories of historical figures – Cyrus the Great, Alexander, Genghis Khan – and mytho-poetic warriors such as Beowulf achieve a cultural significance that transcends their moment in the chronicles of humankind. Myth, history and literature have become powerful, intwined instruments of perception, with echoes of reported fact and symbolic truths that convey the sweep of human experience. In this series of books we are glad to share with you the wonderful traditions of the past.

Jake Jackson
General Editor

Introduction to Ramses the Great

T HE LONG REIGN OF RAMSES II (1279–12 BCE) of the Nineteenth Dynasty, better known today as Ramses the Great, was considered to be the second high point of the New Kingdom, following the reign of Amenhotep III a century before. Egypt slowly lost stability and wealth following Ramses' death. He was a larger-than-life king who built more monuments, had a bigger tomb, had more children and wives, and, dying after 66 years on the throne, ruled longer than most other kings (with only Pepy II of the Sixth Dynasty ruling longer, at 94 years).

Ramses II is a king who is as well known in the modern day as perhaps he was in ancient times. He was immortalized in Percy Bysshe Shelley's poem 'Ozymandias' (1817), which was inspired by the colossal statue from the Ramesseum (the funerary temple of Ramses II at Thebes), which is now in the British Museum.

I met a traveller from an antique land
Who said: 'two vast and trunkless legs of stone
Stand in the desert. Near them on the sand,
Half sunk, a shattered visage lies, whose frown
And wrinkled lip and sneer of cold command
Tell that its sculptor well those passions read
Which yet survive, stamped on these lifeless things,
The hand that mocked them and the heart that fed.
And on the pedestal these words appear:
"My name is Ozymandias, king of kings:
Look on my works, ye mighty, and despair!"
Nothing besides remains. Round the decay
Of that colossal wreck, boundless and bare,
The lone and level sands stretch faraway.'

Pharaoh of the Bible

Even prior to this 1817 poem, Ramses was famous as the most popular candidate to have been the pharaoh from the biblical Exodus, even though in the Bible the king is never actually named and is simply referred to as 'pharaoh'.

The biblical references that led to this belief were to be found in place names: 'the land of Ramses' (Genesis 47:11), and 'treasure cities Pithom and Ramses' (Exodus 1:11). Such references were enough to associate Ramses II with the pharaoh of the Exodus, even though Pithom was thought to have been built by Necho II (610–595 BCE) many centuries after Ramses II, and there were in fact 11 kings called Ramses.

Pithom (Tell el Maskhuta) was not discovered until 1883, and then only excavated and confirmed as this city in the 1970s by a team from the University of Toronto, a long time after the biblical texts had been written. The site had been occupied during the Hyksos period (1663–1555 BCE) but was then abandoned until the reign of Necho II, indicating that the city was empty during the reign of all 11 of the Ramses.

As Ken Kitchen, an expert on Ramses II, said in 1990:

> *The Bible and the classics no longer stood in lonely isolation against aeons of dark, 'prehistoric night', but could be viewed against the breath-taking, richly tapestried background of millennially-ancient and brilliant civilisations.*

However, even Kitchen presents Ramses as the pharaoh of the Exodus with no evidence other than the biblical references that may have been written in the sixth century BCE, some 600 years after the event.

The texts in the following book discuss the pharaoh of the Exodus, with E.A. Wallis Budge (1902) dedicating his second chapter to the Exodus and the identity of Moses. Budge discusses theories regarding the Hyksos expulsion at the start of the Eighteenth Dynasty as the Exodus of the Jews, and that Merenptah, the successor of Ramses II, was the pharaoh who instigated the event. However, Budge is clear that the word 'pharaoh' comes from the Egyptian for 'Great House' (Palace) *per-aa* and was 'a title which was borne by every king of Egypt, and it therefore does not enable us to identify the oppressor king'.

James Henry Breasted (1909), on the other hand, briefly discusses the theory of Merenptah being the king of the Exodus and comments that 'his body has recently been found there [Thebes], quite discomfiting the adherents of the theory that, as the undoubted Pharaoh of the Hebrew Exodus, he must have drowned in the Red Sea'. Budge also makes it clear that Ramses II did not die in the Red Sea.

Archaeology and the written record were able to challenge such long-held ideas, with scientific proof bringing to life the ancient Egyptian civilization. However, many of these ideas are so long held and deep-rooted that no amount of archaeological evidence will change some people's minds, as the idea is tied in with religious belief and faith. The discussions are as passionate in 2023 as they were in 1903.

Ramses' Inheritance

The importance of the biblical beliefs surrounding the reign of Ramses II and his son Merenptah led to an interest in the Hyksos period of Egyptian history at the turn of the twentieth century. This period (1663–1555 BCE) was characterized by Asiatic rulers of Egypt, governing initially from their capital of Tell el-Dab'a in the Delta. Early twentieth-century scholars emphasized the importance of this era as they believed it eventually led to the Exodus of the Jews from Egypt. However, this was long before the Hyksos period was understood properly.

In 1909, when Breasted was writing about this period of history, his evidence was primarily a text by Manetho written 1,300 years after the Hyksos rulers were overthrown. Breasted was also writing some 60 years before the discoveries at Avaris and Tell el-Dab'a, the Hyksos capital, by archaeologist Manfred Bietak in the 1960s and 1970s. These discoveries totally rewrote this period of history, showing the inhabitants here were not of Jewish faith, but instead worshipped traditional Canaanite and Syrian deities such as Anath, Ba'al, Astarte and Reshef, with the Hyksos kings also showing an adoption of traditional Egyptian deities. This period therefore seems little connected to Ramses II, as the Eighteenth Dynasty kings including Thutmose III (1504–1450 BCE) and Amenhotep III (1386–49 BCE) re-established lost traditions and abandoned temples and political alliances.

The timeline that genuinely leads to Ramses II ascending the throne starts in the Amarna period (1350–34 BCE), when Akhenaten was pharaoh. Akhenaten would today be known as a 'disruptor', as he altered the lives of the Egyptian people by abandoning the traditional pantheon of gods and replacing it with the sun disc Aten, himself and his wife Nefertiti. Instead of having a complex pantheon of gods to approach for every aspect of life, health and death, the people were expected to go through the king, who could commune personally with the Aten.

The capital city was moved from Thebes and Memphis and transferred to Akhetaten (Amarna) in a previously uninhabited area of desert in Middle Egypt. Akhenaten rarely left the city, and was totally absorbed by his new religion, eschewing his other royal duties. However, these changes were not to last, and Akhenaten's son Tutankhamun, when he came to the throne at age nine, reinstated the traditional religion and moved the capital city back to Thebes. He effectively undid the 17 years of damage that his father had caused.

Tutankhamun was supported in his endeavours to reinstate the splendours of the Golden Age of his grandfather, Amenhotep III (1386–49 BCE), by two officials: Ay, who may have been an uncle, and Horemheb, the general of the army. Both succeeded Tutankhamun on the throne in the absence of any sons.

Horemheb was also lacking in sons to take over once he died, and he instead turned to his vizier and friend, Ramses – who was Ramses II's grandfather. Horemheb chose Ramses as he already had a son, Sety, and a grandson, Ramses, meaning he was placing a new dynasty on the throne, not just one man. Horemheb was later deified by the family, and was seen as the head of their lineage, right until the end of the reign of Ramses II.

Although Horemheb, Ramses I and Sety I had done their bit to reinstate the majesty of Egypt, restore monuments that had been neglected, reinstate borders and renegotiate political alliances, Ramses II, throughout his long reign, continued their work.

The Royal Harem

With so many monuments surviving, including tombs, temples and written documents, we have a clear idea of Ramses' family life. He was born in 1304 BCE to Sety I and Muttuya. She was the daughter of the lieutenant of chariotry named Raia. There is evidence that he had at least two sisters, Tia and Hunetmire, although it is likely that he had more siblings and half siblings, as was traditional for Egyptian royalty.

Ramses had a number of wives, which included his sister Hunetmire. This marriage did not bear any children. She was, however, given the honour of a tomb in the Valley of the Queens (QV75) when she died in the 40th year of his reign.

It was traditional for Egyptian kings to marry their sisters, often just to prevent them from marrying elsewhere. Thutmose II (1518–04 BCE), Thutmose III (1504–1450 BCE) and Tutankhamun (1334–25 BCE) had all married their sisters, and Akhenaten (1350–34 BCE) and Ramses II also married their daughters, with Ramses' daughter Bintanath bearing him a child.

In the New Kingdom, princesses were generally not permitted to marry anyone of lower status than a prince, and even foreign princes were out of bounds. Any unsuitable marriages could end up being a threat, so limiting the number of grandchildren and relatives with a claim to the throne was a strong incentive.

For many years, Egyptologists believed these marriages were part of the 'heiress theory' where the royal line passed through the women, meaning it was necessary to marry and have children through the females of the family. This theory has long been debunked, however, due to the number of queens and king's mothers who were not of royal blood.

As only the royal family was permitted to marry incestuously, it further connected them with the deities. All kings were viewed as the living Horus, becoming Osiris upon death, as well as holding the royal title of Son of Ra. Many kings, including Ramses II, further legitimized their divine status with a divine birth scene in which the god Amun impregnates their mother. In the mythology surrounding the gods, they were known for their brother/sister marriages (Isis/Osiris, Nut/Geb, Shu/Tefnut) and this was therefore another way of emphasizing divinity.

Even if these incestuous marriages were necessary for political reasons, not all ended in children, and the king was able to choose his principal wife from his harem.

Ramses II's principal wife was Nefertari, who is also buried in the Valley of the Queens (QV66). Little personal information is known about her to the extent that her parents' names are unrecorded and, as she does not hold the title of King's Daughter, she is likely to be of non-royal descent. It is thought Amenmose, the mayor of Thebes, was her brother, although his parents are also unknown.

Nefertari is likely to have come from the harem of Ramses II, and it is no surprise that he had dozens of wives. His father, Sety I, as a gift to mark their co-regency, gave him a harem of 'female royal attendants, who were like the great beauties of the palace'. These beauties would have comprised a number of eligible unmarried women who could be potential wives or concubines. Two of Ramses' children were named Meher-anath (Child of Anath) and Astarteherwenemef (Astarte is on his right), which were Asiatic and suggests he may have had Asiatic women in the harem as well.

In fact, Ramses' Marriage Stela records his marriage with the daughter of the Hittite king. She was given the title of Great Royal Wife, which was generally unheard of for a foreign princess. There are also a number of letters between Ramses and Queen Padukhepa, the mother of the princess, as the pharaoh was anxious about the delayed arrival of his bride. The princess, her entourage and her dowry had been escorted to southern Syria, where she had been further delayed by snow. When she was able to continue her journey to Egypt she was 'beautiful in the heart of his majesty and he loved her more than anything', and she was given the Egyptian name of Maat-hor-neferura. Despite the apparent excitement at a new bride, the Marriage Stela, which was recorded at Abu Simbel, Amara, Karnak and Elephantine, reflects the political nature of the marriage, showing Maat-hor-neferura was little more than a tribute from an inferior ruler. Ten years later, the Hittite king agreed to another marriage, possibly following the death of Maat-hor-neferura.

Another principal wife was a woman called Isetnofret, who replaced Nefertari on the monuments as principal wife following her death in or around year 24 of the king. She does not hold the title King's Daughter either and, more than likely, was also of non-royal birth. Nefertari and Isetnofret between them had 11 children of all Ramses' offspring: the four oldest sons, and the seven oldest daughters.

However, a list of Ramses' children at Karnak shows he had at least 46 sons and 55 daughters. It is thought that a number of them may have died before reaching child-bearing age, and many of the girls married their father to prevent becoming a threat to the throne. Many died before their father. It was Merenptah, the 13th son, in fact, who took over the throne following Ramses' death. Merenptah was already in his 60s by the time he became king, which in ancient Egypt was of advanced age.

Battle of Kadesh

Ramses was only really involved in one military campaign, which he recorded in great detail on the walls of his monuments. This was the battle of Kadesh, against the Hittites. The conflict had started during his father's reign as a means of regaining territory that was lost during the reign of Akhenaten and the Amarna period. Ramses II wanted to finish the job.

There were two battle reports: the bulletin and the poem. The bulletin was recorded at the temples of Luxor, Karnak, Abydos and the Ramesseum, and the poem was at the same sites as well as at Abu Simbel. Two hieratic copies were also discovered at Deir el Medina, which may have been designed to have been read out to the villagers. The bulletin is a concise record, focusing on the day of the battle and the activities at Kadesh, whereas the poem has more epic tendencies and starts about a month before the battle, recording the run up to the final conflict. The poem is also more bombastic in nature as it emphasizes the divinity of the king and how the Hittites were quaking in fear of him. The images accompanying the text follow some formulaic scenes, such as the piles of dismembered hands as a means of counting the fallen enemy, and smiting scenes with the king standing upon a fallen figure of a Hittite soldier as he is ready to club another. However, one aspect of the imagery accompanying these battle records that is remarkable is the utter chaos that is presented. Even the Egyptians are shown as being central to the chaos of fallen Hittite soldiers; piles of bodies with the Egyptian chariots and horses riding over them. However, despite this unusual approach, this imagery is mere propaganda, as no victories of the Hittites or weaknesses of the Egyptians are recorded.

Battle reports are always written by the winners, and Ramses' reports show his great victory in this battle, even though in reality it appeared to have ended in a stalemate. The reports hint at Ramses' poor skills as a general due to his trusting nature, which affected his military judgement. For example, when two men approached the king, he believed their story that they had abandoned the Hittite army and wanted to join the Egyptians. To show their legitimacy, they told the king of the location of the Hittite army. However, when two Hittite scouts were later picked up and beaten, it turns out the army was actually a lot closer than Ramses had been told, putting him on the back foot, unprepared when the Hittites attacked. The Egyptian army fled, leaving Ramses to deal with the ambush alone. Luckily, he had the support of Amun, who helped him win the battle single-handedly, although the back-up corps of the Egyptian army arriving in time to save the battle may also have had something to do with it.

Ramses II was all about hyperbole and bombastic claims, and a casual onlooker need look no further than the monuments he left behind to see this 'look at me' nature.

Building Works

Ramses is known as one of the most prolific builders in ancient Egypt, and his monuments cover the length and breadth of the land, from Abu Simbel at Aswan in the far south to his city at Pi-Ramses in the north. Not only did he build his own monuments from scratch, but he also made additions to the works of others to expand them, or simply to carve his name onto monuments dating back to the Middle Kingdom and therefore taking ownership of them. Just a few of his works include:

- Moving the capital city from Thebes and Memphis, building a new city at Pi-Ramses in the Delta.
- Adding a pylon to Luxor temple and completing the Hypostyle Hall at Karnak that had been started by his grandfather Ramses I and designed by Horemheb.

- Completing his father's mortuary temple on the west bank at Thebes.
- Completing his father's temple at Abydos, as well as making his own extension to the temple. The artwork of Sety I is in raised relief, and Ramses II's is in the easier-to-produce sunken relief.
- Building his own mortuary temple, the Ramesseum, on the west bank at Thebes, using 3,000 workmen at Gebel el Silsila to quarry the stone for the temple.
- Building numerous temples in Nubia, including Beit el Wali, Gerf Hussein, Wadi es Sebua, Derr and Napata.
- Building the two temples at Abu Simbel, one dedicated to Amun but fronted by four colossal statues of himself, and the other to Hathor with colossal statues of his wife Nefertari on the façade, with even larger images of himself.
- Commissioning the longest tomb in the Valley of the Kings for his burial (KV7), as well as finishing the tomb of his father, Sety I (KV17).
- Commissioning a tomb for the burial of his sons in the Valley of the Kings (KV5) and, although it had been recorded in 1835, it was not properly excavated until 1985 when it was rediscovered by Kent Weeks. So far, 95 chambers have been recovered.
- Building a tomb for Nefertari in the Valley of the Queens (QV66), as well as one (QV75) for his sister wife Hunetmire.

It is little surprise that Ramses II became such a well-known king and was considered to be the greatest king of all time, as his cartouche can be seen on various monuments throughout the full length of Egypt.

Modern Discoveries

Pi-Rameses

One of the greatest discoveries associated with the reign of Ramses II was the excavation of the capital city Pi-Rameses in the Delta. Ramses had wanted to build a capital city to rival Thebes and Memphis and expanded the harbour town founded by his father due to the perfect position on a feeder channel from the

Pelusaic branch of the Nile. The city was, unfortunately, a short-term capital, and by the end of the Twenty-First Dynasty it had been abandoned, and the capital moved north to Tanis, probably due to the branch of the Nile drying up.

Egyptologist Flinders Petrie thought he had discovered Pi-Ramses when he was excavating at Tanis in 1884. There were numerous blocks and monuments carved with Ramses' name, and it is thought the site of Pi-Rameses was being used as a quarry for cut blocks to build this new city.

However, in the 1920s at Qantir, tiles were discovered bearing the names of Sety I and Ramses II, shifting the attention to this site. It was not until the 1970s and the work of Manfred Bietak with the Austrian Archaeological Institute that it was confirmed.

Using a magnetometer, Bietak and his team were able to map out the city in a non-intrusive manner and by 1999 they had identified the domestic areas, the administrative quarters of the palace, a cemetery and a village that housed poorer residents. Excavations have uncovered stables that had 24 rooms over two hallways. The archaeologists have also discovered chariot and arms workshops, including remnants of chariots, arrow shafts and arrowheads, javelin heads, body armour and daggers.

The site of Pi-Ramses covered about 30 square kilometres, stretching southwards to the site of Tell el-Dab'a, which was the Hyksos capital.

His Mummy

Ramses II's mummy was discovered as part of the mummy cache in Luxor in 1881. Ramses sadly had not been allowed to rest in peace, and his body had initially been moved to his father's tomb (KV17), where it slumbered for 80 years. Then in the Twenty-First Dynasty, in order to protect them from plunder, the priests gathered the mummies of the kings from the valley and stored them in the tomb of Ahmose-Inhapi. Forty years later, after being re-wrapped and placed into new coffins, they were moved to the Royal Cache at DB320 in year 11 of Shoshenq II's reign (c. 890 BCE). The coffin Ramses II was found in is likely to have been the coffin of Horemheb (1321–1293 BCE), the last king of the Eighteenth Dynasty, and the one who named Ramses I as king.

Whilst the texts used in this book were written after the discovery, in the following 140 years science has progressed, and there is much the mummy can tell us. Budge, writing in 1902, describes the appearance of the mummy, and how it matches with his character from the classical sources, but nothing further about the body, as the studies had not been carried out at this time. In 1976, the mummy was flown to Paris for an exhibition, but also for much-needed conservation. Ramses was met at the airport by a full presidential guard of honour.

Studies of his mummy have shown he suffered from severe arthritis in his hips and atherosclerosis in his legs, which may have made walking difficult in his later years and could have led to heart disease or stroke. A study of his teeth also showed they were badly decayed, as well as having a number of tooth abscesses, which would have been painful if not fatal. As a man who lived until he was more than 90 years old in a civilization where the average age of death was 35, it is likely Ramses died due to old age, although this is something that may be determined in further studies.

Examination of the mummy also uncovered that the embalmers had made a bit of a botched job, as they accidently removed his heart with the lungs, when traditionally this was required to remain within the chest cavity. To disguise their mistake, they sewed the heart back into the chest using gold thread, although they placed it on the right rather than the left side. Studies in 1976 also showed that his nose had managed to retain its regal shape because the embalmers had packed it with peppercorns, whereas normally the noses were often misshapen by the bandages.

At the end of 2022, Dr. Sahar Saleem of Cairo University, alongside the Face Lab at Liverpool John Moores University, made a facial reconstruction of Ramses II based on a CT scan of his head. Using software designed for forensic applications, they were able to rebuild the face and then turn back the clock to show what he would have looked like as a young man at the height of his reign. Dr. Caroline Wilkinson from the Face Lab believes the reconstruction of face shape and proportions will have only a 2mm margin of error.

The Future

Although archaeologists and Egyptologists have a pretty comprehensive understanding of the reign of Ramses II and the politics surrounding his era, there are still gaps in our knowledge. Ancient Egypt is very much like a jigsaw puzzle where half of the pieces are missing and there is no picture on the box to tell us what we are aiming for. But in the 120 years since these Egyptological texts were published, we have learned more about Ramses II and his time. Scientific research has enabled us to study his mummy and reconstruct his face and, in another 50 or 120 years, technology may provide insights that we are unable to discover today. In an exhibition in the USA in 2022–23 called '*Ramses the Great and the Gold of the Pharaohs*', virtual-reality headsets enable visitors to travel with Nefertari through Abu Simbel, as multi-media and drone photography recreates the many elements of her husband's reign. Whilst this may not teach us anything new about the king, it enables visitors to experience his life in a novel way and keep this pharaoh alive for eternity.

Charlotte Booth (Introduction) has a PhD in Egyptology from the University of Birmingham, where she studied paper squeezes and their value as an archaeological tool. She obtained her BA (Hons) and MA from UCL in Egyptian Archaeology. She worked in Cairo for the EAIS project and in Luxor for ARCE. She has published extensively in Egyptology, including 17 books, and numerous articles and papers.

The New Kingdom Before Ramses II

ook V of *A History of Egypt* by James Henry Breasted, which is presented here, gives an introduction on the kings of the Eighteenth Dynasty including Hatshepsut, Thutmose III and Amenhotep III, and how they were able to rebuild after the Hyksos period, setting up a strong foundation until the Amarna period and the reign of Akhenaten (Amenhotep IV) tore it down again.

Each reign is outlined in great detail, examining the pharaohs' lives, their political deeds and their deaths and burials using the evidence available at the time of writing.

The New State: Society and Religion

☥

THE TASK OF BUILDING UP A STATE, which now confronted Ahmose I, differed materially from the reorganization accomplished at the beginning of the Twelfth Dynasty by Amenemhet I. The latter dealt with social and political factors no longer new in his time, and manipulated to his own ends the old political units without destroying their identity, whereas Ahmose had now to begin with the erection of a fabric of government out of elements so completely divorced from the old forms as to have lost their identity, being now in a state of total flux. The course of events, which culminated in the expulsion of the Hyksos, determined for Ahmose the form which the new state was to assume.

He was now at the head of a strong army, effectively organized and welded together by long campaigns and sieges protracted through years, during which he had been both general in the field and head of the state. The character of the government followed involuntarily out of these conditions. Egypt became a military state. It was quite natural that it should remain so, in spite of the usually unwarlike character of the Egyptian. The long war with the Hyksos had now educated him as a soldier, the large army of Ahmose had spent years in Asia and had even been for a longer or shorter period among the rich cities of Syria. Having thoroughly learned war and having perceived the enormous wealth to be gained by it in Asia, the whole land was roused and stirred with a lust of conquest, which was not quenched for several centuries. The wealth, the rewards and the promotion open to the professional soldier were a constant incentive to a military career, and the middle classes, otherwise so unwarlike, now entered the ranks with ardour. Among the survivors of the noble class, chiefly those who had attached themselves to the Theban house, the profession of arms became the most attractive of all careers, and in the biographies which they have left in their tombs at Thebes they narrate with the greatest satisfaction the campaigns which they went through at the pharaoh's side, and the honours which he bestowed upon them. Many a campaign, all record of which would have been irretrievably lost, has thus come to our knowledge through one of these military biographies, like that of Ahmose, son of Ebana, from which we have quoted.

The sons of the pharaoh, who in the Old Kingdom held administrative offices, are now generals in the army. For the next century and a half, the story of the achievements of the army will be the story of Egypt, for the army is now the dominant force and the chief motive power in the new state. In organization it quite surpassed the militia of the old days, if for no other reason than that it was now a standing army. It was organized into two grand divisions, one in the Delta and the other in the upper country. In Syria it had learned tactics and proper strategic disposition of forces, the earliest of which we know anything in history. We shall now find partition of an army into divisions, we shall hear of wings and centre, we shall even trace a flank movement and define battle lines. All this is fundamentally different from the disorganized plundering expeditions naively reported as wars by the monuments of the older periods. Besides the old bow and spear, the troops henceforth carry also a war axe. They have learned archery fire by volleys and the dreaded archers of Egypt now gained a reputation which followed and made them feared even in classic times. But more than this, the Hyksos having brought the horse into Egypt, the Egyptian armies now for the first time possessed a large proportion of chariotry. Cavalry in the modern sense of the term was not employed. The deft craftsmen of Egypt soon mastered the art of chariot-making, while the stables of the pharaoh contained thousands of the best horses to be had in Asia. In accordance with the spirit of the time, the pharaoh was accompanied on all public appearances by a bodyguard of elite troops and a group of his favourite military officers.

With such force at his back, he ruled in absolute power; there was none to offer a breath of opposition; there was not a whisper of that modern monitor of kings, public opinion, an inconvenience with which rulers in the orient are rarely obliged to reckon, even at the present day. With a man of strong powers on the throne, all were at his feet, but let him betray a single evidence of weakness, and he was quickly made the puppet of court coteries and the victim of harem intrigues as of old. At such a time, as has happened so often since in Egypt, an able minister might overthrow the dynasty and found one of his own. But the man who expelled the Hyksos was thoroughly master of the situation. It is evidently in large measure to him that we owe the reconstruction of the state which was now emerging from the turmoils of two centuries of internal disorder and foreign invasion.

This new state is revealed to us more clearly than that of any other period of Egyptian history under native dynasties, and while we shall recognize many elements surviving from earlier times, we shall be able to discern much that is new in the great structure of government which was now rising under the hands of Ahmose I and his successors. The supreme position occupied by the pharaoh meant a very active participation in the affairs of government. He was accustomed every morning to meet the vizier, still the main spring of the administration, to consult with him on all the interests of the country and all the current business which necessarily came under his eye. Immediately thereafter he held a conference with the chief treasurer. These two men headed the chief departments of government: the treasury and the judiciary. The pharaoh's office, in which they made their daily reports to him, was the central organ of the whole government where all its lines converged. All other reports to government were likewise handed in here, and theoretically they all passed through the pharaoh's hands. Even in the limited number of such documents preserved to us, we discern the vast array of detailed questions in practical administration which the busy monarch decided. The punishment of condemned criminals was determined by him, the documents in the case being sent up to him for a decision while the victims awaited their fate in the dungeon. Besides frequent campaigns in Nubia and Asia, he visited the quarries and mines in the desert or inspected the desert routes, seeking suitable locations for wells and stations. Likewise, the internal administration required frequent journeys to examine new buildings and check all sorts of official abuses. The official cults in the great temples, too, demanded more and more of the monarch's time and attention as the rituals in the vast state temples increased in complexity with the development of the elaborate state religion. Under these circumstances the burden inevitably exceeded the powers of one man, even with the assistance of his vizier. From the earliest days of the Old Kingdom, as the reader will recall, there had been but one vizier. Early in the Eighteenth Dynasty, however, the business of government and the duties of the pharaoh had so increased that he appointed two viziers, one residing at Thebes, for the administration of the South, from the cataract as far as the nome of Siut; while the other, who had charge of all the region north of the latter point, lived at Heliopolis. This innovation probably took place after the transfer of the southern country between El Kab and the cataract from the jurisdiction of the Nubian province to that of the vizier.

For administrative purposes the country was divided into irregular districts, some of which consisted of the old and strong towns of feudal days, each with its surrounding villages; while others contained no such town centre, and were evidently arbitrary divisions established solely for governmental reasons. There were at least 27 such administrative districts between Siut and the cataract, and the country as a whole must have been divided into over twice that number. The head of government in the old towns still bore the feudal title 'count', but it now indicated solely administrative duties and might better be translated 'mayor' or 'governor'. Each of the smaller towns had a 'town-ruler', but in the other districts there were only recorders and scribes, with one of their number at their head. As we shall see, these men were both the administrators, chiefly in a fiscal capacity, and the judicial officials within their jurisdictions.

The great object of government was to make the country economically strong and productive. To secure this end, its lands, now chiefly owned by the crown, were worked by the king's serfs, controlled by his officials, or entrusted by him as permanent and indivisible fiefs to his favourite nobles, his partisans and relatives. Divisible parcels might also be held by tenants of the untitled classes. Both classes of holdings might be transferred by will or sale in much the same way as if the holder actually owned the land. Other royal property, like cattle and asses, was held by the people of both classes, subject, like the lands, to an annual assessment for its use. For purposes of taxation all lands and other property of the crown, except that held by the temples, were recorded in the tax registers of the White House, as the treasury was still called. All 'houses' or estates and the 'numbers belonging thereto', were entered in these registers. On the basis of these, taxes were assessed. They were still collected in naturalia: cattle, grain, wine, oil, honey, textiles and the like. Besides the cattle yards, the 'granary' was the chief sub-department of the White House, and there were innumerable other magazines for the storage of its receipts. All the products which filled these repositories were termed 'labour', the word employed in ancient Egypt as we use 'taxes'. If we may accept Hebrew tradition as transmitted in the story of Joseph, such taxes comprised one fifth of the produce of the land. It was collected by the local officials, whom we have already noticed, and its reception in and payment from the various magazines demanded a host of scribes and subordinates, now more numerous than ever before in the history of the country. The chief treasurer at their head was under the authority of the vizier, to whom he made a report every morning, after which he received permission to open the offices and magazines for the day's business. The collection of a second class of revenue, that paid by the local officials themselves as a tax upon their offices, was exclusively in the hands of the viziers. The southern vizier was responsible for all the officials of Upper Egypt in his jurisdiction from Elephantine to Siut; and in view of this fact, the other vizier doubtless bore a similar responsibility in the North. This tax on the officials consisted chiefly of gold, silver, grain, cattle and linen; the mayor of the old city of El Kab, for example, paid some 5,600 grains of gold, 4,200 grains of silver, one ox and one 'two-year-old' into the vizier's office every year, while his subordinate paid 4,200 grains of silver, a bead necklace of gold, two oxen and two chests of linen. Unfortunately the list from which these numbers are taken, recorded in the tomb of the vizier Rekhmire at Thebes, is too mutilated to permit the calculation of the exact total of this tax on all the officials under the jurisdiction of the southern vizier; but they paid him annually at least some 220,000 grains of gold, nine gold necklaces, over 16,000 grains of silver, some 40 chests and other measures of linen, 106 cattle of all ages and some grain; and these figures are short by probably at least 20 percent of the real total. As the king presumably received a similar amount from the northern vizier's collections, this tax on the officials formed a stately sum in the annual revenues. We can unfortunately form no estimate of the total of all revenues. Of the royal income from all sources in the Eighteenth Dynasty the southern vizier had general charge. The amount of all taxes to be levied and the distribution of the revenue when collected were determined in his office, where a constant balance sheet was kept. In order to control both income and outgo, a monthly fiscal report was made to him by all local officials, and thus the southern vizier was able to furnish the king from month to month with a full statement of prospective resources in the royal treasury. The taxes were so dependent, as they still are, upon the height of the inundation and the consequent prospects for a plentiful or scanty harvest, that the level of the rising river was also reported to him. He held also all the records of the temple estates, and in the case of Amon, whose chief sanctuary was in the city of which the vizier was governor, he naturally had charge of the rich temple fortune, even ranking the High Priest of Amon in the affairs of the god's estate. As the income of the crown was, from now on, so largely augmented by foreign tribute, this was also received by the southern vizier and by him communicated to the king. The great vizier, Rekhmire, depicts himself in the gorgeous reliefs in his tomb receiving both the taxes of the officials who appeared before him each year with their dues, and the tribute of the Asiatic vassal-princes and Nubian chiefs.

In the administration of justice, the southern vizier played even a greater role than in the treasury. Here he was supreme. The old magnates of the Southern Tens, once possessed of important judicial functions, have sunk to a mere attendant council at the vizier's public audiences, where they seem to have retained not even advisory functions. They are never mentioned in the court records of the time, though they still live in poetry and their old fame survived even into Greek times. The vizier continues to bear his traditional title, 'chief of the six great houses' or courts of justice, but these are never referred to in any of the surviving legal documents and have evidently disappeared save in the title of the vizier. As always heretofore the officers of administration are incidentally the dispensers of justice. They constantly serve in a judicial capacity. Although there is no class of judges with *exclusively* legal duties, every man of important administrative rank is thoroughly versed in the law and is ready at any moment to serve as judge. The vizier is no exception. All petitioners for legal redress applied first to him in his audience hall; if possible in person, but in any case in writing. For this purpose he held a daily audience or 'sitting' as the Egyptian called it. Every morning the people crowded into the 'hall of the vizier', where the ushers and bailiffs jostled them into line that they might 'be heard', in order of arrival, one after another. In cases concerning land located in Thebes he was obliged by law to render a decision in three days, but if the land lay in the 'South or North' he required two months. This was while he was still the only vizier; when the North received its own vizier such cases there were referred to him at Heliopolis. All crimes in the capital city were denounced and tried before him, and he maintained a criminal docket of prisoners awaiting trial or punishment, which strikingly suggests modern documents of the same sort. All this, and especially the land cases, demanded rapid and convenient access to the archives of the land. They were therefore all filed in his offices. No one might make a will without filing it in the 'vizier's hall'. Copies of all name archives, boundary records and all contracts were deposited with him or with his colleague in the North. Every petitioner to the king was obliged to hand in his petition in writing at the same office.

Besides the vizier's 'hall', also called the 'great council', there were local courts throughout the land, not primarily of a legal character, being, as we have already explained, merely the body of administration officials in each district, who were corporately empowered to try cases with full competence. They were the 'great men of the town', or the local 'council', and acted as the local representatives of the 'great council'. In suits involving real estate titles, a commissioner of the 'great council' was sent out to execute the decisions of the 'great council' in cooperation with the nearest local 'council'. Or sometimes a hearing before the local 'council' was necessary before the 'great council' could render a decision. The number of these local courts is entirely uncertain, but the most important two known were at Thebes and Memphis. At Thebes its composition varied from day to day; in cases of a delicate nature, where the members of the royal house were implicated, it was appointed by the vizier, and in case of conspiracy against the ruler, the monarch himself commissioned them, though without partiality, and with instructions merely to determine who were the guilty, accompanied by power to execute the sentence. All courts were largely made up of priests. It is difficult to discern the relation of these courts to the 'hall of the vizier', but in at least one case, when satisfaction was not obtained at the vizier's hall, the petitioner recorded a stolen slave by suit before one of these courts. They did not, however, always enjoy the best reputation among the people, who bewailed the hapless plight of 'the one who stands alone before the court when he is a poor man and his opponent is rich, while the court oppresses him (saying), "Silver and gold for the scribes! Clothing for the servants!"' For of course the bribe of the rich was often stronger than the justice of the poor man's cause, as it frequently is at the present day. The law to which the poor appealed was undoubtedly just. The vizier was obliged to keep it constantly before him, contained in 40 rolls which were laid out before his dais at all his public sessions where they were doubtless accessible to all. Unfortunately the code which they contained has perished, but of its justice we can have no doubt, for the vizier was said to be a judge 'judging justly, not showing partiality, sending two men [opponents] forth satisfied, judging the weak and the powerful', or again, 'not preferring the great above the humble, rewarding the oppressed... bringing the evil to him who committed it'. Even the king dealt according to law; Amenhotep III called himself in his titulary 'establisher of law', and when before one of the courts which we have already described, the king boasts that 'the law stood firm; I did not reverse judgment, but in view of the facts I was silent that I might cause jubilation and joy'. Even conspirators against the king's life were not summarily put to death, but, as we have seen, were handed over to a legally constituted court to be properly tried, and condemned only when found guilty. The punishments inflicted by Haremhab upon his corrupt officials who robbed the poor, were all according to 'law'. The great body of this law was undoubtedly very old, and some of it, like the old texts of the *Book of the Dead*, was ascribed to the gods; but Haremhab's new regulations were new law enacted by him. Diodorus tells of five different kings before Persian times who enacted new laws, and in the Middle Kingdom even a nobleman relates having made laws, meaning, of course, that he had formulated them at the king's request. The social, agricultural and industrial world of the Nile-dwellers under the empire was therefore not at the mercy of arbitrary whim on the part of either king or court, but was governed by a large body of long respected law, embodying the principles of justice and humanity.

The southern vizier was the motive power behind the organization and operation of this ancient state. We recall that he went in every morning and took council with the pharaoh on the affairs of the country; and the only other check upon his untrammelled control of the state was a law constraining him to report the condition of his office to the chief treasurer. Every morning as he came forth from his interview with the king he found the chief treasurer standing by one of the flag staves of the palace front, and there they exchanged reports. The vizier then unsealed the doors of the court and of the offices of the royal estate so that the day's business might begin; and during the day all ingress and egress at these doors was reported to him, whether of persons or of property of any sort. His office was the means of communication with the local authorities, who reported to him in writing on the first day of each season, that is, three times a year. It is in his office that we discern with unmistakable clearness the complete centralization of all local government in all its functions. This supervision of the local administration required frequent journeys and there was therefore an official barge of the vizier on the river in which he passed from place to place. It was he who detailed the king's bodyguard for service as well as the garrison of the residence city; general army orders proceeded from his office; the forts of the South were under his control; and the officials of the navy all reported to him. He was thus minister of war for both army and navy, and in the Eighteenth Dynasty at least, 'when the king was with the army', he conducted the administration at home. He had legal control of the temples throughout the country, or, as the Egyptian put it, 'he established laws in the temples of the gods of the South and the North', so that he was minister of ecclesiastical affairs. He had economic oversight of many important resources of the country; no timber could be cut without his permission, and the administration of irrigation and water supply was also under his charge. In order to establish the calendar for state business, the rising of Sirius was reported to him. He exercised advisory functions in all the offices of the state; so long as his office was undivided with a vizier of the North he was grand steward of all Egypt, and there was no prime function of the state which did not operate immediately or secondarily through his office, while all others were obliged to report to it or work more or less closely in connection with it. He was a veritable Joseph and it must have been this office which the Hebrew narrator had in mind as that to which Joseph was appointed. He was regarded by the people as their great protector and no higher praise could be proffered to Amon when addressed by a worshipper than to call him 'the poor man's vizier who does not accept the bribe of the guilty'. His appointment was a matter of such importance that it was conducted by the king himself, and the instructions given him by the monarch on that occasion were not such as we should expect from the lips of an oriental conqueror 3,500 years ago. They display a spirit of kindness and humanity and exhibit an appreciation of state craft surprising in an age so remote. The king tells the vizier that he shall conduct himself as one 'not setting his face toward the princes and councillors, neither one making brethren of all the people'; again he says, 'It is an abomination of the god to show partiality. This is the teaching: thou shalt do the like, shalt regard him who is known to thee like him who is unknown to thee, and him who is near ... like him who is far.... Such an official shall flourish greatly in the place.... Be not enraged toward a man unjustly ... but show forth the fear of thee; let one be afraid of thee, for a prince is a prince of whom one is afraid. Lo, the true dread of a prince is to do justice.... Be not known to the people and they shall not say, "He is only a man."' Even the vizier's subordinates are to be men of justice, for the king admonishes the new vizier, 'Lo, one shall say of the chief scribe of the vizier, "A scribe of justice" shall one say of him'. In a land where the bribery of the court still begins with the lowest subordinates before access is gained to the magistrates, such 'justice' was necessary indeed. The viziers of the Eighteenth Dynasty desired the reputation of hard working, conscientious officials, who took the greatest pride in the proper administration of the office. Several of them have left a record of their installation, with a long list of the duties of the office, engraved and painted upon the walls of their Theban tombs, and it is from these that we have drawn our account of the vizier.

Such was the government of the imperial age in Egypt. In society the disappearance of the landed nobility, and the administration of the local districts by a vast army of petty officials of the crown, opened the way more fully than in the Middle Kingdom for innumerable careers among the middle class. These opportunities must have worked a gradual change in their condition. Thus one official relates his obscure origin thus: 'Ye shall talk of it, one to another, and the old men shall teach it to the youth. I was one whose family was poor and whose town was small, but the Lord of the Two Lands [the king] recognized me; I was accounted great in his heart, the king in his role as sun god in the splendour of his palace saw me. He exalted me more than the [royal] companions, introducing me among the princes of the palace.... He appointed me to conduct works while I was a youth, he found me, I was made account of in his heart, I was introduced into the gold-house to fashion the figures and images of all the gods.' Here he administered his office so well in overseeing the production of the costly images of gold that he was rewarded publicly with decorations of gold by the king and even gained place in the councils of the treasury. Such possibilities of promotion and royal favour awaited success in local administration; for in some local office the career of this unknown official in the small town must have begun. There thus grew up a new official class, its lower ranks drawn from the old middle class, while on the other hand in its upper strata were the relatives and dependents of the old landed nobility, by whom the higher and more important local offices were administered. Here the official class gradually merged into the large circle of royal favourites who filled the great offices of the central government or commanded the pharaoh's forces on his campaigns. As there was no longer a feudal nobility, the great government officials became the nobles of the empire. The old middle class of merchants, skilled craftsmen and artists also still survived and continued to replenish the lower ranks of the official class. Below these were the masses who worked the fields and estates, the serfs of the pharaoh. They formed so large a portion of the inhabitants that the Hebrew scribe, evidently writing from the outside, knew only this class of society beside the priests. These lower strata passed away and left little or no trace, but the official class was now able to erect tombs and mortuary stela in such surprising numbers that they furnish us a vast mass of materials for reconstructing the life and customs of the time. An official who took a census in the Eighteenth Dynasty divided the people into 'soldiers, priests, royal serfs and all the craftsmen', and this classification is corroborated by all that we know of the time; although we must understand that all callings of the free middle class are here included among the 'soldiers'. The soldier in the standing army has therefore now also become a social class. The free middle class, liable to military service, are called 'citizens of the army', a term already known in the Middle Kingdom; but now very common; so that liability to military service becomes the significant designation of this class of society. Politically the soldier's influence grows with every reign and he soon becomes the involuntary reliance of the pharaoh in the execution of numerous civil commissions where formerly the soldier was never employed. Side by side with him appears another new and powerful influence, the ancient institution of the priesthood. As a natural consequence of the great wealth of the temples under the empire, the priesthood becomes a profession, no longer merely an incidental office held by a layman, as in the Old and Middle Kingdoms. As the priests increase in numbers they gain more and more political power; while the growing wealth of the temples demands for its proper administration a veritable army of temple officials of all sorts, who were unknown to the old days of simplicity. Probably one fourth of all the persons buried in the great and sacred cemetery of Abydos at this period were priests. Priestly communities had thus grown up. Heretofore the priests of the various sanctuaries had never been united by any official ties, but existed only in individual and entirely separated communities without interrelation. All these priestly bodies were now united in a great sacerdotal organization embracing the whole land. The head of the state temple at Thebes, the High Priest of Amon, was the supreme head of this greater body also and his power was thereby increased far beyond that of his older rivals at Heliopolis and Memphis. The members of the sacerdotal guild thus became a new class, so that priest, soldier and official now stood together as three great social classes, yet possessing common interests; their leaders were the pharaoh's nobles, who replaced the old aristocracy; but their lower ranks were not to be distinguished from the free middle class, the tradesmen and craftsmen; while at the bottom, as the chief economic basis of all, were the peasant serfs.

The priests whom we now find so numerous as to have become a class of society, were the representatives of a richer and more elaborate state religion than Egypt had ever seen. The days of the old simplicity were forever past. The wealth gained by foreign conquest enabled the pharaohs from now on to endow the temples with such riches as no sanctuary of the old days had ever possessed. The temples grew into vast and gorgeous palaces, each with its community of priests, and the high priest of such a community in the larger centres was a veritable sacerdotal prince, ultimately wielding considerable political power. The high priest's wife at Thebes was called the chief concubine of the god, and his real consort was no less a person than the queen herself, who was therefore known as the 'Divine Consort'. In the gorgeous ritual which now prevailed, her part was to lead the singing of the women who were also still permitted to participate in the service in large numbers. She possessed also a fortune, which belonged to the temple endowment, and for this reason it was desirable that the queen should hold the office in order to retain this fortune in the royal house.

The triumph of a Theban family had brought with it the supremacy of Amon. He had not been the god of the residence in the Middle Kingdom, and although the rise of a Theban family had then given him some distinction, it was not until now that he became the great god of the state. His essential character and individuality had already been obliterated by the solar theology of the Middle Kingdom, when he had become Amon-Re, and with some attributes borrowed from his ithyphallic neighbour, Min of Coptos, he now rose to a unique and supreme position of unprecedented splendour. He was popular with the people, too, and as a Moslem says, 'Inshallah', 'If Allah will', so the Egyptian now added to all his promises 'If Amon spare my life'. They called him the 'vizier of the poor', the people carried to him their wants and wishes, and their hopes for future prosperity were implicitly staked upon his favour. But the fusion of the old gods had not deprived Amon alone of his individuality, for in the general flux almost any god might possess the qualities and functions of the others, although the dominant position was still occupied by the sun god.

The mortuary beliefs of the time are the outgrowth of tendencies already plainly observable in the Middle Kingdom. The magical formula by which the dead are to triumph in the hereafter become more and more numerous, so that it is no longer possible to record them on the inside of the coffin, but they must be written on papyrus and the roll placed in the tomb. As the selection of the most important of these texts came to be more and more uniform, the *Book of the Dead* began to take form. All was dominated by magic; by this all-powerful means the dead might effect all that he desired. The luxurious lords of the empire no longer look forward with pleasure to the prospect of plowing, sowing and reaping in the happy fields of Yaru. They would escape such peasant labour, and a statuette bearing the implements of labour in the field and inscribed with a potent charm is placed in the tomb, thereby ensuring to the deceased immunity from such toil, which will always be performed by this representative whenever the call to the fields is heard. Such 'Ushebtis', or 'respondents', as they were termed, were now placed in the necropolis by scores and hundreds. But this means of obtaining material good was now unfortunately transferred also to the ethical world, in order to secure exemption from the consequences of an evil life. A sacred beetle or scarabaeus is cut from stone and inscribed with a charm, beginning with the significant words, 'O my heart, rise not up against me as a witness'. So powerful is this cunning invention when laid upon the breast of the mummy under the wrappings that when the guilty soul stands in the judgment hall in the awful presence of Osiris, the accusing voice of the heart is silenced and the great god does not perceive the evil of which it would testify. Likewise the rolls of the *Book of the Dead* containing, besides all the other charms, also the scene of judgment, and especially the welcome verdict of acquittal, are now sold by the priestly scribes to anyone with the means to buy; and the fortunate purchaser's name is then inserted in the blanks left for this purpose throughout the document; thus securing for himself the certainty of such a verdict, before it was known whose name should be so inserted. The invention of these devices by the priests was undoubtedly as subversive of moral progress and the elevation of the popular religion as the sale of indulgences in Luther's time. The moral aspirations which had come into the religion of Egypt with the ethical influences so potent in the Osiris myth, were now choked and poisoned by the assurance that, however vicious a man's life, exemption in the hereafter could be purchased at any time from the priests. The priestly literature on the hereafter, produced probably for no other purpose than for gain, continued to grow. We have a *Book of What is in the Netherworld*, describing the 12 caverns, or hours of the night through which the sun passed beneath the earth; and a *Book of the Portals*, treating of the gates and strongholds between these caverns. Although these edifying compositions never gained the wide circulation enjoyed by the *Book of the Dead*, the former of the two was engraved in the tombs of the Nineteenth and Twentieth Dynasty kings at Thebes, showing that these grotesque creations of the perverted priestly imagination finally gained the credence of the highest circles.

The tomb of the noble consists as before of chambers hewn in the face of the cliff, and in accordance with the prevailing tendency it is now filled with imaginary scenes from the next world, with mortuary and religious texts, many of them of a magical character. At the same time the tomb has become more a personal monument to the deceased and the walls of the chapel bear many scenes from his life, especially from his official career, particularly as a record of the honours which he received from the king. Thus the cliffs opposite Thebes, honeycombed as they are with the tombs of the lords of the empire, contain whole chapters of the life and history of the period, with which we shall now deal. In a solitary valley behind these cliffs, as we shall see, the kings now likewise excavate their tombs in the limestone walls and the pyramid is no longer employed. Vast galleries are pierced into the mountain, and passing from hall to hall, they terminate many hundreds of metres from the entrance in a large chamber, where the body of the king is laid in a huge stone sarcophagus. It is possible that the whole excavation is intended to represent the passages of the nether world along which the sun passes in his nightly journey. On the western plain of Thebes, the plain east of this valley, as on the east side of the pyramid, arose the splendid mortuary temples of the emperors, of which we shall later have occasion to say more. But these elaborate mortuary customs are now no longer confined to the pharaoh and his nobles; the necessity for such equipment in preparation for the hereafter is now felt by all classes. The manufacture of such materials, resulting from the gradual extension of these customs, has become an industry; the embalmers, undertakers and manufacturers of coffins and tomb furniture occupy a quarter at Thebes, forming almost a guild by themselves, as they did in later Greek times. The middle class were now frequently able to excavate and decorate a tomb; but when too poor for this luxury, they rented a place for their dead in great common tombs maintained by the priests, and here the embalmed body was deposited in a chamber where the mummies were piled up like cord-wood, but nevertheless received the benefit of the ritual maintained for all in common. The very poor still buried in the sand and gravel on the desert margin as of old, but even they looked with longing upon the luxury enjoyed in the hereafter by the rich, and at the door of some luxurious tomb they buried a rude statuette of their dead, bearing his name, in the pathetic hope that thus he might gain a few crumbs from the bounty of the rich man's mortuary table.

Out of the chaos which the rule of foreign lords had produced, the new state and the new conditions slowly emerged as Ahmose I gradually gained leisure from his arduous wars. With the state religion, the foreign dynasty had shown no sympathy and the temples lay wasted and deserted in many places. We find Ahmose therefore in his 22nd year opening new workings in the famous quarries of Ayan or Troja, opposite Gizeh, from which the blocks for the Gizeh pyramids were taken, in order to secure stone for the temples in Memphis, Thebes (Luxor) and probably elsewhere. For these works he still employed the oxen which he had taken from the Syrians in his Asiatic wars. None of these buildings of his, however, has survived. For the ritual of the state temple at Karnak he furnished the sanctuary with a magnificent service of rich cultus utensils in precious metals, and he built a new temple-barge upon the river of cedar exacted from the Lebanon princes. His greatest work remains the Eighteenth Dynasty itself, for whose brilliant career his own achievements had laid so firm a foundation. Notwithstanding his reign of at least 22 years, Ahmose must have died young (1557 BCE) for his mother was still living in the 10th year of his son and successor, Amenhotep I. By him he was buried in the old Eleventh Dynasty cemetery at the north end of the western Theban plain in a masonry tomb, which has now long perished. The jewellery of his mother, stolen from her neighbouring tomb at a remote date, was found by [French Egyptologist Auguste] Mariette concealed in the vicinity. The body of Ahmose I, as well as this jewellery, are now preserved in the Museum at Cairo.

The Consolidation of the Kingdom; The Rise of the Empire

☥

THE TIME WAS NOT YET RIPE for the great achievement which awaited the monarchs of the new dynasty. The old dominion of the Middle Kingdom, from the second cataract to the sea, was still far from the consolidation necessary to retain it in administrative and industrial stability. Nubia had been long without a strong arm from the north and the southern rebels in Egypt had prevented Ahmose I from continuous exertion of force above the cataract. The Troglodytes, who later harassed the Romans on this same frontier, and who were never thoroughly subdued by them, now possessed a leader, and Ahmose's campaign against them had not been lasting in its effects. It was easy for these barbarians to retreat into the eastern desert as the Egyptians approached, and then return after the danger had passed.

Amenhotep I, Ahmose's successor, was therefore obliged to invade Nubia in force and penetrated to the Middle Kingdom frontier at the second cataract, where the temple of the Sesostrises and Amenemhets had long been in the hands of the barbarians, and was doubtless in ruin. The two Ahmoses of El Kab were with the king, and Ahmose, son of Ebana, reports that 'his majesty captured that Troglodyte of Nubia in the midst of his soldiers'. With the loss of their leader, there was but one outcome for the action; both the Ahmoses captured prisoners, displayed great gallantry and were rewarded by the king. Northern Nubia was now placed under the administration of the mayor or governor of the old city of Nekhen, which now became the northern limit of a southern administrative district, including all the territory on the south of it, controlled by Egypt, at least as far as northern Nubia, or Wawat. From this time the new governor was able to go north with the tribute of the country regularly every year.

Hardly had Amenhotep I won his victory at the second cataract than another danger on the opposite frontier in the north recalled him thither. Ahmose, son of Ebana, boasts that he brought the king back to Egypt in his ship, probably from the second cataract, that is some 322 kilometres (200 miles), in two days. The long period of weakness and disorganization accompanying the rule of the Hyksos had given the Libyans the opportunity, which they always improved, of pushing in and occupying the rich lands of the Delta. Though our only source does not mention any such invasion, it is evident that Amenhotep I's war with the Libyans at this particular time can be explained in no other way. Finding their aggressions too threatening to be longer ignored, the pharaoh now drove them back and invaded their country. We know nothing of the battles that may have been fought, but Amose-Pen-Nekhbet of El Kab states that he slew three of the enemy and brought away their severed hands, for which he was of course rewarded by the king. Having relieved his frontiers and secured Nubia, Amenhotep was at liberty to turn his arms toward Asia. Unfortunately we have no records of his Syrian war, but he possibly penetrated far to the north, even to the Euphrates. In any case he accomplished enough to enable his successor to boast of ruling as far as the Euphrates, before the latter had himself undertaken any Asiatic conquests. Whether from this war or some other source he gained wealth for richly wrought buildings at Thebes, including a chapel on the western plain for his tomb there, and a superb temple gate at Karnak, later demolished by Thutmose III. The architect who erected these buildings, all of which have perished, narrates the king's death at Thebes, after a reign of at least 10 years.

Whether Amenhotep left a son entitled to the throne or not, we do not know. His successor, Thutmose I, was the son of a woman whose birth and family are of doubtful connection, and she was almost certainly not of royal blood. Her great son evidently owed his accession to the kingship to his marriage with a princess of the old line, named Ahmose, through whom he could assert a valid claim to the throne. On making good this claim, he lost no time in issuing a proclamation announcing throughout the kingdom that he had been crowned. This occurred about January 1540 or 1535 BCE. The officials in Nubia regarded the proclamation of sufficient importance to engrave it on tablets which they set up at Wadi Halfa, Kubban and perhaps elsewhere. The official to whom this action was due had reason to make evident his adherence to the new king, for he had been appointed to a new and important office immediately on the king's accession. It was no longer possible for the mayor of Nekhen to administer Nubia and collect the tribute. The country demanded the sole attention of a responsible governor who was practically a viceroy. He was given the title 'Governor of the south countries, king's-son of Kush', although he was not necessarily a member of the royal household or of royal birth. With great ceremony, in the presence of the pharaoh, one of the treasury officials was wont to deliver to the incumbent the seal of his new office, saying: 'This is the seal from the pharaoh, who assigns to thee the territory from Nekhen to Napata.' The jurisdiction of the viceroy thus extended to the fourth cataract, and it was the region between this southern limit and the second cataract which was known as Kush. There was still no great or dominant kingdom in Kush, nor in lower Nubia, but the country was under the rule of powerful chiefs, each controlling a limited territory. It was impossible to suppress these native rulers at once and nearly 200 years after this we still find the chiefs of Kush and a chief of Wawat as far north as Ibrim. Although possessing only a nominal authority, it was but slowly that they were replaced by Egyptian administrative officers. Moreover, in Thutmose I's time the southern half of the new province was far from being sufficiently pacified. The appointment of Thure, the first viceroy, therefore brought him a serious task. The turbulent tribes from the hills above the Nile valley were constantly raiding the towns along the river and making stable government and the orderly development of the country's natural resources impossible. Seeing that Thure was unable to stop this, the king went south early in his second year personally to oversee the task of more thorough subjugation. Arriving at the first cataract in February or March, he found the canal through the rapids obstructed with stone, just as it had perhaps been since Hyksos days. Desirous of losing no time, and anxious to take advantage of the fast-falling water, he did not stop to clear it, but forced the rapids with the aid of the admiral, Ahmose, son of Ebana, whose exploits we have followed so long. This officer now again distinguished himself 'in the bad water in the passage of the ship by the bend', presumably in the cataract, and was again liberally rewarded by the king. By early April Thutmose had reached Tangur, about 120 kilometres (75 miles) above the second cataract! Ahmose, son of Ebana, describes the battle, which probably took place somewhere on this advance, between the second and third cataracts. The king engaged in hand-to-hand combat with a Nubian chief; 'his majesty cast the first lance, which remained in the body of that fallen one'. The enemy were totally defeated and many prisoners were taken. Of these, the other hero of El Kab, Ahmose-Pen-Nehkbet, captured no less than five. The water was now so low that the advance was necessarily for the most part by land: but the king pressed on to the third cataract. He was the first pharaoh to stand here at the northern gateway of the Dongola Province, the great garden of the Upper Nile, through which there wound before him over 320 kilometres (200 miles) of unbroken river. With the long advance now behind him, he erected here five triumphant stela commemorating the new conquest. On the Island of Tombos he erected a fortress, of which some remains still survive, and garrisoned it with troops from the army of conquest. In August of the same year, five months after he had passed Tangur on the way up, he erected a tablet of victory on Tombos, on which he boasts of ruling from the frontier at Tombos on the south, to the Euphrates on the north, a statement to which his own achievements in Asia did not yet entitle him. Returning slowly northward with the Nubian chief, whom he had slain, hanging head downward at the prow of his royal barge, he reached the first cataract again some seven months after he had erected the stele on Tornbos.

We can only explain the slowness of his return by supposing that he devoted much time to the reorganization and thorough pacification of the country on his way. It was now April, and as the low water of that season was favourable to the enterprise, the king ordered the canal at the first cataract cleared. The viceroy, Thure, had charge of the work, and he has left three records of its successful accomplishment inscribed on the rocks by the stream, two on the island of Sehel and one on the neighbouring shore. The king then sailed through the canal in triumph with the body of the Nubian chief still hanging head downward at the bow of his barge, where it remained till he landed at Thebes.

The subjugation of the Nubian province was now thoroughly done, and Thutmose was able to give his attention to a similar task at the other extremity of his realm, in Asia. Evidently the conquest of Amenhotep I, which had enabled Thutmose to claim the Euphrates as his northern boundary, had not been sufficient to ensure to the pharaoh's treasury the regular tribute which he was now enjoying from Nubia, but the conditions in Syria-Palestine were very favourable for a prolonged lease of power on the pharaoh's part.

The geographical conformation of the country along the eastern end of the Mediterranean, which we may call Syria-Palestine, is not such as to permit the gradual amalgamation of small and petty states into one great nation, as that process took place in the valleys of the Nile and the Euphrates. From north to south, roughly parallel with the coast, the region is traversed by rugged mountain ranges, in two main ridges, known as the Lebanon and Anti-Lebanon in the north. In the south, the western ridge, with some interruptions, drops finally into the bare and forbidding hills of Judah, which merge then into the desert of Sinai south of Palestine. South of the plain of Esdraelon, or Jezreel, it throws off the ridge of Carmel, which drops, like a Gothic buttress, abruptly to the sea. The eastern ridge shifts somewhat further eastward in its southern course, interrupted here and there, and spreading on the east of the Dead Sea in the mountains of Moab, its southern flanks are likewise lost in the sandy plateau of northern Arabia. Between the two Lebanons, that is, in the northern half of the depression between the eastern and western ridges, is a fertile valley traversed by the river Orontes. This Orontes valley is the only extensive region in Syria-Palestine not cut up by the hills and mountains, where a strong kingdom might develop. The coast is completely isolated from the interior by the ridge of Lebanon, on whose western base a people might rise to wealth and power only by the exploitation of the resources of the sea; while in the south, Palestine with its harbourless coast and its large tracts of unproductive soil, hardly furnished the economic basis for the development of a strong nation. It is moreover badly cut up by the ridge of Carmel and the deep clove in which lie the Jordan and the Dead Sea. Along almost its entire eastern frontier, Syria-Palestine merges into the northern extension of the Arabian desert, save in the extreme north, where the valley of the Orontes and that of the Euphrates almost blend, just as they part, the one to seek the Mediterranean, while the other turns away toward Babylon and the Persian Gulf. The country was settled chiefly by Semites, probably the descendants of an early overflow of population from the deserts of Arabia, such as has occurred in historic times over and over again. In the north these were subsequently Aramaeans, while in the south they may be designated as Canaanites. In general these peoples showed little genius for government, and were totally without any motives for consolidation. Divided by the physical conformation of the country, they were organized into numerous city-kingdoms, that is, petty principalities, consisting of a city, with the surrounding fields and outlying villages, all under the rule of a local dynast, who lived in the said city. Each city had not only its own kinglet, but also its own god, a local ba'al (Baal) or 'lord', with whom was often associated a ba'lat or 'lady', a goddess like her of Byblos. These miniature kingdoms were embroiled in frequent wars with one another, each dynast endeavouring to unseat his neighbour and absorb the latter's territory and revenues. Exceeding all the others in size was the kingdom of Kadesh, the surviving nucleus of Hyksos power. It had developed in the only place where the conditions permitted such an expansion, occupying a very advantageous position on the Orantes. It thus commanded the road northward through inner Syria, the route of commerce from Egypt and the south, which, following the Orantes, diverged thence to the Euphrates, to cross to Assyria or descend the Euphrates to Babylon. Being likewise at the northern end of both Lebanons, Kadesh commanded also the road from the interior seaward through the Eleutheros valley. These advantages had enabled it to subjugate the smaller kingdoms and to organize them into a loose feudal state, in which we should, in the author's opinion, recognize the empire of the Hyksos, as already indicated. We shall now discern it for two generations, struggling desperately to maintain its independence, and only crushed at last by 20 years of warfare under Thutmose III.

While, with this exception, these kingdoms of the interior showed small aptitude for government, some of them nevertheless possessed a high degree of civilization. in other directions. In the art of war especially they had during Hyksos supremacy taught the Egyptian much. They were masters of the art of metalworking, they wrought weapons of high quality, and the manufacture of chariots was a considerable industry. Metal vessels of varied designs were also produced. Their more strenuous climate demanded woollen clothing, so that they had mastered the art of dyeing and weaving wool, in which they produced textile fabrics of the finest quality and of rich and sumptuous design. These Semites were already inveterate traders, and an animated commerce was passing from town to town, where the marketplace was a busy scene of traffic as it is today. On the scanty foothold available on the western declivities of the Lebanon some of these Semites, crossing from the interior, had early gained a footing on the coast, to become the Phoenicians of historic times. They rapidly subdued the sea, and from being mere fishermen, they soon developed into hardy mariners. Bearing the products of their industries, their galleys were now penetrating beyond the harbours of Cyprus, where they exploited the rich copper mines, and creeping along the coast of Asia Minor they gained Rhodes and the islands of the Aegean. In every favourable harbour they established their colonies, along the southern litoral of Asia Minor, throughout the Aegean, and here and there on the mainland of Greece. Their manufactories multiplied in these colonies, and everywhere throughout the regions which they reached, their wares were prominent in the markets. As their wealth increased, every harbour along the Phoenician coast was the seat of a rich and flourishing city, among which Tyre, Sidon, Byblos, Arvad and Simyra were the greatest, each being the seat of a powerful dynasty. Thus it was that in the Homeric poems the Phoenician merchant and his wares were proverbial, for the commercial and maritime power enjoyed by the Phoenicians at the rise of the Egyptian Empire continued into Homeric times.

How far west these Phoenician mariners penetrated it is now difficult to determine, but it is not impossible that their Spanish and Carthaginian colonies already existed. The civilization which they found in the northern Mediterranean was that of the Mycenaean age, and these Phoenician avenues of commerce served as a link connecting Egypt and the Mycenaean civilization of the north. The people who appear with Mycenaean vessels as gifts and tribute for the pharaoh in this age, are termed by the Egyptian monuments Keftyew, and so regular was the traffic of the Phoenician fleets with these people that the Phoenician craft plying on these voyages were known as 'Keftyew ships'. It is impossible to locate the Keftyew with certainty, but they seem to have extended from the southern coast of Asia Minor as far west as Crete. All this northern region was known to the Egyptians as the 'Isles of the Sea', for having no acquaintance with the interior of Asia Minor, they supposed it to be but island coasts, like those of the Aegean. In northern Syria, on the upper reaches of the Euphrates, the world, as conceived by the Egyptian, ended in marshes in which the Euphrates had its rise, and these again were encircled by the 'Great Circle', the ocean, which was the end of all.

In this Semitic world of Syria-Palestine, now dominated by Egypt, she was to learn much; nevertheless throughout this region the influence of Egyptian art and industry was supreme. Much more highly organized than the neighbouring peoples of Asia, the mighty kingdom on the Nile had from time immemorial been regarded with awe and respect, while its more mature civilization, by its very presence on the threshold of hither Asia, was a powerful influence upon the politically feeble states there. There was little or no native art among these peoples of the western Semitic world, but they were skilful imitators, ready to absorb and adapt to their uses all that might further their industries and their commerce. The products which their fleets marketed throughout the eastern Mediterranean were therefore tinctured through and through with Egyptian elements, while the native Egyptian wares which they carried to Europe and the Aegean introduced there the unalloyed art of the Nile valley. In these Phoenician galleys the civilization of the Orient was being gradually disseminated through southern Europe and the west. Babylonian influences, while not so noticeable in the art of Syria-Palestine, were nevertheless powerfully present there. Since the days of the brief empire of Sargon of Agade, about the middle of the third thousand years BCE, Babylon had gained in the west a commercial supremacy, which had gradually introduced there the cuneiform system of writing. It was readily adaptable to the Semitic dialects prevalent in Syria-Palestine and gained a footing by a process similar to that which, during the commercial dominance of Phoenicia, brought the Phoenician alphabet to Greece. It was even adopted also by the Hittites, who were not Semites, and likewise by another non-Semitic nation in this region, the kingdom of Mitanni. Thus Syria-Palestine became common ground, where the forces of civilization from the Nile and the Euphrates mingled at first in peaceful rivalry, but ultimately to meet upon the battlefield. The historical significance of this region is found in the inevitable struggle for its possession between the kingdom of the Nile on the one hand and those of the Tigro-Euphrates valley and hither Asia on the other. It was in the midst of this struggle that Hebrew national history fell, and in its relentless course the Hebrew monarchies perished.

Other non-Semitic peoples were also beginning to appear on Egypt's northern horizon. A group of warriors of Iran, now appearing for the first time in history, had by 1500 BCE pushed westward to the upper Euphrates. At the rise of the Egyptian Empire therefore, these Iranians were already settled in the country east of the Euphrates, within the huge bend where the river turns away from the Mediterranean, and there established the kingdom of Mitanni. It was the earliest and westernmost outpost of the Aryan race as yet disclosed to us. The source from which they had come must have been the original home of that Aryan race behind the north-eastern mountains at the sources of the Oxus and Jaxartes rivers. The influence and language of Mitanni extended westward to Tunip in the Orontes valley and eastward to Nineveh. They formed a powerful and cultivated state, which, planted thus on the road leading westward from Babylon along the Euphrates, effectively cut off the latter from her profitable western trade, and doubtless had much to do with the decline in which Babylon, under her foreign Kassite dynasty, now found herself. Assyria was as yet but a new and insignificant city-kingdom, whose coming struggle with Babylon only rendered the pharaohs less liable to interference from the east, in the realization of their plans of conquest in Asia. Everything thus conspired to favour the permanence of Egyptian power there.

Under these conditions Thutmose I prepared to quell the perpetual revolt in Syria and bring it into such complete subjection as he had achieved in Nubia. None of his records of the campaign has survived, but the two Ahmoses of El Kab were still serving with the army of conquest and in their biographies they refer briefly to this war also. Kadesh must have been cowed for the time by Amenhotep I, for, in so far as we know, Thutmose met with no resistance from her, which the two Ahmoses considered worthy of mention. Thus, without serious opposition, the pharaoh reached Naharin, or the land of the 'rivers', as the name signifies, which was the designation of the country from the Orontes to the Euphrates and beyond, merging into Asia Minor. Here the revolt was naturally the most serious as it was farthest removed from the pharaoh's vengeance. The battle resulted in a great slaughter of the Asiatics, followed by the capture of large numbers of prisoners. 'Meanwhile', says Ahmose, son of Ebana, 'I was at the head of our troops and his majesty beheld my bravery. I brought off a chariot, its horses and him who was upon it as a living prisoner, and I took them to his majesty. One presented me with gold in double measure.' His namesake of El Kab, who was younger and more vigorous, was even more successful, for he captured no less than 21 hands severed from the dead, besides a horse and a chariot. These two men are typical examples of the followers of the pharaoh at this time. And it is evident that the king understood how to make their own prosperity dependent upon the success of his arms. Unfortunately for our knowledge of Thutmose I's further campaigns, if there were any, the first of these biographies and of course also the warlike career which it narrates, closes with this campaign, though the younger man campaigned with Thutmose II and lived on in favour and prosperity till the reign of Thutmose III.

Somewhere along the Euphrates at its nearest approach to the Mediterranean, Thutmose now erected a stone boundary tablet, marking the northern and at this point the eastern limit of his Syrian possessions. He had made good the boast so proudly recorded, possibly only a year before, on the tablet marking the other extreme frontier of his empire at the third cataract of the Nile. Henceforth he was even less measured in his claims; for he later boasted to the priests of Abydos, 'I made the boundary of Egypt as far as the circuit of the sun', which, in view of the limited and vague knowledge of the world possessed by the Egyptians of that day, was almost true.

Two pharaohs had now seen the Euphrates, the Syrian dynasts were fully impressed with the power of Egypt, and their tribute, together with that of the Beduin and other inhabitants of Palestine, began to flow regularly into the Egyptian treasury. Thus Thutmose I was able to begin the restoration of the temples so neglected since the time of the Hyksos. The modest old temple of the Middle Kingdom monarchs at Thebes was no longer in keeping with the pharaoh's increasing wealth and pomp. His chief architect, Ineni, was therefore commissioned to erect two massive pylons, or towered gateways, in front of the old Amon temple, and between these a covered hall, with the roof supported upon large cedar columns, brought of course, like the splendid silver-gold-tipped flag staves of cedar at the temple front, from the new possessions in the Lebanon. The huge door was likewise of Asiatic bronze, with the image of the god upon it, inlaid with gold. He likewise restored the revered temple of Osiris at Abydos, equipping it with rich ceremonial implements and furniture of silver and gold, with magnificent images of the gods, such as it had doubtless lost in Hyksos days. Admonished by his advancing years he also endowed it with an income for the offering of mortuary oblations to himself, giving the priests instructions regarding the preservation of his name and memory.

The Feud of the Thutmosids and the Reign of Queen Hatshepsut

☥

AS THUTMOSE I APPROACHED the 30th anniversary of his accession to the heirship of the throne, which was also the 30th anniversary of his coronation, he dispatched his faithful architect, Ineni, to the granite quarries of the first cataract to procure two obelisks with which to celebrate the coming Hebsed festival, or 30 years' jubilee. In a barge over 60 metres (200 feet) long and one third as wide, Ineni floated the great shafts down the river to Thebes, and erected them before the pylons of the Karnak temple, which he had likewise constructed for the king. He inscribed one of them, which stands to this day before the temple door, with the king's names and titles, but before he had begun the

inscription upon the other unexpected changes interfered, so that it never bore the name of Thutmose I.

He was now an old man and the claim to the throne which he had thus far successfully maintained, was probably weakened by the death of his queen, Ahmose, through whom alone he had any valid title to the crown. She was the descendant and representative of the old Theban princes who had fought and expelled the Hyksos, and there was a strong party who regarded the blood of this line as alone entitled to royal honours. She had borne Thutmose I four children, two sons and two daughters; but both sons and one of the daughters had died in youth or childhood. The surviving daughter, Makere-Hatshepsut, was thus the only child of the old line, and so strong was the party of legitimacy, that they had forced the king, years before, at about the middle of his reign, to proclaim her his successor, in spite of the disinclination general throughout Egyptian history to submit to the rule of a queen. Among other children, Thutmose I had also two sons by other queens: one, who afterward became Thutmose II, was the son of a princess Mutnofret; while the other, later Thutmose III, had been born to the king by an obscure concubine named Isis.

The close of Thutmose I's reign is involved in deep obscurity, and the following reconstruction is not without its difficulties. The traces left by family dissensions on temple walls are not likely to be sufficiently decisive to enable us to follow the complicated struggle with certainty 3,500 years later. In the period of confusion at the close of Thutmose I's reign probably fall the beginning of Thutmose III's reign and all of the reign of Thutmose II. When the light finally breaks Thutmose III is on the throne for a long reign, the beginning of which had been interrupted for a short time by the ephemeral rule of Thutmose II. Thus, although Thutmose III's reign really began before that of Thutmose II, seven eighths of it falls after Thutmose II's death, and the numbering of the two kings is most convenient as it is, involved in the obscure struggle, with touches of romance and dramatic incidents interspersed, are the fortunes of the beautiful and gifted princess of the old line, Hatshepsut, the daughter of Thutmose I.

Possibly after the death of her brothers she had been married to her half-brother, the concubine's son, whom we must call Thutmose III. As he was a young prince of no prospects, having, through neither his father nor his mother, any claim to the succession, he had been placed in the Karnak temple as a priest with the rank of prophet. Ere long he had won the priesthood to his support, for, on the death of the old queen, Ahmose, Thutmose III had the same right to the throne which his father had once asserted, that is, by inheritance through his wife. To this legal right the priesthood of Amon, who supported him, agreed to add that of divine sanction. Whether by previous peaceful understanding with Thutmose I, or as a hostile revolution totally unexpected on his part, the succession of Thutmose III was suddenly affected by a highly dramatic coup d'état in the temple of Amon.

On a feast day, as the image of the god was borne, amid the acclamations of the multitude, from the holy place into the court of the temple, the priest, Thutmose III, was stationed with his colleagues in the northern colonnade in Thutmose I's hall of the temple. The priests bore the god around both sides of the colonnade, as if he were looking for someone, and he finally stopped before the young prince, who prostrated himself upon the pavement. But the god raised him up, and as an indication of his will, had him placed immediately in the 'Station of the King', which was the ceremonial spot where only the king might stand in the celebration of the temple ritual. Thutmose I, who had but a moment before been burning incense to the god, and presenting him with a great oblation, was thus superseded by the will of the same god, clearly indicated in public. Thutmose III's five-fold name and titulary were immediately published, and on the third of May, in the year 1501 BCE, he suddenly stepped from the duties of an obscure prophet of Amon into the palace of the pharaohs. Years afterward, on the occasion of inaugurating some of his new halls in the Karnak temple of Amon, he repeated this incident to his assembled court, and added that instead of going to Heliopolis to receive there the acknowledgment of the sun god as king of Egypt, he was taken up into the heavens where he saw the sun god in all his most glorious splendour, and was duly crowned and given his royal names by the god himself. This account of unparalleled honour from the gods he then had engraved upon a wall of the temple, that all might know of it for all time.

Thutmose I was evidently not regarded as a source of serious danger, for he was permitted to live on. Thutmose III early shook off the party of legitimacy. When he had been ruling for 13 months e restored the ancient brick temple of his ancestor, Sesostris III, at Semneh, by the second cataract, putting in its place a temple of fine Nubian sandstone, in which he carefully re-erected the old boundary stela of the Middle Kingdom and re-enacted the decree of Sesostris endowing the offerings in the temple with a permanent income. Here he makes no reference to any co-regency of Hatshepsut, his queen, in the royal titulary preceding the dedication. Indeed, he allowed her no more honourable title than 'great or chief royal wife'. But the party of legitimacy was not to be so easily put off. The nomination of Hatshepsut to the succession some 15 years before, and, what was still more important, her descent from the old Theban family of the Sekenenres and the Ahmoses, were things taken seriously by the nobles of this party. As a result of their efforts Thutmose III was forced to acknowledge the co-regency of his queen and actually to give her a share in the government. Before long, her partisans had become so strong that the king was seriously hampered, and eventually even thrust into the background. Hatshepsut thus became king, an enormity with which the state fiction of the pharaoh's origin could not be harmonized. She was called 'the female Horus!' The word 'majesty' was put into a feminine form (as in Egyptian it agrees with the sex of the ruler) and the conventions of the court were all warped and distorted to suit the rule of a woman.

Hatshepsut immediately undertook independent works and royal monuments, especially a magnificent temple for her own mortuary service, which she erected in a bay of the cliffs on the west side of the river at Thebes. It is the temple now known as that of Der el-Bahri; we shall have occasion to refer to it more fully as we proceed. Whether the priestly party of Thutmose III and the party of legitimacy so weakened themselves in the struggle with each other as to fall easy victims of a third party, or whether some other varying wind of fortune favoured the party of Thutmose II, we cannot now discern. In any case, when Thutmose III and his aggressive queen had ruled about five years, Thutmose II, allying himself with the old dethroned king, Thutmose I, succeeded in thrusting aside Thutmose III and Hatshepsut and seizing the crown. Then Thutmose I and II, father and son, began a bitter persecution of the memory of Hatshepsut, cutting out her name on the monuments and placing both their own over it wherever they could find it.

News of the enmities within the royal house had probably now reached Nubia, and on the very day of Thutmose II's accession, the report of a serious outbreak there was handed to him. It was of course impossible to leave the court and the capital to the intrigues of his enemies at the moment when he had barely grasped the sceptre. He was therefore obliged to dispatch an army under the command of a subordinate, who, however, immediately advanced to the third cataract, where the cattle of the Egyptians settled in the country had been in grave danger. According to instructions the Egyptian commander not merely defeated the enemy, but slew all their males whom he could find. They captured a child of the rebellious Nubian chief and some other natives, who were carried to Thebes as hostages and paraded in the presence of the enthroned pharaoh. After this chastening Nubia again relapsed into quiet; but in the north the new pharaoh was obliged to march against the Asiatic revolters as far as Niy, on the Euphrates. On the way out, or possibly on the return, he was obliged to conduct a punitive expedition in southern Palestine against the marauding Beduin. He was accompanied by Ahrnose-Pen-Nekhbet of El Kab, who captured so many prisoners that he did not count them. This was the last campaign of the old warrior, who, like his relative and townsman, Ahmose, son of Ebana, then retired to an honoured old age at El Kab. The imposing temple of Hatshepsut, now standing gaunt and unfinished, abandoned by the workmen, was used by Thutmose II on his return from the north for recording a memorial of his Asiatic campaign. On one of the vacant walls he depicted his reception of tribute from the vanquished, the words 'horses' and 'elephants' being still legible in the accompanying inscription. At this juncture it is probable that the death of the aged Thutmose I so weakened the position of the feeble and diseased Thutmose II that he made common cause with Thutmose III, then apparently living in retirement, but of course secretly seeking to reinstate himself. In any case we find them together for a brief co-regency, which was terminated by the death of Thutmose II, after a reign of not more than three years at most.

Thutmose III thus held the throne again, but he was not able to maintain himself alone against the partisans of Hatshepsut, and was forced to a compromise, by which the queen was recognized as coregent. Matters did not stop here; her party was so powerful, that, although they were unable to dispose of Thutmose III entirely, he was again relegated to the background, while the queen played the leading role in the state. Both she and Thutmose III numbered the years of their joint reign from the first accession of Thutmose III, as if it had never been interrupted by the short reign of Thutmose II. The queen now entered upon an aggressive career as the first great woman in history of whom we are informed. Her father's architect, Ineni, thus defines the position of the two: after a brief reference to Thutmose III as 'the ruler upon the throne of him who begat him', he says: 'His sister, the Divine Consort, Hatshepsut, adjusted the affairs of the Two Lands by reason of her designs; Egypt was made to labour with bowed head for her, the excellent seed of the god, who came forth from him. The bow cable of the South, the mooring stake of the southerners, the excellent stern cable of the Northland is she; the mistress of command, whose plans are excellent, who satisfies the Two Regions when she speaks'. Thus, in perhaps the first occurrence of the ship of state, Ineni likened her, in vivid oriental imagery, to the mooring cables of a Nile boat.

This characterization is confirmed by the deeds of the queen. Her partisans had now installed themselves in the most powerful offices. Closest to the queen's person stood one Senmut, who deeply ingratiated himself in her favour. He had been the tutor of Thutmose III as a child, and he was now entrusted with the education of the queen's little daughter Nefrure, who had passed her infancy in charge of the ancient Ahmose-Pen-Nekhbet of El Kab, now no longer capable of any more serious commission. Senmut was then placed in control of the young girl's fortune as her steward. He had a brother named Senmen, who likewise supported Hatshepsut's cause. The most powerful of her coterie was Hapuseneb, who was both vizier and High Priest of Amon. He was also head of the newly organized priesthood of the whole land; he thus united in his person all the power of the administrative government with that of the strong priestly party, which was now enlisted in Hatshepsut's favour. With such new forces Hatshepsut's party was now operating. The aged Ineni was succeeded as 'overseer of the gold and silver treasury' by a noble named Thutiy, while one Nehsi was chief treasurer and colleague of Hapuseneb. The whole machinery of the state was thus in the hands of these partisans of the queen. It is needless to say that the fortunes, and probably the lives of these men were identified with the success and the dominance of Hatshepsut; they therefore took good care that her position should be maintained. In every way they were at great pains to show that the queen had been destined for the throne by the gods from the beginning. In her temple at Der el-Bahri, where work was now actively resumed, they had sculptured on the walls a long series of reliefs showing the birth of the queen. Here all the details of the old state fiction that the sovereign should be the bodily son of the sun god were elaborately depicted. Thutmose I's queen, Ahmose, is shown in converse with Amon (the successor of the sun god Re in Theban theology), who tells her as he leaves, 'Hatshepsut shall be the name of this my daughter [to be born].... She shall exercise the excellent kingship in this whole land'.

The reliefs thus show how she was designed by the divine will from the first to rule Egypt, and hence they proceed to picture her birth, accompanied by all the prodigies, which both the conventions of the court and the credulity of the folk associated with the advent of the sun god's heir. The artist who did the work followed the current tradition so closely that the newborn child appears as a *boy,* showing how the introduction of a woman into the situation was wrenching the inherited forms. To such scenes they added others, showing her coronation by the gods, and then the acknowledgment of her as queen by Thutmose I before the assembled court on New Year's day. The accompanying narrative of these events they copied from the old Twelfth Dynasty records of Amenemhet III's similar appointment by his father, Sesostris III. As a discreet reminder to any who might be inclined to oppose the queen's rule, these inscriptions were so framed by the queen's party that they represent Thutmose I as saying to the court, 'Ye shall proclaim her word, ye shall be united at her command. He who shall do her homage shall live, he who shall speak evil in blasphemy of her majesty shall die'. On the pylon, which Thutmose I built as a southern approach to the Karnak temple, he was even depicted before the Theban gods praying for a prosperous reign for his daughter. With such devices as these it was sought to overcome the prejudice against a queen upon the throne of the pharaohs.

Hatshepsut's first enterprise was, as we have intimated, to continue the building of her magnificent temple against the western cliffs at Thebes where her father and brother had inserted their names over hers. The building was in design quite unlike the great temples of the age. It was modelled after the little terraced temple of Mentuhotep II in a neighbouring bay of the cliffs.

In a series of three terraces it rose from the plain to the level of an elevated court, flanked by the massive yellow cliffs, into which the holy of holies was cut. In front of the terraces were ranged fine colonnades, which, when seen from a distance, to this day exhibit such an exquisite sense of proportion and of proper grouping, as to quite disprove the common assertion that the Greeks were the first to understand the art of adjusting external colonnades, and that the Egyptian understood only the employment of the column in interiors. The architect of the temple was Senmut, the queen's favourite, while Ineni's successor, Thutiy, wrought the bronze doors, chased with figures in electrum, and other metal work. The queen found especial pleasure in the design of the temple. She saw in it a paradise of Amon and conceived its terraces as the 'myrrh terraces' of Punt, the original home of the gods. She refers in one of her inscriptions to the fact that Amon had desired her 'to establish for him a Punt in his house'. To carry out the design fully it was further necessary to plant the terraces with the myrrh trees from Punt. Her ancestors had often sent expeditions thither, but none of these parties had ever been equipped to bring back the trees; and indeed for a long time, as far back as anyone could remember, even the myrrh necessary for the incense in the temple service had been passed from hand to hand by overland traffic until it reached Egypt. Foreign traffic had suffered severely during the long reign of the Hyksos. But one day as the queen stood before the shrine of the god, 'a command was heard from the great throne, an oracle of the god himself, that the ways to Punt should be searched out, that the highways to the myrrh terraces should be penetrated'. For, so says the god, 'It is a glorious region of God's Land, it is indeed my place of delight; I have made it for myself in order to divert my heart'. The queen adds, 'it was done according to all that the majesty of this god commanded'.

The organization and dispatch of the expedition were naturally entrusted by the queen to the chief treasurer, Nehsi, in whose coffers the wealth brought back by the expedition were to be stored. With propitiatory offerings to the divinities of the air to ensure a fair wind, the five vessels of the fleet set sail early in the ninth year of the queen's reign. The route was down the Nile and through a canal leading from the eastern Delta through the Wadi Tumilat, and connecting the Nile with the Red Sea. This canal, as the reader will recall, was already in regular use in the Middle Kingdom. Besides plentiful merchandise for barter, the fleet bore a great stone statue of the queen, to be erected in Punt. If still surviving there, it is the most remote statue ever erected by an Egyptian ruler. They arrived in Punt in safety; the Egyptian commander pitched his tent on the shore, where he was received with friendliness by Perehu, the chief of Punt, followed by his absurdly corpulent wife and three children. It was so long since any Egyptians had been seen in Punt that the Egyptians represented the Puntites as crying out, 'Why have ye come hither unto this land, which the people [of Egypt] know not. Did ye descend upon the roads of heaven, or did ye sail upon the waters, upon the sea of God's Land?'

The Puntite chief having been won with gifts, a stirring traffic is soon in progress, the ships are drawn up to the beach, the gangplanks run out, and the loading goes rapidly forward, until the vessels are laden 'very heavily with marvels of the country of Punt; all goodly fragrant woods of God's Land, heaps of myrrh resin, of fresh myrrh trees, with ebony and pure ivory, with green gold of Emu, with cinnamon wood, with incense, eye cosmetic, with baboons, monkeys, dogs, with skins of the southern panther, with natives and their children. Never was the like of this brought for any king who has been since the beginning'. After a fair voyage, without mishap, and with no transfer of cargo as far as our sources inform us, the fleet finally moored again at the docks of Thebes. Probably the Thebans had never before been diverted by such a sight as now greeted them, when the motley array of Puntites and the strange products of their far-off country passed through the streets to the queen's palace, where the Egyptian commander presented them to her majesty.

After inspecting the results of her great expedition, the queen immediately presented a portion of them to Amon, together with the impost of Nubia, with which Punt was always classed. She offered to the god 31 living myrrh trees, electrum, eye cosmetic, throw sticks of the Puntites, ebony, ivory shells, a live southern panther, which had been especially caught for her majesty, many panther skins and 3,300 small cattle. Huge piles of myrrh of twice a man's stature were now measured in grain measures under the oversight of the queen's favourite, Thutiy, and large rings of commercial gold were weighed in tall balances three metres (10 feet) high. Then, after formally announcing to Amon the success of the expedition which his oracle had called forth,

Hatshepsut summoned the court, giving to her favourites, Senmut, and the chief treasurer, Nehsi, who had dispatched the expedition, places of honour at her feet, while she told the nobles the result of her great venture.

She reminded them of Amon's oracle commanding her 'to establish for him Punt in his house, to plant the trees of God's Land beside his temple in his garden, according as he commanded'. She proudly continues, 'It was done.... I have made for him a Punt in his garden, just as he commanded me.... It is large enough for him to walk abroad in it.' Thus the splendid temple was made a terraced myrrh garden for the god, though the energetic queen was obliged to send to the end of the known world to do it for him. She had all the incidents of the remarkable expedition recorded in relief on the wall once appropriated by Thutmose II for the record of his Asiatic campaign where they still form one of the great beauties of her temple. All her chief favourites found place among the scenes. Senmut was even allowed to depict himself on one of the walls praying to Hathor for the queen, an unparalleled honour.

This unique temple was in its function the culmination of a new development in the arrangement and architecture of the royal tomb and its chapel or temple. Perhaps because they had other uses for their resources, perhaps because they recognized the futility of so vast a tomb, which yet failed to preserve from violation the body of the builder, the pharaoh, as we have seen, had gradually abandoned the construction of a pyramid. With its mortuary chapel on the east front, it had survived probably into the reign of Ahmose I, but it had been gradually declining in size and importance, while the shaft and chambers under it and the chapel before it remained relatively large. Amenhotep I was the last to follow the old traditions; he pierced a passage 60 metres (200 feet) long into the western cliffs of Thebes, terminating in a mortuary chamber for the reception of the royal body. Before the cliff, at the entrance to the passage, he built a modest mortuary chapel, surmounted by a pyramidal roof, to which we have already adverted. Probably for purposes of safety Thutmose I then took the radical step of separating the tomb from the mortuary chapel before it. The latter was still left upon the plain at the foot of the cliffs, but the sepulchre chamber, with the passage leading to it, was hewn into the rocky wall of a wild and desolate valley, lying behind the western cliffs, some two miles in a direct line from the river, and accessible only by a long detour northward, involving nearly twice that distance. It is evident that the exact spot where the king's body was entombed was intended to be kept secret, that all possibility of robbing the royal burial might be precluded.

Thutmose I's architect, Ineni, says that he superintended 'the excavation of the cliff-tomb of his majesty alone, no one seeing and no one hearing'. The new arrangement was such that the sepulchre was still behind the chapel or temple, which thus continued to be on the east of the tomb as before, although the two were now separated by the intervening cliffs. The valley, now known as the 'Valley of the Kings' Tombs', rapidly filled with the vast excavations of Thutmose I's successors. It continued to be the cemetery of the Eighteenth, Nineteenth and Twentieth Dynasties, and over 40 tombs of the Theban kings were excavated there. Forty-one now accessible form one of the wonders which attract the modern Nile tourists to Thebes, and Strabo speaks of 40 which were worthy to be visited in his time. Hatshepsut's terraced sanctuary was therefore her mortuary temple, dedicated also to her father. As the tombs multiplied in the valley behind, there rose upon the plain before it temple after temple endowed for the mortuary service of the departed gods, the emperors who had once ruled Egypt. They were besides also sacred to Amon as the state god; but they bore euphemistic names significant of their mortuary function. Thus, for example, the temple of Thutmose III was called 'Gift of Life'. Hatshepsut's architect, Hapuseneb, who was also her vizier, likewise excavated her tomb in the desolate valley. In its eastern wall, immediately behind the terraced temple, the passage descended at a sharp decline for many hundred metres, and terminated in several chambers, one of which contained a sarcophagus both for herself and her father, Thutmose I. But the family feud was probably responsible for his construction of his own tomb, on a modest scale, as we have seen, and he doubtless never used the sarcophagus made for him by his daughter. Both sarcophagi, however, had been robbed in antiquity and contained no remains when recently discovered.

The aggressive queen's attention to the arts of peace, her active devotion to the development of the resources of her empire, soon began to bring in returns. Besides the vast income of the crown from internal sources, Hatshepsut was also receiving tribute from her wide empire, extending from the third cataract of the Nile to the Euphrates. As she herself claimed, 'My southern boundary is as far as Punt ... my eastern boundary is as far as the marshes of Asia, and the Asiatics are in my grasp; my western boundary is as far as the mountain of Manu [the sunset] ... my fame is among the Sand-dwellers [Beduin] altogether. The myrrh of Punt has been brought to me ... all the luxurious marvels of this country were brought to my palace in one collection.... They have brought to me the choicest products ... of cedar, of juniper and of Meru wood ... all the goodly sweet woods of God's Land. I brought the tribute of Tehenu [Libya], consisting of ivory and seven hundred tusks which were there, numerous panther skins of five cubits along the back and four cubits wide'. Evidently no serious trouble in Asia had as yet resulted from the fact that there was no longer a warrior upon the throne of the pharaohs. This energetic woman therefore began to employ her new wealth in the restoration of the old temples, which, although two generations had elapsed, had not even yet recovered from the neglect which they had suffered under the Hyksos. She recorded her good work upon a rock temple of Pakht at Beni Hasan, saying, 'I have restored that which was ruins, I have raised up that which was unfinished since the Asiatics were in the midst of Avaris of the Northland, and the barbarians in the midst of them, overthrowing that which had been made while they ruled in ignorance of Re'.

It was now seven or eight years since she and Thutmose III had regained the throne and 15 years since they had first seized it. Thutmose III had never been appointed heir to the succession, but his queen had enjoyed that honour, and it was now nearing the thirtieth anniversary of her appointment, when she might celebrate her jubilee. She must therefore make preparation for the erection of the obelisks, which were the customary memorial of such jubilees. Of this, the queen herself tells us: 'I sat in the palace, I remembered him who fashioned me, my heart led me to make for him two obelisks of electrum, whose points mingled with heaven'. Her inevitable favourite, Semnut, was therefore called in and instructed to proceed to the granite quarries at the first cataract to secure the two gigantic shafts for the obelisks. He levied the necessary forced labour and began work early in February of the queen's 15th year. By early August, exactly seven months later, he had freed the huge blocks from the quarry, was able to employ the high water then rapidly approaching to float them, and towed them to Thebes before the inundation had again fallen.

The queen then chose an extraordinary location for her obelisks, namely, the very colonnaded hall of the Karnak temple erected by her father, where her husband Thutmose III had been named king by oracle of Amon; although this necessitated the removal of all her father's cedar columns in the south half of the hall and four of those in the north half, besides, of course, unroofing the hall, and demolishing the south wall, where the obelisks were introduced. They were richly overlaid with electrum, the work on which was done for the queen by Thutiy. She avers that she measured out the precious metal by the peck, like sacks of grain, and she is supported in this extraordinary statement by Thutiy, who states that by royal command he piled up in the festival hall of the palace no less than nearly 20 bushels of electrum. The queen boasts of their beauty, 'their summits being of electrum of the best of every country, which are seen on both sides of the river. Their rays flood the Two Lands when the sun rises between them as be dawns in the horizon of heaven'. They towered so high above the dismantled hall of Thutmose I that the queen recorded a long oath, swearing by all the gods that they were each of one block'.

They were indeed the tallest shafts ever erected in Egypt up to that time, being 30 metres (97½ feet) high and weighing nearly 350 tons each. One of them still stands, an object of constant admiration to the modern visitor at Thebes. Hatshepsut at the same time erected two more large obelisks at Karnak, though they have now perished. It is possible that she also set up two more, at her terraced temple, making six in all; for she has recorded there the transportation of two great shafts on the river, depicting the achievement in a relief, which shows the obelisks end to end on a huge barge, towed by 30 galleys, with a total of some 960 oarsmen. But this scene may refer to the first two obelisks as they were brought down the river by Senmut.

Besides her obelisks, erected in her 16th year, we learn of another enterprise of Hatshepsut in the same year from a relief in the Wadi Maghara in Sinai, whither the tireless queen had sent a mining expedition, resuming the work there which had been interrupted by the Hyksos invasion. This work in Sinai continued in her name until the 20th year of her reign.

Sometime between this date and the close of the year 21, when we find Thutmose III ruling alone, the great queen must have died. If we have spent some space on her buildings and expeditions, it has been because she was a woman, in an age when warfare was impossible for her sex, and great achievements could only be hers in the arts and enterprises of peace. Great though she was, her rule was a distinct misfortune, falling, as it did, at a time when Egypt's power in Asia had not yet been seriously tested, and Syria was only too ready to revolt.

Thutmose III was not chivalrous in his treatment of her when she was gone. He had suffered too much. Burning to lead his forces into Asia, he had been assigned to such puerile functions as offering incense to Amon on the return of the queen's expedition to Punt; or his restless energies had been allowed to expend themselves on building his mortuary temple of the western plain of Thebes. Considering the age in which he lived, we must not too much blame him for his treatment of the departed queen. Around her obelisks in her father's hall at Karnak he now had a masonry sheathing built, covering her name and the record of her erection of them on the base. Everywhere he had her name erased and in the terraced temple on all the walls both her figure and her name have been hacked out. Her partisans doubtless all fled. If not they must have met short shrift. In the relief scenes in the same temple, where Senmut and Nehsi and Thutiy had been so proud to appear, their names and their figures were ruthlessly chiselled away. The queen had given Senmut three statues in the Theban temples and on all these his name was erased; in his tomb and on his mortuary stela his name vanished. A statue of the vizier Hapuseneb was treated in the same way. Thutiy's tomb was likewise visited and his name obliterated, the tomb of Senmen, Senmut's brother, did not escape, and the name of a colleague of theirs who was buried in the next tomb was so effectually erased that we do not know who he was. Even distant Silsileh was visited at the king's orders that the tomb of the queen's 'chief steward' might be dealt with in the same way. And these mutilated monuments stand to this day, grim witnesses of the great king's vengeance. But in Hatshepsut's splendid temple her fame still lives, and the masonry around her Karnak obelisk has fallen down, exposing the gigantic shaft to proclaim to the modern world the greatness of Hatshepsut.

The Consolidation of the Empire:
Thutmose III

✝

I N THE YEAR 15, Hatshepsut and Thutmose III still controlled their Asiatic dependencies as far north as the Lebanon. From that time until we find him marching into Asia, late in the year 22, we are not informed of what took place there; but the conditions which then confronted him and the course of his subsequent campaigns make it evident how matters had gone with Egyptian supremacy during the interim. Not having seen an Egyptian army for many years, the Syrian dynasts grew continually more restless, and finding that their boldness called forth no response from the pharaoh, the king of Kadesh, once probably the suzerain of all Syria-Palestine, had stirred all the city kings of northern Palestine and Syria to accept his leadership in a great coalition, in which they at last felt themselves strong enough to begin open revolt. Kadesh thus assumed its head with a power in which we should evidently recognize the surviving prestige of her old time more extended and unchallenged suzerainty.

'Behold from Yeraza [in northern Judea] to the marshes of the earth [upper Euphrates], they had begun to revolt against his majesty.' But southern Palestine was loth to take up arms against the pharaoh. Sharuhen, which had suffered a six years' siege at the hands of Ahmose in Hyksos days, was too well aware of what to expect thoughtlessly to assume the offensive against Egypt. Hence the whole region of southern Palestine, which had witnessed that siege, was not differently minded, but a small minority probably desired to join the revolt. Hence civil war arose in Sharuhen, as well as in the south generally, as the allies sought to compel the southern dynasts to join the uprising and send a quota to the army which they were raising. Not only were 'all the allied countries of Zahi', or western Syria, in open rebellion against the pharaoh, but it is also evident that the great kingdom of Mitanni, on the east of the Euphrates, had done all in her power to encourage the rebellion and to support it when once in progress; for Thutmose III was ultimately obliged to invade Mitanni and punish its king before he could maintain Egyptian supremacy in Naharin. It was natural that Mitanni, an aggressive and active power, competing with the infant Assyria on more than equal terms, should view with distrust the presence of a new and great empire on its western borders. The Mitannian king had finally learned what to expect from Egypt and he would naturally exert himself to the utmost to rehabilitate the once great kingdom of Kadesh, as a buffer between himself and Egypt. Against such formidable resources as these, then, Thutmose III was summoned to contend, and no pharaoh before his time had ever undertaken so great a task.

In what condition the long unused Egyptian army may have been, or how long it took Thutmose to reorganize and prepare it for service, we have no means of knowing. The armies of the early orient, at least those of Egypt, were not large, and it is not probable that any pharaoh ever invaded Asia with more than 25,000 or 30,000 men, while less than 20,000 is probably nearer the usual figure. Late in his 22nd year we find Thutmose with his army ready to take the field. He marched from Tharu, the last Egyptian city on the north-eastern frontier, about the 19th of April, 1479 BCE. Nine days later, that is, on April 28th, he reached Gaza, 257 kilometres (160 miles) from Tharu. In the Egyptian calendar the day was the fourth of Pakhons, his coronation day, just 22 years since the oracle of Amon had proclaimed him king in his father's colonnaded temple hall at Karnak.

It had been long indeed, but the opportunity for which he had ceaselessly plotted and planned and striven was at last his. He was not the man to waste the day in a futile celebration, but having arrived in the evening of the coronation anniversary, he was away for the north again the very next morning. Marching along the Shephelah and through the sea plain, he crossed the plain of Sharon, turning inland as he did so, and camped on the evening of May 10th at Yehem, a town of uncertain location, some 125 or 145 kilometres (80 or 90 miles) from Gaza, on the southern slopes of the Carmel range. Meantime, the army of the Asiatic allies under the command of the king of Kadesh, had pushed southward as far as the territory of their adherents extended, and had occupied the strong fortress of Megiddo, in the plain of Jezreel, on the north slope of the Carmel ridge. This place, which here appears in history for the first time, was not only a powerful stronghold, but occupied an important strategic position, commanding the road from Egypt between the two Lebanons to the Euphrates, hence its prominent role in oriental history from this time on. Thutmose, of course, regarded all this country as his own, and hence afterward says: 'The lands of the Fenkhu [Asiatics] had begun to invade my boundary'.

Thus far he had been advancing through friendly towns, or at least through regions where no open disaffection prevailed; but as he neared Carmel it was necessary to move with caution. At Yehem he learned of the enemy's occupation of Megiddo, and he called a council of his officers to ascertain the most favourable route for crossing the ridge and reaching the plain of Esdraelon. There were three roads practicable for an army leading from Yehem over the mountain; one which made a direct line by way of Aruna for the gates of Megiddo; and two involving a detour to either side, the first leading around southward by way of Taanach, about eight kilometres (five miles) southeast of Megiddo; and the other northward through Zefti, emerging on the northwest of Megiddo. Thutmose characteristically favoured the direct route, but his officers urged that the other roads were more open, while the middle one was a narrow pass. 'Will not horse come behind horse,' they asked, 'and man behind man likewise? Shall our advance guard be fighting while our rear guard is yet standing in Aruna?' These objections showed a good military understanding of the dangers of the pass; but Thutmose swore a round oath that he would move against his enemies by the most direct route, and they might follow or not as they pleased. Accordingly, making his preparations very deliberately, he moved to Aruna on the 13th of May. To prevent surprise and also to work upon the courage of his army, he personally took the head of the column, vowing that none should precede him, but that he would go 'forth at the head of his army himself, showing the way by his own footsteps'.

Aruna lay well up in the mountain ridge, accessible only by a stretch of narrow road; but he reached it in safety, and passed the night of the 13th there. At this point his army must have been distributed for a long distance along the road from Aruna back to Yehem; but on the morning of the 14th he pushed quickly forward again. He had not been long on the march when he came in touch with the enemy. Had they been in force he must have suffered, in view of his long and straggling line of march, extended along the narrow mountain road. Fortunately, the pass now widened and he was able to expand his advance in a spreading valley. Here, on the urgent advice of his officers, he held the enemy in check until his rear, which was still in Aruna, came up. The enemy had not been in sufficient force to take advantage of his precarious position, and he now pushed on his advance again. It was just past midday when his forward column emerged from the pass upon the plain of Esdraelon, and by one o'clock Thutmose halted without opposition on the south of Megiddo, 'on the bank of the brook Kina'. The Asiatics had thus lost an inestimable opportunity to destroy him in detail. They seem to have been too far toward the south-east to draw in quickly and concentrate against his thin line of march as it defiled from the mountains.

It is impossible to determine their exact position, but when the skirmishing in the mountains took place their southern wing was at Taanach, doubtless in the expectation that Thutmose would cross the mountain by the Taanach road. From Taanach their line could not have extended as far north as Megiddo, otherwise it would have been impossible for the Egyptians peacefully to emerge from the defile and debouch upon the slope south of Megiddo. Thutmose went into camp on the plain by Megiddo, sending out orders to the entire army to make ready for the battle on the morrow. Preparations for the conflict then went quietly on, and the best of order and spirit prevailed in the camp. Late in the afternoon of the same day (the 14th), or during the ensuing night, Thutmose took advantage of the enemy's position on the east and south-east of his own force to draw his line around the west side of Megiddo and boldly threw out his left wing on the northwest of the city. He thus secured, in case of necessity, a safe and easy line of retreat westward along the Zefti road, while at the same time his extreme left might cut off the enemy from flight northward.

Early the next morning, the 15th of May, Thutmose gave orders to form and move out in order of battle. In a glittering chariot of electrum he took up his position with the centre; his right or southern wing rested on a hill south of the brook of Kina; while, as we have seen, his left was northwest of Megiddo. To protect their stronghold the Asiatics now drew in between Thutmose's line and the city, from which, of course, supplementary forces emerged. He immediately attacked them, leading the onset himself 'at the head of his army'. 'The king himself, he led the way of his army, mighty at its head like a flame of fire, the king who wrought with his sword. He went forth, none like him, slaying the barbarians, smiting Retenu, bringing their princes as living captives, their chariots wrought with gold, bound to their horses.' The enemy gave way at the first charge, 'they fled headlong to Megiddo in fear, abandoning their horses and their chariots of gold and silver, and the people hauled them up, pulling them by their clothing into this city; the people of this city having closed it against them and lowered clothing to pull them up into this city. Now if only the army of his majesty had not given their heart to plundering the things of the enemy they would have captured Megiddo at this moment, when the wretched vanquished king of Kadesh and the wretched vanquished king of this city [Megiddo] were hauled up in haste to bring them into this city'. But the discipline of an oriental army cannot to this day withstand a rich display of plunder; much less could the host of Egypt in the fifteenth century BCE resist the spoil of the combined armies of Syria. 'Then were captured their horses, their chariots of gold and silver were made spoil…. Their champions lay stretched out like fishes on the ground. The victorious army of his majesty went round counting the spoils, their portions. Behold there was captured the tent of that wretched vanquished foe [the king of Kadesh] in which was his son. The whole army made jubilee, giving praise to Amon for the victory which he had granted to his son. They brought in the booty which they had taken, consisting of hands severed from the slain, living prisoners, of horses, chariots, gold and silver.' It is evident that in the disorganized rout the camp of the king of Kadesh fell into the hands of the Egyptians and they brought its rich and luxurious furniture to the pharaoh.

But the stern Thutmose was not to be placated by these tokens of victory; he saw only what had been lost. 'Had ye afterwards captured this city,' said he to the troops, 'behold I would have given [a rich offering to] Re this day; because every chief of every country that has revolted is within it; and because it is the capture of a thousand cities, this capture of Megiddo.' Hereupon he gave orders for the instant investment of the city; 'they measured this city, surrounding it with an enclosure, walled about with green timber of all their pleasant trees. His majesty himself was upon the fortification east of the city, inspecting what was done'. Thutmose boasts after his return to Egypt, saying, 'Amon gave to me all the allied countries of Zahi shut up in one city.... I snared them in one city, I built around them with a rampart of thick wall'. They called this wall of investment: 'Thutmose is the Surrounder of the Asiatics', according to the custom under the empire of naming every royal building after the king. The closest vigilance was enjoined upon the troops that none might escape, and no one from within the city was allowed to approach the siege lines unless with the purpose of surrendering. But, as we shall see, before Thutmose had succeeded in closely investing the place, the king of Kadesh had escaped northward, which was exactly what Thutmose had desired to prevent in swinging his left wing around the northwest angle of the city on the night before the battle.

As the siege went on, the dynasts who were fortunate enough not to be shut up in the city hastened to make their peace with the incensed pharaoh; 'the Asiatics of all countries came with bowed head, doing obeisance to the fame of his majesty'. Of the course of the siege meanwhile and of the assaults of the Egyptians, we are not informed. The priestly scribe of our only source remarks, 'Now all that his majesty did to this city, to that wretched foe and his wretched army was recorded on each day by its [the day's] name ... recorded upon a roll of leather in the temple of Amon to this day'. But this precious roll, like the book of chronicles of the kings of Judah, has perished, and our narrative suffers much from its loss.

The season was far enough advanced so that the Egyptians foraged on the grain fields of the plain of Esdraelon, while its herds furnished them the fat of the land. They were the first host, of whom we have knowledge, to ravage this fair plain, destined to be the battle ground of the east and west from Thutmose III to Napoleon. But within the walls all was different; proper provision for a siege had not been made, and famine finally wrought its customary havoc in the beleaguered town, which, after sustaining the siege for some weeks, at length surrendered. But the king of Kadesh was not among the prisoners. 'These Asiatics who were in the wretched Megiddo ... came forth to the fame of Thutmose III, who is given life, saying, "Give us a chance, that we may present to thy majesty our impost". Then they came, bringing that which belonged to them, to do obeisance to the fame of his majesty, to crave the breath of their nostrils, because of the greatness of his power'. 'Then,' says Thutmose, 'my majesty commanded to give to them the breath of life', and it is evident that he treated them with the greatest leniency. The frightful destruction of whole cities, of which the Assyrian kings boasted when recounting their treatment of rebels, is nowhere found among the records of the pharaohs. To compensate for the failure to capture the dangerous king of Kadesh himself, they secured his family as hostages; for Thutmose says, 'Lo, my majesty carried off the wives of that vanquished one, together with his children, and the wives of the chiefs who were there, together with their children'.

Rich as had been the spoil on the battlefield, it was not to be compared with the wealth which awaited the pharaoh in the captured city. Nine hundred and twenty-four chariots, including those of the kings of Kadesh and Megiddo, 2,238 horses, 200 suits of armour, again including those of the same two kings, the gorgeous tent of the king of Kadesh, some 2,000 large cattle and 22,500 small cattle, the magnificent household furniture of the king of Kadesh, and among it his royal sceptre, a silver statue, perhaps of his god, and an ebony statue of himself, wrought with gold and lapis lazuli. Immense quantities of gold and silver were also taken from the city, but they are combined with the spoil of other cities in Thutmose's account of the plunder, and we cannot determine how much came out of Megiddo alone. The cattle, of course, came from the country round about; otherwise the city would not have suffered from famine. Before they left, the army also harvested the fields of the plain of Esdraelon around Megiddo, and gathered over 113,000 bushels, after the army had foraged on the fields during the siege.

Thutmose lost no time in marching as far northward as the hostile strongholds and the lateness of the season would permit. He reached the southern slopes of Lebanon, where the three cities of Yenoam, Nuges and Herenkeru formed a kind of Tripolis under the government of 'that foe', who was possibly the king of Kadesh. They quickly succumbed, if their king had not already been among those to send in their submission, while Thutmose was still besieging Megiddo. In order to prevent another southward advance of the still unconquered king of Kadesh and to hold command of the important road northward between the Lebanons, Thutmose now built a fortress at this point, which he called 'Thutmose-is-the-Binder-of-the-Barbarians', using the same rare word for 'barbarian' which Hatshepsut applies to the Hyksos. He now began the reorganization of the conquered territory, supplanting the old revolting dynasts, of course, with others who might be expected to show loyalty to Egypt. These new rulers were allowed to govern much as they pleased, if only they regularly and promptly sent in the yearly tribute to Egypt. In order to hold them to their obligations Thutmose carried off with him to Egypt their eldest sons, whom he placed in a special quarter or building called 'Castle in Thebes'. Here they were educated and so treated as to engender feelings of friendliness toward Egypt; and whenever a king of one of the Syrian cities died 'his majesty would cause his son to stand in his place'. Thutmose now controlled all Palestine as far north as the southern end of Lebanon, and further inland also Damascus. In so far as they had rebelled, he stripped all the towns of their wealth, and returned to Egypt with some 194 kilograms (426 pounds) of gold and silver in commercial rings or wrought into magnificent vessels and other objects of art, besides untold quantities of less valuable property and the spoil of Megiddo already mentioned.

Early in October Thutmose had reached Thebes, and we can be certain that it was such a return to the capital as no pharaoh before him had ever enjoyed. In less than six months, that is, within the limits of the dry season in Palestine, he had marched from Tharu, gained a sweeping victory at Megiddo, captured the city after a long and arduous investment, marched to the Lebanon and taken three cities there, built and garrisoned a permanent fort near them, begun reorganizing the government in northern Palestine, and completed the return journey to Thebes. With what difficulties such an achievement was beset we may learn by a perusal of Napoleon's campaign from Egypt through the same country against Akko, which is almost exactly as far from Egypt as Megiddo. We may then understand why it was that Thutmose immediately celebrated three 'Feasts of Victory' in his capital. They were each five days long and coincided with the first, second and fifth calendar feasts of Amon. The last was held in Thutmose's mortuary temple on the western plain of Thebes, which was now completed, and this may have been the first celebration held in it. These feasts were made permanent, endowed with an annual income of plentiful offerings. At the feast of Opet, which was Amon's greatest annual feast and lasted 11 days, he presented to the god the three towns which he had captured in southern Lebanon, besides a rich array of magnificent vessels of gold, silver and costly stones from the prodigious spoil of Retenu. In order to furnish income to maintain the temple on the sumptuous plan thus projected, he gave Amon not only the said three towns, but also extensive lands in Upper and Lower Egypt, supplied them with plentiful herds and with hosts of peasant serfs taken from among his Asiatic prisoners. Thus was established the foundation of that vast fortune of Amon, which now began to grow out of all proportion to the increased wealth of other temples. Hence the state temple, the old sanctuary of his father at Karnak, was no longer adequate for the rich and elaborate state cult; for even his father's great hall had been dismantled by Hatshepsut in order to insert her obelisks.

There it stood, with the obelisks preventing the replacement of over a third of the roof, the south half without roof or columns, and four cedar columns of Thutmose I, with two of sandstone which he had himself inserted, occupying the north half. It was further disfigured by the masonry which Thutmose III had built around Hatshepsut's obelisks. But it was the hall where he had been called to be king of Egypt by the oracle of Amon himself. Hatshepsut's partisan, Thutiy, had now been supplanted by another architect and chief of craftsmen named Menkheperre-seneb, whose very name, 'Thutmose III is Healthy', was indicative of his loyalty. He was called in and an attempt was made to restore the north half of the old hall, replacing the cedar columns by shafts of sandstone. But the southern half was left untouched. In this makeshift hall the great feasts celebrating his victorious return from the first campaign were some of them held, but for others he naturally resorted to his mortuary temple of Amon, which, as we have seen, was now complete on the western plain. Judging from the small temple of Ptah by the great Karnak temple which Thutmose also rebuilt at his return from this campaign, he probably showed like generosity to the two ancient sanctuaries at Heliopolis and Memphis, of which the former was still in a traditional sense the temple of the state god, for Re was now identified with Amon.

The great task of properly consolidating the empire was now fairly begun; but Egyptian power in Asia during the long military inactivity of Hatshepsut's reign had been so thoroughly shaken that Thutmose III was far from ready, as a result of the first campaign, to march immediately upon Kadesh, his most dangerous enemy. Moreover, he desired properly to organize and render perfectly secure the states already under the power of Egypt. In the year 24 therefore he marched in a wide curve through the conquered territory of northern Palestine and southern Syria, while the dynasts came to pay their tribute and do him homage in 'every place of his majesty's circuit where the tent was pitched'. The news of his great victory of the year before had by this time reached Assyria, now just rising on the eastern horizon, with her career as yet all before her. Her king naturally desired to be on good terms with the great empire of the west, and the gifts of costly stone, chiefly lapis lazuli from Babylon, and the horses which he sent to Thutmose, so that they reached him while on this campaign, were, of course, interpreted by the Egyptians as tribute. In all probability no battles were fought on this expedition.

Returning to Thebes as before, in October, the king immediately planned for the enlargement of the Karnak temple, to suit the needs of the empire of which he dreamed. Moreover, the slowly rising bed of the river had now raised the waters of the inundation until they invaded the temple area, and it had become necessary to elevate the temple pavement. The splendid gate of Amenhotep I was sacrificed to this necessity. By the latter part of February, at the feast of the new moon, which happened by a lucky chance to fall upon the day of the 10th feast of Amon, he was able personally to celebrate the foundation ceremonies with the greatest splendour. To render the act especially auspicious the god appeared and even himself participated in the stretching of the measuring cord as the foundation plan was laid out. As the west end, the real front of the temple, was marred by Hatshepsut's obelisks, rising from his father's dismantled hall, and he was unable or unwilling to build around his father's obelisks, which stood before the western entrance of the temple, Thutmose III laid out his imposing colonnaded halls at the other, or east end, of the temple, where they today form one of the great architectural beauties of Thebes. The greatest hall is nearly 42 metres (140 feet) long, and lies transversely across the axis of the temple. This hall was called 'Menkheperre [Thutmose III] is Glorious in Monuments', a name which it still bore 650 years later. Behind it is the sanctuary or holy of holies, while grouped about it are some half a hundred halls and chambers. Among these, on the south side, was a hall for the mortuary service of his ancestors. In the chamber to which this hall led he 'commanded to record the names of his fathers, to increase their offerings and to fashion statues of all these their bodies'. These names formed a great list on the walls, which still exists in the Bibliotheque Nationale at Paris. The statues of his fathers, while many have perished, have recently been discovered in a court south of the temple, where they had been concealed for safety in time of war.

The third campaign of the next year (25) was evidently spent like the first, in organizing the southern half of the future Asiatic empire, the northern half being still unsubdued. When he returned, his building at Karnak was sufficiently far advanced to record upon the walls of one of the chambers the plants and animals of Asia which he had found on his march and brought home with him to beautify the garden of the temple of Amon, the sacred lake of which he supplied with a masonry coping.

No records of the fourth campaign have survived, but the course of his subsequent operations was such that it must have been confined like the others to the territory already regained. It had now become evident to Thutmose that he could not march northward between the Lebanons and operate against Kadesh, while leaving his flank exposed to the unsubdued Phoenician cities of the coast. It was likewise impossible to strike Naharin and Mitanni without first destroying Kadesh, which dominated the Orontes valley. He therefore planned a series of campaigns, directed first against the northern coast, which he might then use as a base of operations against Kadesh; and this being once disposed of, he could again push in from the coast against Mitanni and the whole Naharin region. No modern strategist could have conceived a series of operations better suited to the conditions, nor have gone about putting them into execution with more indomitable energy than Thutmose now displayed. He therefore organized a fleet and placed in command of it a trusty officer named Nibamon, who had served with his father.

In the year 29, on his fifth campaign, he moved for the first time against the northern coast cities, the wealthy commercial kingdoms of Phoenicia. He must have employed the new fleet and transported his army by sea, for he began operations in northern Phoenicia, which, with all southern Phoenicia and Kadesh still unconquered, he could not have reached by land. It is possible that he gained his first foothold by offering to Tyre special inducements to submit, for it is evident that some pharaoh granted this city exceptional privileges, making it practically a free city. It is easily conceivable that the rich harbour town would readily embrace the opportunity to save her commerce from destruction and escape tribute, or at least a portion of the usual obligation in the future. The name of the first city which Thutmose took is unfortunately lost, but it was on the coast opposite Tunip, and must have been a place of considerable importance, for it brought him rich spoils; and there was in the town a temple of Amon, erected by one of Thutmose III's predecessors (either Thutmose I or possibly Amenhotep I). The cities of the interior, seeing that this attack from the coast must be fatal to them if successful, had sent troops to assist in its defence. Thus Tunip sent forces to strengthen the garrison of this unknown city, the fall of which would involve the ultimate capture of Tunip also.

Thutmose now seized the fleet of the city, and was able rapidly to move his army southward against the powerful city of Arvad. A short siege, compelling Thutmose to cut down the groves about the town, as at Megiddo, sufficed to bring the place to terms, and with its surrender a vast quantity of the wealth of Phoenicia fell into the hands of the Egyptians. Besides this, it being now autumn, the gardens and groves 'were filled with their fruit, their wines were found left in their presses as water flows, their grain on the [hillside] terraces ... it was more plentiful than the sand of the shore. The army were overwhelmed with their portions'. Under these circumstances it was useless for Thutmose to attempt to maintain discipline, and during the first days following the surrender, 'behold the army of his majesty was drunk and anointed with oil every day as at a feast in Egypt'. The dynasts along the coast now came in with their tribute and offered submission. Thutmose had thus gained a secure footing on the northern coast, easily accessible by water from Egypt, and forming an admirable base for operations inland as he had foreseen. He then returned to Egypt, possibly not for the first time, by water.

All was now in readiness for the long-planned advance upon Kadesh. It had taken five campaigns to gain the south and the coast; the sixth was at last directed against his long invulnerable enemy. In the year 30 the close of the spring rains found Thutmose disembarking his army from the fleet at Simyra, by the mouth of the Eleutheros, up the valley of which he immediately marched upon Kadesh. It was a convenient and easy road, and the shortest route from the sea to Kadesh to be found anywhere along the coast; indeed it was then, as it is now, the only practicable highway for a military advance inland across the mountains toward the region of Kadesh. The city lay on the west side of the Orontes river at the north end of the high valley between the two Lebanons, the ridge of Anti-Lebanon dropping to the plain just south and east of the town. A small tributary of the Orontes from the west joined the larger stream just below the city, so that it lay on a point of land between the two. A canal, still traceable and doubtless in existence in Thutmose's day, was cut across the tongue of land above the town, thus connecting the two streams and entirely surrounding the place by water. An inner moat encircling the high curtain walls within the banks of the rivers reenforced the natural water defences, so that, in spite of its location in a perfectly level plain, it was a place of great strength, and probably the most formidable fortress in Syria.

In its relation to the surrounding country also the place was skilfully chosen as one of great strategic importance; for, as the reader recalls, it commanded the Orontes valley, and, as Thutmose had found, it was impossible to advance northward without reckoning with it. It will be remembered, furthermore, that it also dominated the only road inland from the coast for a long distance both north and south. This was the road up the Eleutheros valley, along which we have followed Thutmose. The capture of such a place by siege was an achievement of no slight difficulty, and it is with peculiar regret that one reads in the narrative of the priestly scribe who excerpted Thutmose's annals, merely these words regarding it: 'His majesty arrived at the city of Kadesh, overthrew it, cut down its groves, harvested its grain'. We can only discern from these laconic words that as at Megiddo Thutmose was obliged to fell the groves to build his siege walls, and that the army lived on the forage from the surrounding grain fields during the investment, which must therefore have continued from early spring into harvest time. At least one assault was made, in which Amenemhab, one of Thutmose's commanders, whom we shall meet in later campaigns also, captured two of the patricians of the city. He was rewarded in the presence of the army with two orders or decorations for distinguished service: 'a lion of the finest gold' and 'two flies', besides rich ornaments.

The siege had now continued long enough to encourage the coast cities in the hope that Thutmose had suffered a reverse. In spite of the chastisement inflicted upon Arvad the year before, the opulent harbour town could not resist an attempt to rid itself of the annual obligation to Thutmose, which cost it so large a portion of its yearly gains. As soon as Kadesh fell and Thutmose was able to leave it, he quickly returned to Simyra, embarked his army on his waiting fleet and sailed to Arvad to inflict swift retribution. Sailing for Egypt as the rainy season drew on, he took with him the sons of the north Syrian kings and dynasts, to be educated at Thebes, as he had already done with the young princes of the south in former years.

The revolt of Arvad, while Thutmose was still besieging Kadesh, showed him that he must devote another campaign to the thorough subjugation of the coast before he could safely push inland beyond the valley of the Orontes on the long-planned advance into Naharin. He therefore spent the summer of the year 31, the seventh campaign, in completely quenching any slumbering embers of revolt in the coast cities. In spite of his display of force at Simyra, Ullaza, a harbour town near Simyra, had showed serious disaffection, owing to encouragement from the king of Tunip, who sent his two sons to conduct the revolt. On the 27th of April, Thutmose appeared in the harbour of the recreant city; he made short work of the place and captured the king of Tunip's son. The local dynasts came in as usual with their submission and Thutmose collected about 85 kilograms (185 pounds) of silver from them and the captured city, besides great quantities of natural produce. He then sailed from harbour to harbour along the coast, displaying his force and thoroughly organizing the administration of the cities. In particular he saw to it that every harbour town should be liberally supplied with provisions for his coming campaign in Naharin. On his return to Egypt he found envoys from the extreme south, probably eastern Nubia, bringing to the pharaoh their tribute, showing that he was maintaining an aggressive policy in the far south while at the same time so active in the north.

The organization and the collection of resources necessary for the great campaign now before him evidently occupied Thutmose all the year following his return from this expedition; for it was not until the spring of the year 33 that he landed his forces in the harbour of Simyra, on his eighth campaign, and marched inland for the second time along the Kadesh road. He turned northward and captured the town of Ketne. Continuing the march down the Orontes, he fought a battle at the city of Senzar, which he also took. In this action his general, Amenemhab, again won distinction. Thutmose probably crossed and forsook the Orontes at this point; in any case, he now entered Naharin and marched rapidly on. He soon met resistance and fought a slight action in which Amenemhab captured three prisoners. But no serious force confronted him until he had arrived at 'The Height of Wan, on the west of Aleppo', where a considerable battle was fought, in the course of which Amenemhab took 13 prisoners, each bearing a bronze spear inlaid with gold. This doubtless shows that the royal troops of the king of Aleppo were engaged. Aleppo itself must have fallen, for the pharaoh could otherwise hardly have pushed on without delay, as he evidently did. 'Behold his majesty went north, capturing the towns and laying waste the settlements of that foe of wretched Naharin', who was, of course, the king of Mitanni. Egyptian troops were again plundering the Euphrates valley, a license which they had not enjoyed since the days of their fathers under Thutmose I, some 50 years before.

As he advanced northward, Thutmose now turned slightly toward the Euphrates, in order to reach Carchemish. In the battle fought at that city it must have been his long unscathed foe, the King of Mitanni, whose army Thutmose scattered far and wide, 'not one looked behind him, but they fled forsooth like a herd of mountain goats'. Amenemhab seems to have pushed the pursuit across the Euphrates to the east side, as he was obliged to cross it in bringing back to the king the prisoners whom he had taken. This battle at last enabled Thutmose to do what he had been fighting 10 years to attain, for he himself now crossed the Euphrates into Mitanni and set up his boundary tablet on the east side, an achievement of which none of his fathers could boast. But without wintering in Naharin, it was impossible for Thutmose to advance further, and he was too wise a soldier to risk exposing to the inclement northern winter the seasoned veterans of so many campaigns, whom it would have taken him years to replace. He therefore returned unmolested to the west shore, where he found the tablet of his father, Thutmose I, and with the greatest satisfaction he set up another of his own alongside it.

It was now late in the season, his troops had already harvested the fields of the Euphrates valley, and he was obliged to begin the return march. But one serious enterprise still awaited him before he could return to the coast.

The city of Niy, further down the Euphrates, was still unconquered and all his work in Naharin might be undone were this place left unscathed. Having set up his boundary tablets, therefore, he marched down the river and took Niy without trouble so far as we know. The object of the campaign having been accomplished and its arduous duties past, Thutmose organized a great elephant hunt in the region of Niy, where these animals have now been extinct for ages. He and his party attacked the North Syrian herd of 120 animals. In the course of the hunt the king came to close quarters with one great beast and was in some danger when his general, Amenemhab, rushed between and cut off the animal's trunk; whereupon the infuriated beast charged upon his hardy assailant, who escaped between two rocks overhanging a neighbouring pool. For thus diverting the animal at the critical moment the faithful Amenemhab was of course liberally rewarded by the king.

Meantime, all the local princes and dynasts of Naharin appeared at his camp and brought in their tribute as a token of their submission. Even far off Babylon was now anxious to secure the goodwill of the pharaoh, and its king sent him gifts wrought of lapis lazuli. But what was still more important, the mighty people of the Kheta, whose domain stretched far away into the unknown regions of Asia Minor, sent him a rich gift. As he was on the march from Naharin to reach the coast again their envoys met him, with eight massive commercial rings of silver, weighing nearly 45 kilograms (98 pounds), beside some unknown precious stone and costly wood. Thus the Kheta, probably the Biblical Hittites, enter for the first time, as far as we know, into relations with the Egyptian pharaohs. On Thutmose's arrival at the coast, he laid upon the chiefs of the Lebanon the yearly obligation to keep the Phoenician harbours supplied with the necessary provision for his campaigns. From any point in this line of harbours, which he could reach from Egypt by ship in a few days, he was then able to strike inland without delay and bring delinquents to an immediate accounting. His sea power was such that the king of Cyprus became practically a vassal of Egypt, as later in Saitic times. Moreover, his fleet made him so feared in the islands of the north that he was able to exert a loose control over the eastern Mediterranean, westward an indefinite distance to the Aegean. Thus his general, Thutiy, includes 'the isles in the midst of the sea' as within his jurisdiction as governor of the north countries; although his control will doubtless have consisted in little more than the reception of the annual gifts which the island dynasts thought it wise to send him.

His arrival at Thebes in October found awaiting him a newly returned expedition which in the midst of his responsibilities in Asia he had found time to dispatch to Punt. His emissaries brought back the usual rich and varied cargo of ivory, ebony, panther skins, gold and over 223 bushels of myrrh, besides male and female slaves and many cattle. At some time during these wars Thutmose is also found in possession of the entire oasis region on the west of Egypt. The oases thus became pharaonic territory and were placed under the government of Intef, Thutmose III's herald, who was a descendant of the old line of lords of Thinis-Abydos, whence the Great Oasis was most easily reached. The oasis region remained an appanage of the lords of Thinis and became famous for its fine wines.

The great object for which Thutmose had so long striven was now achieved; he had followed his fathers to the Euphrates. The kings whom they had been able to defeat singly and in succession, he had been obliged to meet united, and against the combined military resources of Syria and northern Palestine under their old time Hyksos suzerain of Kadesh, he had forced his way through to the north. In 10 long years of scattered and often guerrilla warfare he had crushed them with blow on blow, until he had at last planted his boundary stone beside that of his father on the frontier, won two generations before. He had even surpassed his father and crossed the Euphrates, an unprecedented feat in the annals of Egyptian conquest. He might pardonably permit himself some satisfaction in the contemplation of what he had accomplished. Nearly 33 years had elapsed since the day when Amon called him to the throne. Already on his 30th anniversary his architect, Puemre, had erected the jubilee obelisks at Thebes; but on his return from the great campaign the date for the customary second jubilee celebration was approaching. A pair of enormous obelisks, which had been in preparation for the event, were erected at the Karnak temple and one of them bore the proud words, 'Thutmose, who crossed the great "Bend of Naharin" [the Euphrates] with might and with victory at the head of his army'. The other obelisk of this pair has perished, but this one now stands in Constantinople. Indeed, all of the great king's obelisks in Egypt have either perished or been removed, so that not a single obelisk of his still stands in the land he ruled so mightily, while the modern world possesses a line of them reaching from Constantinople, through Rome and London to New York. The last two, which commemorate his fourth jubilee celebration, now rise on opposite shores of the Atlantic, as they once stood on either side of the approach to the sun temple at Heliopolis.

With such monuments as these before them the people of Thebes soon forgot that he who erected them was once a humble priest in the very temple where his giant obelisks now rose. On its walls, moreover, they saw long annals of his victories in Asia, endless records of the plunder he had taken, with splendid reliefs picturing the rich portion which fell to Amon. A list of 119 towns which he captured on his first campaigns was three times displayed upon the pylons, while from his recent successes in the north the same walls bore a record of no less than 248 towns which had submitted to him. However much they may have impressed the Thebans, these records are for us of priceless value. Unfortunately, they are but excerpts from the state records, made by priests who wished to explain the source of the gifts received by the temple, and to show how Thutmose was repaying his debt to Amon for the many victories which the favouring god had vouchsafed him. Hence they are but meagre sources from which to reconstruct the campaigns of the first great strategist of whom we know anything in history.

But the Thebans were not obliged to study the monuments of Karnak for witness to the greatness of their king. In the garden of Amon's temple, as we have seen, grew the strange plants of Syria-Palestine, while animals unknown to the hunter of the Nile valley wandered among trees equally unfamiliar. Envoys from the north and south were constantly appearing at the court. Phoenician galleys, such as the upper Nile had never seen before, delighted the eyes of the curious crowd at the docks of Thebes; and from these landed whole cargoes of the finest stuffs of Phoenicia, gold and silver vessels of magnificent workmanship, from the cunning hand of the Tyrian artificer or the workshops of distant Asia Minor, Cyprus, Crete and the Aegean islands; exquisite furniture of carved ivory, delicately wrought ebony, chariots mounted with gold and electrum and bronze implements of war; besides these, fine horses for the pharaoh's stables and untold quantities of the best that the fields, gardens, vineyards, orchards and pastures of Asia produced. Under heavy guard emerged from these ships, too, the annual tribute of gold and silver in large commercial rings, some of which weighed as much as five kilograms (12 pounds) each, while others for purposes of daily trade were of but a few grains weight. Winding through the streets, crowded with the wondering Theban multitude, the strange tongued Asiatics in long procession bore their tribute to the pharaoh's treasury. They were received by the vizier, Rekhmire, and when unusually rich tribute was presented, he conducted them into the pharaoh's presence, who, enthroned in splendour, reviewed them and praised the vizier and his officials for their zeal in his behalf. The Asiatics then delivered their tribute at the office of the vizier, where all was duly entered on his books, even to the last measure of grain.

It was such scenes as this that the vizier and treasury officials loved to perpetuate in gorgeous paintings on the walls of their tombs, where they are still preserved at Thebes. The amount of wealth which thus came into Egypt must have been enormous for those times, and on one occasion the treasury was able to weigh out some 4,050 kilograms (8,943 pounds) of gold-silver alloy. Nubia also, under the Egyptian viceroy, was rendering with great regularity her annual impost of gold, negro slaves, cattle, ebony, ivory and grain; much of the gold in the above hoard must have come from the Nubian mines. It was a great day, too, for the Theban crowds when the Nubian barges landed their motley cargo. Similar sights diverted the multitudes of the once provincial Thebes when every year, toward the close of September or the opening days of October, Thutmose's war galleys moored in the harbour of the town; but at this time not merely the *wealth* of Asia was unloaded from the ships; the Asiatics themselves, bound one to another in long lines, were led down the gangplanks to begin a life of slave labour for the pharaoh. They wore long matted beards, an abomination to the Egyptians; their hair bung in heavy black masses upon their shoulders, and they were clad in gaily coloured woollen stuffs, such as the Egyptian, spotless in his white linen robe, would never put on his body. Their arms were pinioned behind them at the elbows or crossed over their heads and lashed together; or, again, their bands were thrust through odd pointed ovals of wood, which served as handcuffs. The women carried their children slung in a fold of the mantle over their shoulders. With their strange speech and uncouth postures the poor wretches were the subject of jibe and merriment on the part of the multitude; while the artists of the time could never forbear caricaturing them. Many of them found their way into the houses of the pharaoh's favourites, and his generals were liberally rewarded with gifts of such slaves; but the larger number were immediately employed on the temple estates, the pharaoh's domains, or in the construction of his great monuments and buildings, especially the last, a custom which continued until Saladin built the citadel at Cairo with the labour of the knights whom he captured from the ranks of the crusaders. We shall later see how this captive labour transformed Thebes.

The return of the king every autumn, under such circumstances, with the next campaign but six months distant, began for him a winter, if not so arduous, at least as busily occupied as the campaigning season in Asia. At the time of the feast of Opet, that is in October, shortly after his return, Thutmose made a tour of inspection throughout Egypt, closely questioning the local authorities wherever he landed, for the purpose of suppressing corruption in the local administration by preventing all collusion between them and the officers of the central government in extortionate oppression of the people while collecting taxes. On these journeys, too, he had opportunity of observing the progress on the noble temples which he was either erecting, restoring or adorning at over 30 different places of which we know, and many more which have perished. He revived the long-neglected Delta and from there to the third cataract his buildings were rising, strung like gems, along the river. He built a new town with its temple at the mouth of the Fayum; while at Dendereh, Coptos, El Kab, Edfu, Kom Ombo, Elephantine and many other places his captives of war and his imperial revenues were producing the magnificent works which he and his architects planned. Returning to Thebes his interests were wide and his power was felt in every avenue of administration. Besides the attention continually demanded by Nubian affairs, of which we shall speak more fully later, he organized the other gold country, that on the Coptos road, placing it under a 'governor of the gold country of Coptos'. It is evident that every resource of his empire was being thus exploited. The increasing wealth of the Amon temple demanded reorganization of its management. This the king personally accomplished, giving the priests full instructions and careful regulations for the conduct of the state temple and its growing fortune. As the fruit of a moment's respite from the cares of state, he even handed to his chief of artificers in the state and temple workshops designs sketched by his own royal hand for vessels which he desired for the temple service. Thutmose himself thought sufficiently well of this accomplishment to have it noted over a relief depicting these vessels on the temple walls at Karnak, after they had been presented to the god; while in the opinion of the official who received the commission it was a fact so remarkable that he had the execution of these vessels by his artificers shown in the paintings on the walls of his tomb chapel. Both these evidences of Thutmose's restless versatility still survive at Thebes. The great state temple received another pylon on the south and the whole mass of buildings, with the adjoining grove and garden, was given unity by an enclosure wall, with which Thutmose surrounded them.

His campaigning was now as thoroughly organized as the administration at Thebes. As soon as the spring rains in Syria and Palestine had ceased, he regularly disembarked his troops in some Phoenician or north Syrian harbour. Here his permanent officials had affected the collection of the necessary stores from the neighbouring dynasts, who were obligated to furnish them. His palace herald, or marshal, Intef, who was of the old princely line of Thinis, and still held his title as 'count of Thinis and lord of the entire oasis region', accompanied him on all his marches, and as Thutmose advanced inland Intef preceded him until the proximity of the enemy prevented. Whenever he reached a town in which the king was expected to spend the night, he sought out the palace of the local dynast and prepared it for Thutmose's reception, 'When my lord arrived in safety where I was, I had prepared it, I had equipped it with everything that is desired in a foreign country, made better than the palaces of Egypt, purified, cleansed, set apart, their mansions adorned, each chamber for its proper purpose. I made the king satisfied with that which I did'. One is reminded of the regular and detailed preparation of Napoleon's tent, which he always found awaiting him after his day's march, as he rode into the quarters each night. All the king's intercourse with the outside world, and the regulation of the simple court state maintained on the campaigns, was in Intef's hands. When the Syrian princes came in to offer their allegiance and pay their tribute, it was Intef also who had charge of the interview; he informed the vassals what they were expected to contribute and he counted the gold, silver and *naturalia* when they were paid in at the camp. When any of the pharaoh's captains distinguished himself upon the battlefield, it was again Intef who reported it to the king, that the proper reward might be rendered to the fortunate hero.

Had it been preserved, the life of these warriors of Thutmose would form a stirring chapter in the history of the early east. The career of his general, Amenemhab, who cut off the elephant's trunk and rescued the king, is but a hint of the life of the pharaoh's followers in bivouac and on battlefield, crowded to the full with perilous adventure and hard-won distinction. We shall meet one more exploit of this same Amenemhab, but his is the only such career which has survived in authentic narrative. The fame of these tried veterans of Thutmose, of course, found its way among the common people and doubtless many a stirring adventure from the Syrian campaigns took form in folktales, told with eager interest in the marketplaces and the streets of Thebes. A lucky chance has rescued one of these tales written by some scribe on a pagé or two of papyrus. It concerns one Thutiy, a great general of Thutmose, and his clever capture of the city of Joppa by introducing his picked soldiers into the town, concealed in panniers, borne by a train of donkeys. The tale is probably the prototype of 'Ali Baba and the Forty Thieves'. But Thutiy was not a creation of fancy; his tomb, though now unknown, must exist somewhere in Thebes, for it was plundered many years ago by the natives, who took from it some of the rich gifts which Thutmose gave him as a reward for his valour. A splendid golden dish, which found its way into the Louvre, bears the words: 'Given as a distinction from king Thutmose III to the prince and priest who satisfies the king in every country, and the isles in the midst of the sea, filling the treasury with lapis lazuli, silver and gold, the governor of countries, commander of the army, favourite of the king, the king's scribe, Thutiy'. A jewel of his in the Leyden museum calls him 'governor of the north countries', so that he must have administered Thutmose's northern vassal kingdoms.

Had chance so decreed we might have known not only the whole romance of Thutmose's personal adventures on the field and those of his commanders, but also the entire course of his campaigns, which we could have followed step by step; for a record of every day's happenings throughout each campaign was carefully kept by one Thaneni, a scribe appointed for the purpose by Thutmose. Thaneni tells us of his duties with great pride, saying: 'I followed king Thutmose III; I beheld the victories of the king which he won in every country. He brought the chiefs of Zahi [Syria] as living prisoners to Egypt; he captured all their cities, he cut down their groves.... I recorded the victories which he won in every land, putting them into writing according to the facts'. It is these records of Thaneni upon rolls of leather which are referred to in the account of the first campaign during the siege of Megiddo. But the priceless rolls have perished and we have upon the wall at Karnak only the capricious extracts of a temple scribe, more anxious to set forth the spoil and Amon's share therein than to perpetuate the story of his king's great deeds. How much he has passed over, the biography of Amenemhab shows only too well; and thus all that we have of the wars of Egypt's greatest commander has filtered through the shrivelled soul of an ancient bureaucrat, who little dreamed how hungrily future ages would ponder his meagre excerpts.

The advancement of Egypt's Asiatic frontier to the Euphrates again was, in the light of past experience, not an achievement from which he might expect lasting results; nor was Thutmose III the man to drop the work he had begun as if it were complete with the campaign of the year 33. The spring of the 34th year therefore found him again in Zahi on his ninth campaign. Some disaffection, probably in the Lebanon region, obliged him to take three towns, one of which at least was in the district of Nuges, where he had erected a fortress at the close of the first campaign. Considerable spoil was captured and the Syrian dynasts as usual hastened to pay their tribute and express their loyalty. Meanwhile, the magazines of the harbour towns were replenished as formerly, but especially with ships for the fleet, and with masts and spars for naval repairs. The tribute of the year was rendered notable by a present of 108 blocks of copper, weighing nearly two kilograms (four pounds) apiece, beside some lead and costly stones from the king of Cyprus, who had not heretofore recognized the might of Thutmose in this manner.

This year evidently saw the extension of his power in the south also; for he secured the son of the chief of Irem, the neighbour of Punt as a hostage; and the combined tribute of Nubia amounted to over 60 kilograms (134 pounds) of gold alone, besides the usual ebony, ivory, grain, cattle and slaves. The sway of Thutmose was absolute from above the third cataract to the Euphrates and his power was at its zenith when he learned of a general revolt in Naharin. It was now nearly two years since he had seen that region and in so short a time its princes had ceased to fear his power. They formed a coalition, with some prince at its head, possibly the king of Aleppo, whom Thutmose's Annals call 'that wretched foe of Naharin'. The alliance was strong in numbers, for it included the far north, or 'the ends of the earth', as the Egyptians called the distant regions of Asia where their knowledge of the country ceased. Thutmose's continual state of preparation enabled him to appear promptly on the plains of Naharin in the spring of the year 35. He engaged the allies in battle at a place called Araina, which we are unable to locate with certainty, but it was probably somewhere in the lower Orontes valley. 'Then his majesty prevailed against these barbarians.... They fled headlong, falling one over another before his majesty'. It is perhaps this battle which Amenemhab mentions as occurring in the land of Tikhsi. If so, he fought before Thutmose, as the latter advanced against the enemy and both took booty from the field: the king several pieces of armour, and his general three prisoners, for which act he was again decorated by Thutmose. The troops, of course, found rich plunder on the field: horses, bronze armour and weapons, besides chariots richly wrought with gold and silver. The alliance of the Naharin dynasts was completely shattered and its resources for future resistance destroyed or carried off by the victorious Egyptians. Far as were these Syrian princes from Egypt, they had learned the length and the might of the pharaoh's arm, and it was seven years before they again revolted.

Thutmose's annals for the next two years are lost, and we know nothing of the objective of his 11th and 12th campaigns; but the year 38 found him in the southern Lebanon region on his 13th campaign, again chastising the region of Nuges, which had felt his power for the first time 15 years before on the first campaign. On this expedition he received not only another gift from the king of Cyprus, but also one from far off Arrapakhitis, later a province of Assyria. The turbulent Beduin of southern Palestine forced him to march through their country the next year, and the inevitable Amenemhab captured three prisoners in an action in the Negeb. He then spent the rest of this 14th campaign in Syria, where it became merely a tour of inspection; but in both years he kept the harbours supplied as before, ready for every emergency. The tribute seems to have come in regularly for the next two years (40 and 41), and again the king of 'Kheta the great' sent gifts, which Thutmose as before records among the 'tribute'.

The princes of Syria, sorely chastised as they had been, were nevertheless unwilling to relinquish finally their independence, and regard the suzerainty of Egypt as an inevitable and permanent condition of their rule. Incited by Kadesh, Thutmose's inveterate enemy, they again rose in a final united effort to shake off the pharaoh's strong hand. All Naharin, especially the king of Tunip, and also some of the northern coast cities, had been induced to join the alliance. The great king was now an old man, probably over 70 years of age, but with his accustomed promptitude he appeared with his fleet off the north coast of Syria in the spring of the year 42. It was his 17th and last campaign. Like his first, it was directed against his arch enemy, Kadesh. Instead of approaching the place from the south, as before, Thutmose determined to isolate her from her northern support and to capture Tunip first. He therefore landed at some point between the mouth of the Orontes and the Nahr el-Kebir and captured the coast city of Erkatu, the exact location of which is not certain; but it must have been nearly opposite Tunip, against which he then marched. He was detained at Tunip until the harvest season, but he captured the place after a short resistance. He then accomplished the march up the Orontes to Kadesh without mishap and wasted the towns of the region. The king of Kadesh, knowing that his all was lost unless he could defeat Thutmose's army, made a desperate resistance. He engaged the Egyptians in battle before the city, and in the effort to make head against Thutmose's seasoned troops the Syrian king resorted to a stratagem. He sent forth a mare against the Egyptian chariotry, hoping thus to excite the stallions and produce confusion, or even a break in the Egyptian battle line, of which he might take advantage. But Amenemhab leaped from his chariot, sword in hand, pursued the mare on foot, ripped her up and cut off her tail, which he carried in triumph to the king. Thutmose's siege lines now closed in on the doomed city, and the first assault was ordered. For this purpose he selected all the elite of his army, in order to breach the walls. Amenemhab was placed in command. The dangerous feat was successfully accomplished, the flower of Thutmose's tried veterans poured in through the breach, Amenemhab at their head, and the strongest city of Syria was again at the pharaoh's mercy. The Naharin auxiliaries in the city fell into Thutmose's hands, and it was not even necessary for him to march into the north. In any case, at his advanced age he might have been pardoned for avoiding so arduous an expedition after a long campaign. It is also probable that the season was too far advanced for him to undertake so long a march before the cold of winter should set in. However, as the event proved, no further display of force in the north was necessary.

Never again as long as the old king lived did. the Asiatic princes make any attempt to shake off his yoke. In 17 campaigns, during a period of 19 years, he had beaten them into submission, until there was no spirit for resistance left among them. With the fall of Kadesh disappeared the last vestige of that Hyksos power which had once subdued Egypt. Thutmose's name became a proverb in their midst, and when, four generations later, his successors failed to shield their faithful vassals in Naharin from the aggression of the Kheta, the forsaken unfortunates remembered Thutmose's great name, and wrote pathetically to Egypt: 'Who formerly could have plundered Tunip without being plundered by Manakhbiria (Thutmose III)?' But even now, at three score and 10 or more, the indomitable old warrior had the harbours equipped with the necessary supplies, and there is little doubt that if it had been necessary he would have led his army into Syria again. For the last time in Asia he received the envoys of the tribute-paying princes in his tent, and then returned to Egypt. There the Nubian envoys brought him over 260 kilograms (578 pounds) of gold from Wawat alone.

One would have thought that the old king might now enjoy a well-earned repose for the few years that remained to him; but having at last established the sovereignty of Egypt in Asia on a permanent basis, he turned his attention to Nubia. It is evident that Menkheperreseneb, the head of his gold and silver treasury, was now receiving thence 270 to 360 kilograms (600 to 800 pounds) of gold every year, for, as we now see, even the incomplete data at our command show in his 41st year nearly 360 kilograms (800 pounds). His viceroy, Nehi, had now been administering Kush for 20 years and had placed the productivity of the country on a high plane; but it was the desire of the great king to extend still further his dominions in the south. In his last years his buildings show that he was extremely active throughout the province; as far as the third cataract we trace his temples at Kalabsheh, Amada, Wadi Halfa, Kummeh and Semneh, where he restored the temple of his great ancestor Sesostris III, and at Soleb. We learn through the clearance of the canal at the first cataract, which he was obliged to effect in the 50th year, that an expedition of his was then returning from a campaign against the Nubians. It is impossible to suppose that the aged Thutmose accompanied it. There must have been earlier expeditions also in the same region, for Thutmose was able to record in duplicate upon the pylons of his Karnak temple a list of 115 places which he conquered in Nubia and another containing some 400 such names. The geography of Nubia is too little known to enable us to locate the territory represented, and it is uncertain exactly how far up the Nile his new frontier may have been, but it was doubtless well up toward the fourth cataract, where we find it under his son.

Twelve years more were vouchsafed the great king after he had returned from his last campaign in Asia. As he felt his strength failing, he made co-regent his son, Amenhotep II, born to him by Hatshepsut-Meretre, a queen of whose origin we know nothing. About a year later, on the 17th of March, in the year 1447 BCE, when he was within five weeks of the end of his 54th year upon the throne, he closed his eyes upon the scenes among which he had played so great a part. He was buried in his tomb in the Valley of the Kings by his son, and his body still survives. Before his death the priests of Amon had put into the mouth of their god a hymn of praise to him, which, although a highly artificial composition, is not without effectiveness as literature; and shows at the same time not only how universal was his sway as the priests saw it, but also how deeply he had wrought upon the imagination of his contemporaries. After a long introduction in praise of Thutmose, Amon, his god says to him:

I have come, giving thee to smite the princes of Zahi,
I have hurled them beneath thy feet among their highlands:
I have made them see thy majesty as lord of radiance,
So that thou hast shone in their faces like my image.

I have come, giving thee to smite the Asiatics,
Thou hast made captive the heads of the Asiatics of Retenu;
I have made them see thy majesty equipped with thy adornment,
When thou hast taken the weapons of war in the chariot.

I have come, giving thee to smite the eastern land,
Thou hast trampled those who are in the districts of God's Land;
I have made them see thy majesty as a circling star,
When it scatters its flame in fire and gives forth its dew.

I have come, giving thee to smite the western land,
Keftyew and Cyprus are in terror;
I have made them see thy majesty as a young bull,
Firm of heart, ready horned and irresistible.

I have come, giving thee to smite those who are in their marshes,
The lands of Mitanni tremble under fear of thee;
I have made them see thy majesty as a crocodile,
Lord of fear in the water, inapproachable.

I have come, giving thee to smite those who are in their isles,
Those who are in the midst of the great sea hear thy roarings;
I have made them see thy majesty as an avenger,
Rising upon the back of his slain victim.

I have come, giving thee to smite the Libyans,
The isles of the Utentyew belong to the might of thy prowess;
I have made them see thy majesty as a fierce-eyed lion,
While thou makest them corpses in their valleys.

I have come, giving thee to smite the uttermost ends of the lands;
The circuit of the Great Curve (Okeanos) is enclosed in thy grasp;
I have made them see thy majesty as a soaring hawk,
Seizing that which he seeth, as much as he desires.

I have come, giving thee to smite those who are nigh thy border,
Thou hast smitten the Sand-Dwellers as living captives;
I have made them see thy majesty as a southern jackal,
Swift-footed, stealthy going, who roves the Two Lands.

We have seen enough of Thutmose to know that this was not all poetry, the adulation of a fawning priesthood. His character stands forth with more of colour and individuality than that of any king of early Egypt, except Ikhnaton [Akhenaten]. We see the man of a tireless energy unknown in any pharaoh before or since; the man of versatility, designing exquisite vases in a moment of leisure; the lynx-eyed administrator, who launched his armies upon Asia with one hand and with the other crushed the extortionate tax-gatherer. His vizier, Rekhmire, who stood closest to his person, says of him: 'Lo, his majesty was one who knew what happened; there was nothing of which he was ignorant; he was Thoth [the god of knowledge] in everything;

there was no matter which he did not carry out'. While he was proud to leave a record of his unparalleled achievements, Thutmose protests more than once his deep respect for the truth in so doing. 'I have not uttered exaggeration,' says he, 'in order to boast of that which I did, saying, "I have done something," although my majesty had not done it. I have not done anything ... against which contradiction might be uttered. I have done this for my father, Amon ... because he knoweth heaven and he knoweth earth, he seeth the whole earth hourly.' Such protestations, mingled with reverence for his god as demanding the truth, are not infrequently on his lips.

His reign marks an epoch not only in Egypt but in the whole east as we know it in his age. Never before in history had a single brain wielded the resources of so great a nation and wrought them into such centralized, permanent and at the same time mobile efficiency, that for years they could be brought to bear with incessant impact upon another continent as a skilled artisan manipulates a 100-ton forge hammer; although the figure is inadequate unless we remember that Thutmose forged his own hammer. The genius which rose from an obscure priestly office to accomplish this for the first time in history reminds us of an Alexander or a Napoleon. He built the first real empire, and is thus the first character possessed of universal aspects, the first world hero. From the fastnesses of Asia Minor, the marshes of the upper Euphrates, the islands of the sea, the swamps of Babylonia, the distant shores of Libya, the oases of the Sahara, the terraces of the Somali coast and the upper cataracts of the Nile, the princes of his time rendered their tribute to his greatness. He thus made not only a worldwide impression upon his age, but an impression of a new order. His commanding figure, towering like an embodiment of righteous penalty among the trivial plots and treacherous schemes of the petty Syrian dynasts, must have clarified the atmosphere of oriental politics as a strong wind drives away miasmic vapours. The inevitable chastisement of his strong arm was held in awed remembrance by the men of Naharin for three generations. His name was one to conjure with, and centuries after his empire had crumbled to pieces it was placed on amulets as a word of power. It should be a matter of gratification to us of the western world that one of this king's greatest monuments, his Heliopolitan obelisks, now rises on our own shores as a memorial of the world's first empire builder.

The Empire

☥

THE IMPERIAL AGE WAS NOW at its full noontide in the Nile valley. The old reclusiveness had totally disappeared, the wall of partition between Asia and Africa, already shaken by the Hyksos, was now broken down completely by the wars of Thutmose III. Traditional limits disappeared, the currents of life eddied no longer within the landmarks of tiny kingdoms but pulsed from end to end of a great empire, embracing many kingdoms and tongues, from the upper Nile to the upper Euphrates. The wealth of Asiatic trade, circulating through the eastern end of the Mediterranean, which once flowed down the Euphrates to Babylon, was thus diverted to the Nile Delta, centuries earlier united by canal with the Red Sea. All the world traded in the Delta markets. Assyria was still in her infancy and Babylonia no longer possessed any political influence in the west. The pharaoh looked forward to an indefinite lease of power throughout the vast empire which he had conquered.

Of his administration in Asia we know very little. The whole region was under the general control of a 'governor of the north countries'; Thutmose III's general, Thutiy, being the first to hold that office. To bridle the turbulent Asiatic dynasts, it was necessary permanently to station troops throughout Syria-Palestine. Strongholds named after the pharaoh were established and the troops placed in them as garrisons under deputies with power to act as the pharaoh's representatives. Thutmose III erected one such at the south end of Lebanon; he resuscitated another founded by his predecessors at some city on the Phoenician coast, where we find a sanctuary of Amon, the state god of Egypt, and there was probably such a temple in each of the garrison towns. Yet another stronghold at Ikathi, in furthest Naharin, was doubtless his foundation. Remains of an Egyptian temple found by Renan at Byblos, doubtless belong to this period.

As we have seen, the city kings were allowed to rule their little states with great freedom, as long as they paid the annual tribute with promptness and regularity. When such a ruler died, his son, who had been educated at Thebes, was installed in the father's place. The Asiatic conquests were therefore rather a series of tributary kingdoms than provinces, which indeed represent a system of foreign government as yet in its infancy, or only roughly foreshadowed in the rule of the viceroy of Kush. How the local government of the city kings was related to the administration of the 'governor of the north countries' is entirely uncertain. His office was apparently largely a fiscal one, for Thutiy, Thutmose III's governor, adds to his name the phrase 'filling the treasury with lapis lazuli, silver and gold'. But it is evident that the dynasts collected their own taxes and rendered a part to the pharaoh. We are unable to determine what portion of his income the Asiatic vassal was thus obliged to contribute; nor have we the slightest idea how large was the pharaoh's total revenue from Asia.

As so often in similar empires of later age, when the great king died the tributary princes revolted. Thus when the news of Thutmose III's death reached Asia the opportunity was improved and the dynasts made every preparation to throw off the irksome obligation of the annual tribute. Amenhotep II had reigned as co-regent but a year when his father died and the storm broke. All Naharin, including the Mitanni princes, and probably also the northern coast cities, were combined or at least simultaneous in the uprising. With all his father's energy the young king prepared for the crisis and marched into Asia against the allies, who had collected a large army. The south had evidently not ventured to rebel, but from northern Palestine on, the revolt was general. Leaving Egypt with his forces in April of his second year (1447 BCE), Amenhotep was in touch with the enemy in northern Palestine early in May and immediately fought an action at Shemesh-Edom against the princes of Lebanon. In this encounter he led his forces in person, as his father before him had so often done, and mingled freely in the hand-to-hand fray. With his own hand he took 18 prisoners and 16 horses. The enemy was routed. By the 12th of May he had crossed the Orontes for the last time in his northward advance, probably at Senzar and turned north-eastward for the Euphrates. He fought a skirmish with the Naharin advance just after crossing the river, but pushed rapidly on and captured seven of the rebellious dynasts in the land of Tikhsi.

On the 26th of May, 14 days after leaving the Orontes, he arrived at Niy, which opened its gates to him; and with the men and women of the town acclaiming him from the walls he entered the place in triumph. Ten days later, on the fifth of June, he had rescued a garrison of his troops from the treachery of the revolting town of Ikathi and punished its inhabitants. Whether the march to this town carried him northward from Niy, up the Euphrates or across it and into Mitanni, is uncertain; but the latter is the more probable, for his records say of him, 'The chiefs of Mitanni come to him, their tribute upon their backs, to beseech his majesty that there may be given to them his sweet breath of life; a mighty occurrence, it has never been heard since the time of the gods. This country, which knew not Egypt, beseeches the Good God [the pharaoh]'. As he reached his extreme advance, which thus probably surpassed his father's, he set up a boundary tablet, as his father and grandfather had done. His return was a triumphal procession as he approached Memphis, the populace assembled in admiring crowds while his lines passed, driving with them over 500 of the north Syrian lords, 240 of their women, 210 horses and 300 chariots. His herald had in charge for the chief treasurer nearly 750 kilograms (1,660 pounds) of gold in the form of vases and vessels, besides nearly 45,500 kilograms (100,000 pounds) of copper. Proceeding to Thebes, he took with him the seven kings of Tikhsi, who were hung head downward on the prow of his royal barge as he approached the city. He personally sacrificed them in the presence of Amon and hanged their bodies on the walls of Thebes, reserving one for a lesson to the Nubians as we shall see. His unexpected energy had evidently crushed the revolt before it had been able to muster all its forces, and in so far as we know, the lesson was so effective that no further attempt was made against his suzerainty in Asia.

The young pharaoh now directed his energies toward ensuring the security of the other extremity of his empire and establishing his southern frontier. On his arrival at Thebes he dispatched an expedition into Nubia, bearing the body of the seventh king of the land of Tikhsi, which was hung up on the wall of Napata, as a hint of what the Nubians might expect should they attempt revolt against their new sovereign. The operations of Thutmose III in upper Nubia now made it possible for Amenhotep to establish his frontier at the fourth cataract; it was guarded by Napata, just below the cataract, and the region of Karoy, in which the town lay, was from this time on known as the southern limit of Egyptian administration. To this point extended the jurisdiction of the 'viceroy of Kush and governor of the south countries'. This carried the territory of Egypt around the great bend in the river to the region where the stream often flows southward. Here Amenhotep set up tablets marking his southern frontier, and beyond these there was no more control of the rude Nubian tribes than was necessary to keep open the trade routes from the south and prevent the barbarians from becoming so bold as to invade the province in plundering expeditions. About nine months after his return from the Asiatic campaign, the Nubian expedition erected two stelas, one at Amada and the other at Elephantine, recording his completion of the temples begun by his father at these places'. He there tells us of the fate of the Tikhsi kings, and although the second campaign had not yet taken place, he refers to his Naharin war as his 'first campaign', a significant prophecy of the life of conquest which he expected to lead. It was now regarded as a matter of course that Amon had pressed into the eager hand of every pharaoh sceptre and sword alike. The work of Amenhotep's great father was so thoroughly done, however, that, as far as we know, he was not obliged to invade either Asia or Nubia again.

In Thebes he built his now vanished mortuary temple on the west side of the river, by that of his father, while in the Karnak temple he restored the long-dismantled hall of Hatshepsut's obelisks, setting up again the columns which she had removed and richly adorning them with precious metal. He recorded the restoration on the wall which his father had built around the obelisks of Hatshepsut to hide their inscriptions forever from view. Besides a small colonnaded structure at Karnak, he also built at Memphis and Heliopolis, restoring the neighbouring quarries of Troja; but all his works there have perished. We are able to discern little of him personally, but he seems to have been a worthy son of the great king. Physically he was a very powerful man and claims in his inscriptions that no man could draw his bow. The weapon was found in his tomb and bears the words after his name: 'Smiter of the Troglodytes, overthrower of Kush, hacking up their cities ... the great Wall of Egypt, protector of his soldiers'. It is this story which furnished Herodotus with the legend that Cambyses was unable to draw the bow of the king of Ethiopia. He celebrated his jubilee on the 30th anniversary of his appointment as crown prince and erected an obelisk in Elephantine in commemoration of the event. Dying about 1420 BCE, after a reign of some

26 years, he was interred like his ancestors in the valley of the kings' tombs, where his body rests to this day, though even now a prey to the clever tomb robbers of modern Thebes, who in November 1901, forced the tomb and cut through the wrappings of the mummy in their search for royal treasure on the body of their ancient ruler. Their Theban ancestors in the same craft, however, had 3,000 years ago taken good care that nothing should be left for their descendants.

Amenhotep II was followed by his son, Thutmose IV. It is possible that this prince was not at first designed to be his father's successor, if we may believe a folk tale which was in circulation some centuries later. The story recounted how, long before his father's death, a hunting expedition once carried him to the desert near the pyramids of Gizeh, where the pharaohs of the Fourth Dynasty had already slept over 1,300 years. He rested in the shadow of the great Sphinx at noon time, and falling asleep, the sun god, with whom the Sphinx in his time was identified, appeared to him in a dream, beseeching him to clear his image from the sand which already at that early day encumbered it, and at the same time promising him the kingdom. The prince made a vow to do as the great god desired. The god's promise was fulfilled and the young king immediately upon his accession hastened to redeem his vow. He cleared the gigantic figure of the Sphinx and recorded the whole incident on a stela in the vicinity. A later version, made by the priests of the palace, was engraved on a huge granite architrave taken from the neighbouring Osiris temple and erected against the breast of the Sphinx between the forelegs, where it still stands.

He was early called upon to maintain the empire in Asia. We are, however, entirely ignorant of the course of his campaign there, which, like his father, he called his 'first campaign'. It is evident, however, that he was obliged to advance into the far north, eventually invading Naharin, so that he was afterward able to record in the state temple at Thebes the spoil, 'which his majesty captured in Naharin the wretched, on his first victorious campaign'. The immediate result of his appearance in Naharin was completely to quiet all disaffection there as far as the vassal princes were concerned. He returned by way of Lebanon where he forced the chiefs to furnish him with a cargo of cedar for the sacred barge of Amon at Thebes. Arriving at Thebes, he settled a colony of the prisoners, possibly from the city of Gezer in Palestine, in the enclosure of his mortuary temple, which he had erected by those of his ancestors on the plain at Thebes. Perhaps the recognition of a common enemy in the Kheta now produced a *rapprochement* between the pharaoh and Mitanni, for the latter was soon to suffer from the aggressions of the king of Kheta. Thutmose evidently desired a friend in the north, for he sent to Artatama, the Mitannian king, and desired his daughter in marriage. After some proper display of reluctance, Artatama consented, and the Mitannian princess was sent to Egypt, where she probably received an Egyptian name, Mutemuya, and became the mother of the next king of Egypt, Amenhotep III. A firm alliance with Mitanni was thus formed, which forbade all thought of future conquest by the pharaoh east of the Euphrates. A friendly alliance was also cemented with Babylonia. Although it is probable that Thutmose found it unnecessary to invade Asia again, he was called the 'conqueror of Syria' by his nobles, and the tribute of the Syrian princes regularly appeared at the office of the vizier or the treasurer. In the spring of the year eight news of a serious revolt in Nubia reached him. After a triumphant voyage up the river, having stopped to greet the gods in all the larger temples, he passed the first cataract, and advancing into Wawat, he seems to have found the enemy surprisingly near the northern boundary of Nubia. There was of course but one possible issue for the battle which followed, and great quantities of spoil fell into Thutmose's hands. Again he settled the prisoners which he took as serfs of his mortuary temple.

It is probable that Thutmose did not long survive the war in Nubia. He was therefore unable to beautify Thebes and adorn the state temple as his fathers had done. But the respect in which he held his grandfather, Thutmose III, led him to the completion of a notable work of the latter. For 35 years the last obelisk planned by Thutmose III had been lying unfinished at the southern portal of the Karnak temple enclosure or temenos. His grandson now had it engraved in the old conqueror's name, recorded also upon it his own pious deed in continuing the work, and erected the colossal shaft, 32 metres (105½ feet) high, the largest surviving obelisk, at the southern portal of the enclosure, where he had found it lying. It now stands before the Lateran in Rome. Not long after this gracious act, which may possibly have been in celebration of his own jubilee, Thutmose was gathered to his fathers (about 1411 BCE) and was buried in the valley where they slept.

The son who succeeded him was the third of the Amenhoteps and the last of the great emperors. He was but the great grandson of Thutmose III, but with him the high tide of Egyptian power was already slowly on the ebb, and he was not the man to stem the tide. An early evidence of the effeminate character, which he afterward showed, is noticeable in his relation with his queen. Already as crown prince, or at least early in his reign he married a remarkable woman, of uncertain origin, named Tiy. There is not a particle of evidence to prove her of foreign birth, as is so often claimed. In celebration of the marriage, Amenhotep issued a large number of scarabs, or sacred beetles, carved in stone and engraved with a record of the event, in which the untitled parentage of his queen frankly follows her name in the very royal titulary itself, which declares her to be the queen consort. But the record closes with the words: 'She is the wife of a mighty king whose southern boundary is as far as Karoy and northern as far as Naharin'; as if to remind any who might reflect upon the humble origin of the queen of the exalted station which she now occupied. From the beginning the new queen exerted a powerful influence over Amenhotep, and he immediately inserted her name in the official caption placed at the head of royal documents. Her power continued throughout his reign and was the beginning of a remarkable era characterized by the prominence of the queens in state affairs and on public occasions, a peculiarity which we find only under Amenhotep III and his immediate successors. The significance of these events we shall later dwell upon.

In the administration of his great empire Amenhotep III began well. The Asiatics gave him no trouble at his accession, and he ruled in security and unparalleled splendour. Toward the close of his fourth year, however, trouble in Nubia called him south. Early in October he had improved the high water to pass the cataract with his fleet. His viceroy of Nubia, Mermose, had levied an army of Nubians in the region from the vicinity of Kubban for 120 kilometres (75 miles) up to Ibrim. These, with the pharaoh's Egyptians, were to be employed against the Nubians of the upper country, a striking evidence of the very Egyptianized character of lower Nubia. When they had reached Ibhet, which is at least above the second cataract, they found the enemy and engaged them in battle, probably on the anniversary of the king's coronation, the first day of his fifth year. They took 740 prisoners and slew 312, as recorded on a tablet of victory which they set up at the second cataract.

The outlying villages and wells were visited by small parties and the inhabitants punished to prevent further recurrences of insubordination; whereupon Amenhotep marched southward for a month, taking captives and spoil as he went. Arriving finally at the 'height of Hua', a place of uncertain location, which, however, occurs in the lists, together with Punt, and must have been a long distance south, perhaps above the cataracts, he camped in the land of Uneshek on the south of Hua. This marked his extreme southern advance. In the land of Karoy, with which the reader is now acquainted as the region about Napata, he collected great quantities of gold for his Theban buildings, and at Kebehu-Hor, or 'the Pool of Horus', he erected his tablet of victory, but we are unable to locate the place with certainty. It was certainly not essentially in advance of the frontier of his father. This was the last great invasion of Nubia by the pharaohs. It was constantly necessary to punish the outlying tribes for their incessant predatory incursions into the Nile valley; but the valley itself, as far as the fourth cataract, was completely subjugated, and as far as the second cataract largely Egyptianized, a process which now went steadily forward until the country up to the fourth cataract was effectually engrafted with Egyptian civilization. Egyptian temples had now sprung up at every larger town, and the Egyptian gods were worshipped therein; the Egyptian arts were learned by the Nubian craftsmen, and everywhere the rude barbarism of the upper Nile was receiving the stamp of Egyptian culture. Nevertheless, the native chieftains, under the surveillance of the viceroy, were still permitted to retain their titles and honours, and doubtless continued to enjoy at least a nominal share in the government. We find them as far north as Ibrim, which had marked the southern limit of Amenhotep III's levy of negro auxiliaries, and was therefore probably the extreme point to which local administration solely by Egyptian officials extended southward. The annual landing of the viceroy at Thebes, bringing the yearly tribute of all the Nubian lands, was now a long-established custom.

In Asia Amenhotep enjoyed unchallenged supremacy; at the court of Babylon even, his suzerainty in Canaan, as they called Syria-Palestine, was acknowledged; and when the dynasts attempted to invoke Kurigalzu, king of Babylon, in an alliance with them against the pharaoh, he wrote them an unqualified refusal, stating that he was in alliance with the pharaoh, and even threatened them with hostilities if they formed a hostile alliance against Egypt. At least this is the Babylonian version of the affair and whether true or not, it shows Babylon's earnest desire to stand well with the pharaoh. All the powers: Babylonia, Assyria, Mitanni and Alasa-Cyprus, were exerting every effort to gain the friendship of Egypt. A scene of world politics, such as is unknown before in history, now unfolds before us. From the pharaoh's court as the centre radiate a host of lines of communication with all the great peoples of the age. The Tell el-Amarna ma letters, perhaps the most interesting mass of documents surviving from the early east, have preserved to us this glimpse across the kingdoms of hither Asia as one might see them on a stage, each king playing his part before the great throne of the pharaoh. The letters, some 300 in number, are written on clay tablets in the Babylonian cuneiform, and were discovered in 1888 at the capital city of Amenhotep III's son, Ikhnaton, the place known in modern times as Tell el-Amarna, from which the correspondence takes its name. They date from the reign of Amenhotep III and that of his son and successor, Amenhotep IV, or Ikhnaton, being correspondence of a strictly official character between these pharaohs on the one hand, and on the other the kings of Babylonia, Nineveh, Mitanni, Alasa (Cyprus) and the pharaoh's vassal kings of Syria-Palestine. Five letters survive from the correspondence of Amenhotep III with Kallimma-Sin (Kadash-man-Bel), king of Babylonia, one from the pharaoh and the others from Kallimma-Sin. The Babylonian king is constantly in need of gold and insistently importunes his brother of Egypt to send him large quantities of the precious metal, which he says is as plentiful as dust in Egypt according to the reports of the Babylonian messengers. Considerable friction results from the dissatisfaction of Kallimma-Sin at the amounts with which Amenhotep favours him. He refers to the fact that Amenhotep had received from his father a daughter in marriage, and makes this relationship a reason for further gifts of gold. As the correspondence goes on another marriage is negotiated between a daughter of Amenhotep and Kallimma-Sin or his son. Similarly, Amenhotep enjoys the most intimate connection with Shuttarna, the king of Mitanni, the son of Artatmna, with whom his father, Thutmose IV, had enjoyed the most cordial relations. Indeed, Amenhotep was perhaps the nephew of Shuttarna, from whom he now received a daughter, named Gilukhipa, in marriage. In celebration of this union Amenhotep issued a series of scarab beetles of stone bearing an inscription commemorating the event, and stating that the princess brought with her a train of 317 ladies and attendants. This occurred in Amenhotep's 10th year. On the death of Shuttarna the alliance was continued under his son, Dushratta, from whom Amenhotep later received, as a wife for his son and successor, a second Mitannian princess, Tadukhipa, the daughter of Dushratta. The correspondence between the two kings is very illuminating and may serve as an example of such communications. The following is a letter of Dushratta to his Egyptian ally:

'To Nimmuria, the great king, the king of Egypt, my brother, my son-in-law, who loves me, and whom I love – Dushratta, the great king, thy father-in-law, who loves thee, the king of Mitanni, thy brother. It is well with me. With thee may it be well, with thy house, my sister and thy other wives, thy sons, thy chariots, thy horses, thy chief men, thy land, and all thy possessions, may it be very well indeed. In the time of thy fathers, they were on very friendly terms with my fathers, but thou hast increased [this friendship] still more and with my father thou hast been on very friendly terms indeed. Now, therefore, since thou and I are on mutually friendly terms, thou hast made it 10 times closer than with my father. May the gods cause this friendship of ours to prosper. May Tishub [the god of Mitanni], the lord, and Amon eternally ordain it as it is now'.

'Inasmuch as my brother sent his messenger, Mani, saying: "My brother, send me thy daughter for my wife, to be queen of Egypt", I did not grieve the heart of my brother, and I continually ordered what was friendly. And as my brother wished, I presented her to Mani. And he beheld her and when he saw her, he rejoiced greatly; and when he brings her safely to my brother's land, then may Ishtar and Amon make her correspond to my brother's wish'.

'Gilia, my messenger, has brought to me my brother's message; when I heard it, it seemed to me very good, and I was very glad indeed and said: "So far as I am concerned, even if all the friendly relation which we have had with one another had ceased, nevertheless, on account of this message, we would forever continue friendly". Now when I wrote my brother I said: "So far as I am concerned, we will be very friendly indeed, and mutually well disposed";

and I said to my brother: "Let my brother make [our friendship] 10 times greater than with my father", and I asked of my brother a great deal of gold, saying: "More than to my father let my brother give me and send me. Thou sentest my father a great deal of gold: a namkhar of pure (?) gold, and a kiru of pure (?) gold, thou sentest him; but thou sentest me [only] a tablet of gold that is as if it were alloyed with copper.... So let my brother send gold in very great quantity, without measure, and let him send more gold to me than to my father. For in my brother's land gold is as common as dust....'

In this vein the men who were now shaping the destinies of all hither Asia wrote to one another. In response to similar entreaties, Amenhotep sent a gift of 20 talents of gold to the king of Assyria, and gained his friendship also. The vassalship of the king of Alasa-Cyprus continued, and he regularly sent the pharaoh large quantities of copper, save when on one occasion he excuses himself because his country had been visited by a pestilence. So complete was the understanding between Egypt and Cyprus that even the extradition of the property of a citizen of Cyprus who had died in Egypt was regarded by the two kings as a matter of course, and a messenger was sent to Egypt to receive the property and bring it back to Cyprus for delivery to the wife and son of the deceased. Desirous of holding the first place with Egypt, the island king even ventures to advise the pharaoh against any alliance with Kheta or Babylonia, a policy which we shall later find practiced by Babylonia herself.

Thus courted and flattered, the object of diplomatic attention from all the great powers, Amenhotep found little occasion for anxiety regarding his Asiatic empire. The Syrian vassals were now the grandsons of the men whom Thutmose III had conquered; they had grown thoroughly habituated to the Egyptian allegiance. The time was so far past when they had enjoyed independence that they knew no other condition than that of vassals of Egypt. In an age of turbulence and aggression, where might was the only appeal, it finally seemed to them the natural condition of things and it was not without its advantages in rendering them free from all apprehension of attack from without. An Egyptian education at the pharaoh's capital had, moreover, made him many a loyal servant among the children of the dynasts, who had succeeded disloyal or lukewarm fathers in Syria. They protest their fidelity to the pharaoh on all occasions. Thus the prince Akizzi of Katna writes to Amenhotep: 'My lord, here in this place I am thy servant. I am pursuing the way of my lord, and from my lord I do not depart. Since my fathers became thy servants this land has been thy land, the city of Katna thy city, and I am my lord's. My lord, if the troops and chariots of my lord came, food, drink, cattle, sheep, honey and oil were brought for the king's troops and chariots'. Such letters were introduced by the most abject and self-abasing adulation; the writer says: 'To my lord, the king, my gods, my sun: Abimilki, thy servant. Seven and seven times at the feet of my lord I fall. I am the dust under the sandals of my lord, the king. My lord is the sun which rises over the lands every day, etc.'; the vassals fall down before the pharaoh not only seven times but also 'on breast and back'. They are 'the ground upon which thou treadest, the throne upon which thou sittest, the footstool of thy feet'; even 'thy dog'; and one is pleased to call himself the groom of the pharaoh's horse. They have all been installed by the pharaoh's grace, and he sends oil to anoint them at accession to office. They inform the court at the first sign of disloyalty among their fellows and are even commissioned to proceed against rebellious princes. Throughout the land in the larger cities are garrisons of Egyptian troops, consisting of infantry and chariotry. But they are no longer solely native Egyptians, but to a large extent Nubians and Sherden, roving, predatory bands of sea robbers, perhaps the ancestors of the historical Sardinians. From now on they took service in the Egyptian army in ever larger and larger numbers. These forces of the pharaoh were maintained by the dynasts and one of their self-applied tests of loyalty in writing to the pharaoh was, as we have seen above, their readiness and faithfulness in furnishing supplies. Syria thus enjoyed a stability of government which had never before been hers. The roads were safe from robbers, caravans were convoyed from vassal to vassal, and a word from the pharaoh was sufficient to bring any of his subject-princes to his knees. The payment of tribute was as regular as the collection of taxes in Egypt itself. But in case of any delay a representative of the pharaoh, who was stationed in the various larger towns, needed but to appear in the delinquent's vicinity to recall the unfulfilled obligation. Amenhotep himself was never obliged to carry on a war in Asia. On one occasion he appeared at Sidon, and one of his officials mentions prisoners taken by his majesty on the battlefield, but this may refer to the Nubian campaign. It was deemed sufficient, as we shall later see, to send troops under the command of an efficient officer, who found no difficulty in coping with the situation for a generation after Amenhotep's accession. Thus one of the vassal princes later wrote to Amenhotep's son: 'Verily, thy father did not march forth, nor inspect the lands of his vassal princes'.

Under such circumstances Amenhotep was at leisure to devote himself to those enterprises of peace which have occupied all emperors under similar conditions. Trade now developed as never before. The Nile, from the Delta to the cataracts, was alive with the freight of all the world, which flowed into it from the Red Sea fleets and from long caravans passing back and forth through the Isthmus of Suez, bearing the rich stuffs of Syria, the spices and aromatic woods of the East, the weapons and chased vessels of the Phoenicians, and a myriad of other things, which brought their Semitic names into the hieroglyphic and their use into the life of the Nile dwellers. Parallel with the land traffic through the isthmus were the routes of commerce on the Mediterranean, thickly dotted with the richly laden galleys of Phoenicia, converging upon the Delta from all quarters and bringing to the markets of the Nile the decorated vessels or damascened bronzes from the Mycenaean industrial settlements of the Aegean. The products of Egyptian industry were likewise in use in the palace of the sea kings of Cnossos, in Rhodes, and in Cyprus, where a number of Egyptian monuments of this age have been found. Scarabs and bits of glazed ware with the name of Amenhotep III or queen Tiy have also been discovered on the mainland of Greece at Mycenae. The northern Mediterranean peoples were feeling the impact of Egyptian civilization now appearing in the north with more insistent force than ever before. In Crete Egyptian religious forms had been introduced, in one case under the personal leadership of an Egyptian priest. Mycenaean artists were powerfully influenced by the incoming products of Egypt. Egyptian landscapes appear in their metal work, and the lithe animal forms in instantaneous posture, which were caught by the pencil of the Theban artists were now common in Mycenae. The superbly decorated ceilings of Thebes likewise appear in the tombs of Mycenae and Orchomenos. Even the pre-Greek writing of Crete shows traces of the influence of the hieroglyphics of the Nile. The men of the Mycenaean world, the Keftyew, who brought these things to their countrymen, were now a familiar sight upon the streets of Thebes, where the wares which they offered were also modifying the art of Egypt. The plentiful silver of the north now came in with the northern strangers in great quantities, and, although under the Hyksos the baser metal had been worth twice as much as gold, the latter now and permanently became the more valuable medium. The ratio was now about one and two thirds to one, and the value of silver steadily fell until Ptolemaic times (third century BCE on), when the ratio was 12 to one.

Such trade required protection and regulation. Roving bands of Lycian pirates infested the coasts of the eastern Mediterranean; they boldly entered the harbours of Cyprus and plundered the towns, and even landed on the coast of the Delta. Amenhotep was therefore obliged to develop a marine police which patrolled the coast of the Delta and constantly held the mouths of the river closed against all but lawful comers. Custom houses were also maintained by these police officials at the same places, and all merchandise not consigned to the king was dutiable. The income from this source must have been very large, but we have no means of estimating it. All the land routes leading into the country were similarly policed, and foreigners who could not satisfactorily explain their business were turned back, while legitimate trade was encouraged, protected and properly taxed.

The influx of slaves, chiefly of Semitic race, which had begun under Thutmose III, still continued, and the king's chief scribe distributed them throughout the land and enrolled them among the taxpaying serfs. As this host of foreigners intermarried with the natives, the large infusion of strange blood began to make itself felt in a new and composite type of face, if we may trust the artists of the day. The incalculable wealth which had now been converging upon the coffers of the pharaoh for over a century also began to exert a profound influence, which, as under like conditions, in later history, was far from wholesome. On New Year's Day the king presented his nobles with a profusion of costly gifts which would have amazed the pharaohs of the pyramid age. On one such occasion the chief treasurer carried in before the monarch 'chariots of silver and gold, statues of ivory and ebony, necklaces of every costly stone, weapons of warfare, and work of all craftsmen'. They included 13 statues of the king, seven sphinx portraits of the monarch, eight superb necklaces, 680 richly wrought shields and 230 quivers of the same workmanship, 360 bronze swords and 140 bronze daggers, both damascened with precious metal, 30 ebony staves tipped with silver and gold, 220 ivory and ebony whips, seven elaborately wrought chests, many sunshades, chairs, vases and innumerable small objects. In the old days the monarch rewarded a faithful noble with land, which, in order to pay a return, must be properly cultivated and administered, thus fostering simplicity and wholesome country virtues on a large domain; but the favourite now received convertible wealth, which required no administration to be utilized. The luxury and display of the metropolis supplanted the old rustic simplicity and sturdy elemental virtues. From the pharaoh down to the humblest scribe this change was evident, if in nothing else than the externals of costume; for the simple linen kilt from the hips to the knees, which once satisfied all, not excluding the king, has now given way to an elaborate costume, with long plaited skirt, a rich tunic with full flowing sleeves; the unpretentious headdress of the old time has been replaced by an elaborately curled wig hanging down upon the shoulders; while the once bare feet are shod in elegant sandals, with tapering toes curled up at the tips. A noble of the landed class from the court of the Amenemhets or the Sesostrises, could he have walked the streets of Thebes in Amenhotep III's day, would almost have been at a loss to know in what country he had suddenly found himself; while his own antiquated costume, which had survived only among the priests, would have awakened equal astonishment among the fashionable Thebans of the day. He would not have felt less strange than a noble of Elizabeth's reign upon the streets of modern London. All about him he would have found elegant chateaus and luxurious villas, with charming gardens and summer houses grouped about vast temples, such as the Nile-dweller had never seen before.

The wealth and the captive labour of Asia and Nubia were being rapidly transmuted into noble architecture, and at Thebes a new and fundamental chapter in the history of the world's architecture was being daily written. Amenhotep gave himself with appreciation and enthusiasm to such works, and placed at the disposal of his architects all the resources which they needed for an ampler practice of their art than had ever before been possible. There were among them men of the highest gifts, and one of them, who bore the same name as the king, gained such a wide reputation for his wisdom that his sayings circulated in Greek some 1,200 years later among the 'Proverbs of the Seven Wise Men'; and in Ptolemaic times he was finally worshipped as a god, and took his place among the innumerable deities of Egypt as 'Amenhotep, son of Hapu'.

Under the fingers of such men as these the old and traditional elements of Egyptian building were imbued with new life and combined into new forms in which they took on a wondrous beauty unknown before. Besides this, the unprecedented resources of wealth and labour at the command of such an architect enabled him to deal with such vast dimensions that the element of size alone must have rendered his buildings in the highest degree impressive. But of the two forms of temple which now developed, the smaller is not less effective than the larger. It was a simple rectangular cella or holy of holies, 9 or 12 metres (30 or 40 feet) long and four metres (14 feet) high, with a door at each end, surrounded by a portico, the whole being raised upon a base of about half the height of the temple walls. With the door looking out between two graceful columns, and the facade happily set in the retreating vistas of the side colonnades, the whole is so exquisitely proportioned that the trained eye immediately recognizes the hand of a master who appreciated the full value of simple fundamental lines. Little wonder that the architects of Napoleon's expedition who brought it to the notice of the modern world were charmed with it, and thought that they had discovered in it the origin of the Greek peripteral temple; nor can there indeed be any doubt that the architecture of Greece was influenced by this form. The other and larger type of temple, which now found its highest development, differs strikingly from the one just discussed; and perhaps most fundamentally in the fact that its colonnades are all within and not visible from the outside. The holy of holies, as of old, is surrounded by a series of chambers, now larger than before, as rendered necessary by the rich and elaborate ritual which had arisen. Before it is a large colonnaded hall, often called the hypostyle, while in front of this hall lies an extensive forecourt surrounded by a columned portico. In front of this court rise two towers (together called a 'pylon'), which form the facade of the temple. Their walls incline inward, they are crowned by a hollow cornice and the great door of the temple opens between them. While the masonry, which is of sandstone or limestone, does not usually contain large blocks, huge architraves, 9 or 12 metres (30 or 40 feet) long and weighing 100 or 200 tons, are not unknown. Nearly all the surfaces except those on the columns are carved with reliefs, the outside showing the king in battle, while on the inside be appears in the worship of the gods, and all surfaces with slight exception were highly coloured. Before the vast double doors of cedar of Lebanon mounted in bronze, rose, one on either side, a pair of obelisks, towering high above the pylon towers, while colossal statues of the king, each hewn from a single block, were placed with backs to the pylon, on either side of the door. In the use of these elements and this general arrangement of the parts, already common before Amenhotep's reign, his architects created a radically new type, destined to survive in frequent use to this day as one of the noblest forms of architecture.

At Luxor, the old southern suburb of Thebes, which had now grown into the city, there was a small temple to Amon, built by the kings of the Twelfth Dynasty. Amenhotep had, probably early in his reign, pulled it down and built a new sanctuary with surrounding chambers and a hall before it, like that of Thutmose I at Karnak. To this his architects had laid out in front a superb forecourt, with the finest colonnades now surviving in Egypt. Gaining confidence, they determined to erect in front of all this a new and more ambitious hall than had ever been attempted before, to be preceded in all probability by a still larger court. The great hall was laid out with a row of gigantic columns on either side the central axis, quite surpassing in height any pier ever before employed by the Egyptian. Nor were they less beautiful for their great size, being in every respect masterpieces of exquisite proportion, with capitals of the graceful, spreading papyrus flower type. These columns were higher than those ranged on both sides of the middle, thus producing a higher roof over a central aisle or nave and a lower roof over the side aisles, the difference in level being filled with grated stone windows in a clear story. Thus were produced the fundamental elements in basilica and cathedral architecture, which we owe to the Theban architects of Amenhotep III. Unfortunately, the vast hall was unfinished at the death of the king, and his son was too ardent an enemy of Amon to carry out the work of his father. His later successors walled up the magnificent nave with drums from the columns of the side aisles which were never set up, and the whole stands today a mournful wreck of an unfinished work of art, the first example of a type for which the world cannot be too grateful.

Amenhotep now proceeded to give the great buildings of the city a unity which they had not before possessed. He raised a massive pylon before the temple of Karnak, adorned with unsurpassed richness; stelas of lapis lazuli were set up on either side and besides great quantities of gold and silver, nearly 550 kilograms (1,200 pounds) of malachite were employed in the inlay work. From the river an avenue led up to it between two tall obelisks, and before it his architect, Amenhotep, set up for him his portrait colossus, the largest thus far erected, having been hewn from a single block of tough gritstone 20 metres (67 feet) long, brought up the river from the quarry near modern Cairo by an army of men. The king also built a temple to Mut, the goddess of Thebes, where his ancestors had begun it, on the south of Karnak, and excavated a lake beside it. He then laid out a beautiful garden in the interval of over a mile and a half, which separates the Karnak from the Luxor temple and connected the great temples by avenues of rams carved in stone, each bearing a statue of the pharaoh between the forepaws. The general effect must have been imposing in the extreme; the brilliant hues of the polychrome architecture, with columns and gates overwrought in gold and floors overlaid with silver, the whole dominated by towering obelisks clothed in glittering metal, rising high above the rich green of the nodding palms and tropical foliage which framed the mass – all this must have produced an impression both of gorgeous detail and overwhelming grandeur, of which the sombre ruins of the same buildings, impressive as they are, offer little hint at the present day.

As at Athens in the days of her glory, the state was fortunate in the possession of men of sensitive and creative mind, upon whose quick imagination her greatness had profoundly wrought, until they were able to embody her external manifestations in forms of beauty, dignity and splendour. Thebes was now rapidly becoming a worthy seat of empire, the first monumental city of antiquity. Nor did the western plain on the other side of the river, behind which the conquerors slept, suffer by comparison with the new glories of Karnak and Luxor. Along the foot of the rugged cliffs, from the modest chapel of Amenhotep I on the north, there stretched southward in an imposing line the mortuary temples of the emperors. At the south end of this line, but a little nearer the river, Amenhotep III now erected his own mortuary sanctuary, the largest temple of his reign. Two gigantic colossi of the king, nearly 21 metres (70 feet) high, each cut from one block and weighing over 700 tons, besides a pair of obelisks, stood before the pylon, which was approached from the river by an avenue of jackals sculptured in stone. Numerous other great statues of the pharaoh were ranged about the colonnades of the court. A huge stele of sandstone nine metres (30 feet) high, inwrought with gold and encrusted with costly stones marked the ceremonial 'Station of the King', where Amenhotep stood in performing the official duties of the ritual; another over three metres (10 feet) high bore a record of all his works for Amon, while the walls and floors of the temple, overlaid with gold and silver, displayed the most prodigal magnificence. The fine taste and the technical skill required for such supplementary works of the craftsman were now developed to a point of classical excellence, beyond which Egyptian art never passed. In mere mass alone some of these works of industrial art were surprising, for the bronze hinges and other mountings of the vast cedar pylon doors weighed together some tons, and required castings of unprecedented size; while the overlaying of such doors with sheets of bronze exquisitely damascened in precious metal with the figure of the god demanded a combination of aesthetic capacity with mastery of ponderous mechanics, which is not too common even at the present day.

Sculpture also flourished under such circumstances as never before. While there now developed an attention to details which required infinite patience and nicety, such arduous application did not hamper the fine feeling of which these Eighteenth Dynasty sculptors were capable; nor was the old method of a summary rendering of main lines forsaken. There appear in the works of this age a refinement, a delicacy and a flexibility which were heretofore lacking, even in the best works, though perhaps the striking individuality of the Old Kingdom portraits was not so noticeable. These qualities were carried into work of such ample proportions that the sculptor's command of them under such circumstances is surprising, although not all of the colossal portrait statues are successful in these particulars. Especially in relief were the artists of this age masters. In the accompanying relief, now in the Berlin Museum, study the abandoned grief of the two sons of the High Priest of Memphis as they follow their father's body to the tomb, and note how effectively the artist has contrasted with them the severe gravity and conventional decorum of the great ministers of state behind them, who themselves are again in striking contrast with a Beau Brummel of that day, who is affectatiously arranging the perfumed curls of his elaborate wig. The man of whose work we have here a mere fragment was a master of ripe and matured culture, an observer of life, whose work exhibits alike the pathos and the wistful questioning of human sorrow, recognizing both the necessity and the cruel indifference of official conventionality, and seeing amid all the play of the vain and ostentatious fashions of the hour. Here across 35 centuries there speaks to us a maturity in the contemplation of life which finds a sympathetic response in every cultivated observer. This fragmentary sketch not merely surpasses anything to be found among any other early oriental people, but belongs to a class of work totally lacking elsewhere in this age. It is one of the earliest examples of sculpture exhibiting that interpretation of life and appreciation of individual traits (often supposed to have arisen first among the sculptors of Greece), in which art find its highest expression.

Now, too, the pharaoh's deeds of prowess inspired the sculptors of the time to more elaborate compositions than had ever before been approached. The battle scenes on the noble chariot of Thutmose IV exhibit a complexity in drawing unprecedented, and this tendency continues in the Nineteenth Dynasty. While brute life does not afford opportunity for such work as that just discussed, the perfection attained in the sculpture of animal forms by the artists of this time marks again the highest level of achievement attained by Egyptian art, and Ruskin has even insisted with his customary conviction that the two lions of Amenhotep's reign, now in the British Museum, are the finest embodiment of animal majesty which has survived to us from any ancient people. While this may be an over enthusiastic estimate of their value, it must not be forgotten that these noble works were designed as the adornment of a distant provincial sanctuary at Soleb in upper Nubia. If such work as this beautified the courts of a remote Nubian temple, what may we not imagine were the sculptures in the mortuary temple of the pharaoh himself at Thebes? But this sumptuous building, probably the greatest work of art ever wrought in Egypt, has vanished utterly. Only the two weather-beaten colossi which guarded the entrance still look out across the plain, one of them still bearing the scribblings in Greek of curious tourists in the times of the Roman Empire who came to hear the marvellous voice which issued from it every morning. A hundred paces behind lies prostrate and shattered in two the vast stele, once encrusted with gold and costly stones, marking the 'Station of the King', and upon it one may still read the words of Amenhotep regarding the temple: 'My majesty has done these things for millions of years, and I know that they will abide in the earth'. We shall later have occasion to observe how this regal temple fell a prey to the impiety of Amenhotep's degenerate descendants within 200 years of his death. Of the painting of the time, the best examples were in the palaces, and these, being of wood and sun-dried brick, have perished, but a fine perception, which enabled the artist in his representation of animals and birds to depict instantaneous postures is already observable, reaching its highest expression in the next reign. More elaborate drawings than any known in earlier times were, as we have seen, demanded by the pharaoh in the representation of his battles, and the artist's powers of composition were taxed to the utmost. The battle scenes on the temples of this period have perished, but that they existed is certain, in view of such a composition as that on the chariot of Thutmose IV.

Adorned with such works as these, the western plain of Thebes was a majestic prospect as the observer advanced from the river, ascending Amenhotep's avenue of sculptured jackals. On the left, behind the temple and nearer the cliffs, appeared a palace of the king of wooden architecture in bright colours; very light and airy, the facade adorned with flag staves bearing tufts of parti-coloured pennants, and having over the front entrance a gorgeous cushioned balcony with graceful columns, in which the king showed himself to his favourites on occasion. The art which adorned such a palace was as exquisite in its refined aesthetics as in its technical skill. Innumerable products of the industrial artist which fill the museums of Europe indicate with what tempered richness and delicate beauty such a royal chateau was furnished and adorned. Magnificent vessels in gold and silver with figures of men and animals, plants and flowers rising from the rim, glittered on the king's table among crystal goblets, glass vases, and grey porcelain vessels inlaid with pale blue designs. The walls were covered with woven tapestry of workmanship so fine and colour and design so exquisite that skilled judges have declared it equal to the best modern work. Besides painted pavements depicting animal life, the walls also were adorned with fine blue glazed tiles, the rich colour of which shone through elaborate designs in brilliant gold leaf, while glazed figures were employed in encrusting larger surfaces. All this was done with fine and intelligent consideration of the whole colour scheme. In all the refined arts it is an age like that of Louis XV, and the palace everywhere reflects the spirit of the age.

Here too Amenhotep laid out an exclusive quarter which he gave to his queen, Tiy. He excavated a large lake in the enclosure about one and a half kilometres (a mile) long and over 300 metres (1,000 feet) wide, and at the celebration of his coronation anniversary in his 12th year, he opened the sluices for filling it, and sailed out upon it in the royal barge with his queen, in doubtless just such a gorgeous festival 'fantasia' as we find in the *Arabian Nights* in the days of the inevitable Harun er-Rashid. The music on such occasions was more elaborate than ever before, for the art had made progress since the days of the old simplicity. The harp was now a huge instrument as tall as a man, and had some 20 strings; the lyre had been introduced from Asia, and the full orchestra now contained the harp, the lyre, the lute and the double pipes. As a souvenir of the celebration another series of scarabs, or beetle amulets, was issued, inscribed with a brief narrative of the event. Such festivals were now common in Thebes and enriched the life of the fast-growing metropolis with a kaleidoscopic variety which may be only compared with similar periods in Babylon or in Rome under the emperors. The religious feasts of the seventh month were celebrated with such opulent splendour that the month quickly gained the epithet, 'That of Amenhotep', a designation which clung to it until it became the usual name for it in later ages, and in corrupt form it still survives among the natives of modern Egypt, who employ it without the faintest knowledge of the imperial ruler, their ancestor, whose name is perpetuated in it. In such an age literature doubtless throve, but chance has unfortunately preserved to us little of the literature of the Eighteenth Dynasty. We have heard a portion of the triumphant hymn to Thutmose III and we shall read the remarkable sun hymn of Ikhnaton; but of narrative, song and legend, which must have flourished from the rise of the empire, our surviving documents date almost exclusively from the Nineteenth Dynasty.

Among the king's favourite diversions was the hunt, which he practiced on an unprecedented scale. When his scouts brought him word that a herd of wild cattle had appeared among the hills bordering the Delta, he would leave the palace at Memphis in the evening, sail north all night and reach the herd in the early morning. A numerous body of troops, with children from the villages, then surrounded the herd and drove them into a large enclosure, a method also employed in earlier times. On one occasion his beaters counted no less than 170 wild cattle in the enclosure. Entering it in his chariot the king himself slew 56 of the savage beasts on the first day, to which number he added probably 20 more at a second onslaught, which followed after four days' interval of rest. Amenhotep thought the achievement worthy of commemoration and issued a series of scarabs bearing a record of the feat. When the chase-loving king had completed 10 years of lion hunting he distributed to the nobles of the court a similar memorial of his prowess, which, after the usual royal titulary of himself and his queen, bore the words: 'Statement of lions which his majesty brought down with his own arrows from the year one to the year 10: fierce lions, 102'. Some 30 or 40 of these scarabs of the lion hunt still survive.

It will be seen that in these things a new and modern tendency was coming to its own. The divine pharaoh is constantly being exhibited in human relations, the affairs of the royal house are made public property, the name of the queen, not even a woman of royal birth, is constantly appearing at the head of official documents side by side with that of the pharaoh. In constant intercourse with the nations of Asia he is gradually forced from his old superhuman state, suited only to the Nile, into less provincial and more modern relations with his neighbours of Babylon and Mitanni, who in their letters call him 'brother'. This lion-hunting, bull-baiting pharaoh is far indeed from the godlike and unapproachable immobility of his divine ancestors. It was as if the emperor of China or the Dalai Lama of Tibet were all at once to make his personal doings known on a series of medals! To be sure, Amenhotep compromised with the traditions; he built a temple in Memphis, where he was worshipped, and enlarged the Nubian temple at Soleb also for his own worship in conjunction with that of Amon. His queen likewise was goddess of the Nubian temple of Sedeinga. Amenhotep was thus still a god in Nubia, but in fact he had long since broken with this court and priestly fiction. Whether consciously or not he had assumed a modern standpoint, which must inevitably lead to sharp conflict with the almost irresistible inertia of tradition in an oriental country.

Meantime all went well; the lines of the coming internal struggle were not yet clearly drawn, and of the first signs of trouble from without he was unconscious. A veritable 'Caesar divus', he presided over the magnificence of Thebes. In the 30th year of his reign he celebrated the jubilee of his appointment as crown prince, which had coincided with his accession. It was on this occasion probably that the obelisks before the king's mortuary temple were erected. To render the feast still more auspicious the chief treasurer, in presenting to the king the enormous harvest returns from Nubia to Naharin, was able to report a large increase, which so pleased the king that the local officials of the treasury were all received in audience and presented with rich rewards. The second jubilee, probably of the year 34, passed without incident so far as we know; and in the year 36, when the third jubilee was celebrated, the old monarch was still able to grant the court an audience and receive their congratulations.

But ominous signs of trouble had meanwhile appeared on the northern horizon. Mitanni had been invaded by the Hittites (Kheta), but Dushratta, the Mitannian king, had been able to repel them and sent to Amenhotep a chariot and pair, besides two slaves, as a present from the booty which the Hittites had left in his hands. But the provinces of Egypt had not been spared. Akizzi, the pharaoh's vassal king of Katna, wrote him that the Hittites had invaded his territory in the Orontes valley, had carried off the image of Amon-Re, bearing the name of Amenhotep, and had burned the city as they went: Nukhashshi, which lay still further north, suffered a similar invasion, and its king, Hadadnirari, wrote a despairing letter to Amenhotep with assurances of loyalty and an appeal for support against the invaders. All this had not been done without the connivance of treacherous vassals of the pharaoh, who were themselves attempting the conquest of territory on their own account. The afterward notorious Aziru and his father, Abdashirta, were leaders in the movement, entering Katna and Nukhashshi from the south and plundering as they went. Others who had made common cause with them threatened Ubi, the region of Damascus. Akizzi of Katna and Rib-Addi of Byblos quickly reported the defection of the pharaoh's vassals; Akizzi wrote appealing for speedy aid: 'O my lord, just as Damascus, in the land of Ubi, stretches out her hand to thy feet, so also Katna stretches out her hand to thy feet'. The situation was far more critical than it appeared to the pharaoh, for he had no means of recognizing the seriousness of the Hittite advance, and Akizzi assured him that the kings of Naharin were loyal, saying: 'O my lord, even as I love my lord the king, so also do the king of Nukhashshi, the king of Niy, the king of Senzar and the king of Kinanat. For these kings are all servants of my lord the king'. Amenhotep, therefore, instead of marching with his entire army immediately into north Syria, as Thutmose III would have done, sent troops only. These of course had no trouble in momentarily quelling the turbulent dynasts and putting a brief stop to their aggressions against the loyal vassals; but they were quite unable to cope with the southern advance of the Hittites, who secured a footing in northern Naharin of the greatest value in their further plans for the conquest of Syria. Furthermore, the king's long absence from Syria was telling upon Egyptian prestige there, and another threatening danger to his Asiatic possessions is stated to have begun from the day when the king had last left Sidon. An invasion of the Khabiri, desert Semites, such as had periodically inundated Syria and Palestine from time immemorial, was now taking place. It was of such proportions that it may fairly be called an immigration. Before Amenhotep III's death it had become threatening, and thus Ribaddi of Byblos later wrote to Amenhotep III's son: 'Since thy father returned from Sidon, since that time the lands have fallen into the hands of the Khabiri'.

Under such ominous conditions as these the old pharaoh, whom we may well call 'Amenhotep the Magnificent', drew near his end. His brother of Mitanni, with whom he was still on terms of intimacy, probably knowing of his age and weakness, sent the image of Ishtar of Nineveh for the second time to Egypt, doubtless in the hope that the far-famed goddess might be able to exorcise the evil spirits which were causing Amenhotep's infirmity and restore the old king to health. But all such means were of no avail, and about 1375 BCE, after nearly 36 years upon the throne, 'Amenhotep the Magnificent' passed away and was buried with the other emperors, his fathers, in the Valley of the Kings' Tombs.

The Religious Revolution of Ikhnaton

☥

NO NATION EVER STOOD in direr need of a strong and practical ruler than did Egypt at the death of Amenhotep III. Yet she chanced to be ruled at this fatal crisis by a young dreamer, who, in spite of unprecedented greatness in the world of ideas,

was not fitted to cope with a situation demanding an aggressive man of affairs and a skilled military leader – in fine such a man as Thutmose III. Amenhotep IV, the young and inexperienced son of Amenhotep III and the queen Tiy, was indeed strong and fearless in certain directions, but he failed utterly to understand the practical needs of his empire.

He had inherited a difficult situation. The conflict of new forces with tradition, was, as we have seen, already felt by his father. The task before him was such manipulation of these conflicting forces as might eventually give reasonable play to the new and modern tendency, but at the same time to conserve enough of the old to prevent a catastrophe. It was a problem of practical statesmanship, but Amenhotep IV saw it chiefly in its ideal aspects. His mother, Tiy, and his queen, Nofretete, perhaps a woman of Asiatic birth, and a favourite priest, Eye, the husband of his childhood nurse, formed his immediate circle. The first two probably exercised a powerful influence over him, and were given a prominent share in the government, at least as far as its public manifestations were concerned, for in a manner quite surpassing his father's similar tendency, he constantly appeared in public with both his mother and his wife. The lofty and impractical aims which he had in view must have found a ready response in these his two most influential counsellors. Thus, while Egypt was in sore need of a vigorous and skilled administrator, the young king was in close counsel with a priest and two perhaps gifted women, who, however able, were not of the fibre to show the new pharaoh what the empire really demanded. Instead of gathering the army so sadly needed in Naharin, Amenhotep IV immersed himself heart and soul in the thought of the time, and the philosophizing theology of the priests was of more importance to him than all the provinces of Asia. In such contemplations he gradually developed ideals and purposes which make him the most remarkable of all the pharaohs, and the first *individual* in human history.

The profound influence of Egypt's imperial position had not been limited to the externals of life, to the manners and customs of the people, to the rich and prolific art, pregnant with new possibilities of beauty, but had extended likewise to the thought of the age. Such thought was chiefly theological and we must divest it of all the ideas which are connoted by the modern term 'the thought of the age'. Even before the conquests in Asia the priests had made great progress in the interpretation of the gods, and they had now reached a stage in which, like the later Greeks, they were importing semi-philosophical significance into the myths, such as these had of course not originally possessed. The interpretation of a god was naturally suggested by his place or function in the myth. Thus Ptah, the artificer-god of Memphis, furnished the priesthood there with a fruitful line of thought, moving in concrete channels, and thus guiding the thinker, in an age of intellectual beginnings, thinking in a language without terminology for such processes, even when they had once been followed out.

Ptah had been from the remotest ages the god of the architect and craftsman, to whom he communicated plans and designs for architectural works and the products of the industrial arts. Contemplating this god, the Memphite priest, little used as his mind was to abstractions, found a tangible channel, moving along which he gradually gained a rational and with certain limitations a philosophical conception of the world. The workshop of the Memphite temple, where, under Ptah's guidance, were wrought the splendid statues, utensils and offerings for the temple, expands into a world, and Ptah, its lord, grows into the master workman of the universal workshop. As he furnishes all designs to the architect and craftsman, so now he does the same for all men in all that they do; he becomes the supreme mind; he is mind and all things proceed from him. The world and all that is in it existed as thought in his mind; and his thoughts, like his plans for buildings and works of art, needed but to be expressed in spoken words to take concrete form as material realities. Gods and men alike proceeded from mind, and all that they do is but the mind of the god working in them. A priest of Ptah has expressed this in a short poem, a part of which vaguely and indefinitely shows how the minds of the time were explaining the world:

> Ptah, the great, is the mind and tongue of the gods....
> Ptah, from whom proceeded the power
> Of the mind,
> And of the tongue.
> That which comes forth from every mind,

And from every mouth:
Of all gods, of all people, of all cattle, of all reptiles,
That live, thinking and commanding
Everything that he (Ptah) wills.

It (the mind) is the one that bringeth forth every successful issue.
It is the tongue which repeats the thought of the mind:
It (the mind) was the fashioner of all gods….
At a time when every divine word
Came into existence by the thought of the mind,
And the command of the tongue.

Wherever we have used the word 'mind' in this passage the Egyptian has 'heart', which word served him for 'mind' in exactly the same way as the Hebrews and many other peoples frequently employ it; much in the same manner indeed as we ourselves often use it, with the difference that the Egyptian believed the heart and the bowels actually to be the seat of mind. Although such notions could have been entertained by very limited circles, they were not confined to the priests alone. Intef, the court herald of Thutmose III, states on his tombstone that he owed his success to the guidance of his 'heart', to which he listened implicitly; and he adds that the people said: 'Lo, it is an oracle of the god, which is in every body'. 'Body' is here, as commonly, the word for abdomen or bowels, the seat of mind. The Egyptian had thus gained the idea of a single controlling intelligence, behind and above all sentient beings, including the gods. The efficient force by which this intelligence put his designs into execution was his spoken 'word', and this primitive 'logos' is undoubtedly the incipient germ of the later logos doctrine which found its origin in Egypt. Early Greek philosophy may also have drawn upon it.

Similar ideas were now being propagated regarding all the greater gods of Egypt, but as long as the kingdom was confined to the Nile valley the activity of such a god was limited, in their thinking, to the confines of the pharaoh's domain, and the world of which they thought meant no more. From of old the pharaoh was the heir of the gods and ruled the two kingdoms of the upper and lower river which they had once ruled. Thus they had not in the myths extended their dominion beyond the river valley, and that valley originally extended only from the sea to the first cataract. But under the empire all this is changed, the god goes where the pharaoh's sword carries him; the advance of the pharaoh's boundary tablets in Nubia and Syria is the extension of the god's domain. The king is now called 'The one who brings the world to him [the god], who placed him [the pharaoh] on his throne'. For king and priest alike the world is only a great domain of the god. All the pharaoh's wars are recorded upon the temple walls, and even in their mechanical arrangement his wars converge upon the temple door. The theological theory of the state is simply that the king receives the world that he may deliver it to the god, and he prays for extended conquests that the dominion of the god may be correspondingly extended. Thus theological thinking is brought into close and sensitive relationship with political conditions; and theological theory must inevitably extend the active government of the god to the limits of the domain whence the king receives tribute. It can be no accident that the notion of a practically universal god arose in Egypt at the moment when he was receiving universal tribute from the world of that day. Again the analogy of the pharaoh's power unquestionably operated powerfully with the Egyptian theologian at this time; for in the myth-making days the gods were conceived as pharaohs ruling the Nile valley, because the myth-makers lived under pharaohs who so ruled. Living now under pharaohs who ruled a world empire, the priest of the imperial age had before him in tangible form a world dominion and a world concept, the prerequisite of the notion of the world-god. Conquered and organized and governed, it had now been before him for 200 years, and out of the pharaoh-ruled world he gradually began to see the world-god.

We have thus far given this god no name. Had you asked the Memphite priests they would have said his name was Ptah, the old god of Memphis; the priests of Amon at Thebes would have claimed the honour for Amon, the state god, as a matter of course, while the High Priest of Re at Heliopolis would have pointed out the fact that the pharaoh was the son of Re and the heir to his kingdom, and hence Re must be the supreme god of all the empire. Obscure gods in the local sanctuaries would have found similar champions in their priesthoods because they were now identified with Re and claimed his prerogatives. But historically Re's claim was undoubtedly the best. Amon had never succeeded in displacing him. The introduction of official letters still, as of old, commends the addressee to the favour of Re-Harakhte, while in the popular tales of the time it is Re-Harakhte who rules the world. But none of the old divinities of Egypt had been proclaimed the god of the empire, although in fact the priesthood of Heliopolis had gained the coveted honour for their revered sun god, Re. Already under Amenhotep III an old name for the material sun, 'Aton', had come into prominent use, where the name of the sun god might have been expected. Thus he called the royal barge on which he sailed with Tiy on her beautiful lake, 'Aton Gleams'. A company of his bodyguard bore the new god's name, and there was probably a chapel dedicated to him at Heliopolis. The sun god, too, was now and again designated as 'the sole god' by Amenhotep III's contemporaries.

The already existent conflict with traditional tendencies into which the pharaoh had been forced, contained in itself difficulties enough to tax the resources of any statesman without the introduction of a departure involving the most dangerous conflicts with the powerful priesthoods and touching religious tradition, the strongest conservative force of the time. It was just this rash step which the young king now had no hesitation in taking. Under the name of Aton, then, Amenhotep IV introduced the worship of the supreme god, but he made no attempt to conceal the identity of his new deity with the old sun god, Re. Instructing his vizier in the new faith, he said to him, 'The words of Re are before thee … my august father who taught me their essence…. It was known in my heart, revealed to my face, I understood.' He thus attributes the new faith to Re as its source, and claims to have been himself the channel of its revelation. He immediately assumed the office of high priest of his new god with the same title, 'Great Seer', as that of the High Priest of Re at Heliopolis. But, however evident the Heliopolitan origin of the new state religion might be, it was not merely sun worship; the word Aton was employed in place of the old word for 'god' (nuter), and the god is clearly distinguished from the material sun. To the old sun god's name is appended the explanatory phrase 'under his name: "Heat which is in the Sun [Aton]"', and he is likewise called 'lord of the sun [Aton]'. The king, therefore, was deifying the vital heat which he found accompanying all life. It plays in the new faith a similar important part, which we find it assuming in the early cosmogonic philosophies of the Greeks. Thence, as we might expect, the god is stated to be everywhere active by means of his 'rays', and his symbol is a disk in the heavens, darting earthward numerous diverging rays which terminate in hands, each grasping the symbol of life. In his age of the world it is perfectly certain that the king could not have had the vaguest notion of the physico-chemical aspects of his assumption any more than had the early Greeks in dealing with a similar thought; yet the fundamental idea is surprisingly true, and, as we shall see, marvellously fruitful. The outward symbol of his god thus broke sharply with tradition, but it was capable of practical introduction in the many different nations making up the empire and could be understood at a glance by any intelligent foreigner, which was far from the case with any of the traditional symbols of Egyptian religion.

The new god could not dispense with a temple like those of the older deities whom he was ultimately to supersede. Early in his reign Amenhotep IV sent an expedition to the sandstone quarries of Silsileh to secure the necessary stone and the chief nobles of his court were in charge of the works at the quarry. In the garden of Amon, which his father had laid out between the temples of Karnak and Luxor, Amenhotep located his new temple, which was a large and stately building, adorned with polychrome reliefs. Thebes was now called 'City of the Brightness of Aton', and the temple quarter 'Brightness of Aton the Great'; while the sanctuary itself bore the name 'Gem-Aton', a term of uncertain meaning. Although the other gods were still tolerated as of old, it was nevertheless inevitable that the priesthood of Amon should view with growing jealousy the brilliant rise of a strange god in their midst, an artificial creation of which they knew nothing, save that much of the wealth formerly employed in the enrichment of Amon's sanctuary was now lavished on the intruder.

One of Amenhotep III's High Priests of Amon had also been chief treasurer of the kingdom, and another, Ptahmose, was the grand vizier of the realm; while the same thing had occurred in the reign of Hatshepsut, when Hapuseneb had been both vizier and High Priest of Amon. Besides these powers, the High Priest of Amon was also the supreme head of the organization including all the priests of the nation. Indeed, the fact that such extensive political power was now wielded by the High Priests of Amon must have intensified the young king's desire to be freed from the sacerdotal thrall which he had inherited. His father had evidently made some attempt to shake off the priestly hand that lay so heavily on the sceptre, for he had succeeded Ptahmose by a vizier who was not High Priest of Amon. This new vizier, Ramose, was won by the young king's gifts, and a servile court followed him, even superintending the quarry work for the new temple, as we have seen. The priesthood of Amon, however, was now a rich and powerful body. They had installed Thutmose III as king, and could they have supplanted with one of their own tools the young dreamer who now held the throne they would of course have done so at the first opportunity. But Amenhotep IV was the son of a line of rulers too strong and too illustrious to be thus set aside even by the most powerful priesthood in the land; moreover, he possessed unlimited personal force of character, and he was of course supported in his opposition of Amon by the older priesthoods of the north at Memphis and Heliopolis, long jealous of this interloper, the obscure Theban god, who had never been heard of in the north before the rise of the Middle Kingdom. A conflict to the bitter end, with the most disastrous results to the Amonite priesthood ensued. It rendered Thebes intolerable to the young king, and soon after he had finished his new temple he resolved upon radical measures. He would break with the priesthoods and make Aton the sole god, not merely in his own thought, but in very fact; and Amon should fare no better than the rest of the time-honoured gods of his fathers.

It was no 'Gotterdammerung' which the king contemplated, but an immediate annihilation of the gods. As far as their external and material manifestations and equipment were concerned, this could be and was accomplished without delay. The priesthoods, including that of Amon, were dispossessed, the official temple worship of the various gods throughout the land ceased, and their names were erased wherever they could be found upon the monuments. The persecution of Amon was especially severe. The cemetery of Thebes was visited and in the tombs of the ancestors the hated name of Amon was hammered out wherever it appeared upon the stone. The rows on rows of statues of the great nobles of the old and glorious days of the empire, ranged along the walls of the Karnak temple, were not spared, but the god's name was invariably erased. Even the royal statues of his ancestors, including the king's father, were not respected; and, what was worse, as the name of that father, Amenhotep, contained the name of Amon, the young king was placed in the unpleasant predicament of being obliged to cut out his own father's name in order to prevent the name of Amon from appearing 'writ large' on all the temples of Thebes. The splendid stela erected by his father in his mortuary temple, recording all his great buildings for Amon, was mercilessly hacked and rendered illegible. Even the word 'gods' was not permitted to appear on any of the old monuments and the walls of the temples at Thebes were painfully searched that wherever the compromising word appeared it might be blotted out. And then there was the embarrassment of the king's own name, likewise Amenhotep, 'Amon rests', which could not be spoken or placed on a monument. It was of necessity also banished and the king assumed in its place the name 'Ikhnaton', which means 'Spirit of Aton'.

Thebes was now compromised by too many old associations to be a congenial place of residence for so radical a revolutionist. As he looked across the city he saw stretching along the western plain that imposing line of mortuary temples of his fathers which he had violated. They now stood silent and empty. The towering pylons and obelisks of Karnak and Luxor were not a welcome reminder of all that his fathers had contributed to the glory of Amon, and the unfinished hall of his father at Luxor, with the superb columns of the nave, still waiting for the roof, could hardly have stirred pleasant memories in the heart of the young reformer. A doubtless long contemplated plan was therefore undertaken. Aton, the god of the empire, should possess his own city in each of the three great divisions of the empire: Egypt, Asia and Nubia, and the god's Egyptian city should be made the royal residence. It must have been an enterprise requiring some time, but the three cities were duly founded. The Aton-city of Nubia was situated opposite modern Dulgo, at the foot of the Third Cataract, and was thus in the heart of the Egyptian province. It was named 'Gem-Aton' after the Aton temple in Thebes. In Syria the Aton-city is unknown, but Ikhnaton will not have done less for Aton there than his fathers had done for Amon. In the sixth year, shortly after he had changed his name, the king was living in his own Aton-city in Egypt. He chose as its site a fine bay in the cliffs about 250 kilometres (160 miles) above the Delta and nearly 480 kilometres (300 miles) below Thebes. The cliffs, leaving the river in a semi-circle, retreat at this point some five kilometres (three miles) from the stream and return to it again about eight kilometres (five miles) lower down. In the wide plain thus bounded on three sides by the cliffs and on the west by the river Ikhnaton founded his new residence and the holy city of Aton. He called it Akhetaton, 'Horizon of Aton', and it is known in modern times as Tell el-Amarna.

In addition to the town, the territory around it was demarked as a domain belonging to the god, and included the plain on both sides of the river. In the cliffs on either side, 14 large stelas, one of them no less than eight metres (26 feet) in height, were cut into the rock, bearing inscriptions determining the limits of the entire sacred district around the city. As thus laid out the district was about 13 kilometres (eight miles) wide from north to south, and from 20 to over 27 kilometres (12 to over 17 miles) long from cliff to cliff. The king's oath regarding it is recorded on the extreme northern and southern stelas thus: 'His majesty raised his hand to heaven, to him who made him, even to Aton, saying, "This is my testimony forever, and this is my witness forever, this landmark [stela].... I have made Akhetaton for my father as a dwelling.... I have demarked Akhetaton on its south, on its north, on its west, on its east. I shall not pass beyond the southern landmark of Akhetaton toward the south, nor shall I pass beyond the northern landmark of Akhetaton toward the north.... He has made his circuit for his own, he has made his altar in its midst, whereon I make offering to him"'. Whether this statement that he would never pass beyond the boundary of the district, a vow which is found referring to all four cardinal points, is merely a legal phrase by which a property owner recognized that he had no rights beyond his just limit, the boundary of his property; or whether the king actually carried out this vow literally and remained the rest of his life in Akhetaton we cannot say. But the phrase is not found in any other boundary landmarks known to us.

The region thus demarked was then legally conveyed to Aton by the king's own decree, saying; 'Now as for the area within the ... landmarks from the eastern mountain [cliffs] to the western mountain of Akhetaton opposite, it belongs to my father, Aton, who is given life forever and ever: whether mountains or cliffs, or swamps ... or uplands, or fields, or waters, or towns, or shores, or people, or cattle, or trees or anything which Aton, my father has made.... I have made it for Aton, my father, forever and ever'. And on another stela he says that they are to belong to the temple of Aton in Akhetaton forever and ever as offerings. Besides this sacred domain the god was endowed with revenues from other lands in Egypt and Nubia, and probably also in Syria. The city thus established was to be the real capital of the empire, for the king himself said: 'The whole land shall come hither, for the beautiful seat of Akhetaton shall be another seat [capital], and I will give them audience whether they be north or south or west or east'. The royal architect, Bek, was sent to the first cataract to procure stone for the new temple, or we should rather say temples, for no less than three were now built in the new city, one for the queen mother, Tiy, and another for the princess Beketaton ('Maid servant of Aton'), beside the state temple of the king himself. Around the temples rose the palace of the king and the chateaus of his nobles, one of whom describes the city thus: 'Akhetaton, great in loveliness, mistress of pleasant ceremonies, rich in possessions, the offerings of Re in her midst. At the sight of her beauty there is rejoicing. She is lovely and beautiful; when one sees her it is like a glimpse of heaven. Her number cannot be calculated. When the Aton rises in her he fills her with his rays and he embraces [with his rays] his beloved son, son of eternity, who came forth from Aton and offers the earth to him who placed him on his throne, causing the earth to belong to him who made him'.

On the day when the temple was ready to receive the first dues from its revenues the king proceeded thither in his chariot accompanied by his four daughters and a gorgeous retinue. They were received at the temple with shouts of 'Welcome'; a rich oblation filled the high altar in the temple court, while the store chambers around it were groaning with the wealth of the newly paid revenues. The king himself participated in such ceremonies, while the queen 'sends the Aton to rest with a sweet voice, her two beautiful hands bearing the two sistrums'. But Ikhnaton no longer attempted to act as high priest himself; one of his favourites, Merire ('Beloved of Re'), was appointed by him to the office, coming one day for this purpose with his friends to the balcony of the palace, in which the king and queen appeared in state. The king then formally promoted Merire to the exalted office, saying: 'Behold, I am appointing thee for myself to be "Great Seer" [high priest] of the Aton in the temple of Aton in Akhetaton.... I give to thee the office saying, "Thou shalt eat the food of pharaoh, thy lord, in the house of Aton"'. Merire was so faithful in the administration of the temple that the king publicly rewarded him with 'the gold', the customary distinction granted to zealous servitors of the pharaoh. At the door of one of the temple buildings the king, queen and two daughters extend to the fortunate Merire the rewards of fidelity, and the king says to the attendants: 'Hang gold at his neck before and behind, and gold on his legs; because of his hearing the teaching of pharaoh concerning every saying in these beautiful seats which pharaoh has made in the sanctuary in the Aton-temple in Akhetaton'. It thus appears that Merire had given heed to the king's teachings regarding the ritual of the temple, or, as he says, 'every saying in these beautiful seats'.

It becomes more and more evident that all that was devised and done in the new city and in the propagation of the Aton faith is directly due to the king and bears the stamp of his individuality. A king who did not hesitate to erase his own father's name on the monuments in order to annihilate Amon, the great foe of his revolutionary movement, was not one to stop halfway, and the men about him must have been involuntarily carried on at his imperious will. But Ikhnaton understood enough of the old policy of the pharaohs to know that he must hold his party by practical rewards, and the leading partisans of his movement like Merire enjoyed liberal bounty at his hand. Thus one of his priests of Aton, and at the same time his master of the royal horse, named Eye, who had by good fortune happened to marry the nurse of the king, renders this very evident in such statements as the following: 'He doubles to me my favours in silver and gold,' or again, addressing the king, 'How prosperous is he who hears thy teaching of life! He is satisfied with seeing thee without ceasing'. The general of the army, Mai, enjoyed similar bounty, boasting of it in the same way: 'He hath doubled to me my favours like the numbers of the sand. I am the head of the officials, at the head of the people; my lord has advanced me because I have carried out his teaching, and I hear his word without ceasing. My eyes behold thy beauty every day, O my lord, wise like Aton, satisfied with truth. How prosperous is he who hears thy teaching of life!' Although there must have been a nucleus of men who really appreciated the ideal aspects of the king's teaching, it is thus evident that many were chiefly influenced by 'the loaves and the fishes'.

Indeed there was one royal favour which must have been welcome to them all without exception. This was the beautiful cliff tomb which the king commanded his craftsmen to hew out of the eastern cliffs for each one of his favourites. For the old mortuary practices were not all suppressed by Ikhnaton, and it was still necessary for a man to be buried in the 'eternal house', with its endowment for the support of the deceased in the hereafter. But that eternal house was no longer disfigured with hideous demons and grotesque monsters which should confront the dead in the future life; and the magic paraphernalia necessary to meet and vanquish the dark powers of the nether world, which filled the tombs of the old order at Thebes, were completely banished. In thus suppressing these base and repulsive devices, which the perverted imagination of a stupid priesthood had imposed upon an implicit people, the king's reform was most salutary. The tomb now became a monument to the deceased; the walls of its chapel bore fresh and natural pictures from the life of the people in Akhetaton, particularly the incidents in the official career of the dead man, and preferably his intercourse with the king. Thus the city of Akhetaton is now better known to us from its cemetery than from its ruins. Throughout these tombs the nobles take delight in reiterating, both in relief and inscription, the intimate relation between Aton and the king. Over and over again they show the king and the queen together standing under the disk of Aton, whose rays, terminating in hands, descend and embrace the king. The vulture goddess, Mut, who, since the hoary age of the Thinites had appeared on all the monuments extending her protecting wings over the pharaoh's head, had long since been banished. The nobles constantly pray to the god for the king, saying that he 'came forth from thy rays,' or 'thou hast formed him out of thine own rays'; and interspersed through their prayers are numerous current phrases of the Aton faith, which have now become conventional, replacing those of the old orthodox religion, which it must have been very awkward for them to cease using. Thus they demonstrated how zealous they had been in accepting and appropriating the king's new teaching. On state occasions, instead of the old stock phrases, with innumerable references to the traditional gods, every noble who would enjoy the king's favour was evidently obliged to show his familiarity with the Aton faith and the king's position in it by a liberal use of these allusions. Even the Syrian vassals were wise enough to make their dispatches pleasant reading by glossing them with appropriate recognition of the supremacy of the sun god. The source of such phrases was really the king himself, as we have before intimated, and something of the 'teaching' whence they were taken, so often attributed to him, is preserved in the tombs to which we have referred.

Either for the temple service or for personal devotions, the king composed two hymns to Aton, both of which the nobles had engraved on the walls of their tomb chapels. Of all the monuments left by this unparalleled revolution, these hymns are by far the most remarkable; and from them we may gather an intimation of the doctrines which the speculative young pharaoh had sacrificed so much to disseminate. They are regularly entitled: 'Praise of Aton by king Ikhnaton and queen Nefernefruaton'; and the longer and finer of the two is worthy of being known in modern literature. The titles of the separate strophes are the addition of the present author, and in the translation no attempt has been made to do more than to furnish an accurate rendering. The 104th Psalm of the Hebrews shows a notable similarity to our hymn both in the thought and the sequence, so that it seemed desirable to place the most noticeably parallel passages side by side.

The Splendour of Aton

Thy dawning is beautiful in the horizon of heaven,
O living Aton, Beginning of life!
When thou risest in the eastern horizon of heaven,
Thou fillest every land with thy beauty;
For thou are beautiful, great, glittering, high over the earth;
Thy rays, they encompass the lands, even all thou hast made.
Thou art Re, and thou hast carried them all away captive;
Thou bindest them by thy love.
Though thou art afar, thy rays are on earth;
Though thou art on high, thy footprints are the day,

Night

When thou settest in the
*   western horizon of heaven,*
The world is in darkness
*   like the dead.*
They sleep in their chambers,
Their heads are wrapt up,
Their nostrils stopped, and
*   none seeth the other.*
Stolen are all their things, that
*   are under their heads,*
While they know it not.
Every lion cometh forth from his den,
All serpents, they sting.

Thou makest darkness
*   and it is night,*
Wherein all the beasts of the
*   forest do creep forth.*
The young lions roar
*   after their prey.*
They seek their meat from God.
(Psalm 104, 20-21.)

Darkness reigns (?),
The world is in silence,
He that made them has gone to
  rest in his horizon.

Day and Man

Bright is the earth,
When thou risest in the horizon,
When thou shinest as
  Aton by day.
The darkness is banished,
When thou sendest
  forth thy rays,
The Two Lands [Egypt]
  are in daily festivity,
Awake and standing
  upon their feet,
For thou hast raised them up.
Their limbs bathed, they
  take their clothing;
Their arms uplifted in
  adoration to thy dawning.
Then in all the world,
  they do their work.

The sun ariseth, they
  get them away,
And lay them down
  in their dens.
Man goeth forth
  unto his work,
And to his labour
  until the evening.
(Psalm 104, 22-23.)

Day and the Animals and Plants

All cattle rest upon their herbage,
All trees and plants flourish,
The birds flutter in their marshes,
Their wings uplifted in adoration to thee.
All the sheep dance upon their feet,
All winged things fly,
They live when thou hast shone upon them.

Day and the Waters

*The barques sail upstream
and downstream alike.
Every highway is open because
thou hast dawned.
The fish in the river leap
up before thee,
And thy rays are in the
midst of the great sea.*

*Yonder is the sea, great and wide,
Wherein are things
creeping innumerable
Both small and great beasts.
There go the ships;
There is leviathan, whom thou
hast formed to sport with him.*
(Psalm 10-1, 25-26.)

Creation of Man

*Thou art he who createst the man-child in woman,
Who makest seed in man,
Who giveth life to the son in the body of his mother,
Who soothest him that he may not weep,
A nurse [even] in the womb.
Who giveth breath to animate everyone that
he maketh.
When he cometh forth from the body,
… on the day of his birth,
Thou openest his mouth in speech,
Thou suppliest his necessities.*

Creation of Animals

*When the chicklet crieth in the eggshell,
Thou givest him breath therein, to preserve him alive.
When thou hast perfected him
That he may pierce the egg,
He cometh forth from the egg,
To chirp with all his might;
He runneth about upon his two feet,
When he hath come forth therefrom.*

The Whole Creation

How manifold are
  all thy works!
They are hidden from before us,
O thou sole god, whose powers
  no other possesseth.
Thou didst create the earth
  according to thy desire.
While thou wast alone:
Men, all cattle large and small,
All that are upon the earth,
That go about upon their feet;
All that are on high,
That fly with their wings.
The countries of Syria and Nubia,
The land of Egypt;
Thou settest every man in his place,
Thou suppliest their necessities.
Everyone has his possessions,
And his days are reckoned.
Their tongues are divers in speech,
Their forms likewise and their skins,
For thou divider, hast divided the peoples.

O lord, how manifold
  are thy works!
In wisdom hast thou
  made them all;
The earth is full of thy creatures.
(Psalm 104. 24.)

Watering the Earth

Thou makest the Nile in the Nether World,
Thou bringest it at thy desire, to preserve the people alive.
O lord of them all, when feebleness is in them,
O lord of every house, who risest for them,
O sun of day, the fear of every distant land,
Thou makest [also] their life.
Thou hast set a Nile in heaven,
That it may fall for them,

Making floods upon the mountains, like the great sea;
And watering their fields among their towns.

How excellent are thy designs, O lord of eternity!
The Nile in heaven is for the strangers,
And for the cattle of every land, that go upon their feet;
But the Nile, it cometh from the nether world for Egypt.

Thus thy rays nourish every garden,
When thou risest they live, and grow by thee.

The Seasons

Thou makest the seasons, in order to create all thy works:
Winter bringing them coolness,
And the heat [of summer likewise].
Thou hast made the distant heaven to rise therein,
In order to behold all that thou didst make,
While thou wast alone,
Rising in thy form as living Aton,
Dawning, shining afar off and returning.

Beauty Due to Light

Thou makest the beauty of form, through thyself alone.
Cities, towns and settlements,
On highway or on river,
All eyes see thee before them,
For thou art Aton of the day over the earth.

Revelation to the King

Thou art in my heart,
There is no other that knoweth thee,
Save thy son Ikhnaton.

Thou hast made him wise in thy designs
And in thy might.
The world is in thy hand,
Even as thou hast made them.
When thou hast risen, they live;
When thou settest, they die.
For thou art duration, beyond thy mere limbs,
By thee man liveth,
And their eyes look upon thy beauty,
Until thou settest.
All labour is laid aside,
When thou settest in the west;
When thou risest, they are made to grow
... for the king.
Since thou didst establish the earth,
Thou hast raised them up for thy son,
Who came forth from thy limbs,
The king, living in truth,
The lord of the Two Lands Nefer-khepru-Re, Wan-Re,
The son of Re, living in truth, lord of diadems,
Ikhnaton, whose life is long;
[And for] the great royal wife, his beloved,
Mistress of the Two Lands, Nefer nefru aton, Nofretete,
Living and flourishing for ever and ever.

In this hymn the universalism of the empire finds full expression and the royal singer sweeps his eye from the far-off cataracts of the Nubian Nile to the remotest lands of Syria. These are not thoughts which we have been accustomed to attribute to the men of some 1,400 years before Christ. A new spirit has breathed upon the dry bones of traditionalism in Egypt, and he who reads these lines for the first time must be moved with involuntary admiration for the young king who in such an age found such thoughts in his heart. He grasped the idea of a world dominator, as the creator of nature, in which the king saw revealed the creator's beneficent purpose for all his creatures, even the meanest; for the birds fluttering about in the lily-grown Nile marshes to him seemed to be uplifting their wings in adoration of their creator; and even the fish in the stream leaped up in praise to God. It is his voice that summons the blossoms and nourishes the chicklet or commands the mighty deluge of the Nile. He called Aton, 'the father and the mother of all that he had made', and he saw in some degree the goodness of that All-Father as did he who bade us consider the lilies. He based the universal sway of God upon his fatherly care of all men alike, irrespective of race or nationality, and to the proud and exclusive Egyptian he pointed to the all-embracing bounty of the common father of humanity, even placing Syria and Nubia before Egypt in his enumeration.

It is this aspect of Ikhnaton's mind which is especially remarkable; he is the first prophet of history. While to the traditional pharaoh the state god was only the triumphant conqueror, who crushed all peoples and drove them tribute-laden before the pharaoh's chariot, Ikhnaton saw in him the beneficent father of all men. It is the first time in history that a discerning eye has caught this great universal truth. Again his whole movement was but a return to nature, resulting from a spontaneous recognition of the goodness and the beauty evident in it, mingled also with a consciousness of the mystery in it all, which adds just the fitting element of mysticism in such a faith.

> *How manifold are all thy works! They are hidden from before us,*
> *O thou sole god, whose powers no other possesseth.*

While Ikhnaton thus recognized clearly the power, and to a surprising extent, the beneficence of God, there is not here a very spiritual conception of the deity nor any attribution to him of ethical qualities beyond those which Amon had long been supposed to possess. The king has not perceptibly risen from the beneficence to the righteousness in the character of God, nor to his demand for this in the character of men. Nevertheless, there is in his 'teaching', as it is fragmentarily preserved in the hymns and tomb inscriptions of his nobles, a constant emphasis upon 'truth' such as is not found before nor since. The king always attaches to his name the phrase 'living in truth', and that this phrase was not meaningless is evident in his daily life. To him it meant an acceptance of the daily facts of living in a simple and unconventional manner. For him what was was right and its propriety was evident by its very existence. Thus his family life was open and unconcealed before the people. He took the greatest delight in his children and appeared with them and the queen, their mother, on all possible occasions, as if he had been but the humblest scribe in the Aton-temple. He had himself depicted on the monuments while enjoying the most familiar and unaffected intercourse with his family, and whenever he appeared in the temple to offer sacrifice the queen and the daughters she had borne him participated in the service. All that was natural was to him true, and he never failed practically to exemplify this belief, however radically he was obliged to disregard tradition.

Such a principle unavoidably affected the art of the time in which the king took great interest. Bek, his chief sculptor, appended to his title the words, 'whom his majesty himself taught'. Thus the artists of his court were taught to make the chisel and the brush tell the story of what they actually saw. The result was a simple and beautiful realism that saw more clearly than ever any art had seen before. They caught the instantaneous postures of animal life; the coursing hound, the fleeing game, the wild bull leaping in the swamp; for all these belonged to the 'truth', in which Ikhnaton lived. The king's person was no exception to the law of the new art. The monuments of Egypt bore what they had never borne before, a pharaoh not frozen in the conventional posture demanded by the traditions of court propriety. The modelling of the human figure at this time was so plastic that at the first glance one is sometimes in doubt whether he has before him a product of the Greek age. Even complex compositions of grouped figures in the round were now first conceived. Fragments recently discovered show that in the palace court at Akhetaton, a group in stone depicted the king speeding his chariot at the heels of the wounded lion. This was indeed a new chapter in the history of art, even though now lost. It was in some things an obscure chapter; for the strange treatment of the lower limbs by Ikhnaton's artists is a problem which still remains unsolved and cannot be wholly accounted for by supposing a malformation of the king's own limbs. It is one of those unhealthy symptoms which are visible too in the body politic, and to these last we must now turn if we would learn how fatal to the material interests of the state this violent break with tradition has been.

The Fall of Ikhnaton, and the Dissolution of the Empire

☥

W HOLLY ABSORBED IN THE EXALTED religion to which he had given his life, stemming the tide of tradition that was daily as strong against him as at first, Ikhnaton was beset with too many enterprises and responsibilities of a totally different nature, to give much attention to the affairs of the empire abroad. Indeed, as we shall see, he probably did not realize the necessity of doing so until it was far too late.

On his accession his sovereignty in Asia had immediately been recognized by the Hittites and the powers of the Euphrates valley. Dushratta of Mitanni wrote to the queen-mother, Tiy, requesting her influence with the new king for a continuance of the old friendship which he had enjoyed with Ikhnaton's father, and to the young king he wrote a letter of condolence on his father, Amenhotep III's death, not forgetting to add the usual requests for plentiful gold. Burraburyash of Babylon sent similar assurances of sympathy, but only the passport of his messenger, calling on the kings of Canaan to grant him speedy passage, has survived. A son of Burraburyash later sojourned at Ikhnaton's court and married a daughter of the latter, and her Babylonian father-in-law sent her a noble necklace of over 1,000 gems. But such intercourse did not last long, as we shall see.

Meantime the power of the Hittites in northern Syria was constantly on the increase, as they were reinforced by the southern movement of their countrymen behind them. This remarkable race, who still form one of the greatest problems in the study of the early orient, were now emerging from the obscurity which had hitherto enveloped them. Their remains have been found from the western coast of Asia Minor eastward to the plains of Syria and the Euphrates, and southward as far as Hamath. They were a non-Semitic people, or rather peoples, of uncertain racial affinities, but evidently distinct from, and preceding, the Indo-Germanic influx after 1200 BCE which brought in the Phrygians. As shown on the Egyptian monuments, they are beardless, with long hair hanging in two prominent locks before their ears and dropping to the shoulders; but their own native monuments often give them a heavy beard. On the head they most often wore tall, pointed caps like a sugarloaf hat, but with little brim. As their climate demands, they wear heavy woollen clothing, usually in a long, close-fitting garment, descending from the shoulders and reaching to the knees or sometimes the ankles; while the feet are shod in high boots turned up at the toes. They possessed a crude, but by no means primitive, art which produced very creditable monuments in stone still scattered over the hills of Asia Minor. Their skill in the practical arts was considerable, and they produced a red figured pottery above mentioned which was disseminated in trade from the centre of its manufacture in Cappadocia to the Aegean on the west, and eastward through Syria and Palestine to Lachish and Gezer on the south.

Already by 2000 BCE we remember it had perhaps reached the latter place. They were masters of the art of writing, and the king had his personal scribe ever with him. Their pictographic records are still in course of decipherment, and enough progress has not yet been made to enable the scholar to do more than recognize a word here and there. For correspondence they employed the Babylonian cuneiform and must therefore have maintained scribes and interpreters who were masters of Babylonian speech and writing. Large quantities of cuneiform tablets in the Hittite tongue have been found at Boghaz-koi. In war they were formidable opponents. The infantry, among which foreign mercenaries were plentiful, bore bow and arrows, sword and spear and often an axe. They fought in close phalanx formation, very effective at close quarters; but their chief power consisted of chariotry. The chariot itself was more heavily built than in Egypt, as it bore three men, driver, bowman and shield-bearer, while the Egyptian dispensed with the third man. One of the Hittite dynasts had consolidated a kingdom beyond the Amanus, which Thutmose III regularly called 'Great Kheta', as probably distinguished from the less important independent Hittite princes. His capital was a great fortified city called 'Khatti' (identified in 1907), situated at modern Boghaz-koi, east of Angora and the Halys (Kisil-irmak) river in eastern Asia Minor. Active trade and intercourse between this kingdom and Egypt had been carried on from that time or began not long after. This reached such proportions that the king of Cyprus was apprehensive lest too close relations between Egypt and the Hittite kingdom ('Great Kheta') might endanger his own position.

When Ikhnaton ascended the throne Seplel, the king of the Hittites, wrote him a letter of congratulation, and to all appearances had only the friendliest intentions toward Egypt. For the first invasions of the most advanced Hittites, like that which Dushratta of Mitanni repulsed, he may indeed not have been responsible. Even after Ikhnaton's removal to Akhetaton, his new capital, a Hittite embassy appeared there with gifts and greetings. But Ikhnaton must have regarded the old relations as no longer desirable, for the Hittite king asks him why he has ceased the correspondence which his father had maintained. If he realized the situation, Ikhnaton had good reason indeed for abandoning the connection; for the Hittite empire now stood on the northern threshold of Syria, the most formidable enemy which had ever confronted Egypt, and the greatest power in Asia. It is doubtful whether Ikhnaton could have withstood the masses of Asia Minor which were now shifting southward into Syria even if he had made a serious effort to do so; but no such effort was made. Immediately on his accession the disaffected dynasts who had been temporarily suppressed by his father resumed their operations against the faithful vassals of Egypt. One of the latter, in a later letter to Ikhnaton, exactly depicts the situation, saying: 'Verily, thy father did not march forth, nor inspect the lands of the vassal-princes.... And when thou ascendedst the throne of thy father's house, Abd-ashirta's sons took the king's land for themselves. Creatures of the king of Mitanni are they, and of the king of Babylon, and of the king of the Hittites'. With the cooperation of the unfaithful Egyptian vassals Abd-ashirta and his son Aziru, who were at the head of an Amorite kingdom on the upper Orontes; together with Itakama, a Syrian prince, who had seized Kadesh as his kingdom, the Hittites took possession of Amki, the plain on the north side of the lower Orontes, between Antioch and the Amanus.

Three faithful vassal-kings of the vicinity marched to recover the pharaoh's lost territory for him, but were met by Itakama at the head of Hittite troops and driven back. All three wrote immediately to the pharaoh of the trouble and complained of Itakarna. Aziru of Amor had meantime advanced upon the Phoenician and north Syrian coast cities, which he captured as far as Ugarit at the mouth of the Orontes, slaying their kings and appropriating their wealth. Simyra and Byblos held out, however, and as the Hittites advanced into Nukhashshi, on the lower Orontes, Aziru cooperated with them and captured Niy, whose king he slew. Tunip was now in such grave danger that her elders wrote the pharaoh a pathetic letter beseeching his protection. 'To the king of Egypt, my lord: The inhabitants of Tunip thy servant. May it be well with thee, and at the feet of our lord we fall. My lord, Tunip, thy servant speaks, saying: "Who formerly could have plundered Tunip without being plundered by Manakhbiria [Thutmose III]? The gods ... of the king of Egypt, my lord, dwell in Tunip. May our lord ask his old men [if it be not so]. Now, however, we belong no more to our lord, the king of Egypt.... If his soldiers and chariots come too late, Aziru will make us like the city of Kiy. If, however, we have to mourn, the king of Egypt will mourn over those things which Aziru has done, for he will turn his hand against our lord. And when Aziru enters Simyra, Aziru will do to us as he pleases, in the territory of our lord, the king, and on account of these things our lord will have to lament. And now, Tunip, thy city weeps, and her tears are flowing, and there is no help for us. For 20 years we have been sending to our lord, the king, the king of Egypt, but there has not come to us a word, no not one"'. The fears of Tunip were soon realized, for Aziru now concentrated upon Simyra and quickly brought it to a state of extremity.

During all this, Rib-Addi, a faithful vassal of Byblos, where there was an Egyptian temple, writes to the Pharaoh in the most urgent appeals, stating what is going on, and asking for help to drive away Aziru's people from Simyra, knowing full well that if it falls his own city of Byblos is likewise doomed. But no help comes and the Syrian dynasts grow bolder. Zimrida of Sidon falls away and makes terms with Aziru, and, desiring a share of the spoils for himself, moves against Tyre, whose king, Abi-milki, immediately writes to Egypt for aid. The number of troops asked for by these vassals is absurdly small, and had it not been for the Hittite host, which was pressing south behind them, their operations might have caused Egypt very little anxiety. Aziru now captured the outer defences of Simyra and Rib-Addi continued to plead for assistance for his sister city, adding that he himself had suffered from the hostility of Amor for five years, beginning, as we have seen, under Amenhotep III. Several Egyptian deputies had been charged with the investigation of affairs at Simyra, but they did not succeed in doing anything, and the city finally fell. Aziru had no hesitation in slaying the Egyptian deputy resident in the place, and having destroyed it, was now free to move against Byblos. Rib-Addi wrote in horror of these facts to the pharaoh, stating that the Egyptian deputy, resident in Kumidi in northern Palestine, was now in danger. But the wily Aziru so uses his friends at court that he escapes. He wrote to Tutu, one of Ikhnaton's court officials, who interceded for him, and he speciously excuses himself to Khai, the Egyptian deputy in his vicinity. With Machiavellian skill and cynicism he explains in letters to the pharaoh that he is unable to come and give an account of himself at the Egyptian court, as he had been commanded to do, because the Hittites are in Nukhashshi, and he fears that Tunip will not be strong enough to resist them! What Tunip herself thought about his presence in Nukhashshi we have already seen. To the pharaoh's demand that he immediately rebuild Simyra, which he had destroyed (as he claimed, to prevent it from falling into the hands of the Hittites), he replies that he is too hard-pressed in defending the king's cities in Nukhashshi against the Hittites; but that he will do so within a year. Ikhnaton is reassured by Aziru's promises to pay the same tribute as the cities which he has taken formerly paid. Such acknowledgment of Egyptian suzerainty by the turbulent dynasts everywhere must have left in the pharaoh a feeling of security which the situation by no means really justified. He therefore wrote Aziru granting him the year which he had asked for before he appeared at court, but Aziru contrived to evade Khani, the Egyptian bearer of the king's letter, which was thus brought back to Egypt without being delivered. It shows the astonishing leniency of Ikhnaton in a manner which would indicate that he was opposed to measures of force, such as his fathers had employed. Aziru immediately wrote to the king expressing his regret that an expedition against the Hittites in the north had deprived him of the pleasure of meeting the pharaoh's envoy, in spite of the fact that he had made all haste homeward as soon as he had heard of his coming! The usual excuse for not rebuilding Simyra is offered.

During all this time Rib-Addi is in sore straits in Byblos, and sends dispatch after dispatch to the Egyptian court, appealing for aid against Aziru. The claims of the hostile dynasts, however, are so skilfully made that the resident Egyptian deputies actually do not seem to know who are the faithful vassals and who the secretly rebellious. Thus Bikhuru, the Egyptian deputy in Galilee, not understanding the situation in Byblos, sent his Beduin mercenaries thither, where they slew all of Rib-Addi's Sherden garrison. The unhappy Rib-Addi was now at the mercy of his foes and he sent off two dispatches beseeching the pharaoh to take notice of his pitiful plight; while, to make matters worse, the city raised an insurrection against him because of the wanton act of the

Egyptian resident. He has now sustained the siege for three years, he is old and burdened with disease; fleeing to Bernt to secure help from the Egyptian deputy there, he returns to Byblos to find the city closed against him, his brother having seized the government in his absence and delivered his children to Aziru. As Bernt itself is soon attacked and falls, he forsakes it, again returns to Byblos and in some way regains control and holds the place for a while longer. Although Aziru, his enemy, was obliged to appear at court and finally did so, no relief came for the despairing Rib-Addi. All the cities of the coast were held by his enemies and their ships commanded the sea, so that provisions and reinforcements could not reach him: His wife and family urge him to abandon Egypt and join Aziru's party, but still he is faithful to the pharaoh and asks for 300 men to undertake the recovery of Bernt, and thus gain a little room. The Hittites are plundering his territory and the Khabiri, or Beduin mercenaries of his enemy Aziru, swarm under his walls; his dispatches to the court soon cease, his city of course fell, he was probably slain like the kings of the other coast cities, and in him the last vassal of Egypt in the north had perished.

Similar conditions prevailed in the south, where the advance of the Khabiri, the Aramaean Semites, may be compared with that of the Hittites in the north. Knots of their warriors are now appearing everywhere and taking service as mercenary troops under the dynasts. As we have seen, Aziru employed them against Rib-Addi at Byblos, but the other side, that is, the faithful vassals, engaged them also, so that the traitor, Itakama, wrote to the pharaoh and accused his vassals of giving over the territory of Kadesh and Damascus to the Khabiri. Under various adventurers the Khabiri are frequently the real masters, and Palestinian cities like Megiddo, Askalon and Gezer write to the pharaoh for succour against them. The last named city, together with Askalon and Lachish, united against Abdkhiba, the Egyptian deputy in Jerusalem, already at this time an important stronghold of southern Palestine, and the faithful officer sends urgent dispatches to Ikhnaton explaining the danger and appealing for aid against the Khabiri and their leaders. Under his very gates, at Ajalon, the caravans of the king were plundered. 'The king's whole land', wrote he, 'which has begun hostilities with me, will be lost. Behold the territory of Shiri [Seir] as far as Ginti-Kirrnil [Carmel] – its princes are wholly lost, and hostility prevails against me…. As long as ships were upon the sea, the strong arm of the king occupied Naharin and Kash, but now the Khabiri are occupying the king's cities. There remains not one prince to my lord, the king, everyone is ruined.... Let the king take care of his land and ... let him send troops.... For if no troops come in this year, the whole territory of my lord the king will perish.... If there are no troops in this year, let the king send his officer to fetch me and my brothers, that we may die with our lord, the king'.

Abdkhiba was well acquainted with Ikhnaton's cuneiform scribe, and he adds to several of his dispatches a postscript addressed to his friend in which the urgent sincerity of the man is evident: 'To the scribe of my lord, the king, Abdkhiba thy servant. Bring these words plainly before my lord the king: "The whole land of my lord, the king, is going to ruin"'. Fleeing in terror before the Khabiri, who burned the towns and laid waste the fields, many of the Palestinians forsook their towns and took to the hills, or sought refuge in Egypt, where the Egyptian officer in charge of some of them said of them: 'They have been destroyed and their town laid waste, and fire has been thrown [into their grain?].... Their countries are starving, they live like goats of the mountain.... A few of the Asiatics, who knew not how they should live, have come [begging a home in the domain?] of pharaoh, after the manner of your father's fathers since the beginning.... Now the pharaoh gives them into your hand to protect their borders.' The task of those to whom the last words are addressed was hopeless indeed, for the general, Bikhuru, whom Ikhnaton sent to restore order and suppress the Khabiri was entirely unable to accomplish anything. As we have seen, he misunderstood the situation totally in Rib-Addi's case, and dispatched his Beduin auxiliaries against him. He advanced as far north as Kumidi, north of Galilee, but retreated as Rib-Addi had foreseen he would; he was for a time in Jerusalem, but fell back to Gaza; and in all probability was finally slain. Both in Syria and Palestine the provinces of the pharaoh had gradually passed entirely out of Egyptian control, and in the south a state of complete anarchy had resulted, in which the hopeless Egyptian party at last gave up any attempt to maintain the authority of the pharaoh, and those who had not perished joined the enemy. The caravans of Burraburyash of Babylonia were plundered by the king of Akko and a neighbouring confederate, and Burraburyash wrote peremptorily demanding that the loss be made good and the guilty punished, lest his trade with Egypt become a constant prey of such marauding dynasts. But what he feared had come to pass, and the Egyptian Empire in Asia was for the time at an end.

Ikhnaton's faithful vassals had showered dispatches upon him, had sent special ambassadors, sons and brothers to represent to him the seriousness of the situation; but they had either received no replies at all, or an Egyptian commander with an entirely inadequate force was dispatched to make futile and desultory attempts to deal with a situation which demanded the pharaoh himself and the whole available army of Egypt. At Akhetaton, the new and beautiful capital, the splendid temple of Aton resounded with hymns to the new god of the empire, while the empire itself was no more. The tribute of Ikhnaton's 12th year was received at Akhetaton as usual, and the king, borne in his sedan chair on the shoulders of 18 soldiers, went forth to receive it in gorgeous state. The habit of generations and a fast-vanishing apprehension lest the pharaoh might appear in Syria with his army, still prompted a few sporadic letters from the dynasts, assuring him of their loyalty, which perhaps continued in the mind of Ikhnaton the illusion that he was still lord of Asia.

The storm which had broken over his Asiatic empire was not more disastrous than that which threatened the fortunes of his house in Egypt. But he was as steadfast as before in the propagation of his new faith. At his command temples of Aton had now arisen all over the land. Besides the Aton-sanctuary which he had at first built at Thebes, three at least in Akhetaton and Gem-Aton in Nubia, he built others at Heliopolis, Memphis, Hermopolis, Hermonthis and in the Fayum. He devoted himself to the elaboration of the temple ritual and the tendency to theologize somewhat dimmed the earlier freshness of the hymns to the god. His name was now changed and the qualifying phrase at the end of it was altered from 'Heat which is in Aton' to 'Fire which comes from Aton'. Meantime, the national convulsion which his revolution had precipitated was producing the most disastrous consequences throughout the land. The Aton-faith disregarded some of the most cherished beliefs of the people, especially those regarding the hereafter. Osiris, their old-time protector and friend in the world of darkness, was taken from them and the magical paraphernalia which were to protect them from 1,000 foes were gone. Some of them tried to put Aton into their old usages, but he was not a folk god, who lived out in yonder tree or spring, and he was too far from their homely round of daily needs to touch their lives. The people could understand nothing of the refinements involved in the new faith. They only knew that the worship of the old gods had been interdicted and a strange deity of whom they had no knowledge and could gain none was forced upon them. Such a decree of the state could have had no more effect upon their practical worship in the end than did that of Theodosius when he banished the old gods of Egypt in favour of Christianity 1,800 years after Ikhnaton's revolution. For centuries after the death of Theodosius the old so-called pagan gods continued to be worshipped by the people in Upper Egypt; for in the course of such attempted changes in the customs and traditional faith of a whole people, the span of one man's life is insignificant indeed. The Aton-faith remained but the cherished theory of the idealist, Ikhnaton, and a little circle which formed his court; it never really became the religion of the people.

Added to the secret resentment and opposition of the people, we must consider also a far more dangerous force, the hatred of the old priesthoods, particularly that of Amon. At Thebes there were eight great temples of this god standing idle and forsaken; his vast fortune, embracing towns in Syria and extensive lands in Egypt, had evidently been confiscated and probably diverted to Aton. There could not but be, and, as the result shows, there was, during all of Ikhnaton's reign a powerful priestly party which openly or secretly did all in its power to undermine him. The neglect and loss of the Asiatic empire must have turned against the king many a strong man, and aroused indignation among those whose grandfathers had served under Thutmose III. The memory of what had been done in those glorious days must have been sufficiently strong to fire the hearts of the military class and set them looking for a leader who would recover what had been lost. Ikhnaton might appoint one of his favourites to the command of the army, as we have seen he did, but his ideal aims and his high motives for peace would be as unpopular as they were unintelligible to his commanders.

One such man, an officer named Hannhab, was now in the service of Ikhnaton and enjoying the royal favour; he contrived not only to win the support of the military class, but, as we shall later see, he also gained the favour of the priests of Amon, who were of course looking for someone who could bring them the opportunity they coveted. At every point Ikhnaton had offended against the cherished traditions of a whole people. Thus both the people and the priestly and military classes alike were fomenting plans to overthrow the hated dreamer in the palace of the pharaohs, of whose thoughts they understood so little. To increase his danger, fortune had decreed him no son, and he was obliged to depend for support as the years passed upon his son-in-law, a noble named Sakere, who had married his eldest daughter, Meritaton, 'Beloved of Aton'. Ikhnaton had probably never been physically strong; his spare face, with the lines of an ascetic, shows increasing traces of the cares which weighed so heavily upon him. He finally nominated Sakere as his successor and appointed him at the same time co-regent. He survived but a short time after this, and about 1358 BCE, having reigned some 17 years, he succumbed to the overwhelming forces that were against him. In a lonely valley some miles to the east of his city he was buried in a tomb which he had excavated in the rock for himself and family, and where his second daughter, Meketaton, already rested.

Thus disappeared the most remarkable figure in earlier oriental history. To his own nation he was afterward known as 'the criminal of Akhetaton'; but for us, however much we may censure him for the loss of the empire, which he allowed to slip from his fingers; however much we may condemn the fanaticism with which he pursued his aim, even to the violation of his own father's name and monuments; there died with him such a spirit as the world had never seen before, a brave soul, undauntedly facing the momentum of immemorial tradition, and thereby stepping out from the long line of conventional and colourless pharaohs, that he might disseminate ideas far beyond and above the capacity of his age to understand. Among the Hebrews, 700 or 800 years later, we look for such men; but the modern world has yet adequately to value or even acquaint itself with this man, who in an age so remote and under conditions so adverse, became the world's first idealist and the world's first *individual*.

Sakere was quite unequal to the task before him, and after an obscure and ephemeral reign at Akhetaton he disappeared, to be followed by Tutenkhaton ('Living image of Aton'), another son-in-law of Ikhnaton, who had married the king's third daughter, Enkhosnepaaton ('She lives by the Aton'). The priestly party of Amon was now constantly growing, and although Tutenkhaton still continued to reside at Akhetaton, it was not long before he was forced to a compromise in order to maintain himself. He forsook his father-in-law's city and transferred the court to Thebes, which had not seen a pharaoh for 20 years. Akhetaton maintained a precarious existence for a time, supported by the manufactories of coloured glass and fayence, which had flourished there during the reign of Ikhnaton. These industries soon languished, the place was gradually forsaken, until not a soul was left in its solitary streets. The roofs of the houses fell in, the walls tottered and collapsed, the temples fell prey to the vengeance of the Theban party, as we shall see, and the once beautiful city of Aton was gradually transformed into a desolate ruin. Today it is known as Tell el-Arnarna, and it still stands as its enemies, time and the priests of Amon, left it. One may walk its ancient streets, where the walls of the houses are still several metres high, and strive to recall to its forsaken dwellings the life of the Aton worshippers who once inhabited them. Here in a low brick room, which had served as an archive chamber for Ikhnaton's foreign office, were found in 1885 some 300 letters and dispatches in which we have traced his intercourse and dealings with the kings and rulers of Asia and the gradual disintegration of his empire there. Here were the more than 60 dispatches of the unfortunate Rib-Addi of Byblos. After the modern name of the place, the whole correspondence is generally called the Tell el-Amarna letters. All the other Aton-cities likewise perished utterly; but Gem-Aton in distant Nubia escaped. Long afterward its Aton temple became a temple of' Amon, Lord of Gem-Aton, and thus in far-off Nubia the ruins of the earliest temple of monotheism still stand.

On reaching Thebes, Tutenkhaton continued the worship of Aton and made some enlargement or at least repairs of the Aton temple there; but he was obliged by the priests of Amon to permit the resumption of Amon worship. Indeed, he was constrained to restore the old festal calendar of Karnak and Luxor; he himself conducted the first 'feast of Opet', the greatest of all the festivals of Amon, and restored the temples there. Expediency also obliged him to begin restoring the disfigured name of Amon, expunged from the monuments by Ikhnaton, and his restorations are found as far south as Soleb in Nubia. He was then forced to another serious concession to the priests of Amon; he changed his name to Tutankhamun, 'Living image of Amon', showing that he was now completely in the hands of the priestly party.

The empire which he ruled was still no mean one, extending as it did from the Delta of the Nile to the fourth cataract. The Nubian province under the viceroy was now thoroughly Egyptianized, and the native chiefs wore Egyptian clothing, assumed since Thutmose III's time. The revolution in Egypt had not affected Nubia seriously, and it continued to pay its annual dues into the pharaoh's treasury. He also received tribute from the north which, as his viceroy of Kush, Huy claimed, came from Syria. Although this is probably in some degree an exaggeration in view of our information from the Amarna letters; yet one of Ikhnaton's successors fought a battle in Asia, and this can hardly have been any other than Tutenkhaton. He may thus have recovered sufficient power in Palestine to collect some tribute or at least some spoil, which fact may then have been interpreted to include Syria also. Tutenkhaton soon disappeared and was succeeded by another of the worthies of the Akhetaton court, Eye, who had married Ikhnaton's nurse, Tiy, and had excavated for himself a tomb at Akhetaton, from which came the great Aton hymn which we have already read. He was sufficiently imbued with Ikhnaton's ideas to hold his own for a short time against the priests of Amon; and he built to some extent on the Aton-temple at Thebes. He abandoned his tomb at Akhetaton and excavated another in the Valley of the Kings' Tombs at Thebes. He soon had need of it, for ere long he too passed away and it would appear that one or two other ephemeral pretenders gained the ascendancy either now or before his accession. Anarchy ensued. Thebes was a prey of plundering bands, who forced their way into the royal tombs and as we now know robbed the tomb of Thutmose IV. The prestige of the old Theban family which had been dominant for 250 years; the family which 230 years before had cast out the Hyksos and built the greatest empire the east had ever seen, was now totally eclipsed. The illustrious name which it had won was no longer a sufficient influence to enable its decadent descendants to hold the throne, and the Eighteenth Dynasty had thus slowly declined to its end about 1350 BCE. Manetho places Harmhab, the restorer, who now gained the throne, at the close of the Eighteenth Dynasty; but in so far as we know he was not of royal blood nor any kin of the now fallen house. He marks the restoration of Amon, the resumption of the old order and the beginning of a new epoch.

The Ramesside Era

Egypt Under Rameses the Great

Wallis Budge, in his *Egypt Under Rameses the Great* (note Budge's preferred spelling, which we have kept in his text), separates his text into three sections. The first covers the Nineteenth Dynasty from the reign of Ramses I, Ramses II's grandfather, through to the reign of Ramses II's son Merenptah taking over the throne. The second chapter is dedicated to the Exodus of the Israelites from Egypt and the evidence that was available at the time (i.e. the Bible and Manetho). The final section looks at the Twentieth Dynasty, and the reigns of Ramses III to XI.

This coverage looks at the rise and fall of the New Kingdom from the tribal uprisings following the death of Ramses I, to the battle of Kadesh of Ramses II, to the uprising and growth in power of the priests of Amun, which saw the Egyptian rulership overthrown at the end of the Twentieth Dynasty.

The Nineteenth Dynasty

☥

Rameses I
Ra-Men-Peh-Peh, son of the Sun, Ra-Messu

RAMESSU I, OR RAMESES I, the first king of the Nineteenth Dynasty, was apparently related to Heru-em-heb [today better known as Horemheb], but the degree of relationship cannot at present be defined, and its existence is doubted by some writers. There is certainly no evidence that he was of royal descent, and nothing is known of the circumstances under which he ascended the throne. There are grounds for thinking that he held, like Heru-em-heb, high offices under the government for several years before he became king, and that when he succeeded his colleague he was past middle age; it is more than probable that he exercised in the south of Egypt an authority similar to that which Heru-em-heb exercised in the north. Although the name of Amen does not occur in any of his names or titles, he must have been a loyal servant of that god or he would never have been supported by his priests. His reign was very short, certainly less than 10 years, and, but for one thing, of which there is no mention in the Egyptian inscriptions of the period, might have been termed uneventful.

We have already mentioned the prominent part which the confederation of the Kheta tribes took in the breaking of the power of Egypt in Syria in the reign of Amenhetep IV, and since that time Egypt had been able to do nothing to check their advance in Northern Syria. The disruption caused by the heresy of the Disk worshippers prevented the despatch of any army against them during the reigns of the three predecessors of Rameses I, and thus it happened that when this king ascended the throne of Egypt he discovered that he was powerless even to prevent their advance upon territory much nearer to Egypt, still less to regain the old Egyptian possessions near the Euphrates, and he, therefore, made a treaty of peace with Sapalul, the prince

of the Kheta tribes. Reference is made to this treaty in the treaty which
Sapalul's descendant made with Rameses II, and it is clear that in the reign
of Rameses I the Kheta were sufficiently powerful to make it worth the while
of the Egyptians to be at peace with them.

The only military expedition undertaken by Rameses I was against the
Nubians, but whether this took place during the first two years of his reign,
when he was sole monarch, or later, when his son Seti I was co-regent,
cannot be said. As a mark of his devotion to Amen he built the large pylon
through which entrance is gained to the great Hypostyle Hall in the temple
of the god at Karnak, but of this very little now remains; on a wall near it
he is represented in the act of adoring a number of gods. Rameses I made a
tomb for himself in the Valley of the Tombs of the Kings at Thebes, and was
presumably buried in it. It consists of a large hall, with a doorway at each
end; through the further doorway admission is gained to a narrow chamber.
The hall is approached by two corridors, which are not ornamented in any
way, and the second forms a steep flight of steps which leads directly into
the hall or mummy chamber. The walls of the hall are decorated with large
figures of the gods Maat, Ptah, Nefer-Temu, Anubis, Horus, Thoth, Khepera,
etc., and with inscriptions and scenes from the *Book of the Underworld*. The
sarcophagus is made of red granite and is about one and a half metres (five
feet high); it is ornamented with figures of the gods painted in yellow on a
reel background, and is without a cover. The tomb was very difficult to enter,
and its entrance has now been filled up.

Among the coffins and mummies from the great Der al-Bahari 'find' were
the fragments of a wooden coffin which had been painted yellow, and a
cover which seemed to belong to them. The name of the original owner had
been erased and the prenomen of Rameses I inscribed in its place; this king's
prenomen is found on the fragments written both in hieroglyphics and in the
hieratic character. On a piece of the coffin are the fragments of an inscription,
which by the help of other similar documents has been completed, and from
it we learn that on the 13th day of the fourth month of the season Shat of the
16th year of the reign of Sa-Amen, the mummy of Rameses I was taken from
his own tomb into that of queen An-Hapu, which was situated near the tomb
of Amenhetep, in peace. This removal was affected by a priest of Amen-Ra
called Ankh-f-en-Amen, the son of Baki, who held several high ecclesiastical

offices, and was, apparently, a superintendent of the royal tombs. Near the fragments of the coffin was the unswathed mummy of a man of large and powerful build, with short hair and a black skin; this mummy is believed by M. Maspero to have been that of Rameses I, and he thinks that its coffin was broken by the various journeys which it had to undergo when the royal mummies were removed to their hiding place at Der al-Bahari, and that the mummy itself was stripped and plundered by the people who were assisting in hiding it from the professional robbers of royal tombs.

Seti I
Ra-Maat-Men, son of the Sun, Ptah-Meri-en-Seti

Seti I, or 'Seti-Mer-En-Ptah' I, was the son of Rameses I; he married queen Tuaa, during the reign of Heru-em-heb, and by her became the father of Rameses II. According to Manetho he reigned between 50 and 55 years, but there is no monumental evidence in support of this statement. The inscriptions prove that he adopted a large number of Horus names, among which may be mentioned: 'Mighty Bull, rising in Thebes, vivifying the two lands', 'Mighty Bull, image of Menthu', 'Mighty Bull, son of Temu', 'Bull of Ra, beloved of Maat', 'Mighty Bull, resting upon Maat', etc.; some of his titles were, 'He who repeateth [his] births, mighty one of valour, destroyer of the Nine Bows, Mighty one of bows in all lands, subduer of the Menti, stablisher of monuments', etc.

As soon as Rameses I was dead the nomad tribes and peoples who lived in the Eastern Desert and in Palestine revolted, and his son and successor Seti I found himself obliged to take the field at once against a formidable confederation of hostile hosts. He set out from Egypt against the wretched 'Shasu', and marched from the fortress of Tchare to Kanana, a place which has been thought to be to the south of Hebron; but Kanana refers to the whole country and not to any one portion of it. The Shasu were defeated in the first battle, and large numbers of them were slain. He next attacked the rebels of Khare with the same result, and the king, who is described as the 'Sun of Egypt and the moon of all other lands', swept all before him like the god Baru wheresoever he went he slew men, and his soldiers following him up carried away much spoil.

The chiefs of Rethennu, or Northern Syria, submitted peacefully, and sang praises to the king, and of the presents which they brought to him he made rich gifts to Amen-Ra. The city of Kadesh and the fortress of Innuaamu, were also conquered, and the whole country of the Amorites. The tribes of the Kheta, however, refused to follow this example, and therefore Seti I marched into their country; he slew their chiefs and passed through their soldiers like a flame of fire, and all that could fled before him. From every part of Syria he obtained either gifts or tribute, and he then retraced his steps to Egypt, leaving the country through which he had passed a place of desolation and misery. Among the spoil brought back was wood for making a boat for the god Amen-Ra, and trunks of straight and lofty trees which were to be made into the masts intended to be set up in grooves in front of the main pylons of temples; the wood and the tree trunks came from the Lebanon mountains, famous then, as later, for their lofty cedars and other trees.

When Seti I arrived at the frontiers of Egypt he was met by the priests and nobles of the country, who received him with shouts of joy, and with all the spoil which he had brought back he set out on the river to make a triumphant progress up the Nile to Thebes. The principal events of the campaign in Palestine and Syria were sculptured on the north and south walls of the great Hypostyle Hall at Karnak, and near each was added a full description in hieroglyphics for every man to see. The king was very proud of his achievements and caused lists of the countries, cities and villages which he had conquered to be inscribed upon the buildings and monuments which he set up in Egypt and Nubia. Thus on the north wall of the great hall at Thebes, Amen is depicted holding ropes to which are tied by their necks series of representatives of conquered places, each with his name enclosed in a 'turreted cartouche'; the base of a sphinx in the temple of Seti I at Kurna also contains a long list of names of conquered places; and at Redesiyeh or Radassiyeh, about 65 kilometres (40 miles) to the east of Edfu, and at Sesebi in the Third Cataract portions of lists and scenes of conquest have also been found.

Seti I seems to have claimed that he was master of the Libyans, Nubians, people of Punt, nomads of the eastern desert, Palestine, Syria, Cyprus and of western Asia generally as far eastwards as Neherna, but his court scribes must have exaggerated the size of his kingdom, for it is quite certain that the Kheta were not in any way subject to him at this time, and that their territory was under their own rule. That their power was very great at this period is proved by the fact that not very many years later Rameses II was obliged, even after his fierce battle with them, to enter into an agreement which certainly did not restore to Egypt any of the possessions which had been hers in the reign of Thothmes [today more often spelled Thutmose] III.

As soon as his wars were over, Seti I devoted himself to the building of new temples and the restoration of old ones, and the evidences of his great activity in such works are found throughout Egypt from the north of the Delta to the Third Cataract, and in the Sinaitic peninsula and in Wadi Hammamat. The quarries at Hammamat were worked for stone for his buildings; the mines at Sarbut al-Khadim were worked for copper and malachite; and it appears that he either worked regularly or carried on experimental works in all the great mines of the Eastern Desert in Nubia. The temple of Redesiyeh, or Radassiyeh, mentioned above, stands on the old desert road which ran from Edfu to the emerald mines of Mount Zabara, near Berenice on the Red Sea, and it is pretty certain that Seti I only built it because the mines were being worked for his benefit.

As there was a water station, or well, close by, the traveller who had halted there would not only be able to obtain refreshment, but would also become acquainted with the scenes of the prowess of Seti I, which were sculptured inside the temple in the ninth year of his reign. Seti I either bored, or re-bored a well here, and a small building seems to mark its site to this day; it is probable that he caused a series of water stations to be established from the Nile to Berenice. The local mining agents seem to have made plans of the districts wherein gold or mines of precious stones were situated, and to have had them drawn and painted upon papyrus either for the benefit of newcomers or to supply information about the position of the mines to high officials in Egypt. A plan of this kind was published by [Prussian Egyptologist Karl Richard] Lepsius, and on it we see indicated the footpaths running among the mountains, the position of the government building, which in this case was erected by Seti I, and the places where the workmen are boring into the hills; when viewed in comparison with modern maps it appears to be a crude piece of work, but it must be remembered, as [German Egyptologist Alfred] Wiedemann has said, that it is the oldest map in the world.

Among the buildings of Seti I must be specially mentioned those which he carried out at Abydos and Thebes. At Abydos he built the famous temple called after his own prenomen 'Men-Maat-Ra', but more commonly known from its description by Strabo as the 'Memnonium'. Abydos was the centre of Osiris worship in Upper Egypt, for there was supposed to be the tomb of the head of the god, and Egyptians loved to be buried there, first, that their bodies might be near the head of Osiris, and secondly, because there was a widespread belief in the country that close to the city, in the mountains, was the 'Gap', or, 'opening' through which disembodied souls made their way into Paradise. Seti's temple was built of fine white limestone, but when the king died it was not finished, and his son Rameses II completed it. The walls and pillars are ornamented with religious scenes and figures of the gods, and the sculptures and reliefs are among the most beautiful of those to be found in Egypt; for design, proportion, excellence of work and finish, the reliefs are unequalled under the New Empire. At the end of the temple are seven shrines or chapels, dedicated to Horus, Isis, Osiris, Amen, Harmachis, Ptah and Seti I respectively; behind these is the chief shrine of the god Osiris.

One remarkable feature of the temple is the famous King List which Seti I had inscribed upon the main wall of a corridor of the building at the side of the main edifice. Here we have a list of the names of 76 kings, the first being that of Mena or Menes, and the last being that of Seti I; at one end stand Seti I, making an offering of incense, and his son Rameses II, and they pray that to each of the kings named the triune god Ptah-Seker-Asar will give 1,000 cakes, 1,000 vessels of ale, 1,000 cattle, 1,000 feathered fowl, etc. The royal names in this list represent the kings for whose spiritual welfare Seti I prayed at certain seasons, and the list itself is of great importance, for the 'Tablet of Abydos', as it is generally called, has helped us to reconstruct the chronological order of some of the kings of Egypt. It omits many names, and even whole 'dynasties', but its historical value is very great.

At Karnak, Seti I carried out many important new works and restorations, but the greatest of them all was done in connexion with the Hypostyle Hall, or Hall of Columns. This marvellous building measured about 103 metres by 51 metres (340 feet by 168 feet), and contained 134 columns; one of these was set up by Rameses I, 79 by Seti I, and 54 by Rameses II. Twelve columns are 20 metres (68 feet) high and 10 metres (35 feet) in circumference, and 122 are about 13 metres (43 feet) high and eight metres (27 feet) in circumference. Besides all this Seti I restored or rebuilt, in whole or in part, the temples of many of his ancestors in all the important cities of Egypt. At Kurna, on the west bank of the Nile, opposite Thebes, he completed and adopted as his own the funeral chapel which had been begun by Rameses I, and formally dedicated it to the worship of himself and his father. This funeral temple was built in connexion with the wonderful tomb in the Valley of the Kings, and the king appears to have intended that services should be held in it instead of in the tomb, which was, comparatively, a long way from the river. The tomb is nearly 100 metres (350 feet) long, and consists of a large number of halls and corridors, and side chapels, all of which are hewn out of the solid rock; the floor of the lowest room is about 30 metres (100 feet) below the level of the valley. It was discovered by [Italian explorer Giovanni] Belzoni in 1817, and is commonly called 'Belzoni's Tomb', or 'No.17'. It is the most beautiful of all the royal tombs, and strikes the beholder with wonder at the vast amount of labour and the skill displayed in making it.

The paintings on the walls, etc., suggest that the decoration, and probably every part of it, was carried out by the sculptors and artists who built Seti's temple to Osiris at Abydos. The inscriptions on the entrance staircase corridor are selections from the *Book of the Praisings of Ra* and the *Book of [knowing] that which is in the Underworld*. According to this last work, the world beyond the grave was divided into sections, and the texts of this curious book enabled the deceased to make his way safely through them, even as did the Sun. In one of the chambers entered from the main hall with eight pillars is a remarkable text describing how mankind once on a time rebelled against the Sun-god Ra, and made a mock of him because the god had become old and feeble; they were, however, severely punished, for they were slaughtered by the goddess Sekhet, who 'waded about in their blood', and many other calamities came upon them. The goddess Hathor at this time compassed the destruction of mankind.

The large and beautiful white alabaster sarcophagus of the king is preserved in Sir John Soane's Museum in Lincoln's Inn Fields, London, where it was taken by Belzoni; it is said to have been sold to this institution for £2,000. It is inscribed with a long series of extracts and vignettes from the *Book of [knowing] what is in the Underworld*, and the hieroglyphics were inlaid with blue paste, which was intended to represent lapis lazuli. The coffin of Seti I was found with his mummy at Der al-Bahari. The coffin is painted white, and has eyes inlaid with black and white enamel. Three hieratic inscriptions on it tell us that in the sixth year of the high priesthood of Her-Heru the mummy of Seti I was re-bandaged and reinterred by Hen-Amen-pena, that in the 16th year of the reign of Sa-Amen it was removed to the tomb of the queen An-Hapu; and that in the 10th year of Pai-netchem, who reigned about a century later, the mummy was again moved and taken to the 'everlasting abode' of Amenhetep.

The mummy of Seti I was unrolled on June 9, 1886, when most of its swathings were found to be those originally used, but a few were newer and dated from the Twenty-First Dynasty. The nose is well-shaped and aquiline, the mouth is long, the lips are thin, the ears are small and round and are pierced for earrings, the eyebrows are now blackened by bitumen, but were originally white, the head and chin are shaved, the only two teeth visible are well preserved, even as is the whole body. It is thought that Seti died when he was about 60 years of age, and, in view of his knotted fingers, that he suffered from arthritis. [French Egyptologist Gaston] M. Maspero thinks that there is a striking resemblance between the features of Seti I and those of his son Rameses II, only that they are finer and more intelligent; in fact that the father is an idealized type of the son. Everything that we know about the tomb and funeral furniture and mummy of Seti I proves that the burial of the king must have been attended with the greatest pomp and ceremony, and it is interesting to note that the religious inscriptions on the walls of the tomb are extracts, not from the *Chapters of Coming Forth by Day*, or the *Book of the Dead*, but from works of an entirely different character.

In the inscriptions of Rameses II found on the temple built by Seti I at Abydos, we are told that his father associated him with himself in the rule of the kingdom at a very early age, and that he was made the lord of the kingdom when he was a little boy. When as yet he was in the womb of his mother the nobles of the land saluted him and paid homage to him, and when he was still in the habit of sitting on his father's knee the king gave the order and had the child crowned. All this, however, is exaggeration on the part of Rameses II, or we may regard it as oriental hyperbole; in any case, he cannot have been crowned when he was still a little boy being brought up in the women's apartments, for he was not the eldest son of Seti. That Seti I had a son older than Rameses II we know from the reliefs which depict his battle scenes, for this prince's figure and titles are found in them. What happened to this prince we have no means of knowing, but he took part in Seti's great Syrian war, being at that time a mature man, and it is possible that he was slain in battle. It is a curious fact that in every case where his figure and titles occur his name has been cut out, and we are forced to come to the same conclusion as Wiedemann, i.e., that the existence of an elder brother must have been disagreeable to Rameses II, and that 'he who used with predilection the monuments of his ancestors as material for his own, would try by all possible means to destroy his brother's memory; the obliteration of the prince's name will have been made at his instigation.'

The question which has now to be considered is, 'Was Rameses II ever co-regent with Seti I?' When we consider that the reign of Seti I was very short, probably not more than 12 or 15 years, and that extremely few texts exist which can be construed into referring to the co-regency, and that none are dated in it, it is morally certain that the words which Rameses II allowed to be inscribed on the temple of Seti I at Abydos are untrue. Moreover, we know that Rameses II, had he been co-regent with his father at the extremely early age which he indicates, would have been incapable of conducting the war against the Kheta, which he tells us he waged in the fifth year of his reign, and that he would not have been old enough to be the father of the grown-up sons who accompanied him on that memorable occasion. The late [German Egyptologist] Dr. [Heinrich Karl] Brugsch stated at some length his reasons for believing that Rameses II was selected co-regent by his father at a very early age, and thought that Seti I had good reasons for doing so.

Seti I married a lady called Tuaa, who was probably related or connected with the royal house of the Amenhetep kings, and who had, therefore, in the eyes of the Egyptians, a claim to the throne; Seti himself was not of royal descent, and could only assert a right to the throne through his wife. Dr. Brugsch argued that the priests of Amen and the Egyptians hated Tuaa because 'her grandfather's blood flowed in her veins' (he assumes that she was the granddaughter of Khu-en-Aten, of which there is no proof); that Seti, who was himself named after the god Set, or Sutekh, was related to a stock that worshipped foreign gods, at the head of which was the 'Canaanitish Baal-Sutekh', and that Seti I felt himself obliged to 'avoid an open breach, and to soothe the stubborn caste of the priests of Amen', even though they hated Rameses' ancestry, by electing the child as co-regent.

In answer to this it must be stated that the priests of Amen, having regained their old position, would have no reason to fear any act of Seti I; that the views about the name of the king have no foundation; and that, since Seti I had acquired a claim to the throne through his wife, which was held to be a valid claim by the Egyptians, he could not be regarded as an usurper, as Rameses I might well have been considered. Dr. Brugsch concludes, 'While he [Seti I] actually ruled the land as king, Rameses, his son, as legitimate sovereign, gave authority to all the acts of his father.' It is, however, certain that Rameses II counted the years of his reign from the year in which his father died, that the years of his life when he ascended the throne were many more in number than the years of his father's reign, that he was a man when he ascended the throne, and that in his battle with the Kheta, which took place in the fifth year of his reign, he had sons with him who were young men. The inscriptions at Abydos which record the early history of Rameses II have the same pompous and inflated style as the description of the great battle of that king which was composed, or perhaps, strictly speaking, copied, by the court scribe and poet laureate Pentaur, or Pentaurt, and they may be regarded as narratives written rather to please and flatter the king than to serve any historical purpose.

Rameses II
Ra-User-Maat-Setep-En-Ra, son of the Sun, Ra-Messu-Meri-Amen

Ra-Messu II, or Rameses II, was the son of Seti I and the queen Tuaa, who seems to have been connected with the royal house of the Amenhetep kings; the year of his age when he ascended the throne is unknown, but, as he was conducting his great war against the Kheta five years later, accompanied by grown-up sons, he certainly cannot have been less than 25 years of age when he was crowned.

He adopted as his Horus name 'Mighty Bull, beloved of Maat', and a very large number of epithets which we find applied to him in the inscriptions were regarded as Horus names and treated accordingly, being placed in rectangular enclosures within which the Horus, or *ka*, names were usually written. In addition to his titles, 'Lord of the shrines of Nekhebet and Uatchet, master of Egypt, conqueror of foreign countries, Horus of gold, mighty one of years, great of strength', he is called 'Exalter of Thebes, he who rises in Thebes, vivifier of the two lands son of Set, son of Amen, son of Temu, son of Ptah-Tanen, son of Khepera, son of Amen, mighty of two-fold strength, firm of heart, power of two-fold strength, valiant warrior, smiter of the Asiatics, lord of festivals, beloved of the two lands, king of kings, bull of princes, mighty one of valour like his father Set in Nubti, upholder of Maat, possessor of the two lands', etc.

Rameses' Wars in Nubia, Libya and Syria

Although, as we have already seen, it is improbable that Rameses II was crowned king of Egypt when he was still a little child living in the women's quarters in the palace, we are right in thinking that he was trained with the soldiers and accustomed to military command when he was 10 or 12 years of age. Besides his military appointments he held the offices of counsellor and overseer of certain lands, and Seti I spared no pains to qualify him to become a wise and able prince. In the reign of Seti I, Rameses took part in certain raids which were made upon the Libyans and other tribes living on the west and north-west frontiers of Egypt, and he was present at several fights with the Nubians in various parts of their country. He continued the wars in Nubia during the first two or three years of his reign, and they were waged with such fierceness that it seems as if some of the tribes of that country must have tried to shake off the yoke of Egypt, and to cease from the payment of tribute to the new king.

The principal memorial of his wars in Nubia, Libya and Syria is the little rock-hewn temple at Bet al-Walli near Kalabsheh, where, on the two sides of the vestibule, are scenes depicting the principal events of these wars, the capture of prisoners and the receipt of tribute. In the Libyan war the king was accompanied by his son Amen-her-khepesh-f, who is represented as bringing prisoners before his father; Rameses was also accompanied by his favourite dog, which attacked the foe at the same time as his master. The Syrians, as usual, took refuge in their fortresses, but they availed them nought, for their entrances were forced by the Egyptian soldiers and, if we may trust the picture on the wall, the Syrians were put to the sword by the king whilst they were in the very act of tendering submission and pleading for mercy. The scenes which illustrate the Nubian campaigns are more interesting, for we see the king seated in state and receiving the gifts brought to him by the natives. These gifts consisted of gold rings, leopard or panther skins, prisoners, apes, panthers, giraffes, oxen, gazelles, ostriches, ebony, bows, feathers, fans, chairs of state, tusks of elephants, a lion, an antelope, etc., and it is clear that they must, for the most part, have been brought from the country to the south of the Fourth Cataract. On his Nubian campaign Rameses was accompanied by his sons Amen-her-unami-f and Kha-em-Uast who are seen in their chariots charging the Nubians and performing mighty deeds of valour. From the accounts given of the battles in Nubia it does not appear that Rameses did anything more than make certain tribes pay tribute; he does not seem to have made his way as far to the south as some of his predecessors had done, and he certainly added no new territory to the Egyptian possessions in Nubia.

In the fourth year of his reign Rameses was engaged in a military expedition in Syria, a fact proved by the memorial stele which he set up on the rocks overhanging the left or south bank of the Nahr al-Kalb, or 'Dog River', near its mouth. Here the king is seen thrusting into the presence of the god Menthu a Syrian prisoner, who has his hands tied behind him, and whom he holds by a feather placed on the top of his head. At the Dog River there are three stelae of Rameses II, and one of Esarhaddon, king of Assyria, who set his up on his return from the conquest of Egypt, to commemorate the capture of Memphis by him in the year 670 BCE. The inscriptions on all three stelae of Rameses are obliterated and the dates of two of the three; the third stele is perhaps dated in the fourth year of the king's reign, for it is probable that when Dr. Lepsius saw it the four strokes, which stand for the numeral '4', were distinctly legible after the word for 'year' but when the writer saw the stele in October 1890, it was impossible to say what the exact number of the strokes had been.

The Battle of Kadesh

We have already seen that in the Eighteenth Dynasty the Kheta [Hittites] formed an enemy of Egypt who was by no means to be despised, and that though the Egyptian kings of the latter part of the dynasty claimed to have subdued them and reduced them to the state of vassals, it is by no means certain that they really did so. Since the reign of Thothmes III they had been gradually forcing their way into Syria, and by the time that Rameses II had ascended the throne the authority of the prince of the Kheta reached as far as Kadesh. As a result of the arrangements which had been made between the Kheta princes and Heru-em-heb, Rameses I and Seti I, the limit of Egypt's possessions in Syria was marked by the Dog River. The prince of the Kheta in the time of Heru-em-heb was called Saparuru, and he seems to have made a treaty with Egypt; his son and successor Marusaru, also made a treaty with Egypt, and there was peace between the two countries until his son began to rule over the peoples of the Kheta. This young man, who was called Mauthenre, for some reason thought fit to stir up a war against Egypt, and it was to meet and defeat the Kheta in this war that Rameses was obliged to prepare. The prince of the Kheta had gathered together a number of powerful allies, such as the kings of Aleppo, Karkemish, Aradus and Kadesh, and hosts of soldiers belonging to the tribes who had their homes in the country further to the west; on the other hand, Rameses II employed large numbers of mercenaries, among whom were the Shar-tana, the Shirdani of the Tell el-Amarna Tablets. The allies of the Kheta prince included people from Qitchaua [tan], from Mushanth, from Ruka, from Tartenui, from Masa, from Maunna, from Pitasa, from Qarqisha, etc.

One of the best accounts of the battle of Rameses against the Kheta ever drawn up is found on a stele in the rock-hewn temple at Abu Simbel in Nubia, and as it is comparatively brief and to the point a rendering of it is here given:

'On the ninth day of the third month of the season Shemut (i.e., the month Epiphi), under the reign of his majesty of Horus, the Mighty Bull, beloved of Maat, the king of the South and North, Ra-user-Maat-setep-en-Ra, the sun of the Sun, Ramessu, beloved of Amen, the giver of life forever, behold, his majesty was in the country of Tchah, during his second expedition. A very strict guard was being kept in the camp of his majesty on the country to the south of the city of Kadesh. His majesty rose up like the god Ra, and he arrayed himself in the glorious apparel of his father Menthu; the lord continued to move forward, and his majesty arrived at the south of the town of Shabtun. Then two members of the Shasu came and said to him, "Our brethren who are chiefs of the tribes that are with the wretched Kheta have made us come to your majesty to inform you that we are prepared to become servants of your majesty, and that we are not in any way in league with the wretched Kheta. Now the wretched

Kheta have pitched their camp in the country of Khirebu, (i.e., Aleppo), to the north of Tunep, being afraid that your majesty will go out to attack them." In this wise did the two Shasu speak, but they spake these words with foul intent, for the wretched Kheta had made them to go and spy out where his majesty was before he was able to arrange his troops in battle array, and to prepare for his attack; meanwhile the wretched Kheta had gathered themselves together, with the chiefs of all the neighbouring lands, and their soldiers, and their horsemen, whom they had collected in large numbers, and the whole force was drawn up, and lying in ambush behind the wretched city of Kadesh, and his majesty had no information whatever concerning their arrangements.

'Then his majesty drew on to the north-west of the city of Kadesh, where his troops pitched their camp. When his majesty had seated himself upon his throne of gold, certain of his scouts came in bringing with them before him two spies belonging to the wretched Kheta. When these had been brought before his majesty, the king said to them, "Who are ye?" And they replied, "We belong to the wretched Kheta chief who has made his servants to come and find out where your majesty is." And his majesty said unto them, "Where is the wretched Kheta chief? I have heard it said that he is in the country of Khirebu" (i.e., Aleppo). And they said, "Behold, the wretched Kheta chief is with the innumerable hosts of people which he has gathered together unto him, that is to say, all the nations belonging to the country of Kheta, and to the country of Nehiren (i.e., Western Babylonia), and to the country of Qeti (i.e., Phoenicia), and he has soldiers and men with horses that are for number even as the sands on the seashore, and behold, they stand all ready to do battle behind the wretched city of Kadesh." Then his majesty called his officers into his presence in order that he might inform them concerning all the things which the two spies of the Kheta had said unto him there. [And he said to them] "Find out how it is that those who have been in charge of the soldiers and of outpost duty in the region where his majesty hath been, have reported as certain that the wretched Kheta chief was in the country of Khirebu, whither he

had fled as soon as he heard of him. It was their duty to report to his majesty information which is correct. Ye see now that which I have just made known unto you, through the information received from the two spies of the country of the Kheta, how that the chief of that country hath arrived with followers innumerable, and men and horses which are for number even as the sand which is on the sea shore, and that he is now behind the wretched city of Kadesh, and yet the officers who are over the soldiers and outpost duty in the regions where I am have had no knowledge thereof!"

'When these words had been said the generals who had been called into his majesty's presence admitted that a fault of the gravest kind had been committed by those who were in charge of the district, inasmuch as they had not informed his majesty where the wretched chief of the Kheta had taken up his position. And when the generals had spoken his majesty gave the command to hurry on the march of the soldiers who were to the south of the city of Shabtun, and to bring them to the place where he was as soon as possible. Now at that moment whilst his majesty was sitting in council with his officers, the wretched chief of the Kheta came with his soldiers, and his horsemen, and his allies who were gathered together unto him from every nation, and they crossed over the ditch which was at the south of Kadesh, and they made their way into the midst of the soldiers of his majesty as they were on the march, and they knew it not. Then the soldiers and horsemen of his majesty quailed before them, and ran to the place where his majesty was, and the warriors of the wretched Kheta prince hemmed in the bodyguard of his majesty. As soon as his majesty saw them he raged at them like his father Menthu, the lord of Thebes, and having girded on his panoply of war he seized his lance, and being like unto the god Bar, in his hour, he mounted his chariot and charged the enemy rapidly. His majesty dashed into the midst of the mass of the enemy, and like the most mighty god Sutekh, he hewed them down and slew them, and cast their dead bodies headlong into the waters of the Orontes, "I was," said the king, "by myself, for my soldiers and my horsemen had forsaken me, and not one of them had been sufficiently bold to

come to my assistance. I dedicate my love to Ra, and my praise to my father Temu. What I have just described that I myself performed in very truth in the presence of my soldiers and my horsemen.'"

The information to be derived from the above may, however, be supplemented by some important facts which are to be gleaned from the heroic poem usually attributed to the scribe Pentaurt, and composed some little time after the official account which has been translated above. According to this document, the Kheta hosts covered the mountains and filled the valleys like locusts, and every inhabitant of the country was dragged by the prince of Kheta to the fight. The Egyptian host was divided into four great armies, i.e., the army of Amen, which marched with the king, the army of Ra, which occupied the ditch on the west of the town of Shabtun, the army of Ptah, which occupied a middle position, and the army of Sutekh, which marched along the roads of the country. The enemy's host attacked the army of Ra, which retreated before the attack of the pick of the Kheta army, supported as it was by chariots, each containing three warriors; it was then that the king charged into the enemy at headlong speed, but he found soon afterwards that he was surrounded by 'two thousand five hundred pairs of horses', and that his retreat was barred by the bravest of all the Kheta troops.

In these straits Rameses cried out to Amen, and asked the god where he was, and why he did not come to his help, and he spake to the god, saying, 'Have I for nought dedicated to thee temples, and filled them with prisoners, and given thee of all my substance, and made the whole country to pay tribute unto thee, and ten thousand oxen, besides sweet-smelling woods of every kind? I never stayed my hand from doing that which thou wishedst. I have built for thee pylons and other edifices in stones, I have raised up to thee pillars which will last forever, and I have brought obelisks for thee from Abu (i.e., Elephantine). I brought stone for thee, and I made ships to sail on the sea and bring back the products of foreign lands…. Behold, O Amen, I am in the midst of multitudes of men who have banded themselves together against me, and I am alone, and no one is with me, for all my soldiers and charioteers have forsaken me; I cried out unto them, but none hearkened unto me. But thou, O Amen, art more to me than millions of warriors, and hundreds of thousands of horses, and tens of thousands of brothers and sons, even if they were here all together; the acts of hosts of men are as nothing, and Amen is better than them all.'

The god Amen stretched out his hand to the king, and said, 'I am with thee, I am thy father Ra. My power is with thee, and I am better than hundreds of thousands [of men] united.' Then the king charged, and the 5,000 horses of the enemy were crushed before his horses, and no man lifted a hand to oppose his onset; the enemy fell dead beneath his blows, and when they had once fallen they never moved again.

When the prince of Kheta and the other princes saw what was happening they fled. But the king's charioteer, called Menna, became afraid, for he saw that the king's charge had carried him away from the main body of the Egyptian troops, and that they were surrounded by foes, and he begged Rameses to stop. The king laughed at his fears, and told him that he would slay his enemies and dash them down in the dust, and bidding him to be of good courage he charged the enemy for the sixth time. After this charge he reproached his charioteers for being cowards, and told them that they were worthless as friends in the day of adversity; he then enumerated to them the benefits which he had conferred upon Egypt, and roundly abused them for being craven-hearted men.

No weapon wielded by the enemy touched the king, and on the morning following the second day's fight a man could scarcely find a place on the battlefield whereon to set his foot, because the whole plain was covered with corpses. After the battle was over Rameses thought with gratitude of his two noble horses called 'Victory in Thebes', and 'The goddess Mut is content', for it was they that had strengthened his hand and supported him when he was surrounded by that hostile multitude, and he decreed that when he was in his palace again he would always have their fodder brought to them in his presence so that he might see them fed; and he did not forget to mention honourably the charioteer Menna, who alone out of all his band of trusted servants had remained with him in his brave charge, and he named him the 'captain of the horsemen'. There is, unfortunately, no mention of the tame lion which accompanied Rameses in his chariot and attacked the foe from time to time; it is, however, to be hoped that he was not slain by the Kheta.

When the prince of the Kheta saw how serious had been his defeat he sent a messenger to Rameses asking him to stay his hand, for he and his princes saw that the gods Sutekh and Bar were in the king, and that another day's battle would almost depopulate the country. Rameses hearkened to these representations, and decided to fight the Kheta no more, and to return to the land of Egypt. It is noteworthy that there is no mention either of the giving of gifts or of the payment of tribute by the peoples of the Kheta, and it is clear that both sides must have lost heavily. Rameses was, however, very proud of his achievements in the Kheta war, and he caused narratives of it to be inscribed upon the walls of the temples of Abydos and Thebes, and reliefs to be made near them to illustrate the principal events in it, such as the capture of the two spies of the Kheta, and the council of war, and the flight of the defeated to the city of Kadesh, and the siege of Kadesh, and the death of the prince of Aleppo, who was cast down headlong into the waters of the Orontes.

The prince of the Kheta had collected an army 8,000 or 9,000 strong, without reckoning the horsemen and charioteers, who seem to have been in number about 7,500; the number of the Egyptian soldiers and charioteers is not mentioned. The prince of the Kheta kept in reserve a force of the Tuhire, but he had no opportunity of despatching them to the assistance of their comrades who were routed on all sides. The Kheta allies evidently made a great effort to eject the Egyptians from Syria, and it is probable that they would have succeeded but for the incident of the capture of the two spies, who were beaten by the soldiers of Rameses and made to say where the Kheta army had taken up its position. That this incident was regarded by the king as of great importance is evident from the fact that he caused a scene to be sculptured on his temple walls, in which the beating of the spies with long sticks is represented; in fact the Intelligence Department of the Egyptian Army was badly managed, and it is difficult not to think that disaster was only averted from Rameses by the fortunate discovery of the two spies.

In the account of the battle ascribed to Pentaurt, we observe the same foolish exaggeration which is apparent in the texts relating to the early history of Rameses which are found at Abydos, and it must be hoped that the soldiers never read the texts on the temple walls in which the Egyptian Army is so roundly abused; moreover, the sculptures which Rameses himself caused to be made prove that he was not so utterly isolated on the field of battle as he represents. That the battle against the Kheta was a serious affair is quite clear, and it seems as if the Egyptians engaged an enemy numerically superior to themselves and held their own against him, but that is all that can be said for them, for Rameses acquired no new territory as the result of the fight, and he regained none of Egypt's old possessions in Syria.

Renewed Hostitlities and Final Peace Treaty

But the power of the Kheta had not been broken by the Egyptians, and as soon as Rameses had returned to Egypt the prince of the Kheta and his allies began to collect their forces once more and to prepare to fight again with Rameses. In the eighth and three following years of his reign, Rameses was obliged to march into Syria to put down revolts which had broken out in and about the old fortress city of Ascalon; but when this rising had been suppressed another broke out in the north at Tunep, the inhabitants of which never lost an opportunity of rebelling against the Egyptian rule. Rameses claims to have captured the city on the second assault which he delivered against it, and to have made himself master of the neighbouring country, but there is no proof of it, and it is improbable that he did so.

Matters went on in this unsatisfactory manner for Egypt for some years, but at length an arrangement was made between the prince of the Kheta, who was called Kheta-sar, and Rameses II, which was embodied in a definite treaty between the two kings. The Egyptian version of the text of this treaty was inscribed upon the western face of the wall which leads from the south wall of the great Hypostyle Hall at Karnak to the first pylon on the north, and also on the walls of the Ramesseum, and the composition was thought much of by Rameses; from this text we learn that the original document was inscribed upon a tablet of silver which was deposited in the building in the Delta, part palace and part fortress, where the king of Egypt loved to live.

The treaty is dated on the 21st day of the season Pert, of the 21st year of the reign of Rameses II, and sets forth that at this time the king was in the city of Per-Ramessu-meri-Amen, and that he was in the temple making offerings to his father Amen, and to Heru-khuti, and Temu, and Ptah, and Sutekh, the son of Nut, and other gods. Whilst he was there his ambassador to Asia, Ra-mes, came into his presence leading the Kheta ambassador Tarthisebu who carried in his hand a silver tablet inscribed in the Kheta language with the terms of the treaty which Kheta-sar, the king of Kheta, declared himself ready to accept and to abide by. Kheta-sar refers to the old treaties which existed between his ancestors and those of the king of Egypt, and goes on to say that the treaty now proposed is conformable to the will of Amen the god of Egypt, and of Sutekh the god of Kheta land, and that from now onwards and forever friendship and a right understanding shall exist between himself and Rameses. Kheta-sar will be the ally of Rameses, and Rameses shall be his ally. He has always striven to be friendly with the king of Egypt, and he objected strongly to the war which his brother Mauthenure (or Mutallu) waged against Egypt, and after his death (i.e., murder by Kheta-sar) he ascended the throne of Kheta and strove for peace. He and his sons will for evermore be at peace with Rameses and his sons; he will not invade Egypt, and Rameses must not invade Kheta, and he will observe the treaty which his great ancestor Saparere, and his brother made with the kings of Egypt.

If any foe shall invade Egypt he will bring troops and help Rameses to eject them, but he does not promise to command his troops in person, and Rameses must send troops to help him if his territory be invaded by any foe. Each king is, moreover, to restore to the other any subjects who for any reason may wish to escape from their own country. All the terms of the treaty refer to the relations which Kheta-sar wished to exist between himself and Rameses, and he calls all the gods and goddesses of the land of Kheta and of the land of Egypt to be witnesses of his honourable intent. Among these are mentioned Sutekh, lord of heaven; Sutekh, lord of Kheta; Sutekh, lord of Arenna; Sutekh, lord of Thapu-Arenuta; Sutekh, lord of Paireqa; Sutekh, lord of Khisasapa; Sutekh, lord of Saresu; Sutekh, lord of Khirepa (Aleppo); Sutekh, lord of Rekhasna; Sutekh, lord of Mukhipaina; Anthretha of Kheta, the god of Tchai-tath-khereri; Shasakhire, 'mistress of mountains'; and the gods of the land of Qitchauatana.

Then follow a blessing on those who shall observe this treaty and a curse upon those who shall not; the gods of Kheta and Egypt will punish everyone who treats it with contempt, but will give him that honoureth it a good reward, and a long life, and will preserve him and his family, and his servants and their families. Upon the silver tablet were impressed the seal, that is to say a picture, of the god Sutekh, the seal, or picture, of Ra, the lord of heaven, and of Ra, the lord of Arenena, and the seal of the king of Kheta, Rheta-sar, and of the queen of Kheta, whose name is given as Puukhipa, of the country of Qitchauatana. The latter part of the queen's name indicates that this lady was of Mitannian origin, and it at once calls to remembrance the names of Gilukbipa and Tatumkhipa, the sister and daughter of Tushratta, king of Mitanni, who married kings of Egypt. It seems that Khipa itself was a proper name as late as 710 BCE, for under the form it occurs as the name of a female slave on a small tablet in the British Museum, which was perhaps worn as a ticket of identification by the woman herself, who was probably a Mitannian slave.

At the end of the text of the treaty as proposed by Kheta-sar follow a number of lines which seem to represent the additional clauses which Rameses felt bound to add to it on his own initiative, and which refer to the extradition of malefactors, and the sending back to their own country of those who seek to settle in Egypt from Kheta, or in Kheta from Egypt. The treaty proves that the king of Kheta regarded himself as the equal of the king of Egypt, and that Rameses was obliged to admit that he was; in any case, the treaty was one of friendly reciprocity, and precludes all possibility of the existence of Egyptian possessions in Syria.

Rameses Marries a Kheta Princess

Thirteen years after the concluding of the treaty, i.e., in the 34th year of his reign, Rameses married Ur-maa-neferu-Ra, the daughter of the prince of the Kheta, whom he raised to the rank of great queen of Egypt. Her Kheta name is unknown, but on the stele at Abu Simbel she is arrayed like an Egyptian princess, though her father is represented wearing the characteristic conical hat of the Kheta and the long, coat-like garment. An allusion to this queen seems to be made in the speech of the god Ptah, who, in describing the great things which he has done for Rameses, says that he has made the land of Kheta to be subject to his palace, that the inhabitants thereof bring offerings, that the possessions of their chiefs belong to the king of Egypt, and that at the head of them all is the eldest daughter of the prince of Kheta 'who maketh to be at peace the heart of the lord of the two lands'.

Soon after the marriage of his daughter to the king of Egypt the prince of Kheta and his friend the prince of Keti set out to visit the court of Rameses, and in due course they arrived at Thebes, where they saw the glory and state of the princess of Kheta in her new position as queen of Egypt.

The remembrance of this marriage was preserved in a remarkable manner by the priests of Khensu, who set up a stele to commemorate the healing of the queen's sister by the might of their god. Soon after the king had married the

Kheta lady Ra-maa-ur-neferu messengers came to him from her native country to say that her young sister Bent-reshet was very ill, and to ask that a physician might be sent to heal her. Rameses despatched the royal scribe Tehuti-emheb to Bekhten, but when he arrived there he found that the princess was possessed of a devil over which he had no power. The father of the princess, who is described as the Prince of Bekhten, sent to Egypt once more and asked Rameses to send a god to heal his daughter. Thereupon Rameses went into the temple and asked the god Khensu-Nefer-hetep, if he would go to Bekhten and heal the princess, and the god nodded his head and consented to do so.

After a journey of 17 months Khensu arrived in Bekhten, and when he was taken to the place where the sick princess Bent-reshet was, he made use upon her of his marvellous saving power, and she was healed straightway. The devil that had possessed her came forth out of her and acknowledged the supremacy of the god of Egypt; the prince of Bekhten tried to keep the god in the country, but Khensu willed otherwise, and at length the prince sent him back with his priests, boats and cavalcade, and with rich gifts to Egypt, where he arrived in the 33rd year of the reign of Rameses II. The version of the incident here described was drawn up long after the marriage of the king with the Kheta princess, and it seems that the priests made a mistake in supposing that their god went to Bekhten before the king's marriage which, judging from the stele at Abu Simbel, took place in the 34th year of his reign.

The Works and Buildings of Rameses II

During the years which followed his campaigns in Palestine and Syria Rameses devoted himself to the completion of the buildings which his father Seti I had begun, and to the erection of edifices which he adorned with statues of himself, and obelisks, etc., and to the repairs of old shrines in various parts of Egypt and Nubia. The monumental remains which are found from one end of Egypt to the other testify to the vastness of his building operations generally, but it is certain that Rameses was in the habit of usurping statues, sphinxes, etc., and that when he repaired a temple or sanctuary he caused his name to be inscribed upon walls, doorposts, lintels, etc., in such a way as to make the beholder think that the whole edifice had been erected by himself. He added columns of texts containing glorifications of himself to the obelisks set up by his ancestors, and it is wonderful how he contrived to find the means which resulted in his name being found in every temple and fortress, and sanctuary of any importance in Egypt. Besides this, he re-worked the monuments of his ancestors, with the result that the names of those who made them disappeared entirely.

The greatest of all the works of Rameses II is the famous temple in Nubia, which is hewn out of the solid rock of a mountain on the left or west bank of the Nile at Abu Simbel. It is dedicated to Amen of Thebes, Ra-Heru-khuti of Heliopolis, and Ptah of Memphis, and in later times Rameses II was himself worshipped there. Whether the credit for the whole building belongs to this king or not, whether he 're-worked', or modified, or completed what an earlier king had begun matters little to us, for it is certain that this temple is one of the most marvellous architectural works of the ancient Egyptians. The temple is approached by a flight of steps leading to a kind of court; here in front of the temple, two on each side of the door, are four seated colossal statues of Rameses II, each 18 metres (60 feet) high, which have been hewn out of the living rock.

The front of the temple is about 30 metres (100 feet) wide and is over 27 metres (90 feet) in height; above it is a cornice decorated with 21 dog-headed apes. The temple itself is about 56 metres (185 feet) long, and consists of a large hall measuring about 18 metres by 7 metres (60 feet by 25 feet), wherein are, eight square pillars about nine metres (30 feet) high, each with a colossal figure of Osiris five metres (17 feet) high standing against it, and of a small hall measuring about 10 metres by seven metres (35 feet by 25 feet), supported by four pillars; in this hall are the sanctuary and the altar. In connection with this temple may be mentioned that dedicated to the goddess Hathor which lies to the north of it; here the front of the temple measures about 28 metres by 12 metres (92 feet by 40 feet), and four of the six statues, which are over nine metres (30 feet) in height, are of Rameses II, while the other two are of his wife Nefertari-mert-en-Mut.

Passing to the north of Egypt we find that Rameses II practically rebuilt Tanis, which he made his capital and to which he gave an importance almost equal to that of Thebes or Memphis. It is a remarkable fact that few of the kings of the New Empire seemed to realize the great importance of possessing a capital near Syria; Thebes was too far away for the king, when there, to be able to control events effectively in the Delta, and it was impossible to strike quickly in Palestine from that distance. Tanis was a beautiful city in the reign of Rameses, and its temples and obelisks must have provoked the wonder and admiration of all the Semitic settlers in that part of the country; curiously enough, Rameses, who in Thebes was never tired of proclaiming his devotion to Amen and of boasting what great things he had done for the god, was in Tanis always paying honour to Sutekh, Bar and other deities, who were abominated by the Egyptians of Upper Egypt as being the gods of the Hyksos whom they so much detested. It may have been an act of political expedience on the part of Rameses II to proclaim his worship of Semitic gods in a country which was inhabited by Semitic peoples, but it is not an act which would have approved itself to the great warrior kings of the Twenty-Eighth Dynasty; his toleration of the Semites is further proved by the 'Stele of Four Hundred Years', i.e., the stele so-called because it is dated in the 400th year of the era which began with the year of the founding of the city of Tanis by Nubti, a Hyksos king.

At Heliopolis and Memphis Rameses carried out some important architectural works, and at the former place, according to Pliny, he set up four obelisks. At Abydos he completed the temple which his father Seti I had begun to build, and he tells us in the inscriptions which he placed on its walls he had ordered the works to be continued in the very year wherein his father died. Rameses also relates at length the great things which he did for the temple, and gives the texts of the prayers which he made to the god, and of the speeches which he made to his father, and of Seti's reply. At no great distance from the temple of Seti I, or the Memnonium as Strabo calls it, Rameses II built a temple which he dedicated to the god Osiris; it was a solid and handsome edifice, as the ruins of it testify, and it is not easy to understand why so little of it has remained to us. The walls were ornamented with reliefs illustrating events in the Kheta war, and in one of its corridors was a King List (now in the British Museum), which was evidently a copy of that set up by his father in his temple.

At Thebes he began his building works in the early years of his long reign and, as far as can be seen, they were continued almost to the end of it. He completed the great Hypostyle Hall at Karnak and added to it 54 columns; his grandfather Rameses I set up one of the pillars, and his father Seti I [set up] 79.

He built a pylon leading to it, and inscribed upon it a list of the cities and countries which he had conquered. He enclosed a great portion of the temple of Amen with a wall, and at the east end of the temple he erected a small temple and built a colonnade.

He usurped the obelisk which Thothmes I had set up in front of the pylon which he had built, and it is more than probable that Rameses usurped some of the large statues on which his name appears.

He added reliefs illustrating and texts recording his conquests upon many of the walls of the temple buildings, and among the latter is a copy of his treaty with the Kheta. The presence of this text upon the walls of the great sanctuary of Amen which had been built by the great kings of the Twenty-Eighth Dynasty with the tribute that they forced the Kheta and other Asiatic nations to pay is significant of the decline of the power of Egypt in the reign of Rameses II.

To the temple of Amen-hetep III, which this king left unfinished at his death, Rameses II added largely. He built the large front court with a colonnade, and a court with porticoes, and a huge pylon, before which he placed six colossal statues of himself, two seated and four standing, and he set up two huge reel granite obelisks inscribed with his names and titles. One of these obelisks is in the Place de la Concorde in Paris, and the other remains in situ; each obelisk is about 24 metres (80 feet) high and is said to weigh about 250 tons.

Rameses II completed the funeral temple which his father had begun to build at Kurna, and he did some repairs to the temple of Hatshepsut in Der al-Bahari; it would seem that he also carried on works at other temples on the western banks of the Nile. The greatest of all the buildings of Rameses in Western Thebes was the Ramesseum, which was dedicated to Amen-Ra; it is probably the building to which Diodorus refers under the name of 'Tomb of Osymandyas'; Strabo called it the 'Memnonium'. On the first pylon Rameses II caused scenes in the Kheta war to be sculptured, and in front of the second pylon he set up a colossal statue of himself which is probably the largest statue known in Egypt; it was 18 metres (60 feet) in height, and cannot have weighed less than 885 tons. Of the statue Diodorus says, 'The place is not only commendable for its greatness, but admirable for its cut and workmanship, and the excellency of the stone. In so great a work there is not to be discerned the least flaw, or any other blemish. Upon it there is this inscription: "I am Osymandyas, king of kings; if any would know how great I am, and where I lie, let him excel me in any of my works."' The existence of an inscription on the statue with this meaning, is, of course, wholly imaginary.

At El-kab Rameses built a temple in honour of the gods Thoth, Horus and Nekhebet, and remains of works carried out by him are found at Gebel Silsila, Kom Ombo, and at various places in and about Aswan and on the Island of Elephantine. The temples at Bet al-Walli and Abu Simbel have been already referred to, and of the works which he carried out in Nubia may be specially mentioned: 1. The rock temple at Gerf Husen dedicated to Ptah, Hathor, Anuqet and other gods; 2. the temple at Wadi Sebu'a, part of which is hewn out of the rock, with its rows of sphinxes and its statues of the king; 3. the temple at Derr, which is hewn out of the rock.

To carry on all these works must have entailed great expenditure of labour and money, and it is not easy to see whence the latter was obtained. Tribute from the kings of Palestine and Syria had ceased to flow into Egypt, and the products of the Sudan could hardly supply all the needs of Rameses II. One great source of revenue were the famous gold mines which were situated in the Wadi Ulaki, and which had been worked during the reign of Seti I; there are no records to show that these mines were worked by the Egyptians at an earlier period, but it is most probable that they were, and we know that the supply of gold which could be obtained from them was sufficiently large to make them worth working in Roman and even in Arab times. The portion of the Wadi Ulaki worked by Seti I was near the modern village of Kubban, which marks the site of the Roman fortress called Contra Pselchis, and is nearly opposite to the modern Dakkeh, and it was approached from the Nile at Kubban. Near this place was found a large and important stele which is dated in the third year of the reign of Rameses II, and which throws considerable light on the working of the gold mines at that time, and describes how the difficulties which were experienced through want of water were overcome.

After the first few lines which record the king's names and titles, and state that he is the conqueror of Kesh and of the land of the Negroes, and that his territory extends to the south as far as Kari, Rameses is made to say that gold appears in the mountains at the mere mention of his name, even as it does at the name of Horus of Baka, (i.e., the modern Kubban). We are then told that on a certain day Rameses II sat in council with his nobles discussing the affairs of the gold-producing land, when reports were laid before him stating that the mines could not be worked because there was no water to be had on the road, and that both man and beast therefore died of thirst on the road to and from the mines. All agreed that there was much gold in the country of Akaita, but as there was no water on the way to it, except such as fell from the skies in rain, no more gold was forthcoming.

The king then ordered that the overseers of the mines should be brought into his presence, and expressed his willingness to carry out their recommendations. When they had come in and praised his beautiful face, he described to them the configuration of the country, and inquired of them as to the possibility of boring a well on the road; the overseers approved the suggestion joyfully, and praised the king for his wisdom and sense. They referred to the time when he was the deputy ruler of the country, and spoke of the great buildings which he had erected when he was the governor of the whole land, a position which he seems to have occupied for 10 years. Then the governor of Nubia declared that there had never been any water in the country, and that when Seti I worked the mines he dug a well 120 cubits in depth, at a certain place on the road to it, but no water appeared; finally he advised the king to speak to his father, the Nile-god Hapi, on the subject, for he was sure that he would send water into the waste and desert country if Rameses only asked him to do so. Rameses, however, determined to dig a well there, and despatched a royal scribe with workmen to carry out the royal commands; the borers set to work with a will, and at a depth of 12 cubits they found water, which welled up in such quantities that people were able to sail about on it in boats, like the inhabitants of the marshes in the Delta.

Equally useful to the country were the works which Rameses II undertook in connection with the canal which led from Bubastis to the Bitter Lakes, and which he intended to lengthen until it reached the Red Sea. Some part of it seems to have existed in the time of Seti I, but neither he nor his son finished it; Rameses only seems to have widened or deepened it. Nekau, a king of Twenty-Sixth Dynasty, carried the work a step further, and the canal was finally taken to the Red Sea in the reign of Darius.

Wives and Family of Rameses II

Rameses married his two sisters, Nefert-ari-meri-Maat and Ast-nefert, by whom he had several children, both sons and daughters, and he married at least three of his own daughters, namely, Banta-Antu, and Amen-merit, and Nebt-taui. Besides these wives he had a large number of concubines, both foreign and native, by whom he became the father of, literally, scores of children; several lists of his children were made, e.g., at Abydos, Thebes, Wadi Sebu'a and Abu Simbel, but as far as can be seen none of them was intended to be complete, and they contained the names of selections only of his sons and daughters. The longest list is at Wadi Sebu'a, where we find the names of 111 sons and about 51 daughters.

Of his sons who are well known from their frequent mention in the texts may be noticed Amen-her-khepesh-f, Ramessu, Pa-Ra-her-unami-f, Amen-her-unami-f, Amen-Meri and Seti. His son Kha-em-Uast, the son of the queen Ast-Nefert, was a Sem priest of Ptah, and he held several high ecclesiastical offices, and was the true founder of the Serapeum; he was a man of great learning, and was held in high repute as a magician, as we may see from the famous Romance of Setna. He appears to have conducted the government of the country for about 25 years before his death, which took place in the 55th year of the reign of Rameses II, and he was succeeded in this duty by his brother Mer-en-Ptah-hetep-her-Maat, who is 13th in the list of the sons of Rameses II; he had performed the duties of viceroy for about 12 years when his father died, in the 67th year of his reign, aged about 100 years.

Tomb and Mummy of Rameses II

Rameses II built a tomb for himself in the Valley of the Tombs of the Kings at Thebes, and we may assume that he was laid to rest therein with all due pomp and ceremony, and that the funeral furniture was of a character which befitted the rank of the man for whom it had been made. The tomb became the prey of a gang of professional tomb robbers towards the close of the Twentieth Dynasty, and probably everything that could be carried was stolen. In the time of the Ptolemies it was possible to visit the lower chambers, but it would seem that not many centuries later the whole of the corridors and chambers became filled with sand. [French historian and linguist Jean-Francois] Champollion and [Italian Egyptologist Ippolito] Rosellini forced their way into parts of the tomb, and in spite of the heat and want of air succeeded in obtaining some information as to its size, ornamentation, etc. Lepsius cleared out the sand sufficiently to enable him to make a useful plan of the corridors and chambers, but he found that the wall decorations had been almost entirely destroyed by the mud and gravel which had flowed down the steep corridors into the sarcophagus chamber. It seems astonishing that none of the great architects and master builders who were in the employ of Rameses II warned him of what, from the nature of its situation, must happen to his tomb when rain fell.

The mummy of Rameses II was found at Der al-Bahari in a wooden coffin, in which it seems to have been placed under the Twentieth Dynasty, for the decorations of the coffin, and the style of the writing found upon it, indicate that as the period to which it belongs. The original coffin was either broken or had fallen to pieces, and the high priest of Amen, Her-Heru, had a new one made for the mummy; in the troubled times of the Twentieth Dynasty the priests of Amen took Rameses II out of his tomb, and carried him to the tomb of Seti I for safety; and subsequently he was again removed to the tomb of queen An-Hapu, which was situated in that part of the Biban al-Muluk where Amenhetep III had built his tomb. Nearly a century later the high priest of Amen, called Pai-netchem, provided the mummy with new bandages.

The mummy of Rameses II was unrolled by M. Maspero on June 1, 1886, and when the swathing and coverings had been removed the mummified body was found to be about one and a half metres, 15 centimetres (5 feet, 6 inches) in length. The head is small in comparison to the rest of the body, and is rather long; the hair, which was white at the time of death, has been stained a light yellow colour by the medicaments employed in the process of mummification. The forehead is low and narrow, the eyebrows are well arched, and the hair on them is white and bushy, the eyes are small, and lie close to the nose, the nose is long and thin, and somewhat hooked, the temples are hollow, and the cheekbones prominent; the ears are round, and have slits in them in which earrings must have hung before they were stolen by the tomb robbers, the jaws are fine and strong, the chin is prominent, the mouth is large, the lips are thick, and the teeth, though somewhat soft, are white, and were apparently well cared for. When Rameses died his bones were weak and fragile, and his muscles had become atrophied through senile decay.

M. Maspero thinks that at the time of death he must have been almost 100 years old, and he describes the impression which he received, concerning the character of the king after he had unrolled his mummy, in these words: 'En résumé, le masque de la momie donne très suffisamment l'idée de ce qu'était le masque du roi vivant; une expression peu intelligente, peutêtre légèrement bestiale, mais de la fierté de l'obstination, et un air de majesté souveraine qui perce encore sous l'appareil grotesque de l'embaumement.' This summary agrees very well with the character of Rameses II, which we can deduce from his inscriptions and monuments. In his youth he was brave and active, and proved himself to be a capable though hard ruler; in his old age he devoted himself to a life of comparative inactivity, and indulged in the pleasures of his palace and the society of the *harimat*, meanwhile retaining the nominal sovereignty of the whole country. He was vain and boastful, as his inscriptions show, and he allowed his court scribes to write concerning his life that which he must have known to be untrue, or perhaps Egyptologists have misunderstood their statements, because the facts are often buried under heaps of high-sounding words. And finally he was not justified in claiming the sovereignty of Palestine and Western Asia, or of Nubia as far as Kari, for nothing can disguise the fact that under Rameses II the decline of the power of Egypt set in, that she did not regain any of her old possessions, and that her dominions had shrunk to the size which they were before the conquests of the great kings of the Eighteenth Dynasty.

Mythical Exploits of Rameses II a.k.a Sesostris?

In the histories of Herodotus and Diodorus, and in the works of several other classical writers, the mighty deeds and exploits of a hero called Sesostris are described or alluded to; it is not certain that these writers had any clear idea when he lived, but it is quite certain that many of his works correspond with those performed by Rameses II, and that to the history of Rameses II the Greeks united the legends and romance of Sesostris. The name Sesostris is certainly not a form of that of Rameses, and [German Egyptologist] Prof. [Kurt] Sethe is undoubtedly correct in saying that it is derived from the old Egyptian name Senusert, i.e., Usertsen, and that the original hero of the Sesostris legend was a king of this dynasty who bore this name. But a by-name of Rameses II, 'Sesetsu', may very well have contributed to the formation of the legendary name Sesostris, and why any one of the kings who bore the name Usertsen, or Senusert, should be chosen as the popular hero of historic romances cannot be said.

The Sesoses of Pliny, who made the 'third obelisk at Rome', appears, as Prof. Sethe has said, to be Usertsen I, especially as his son's name,

'Nuncoreus', may very well represent the prenomen of Arnen-em-hat II, Nub-kau-Ra, but history does not record that he waged war like Rameses II, or built great temples, or that he did the things which Rameses II is known to have done. On the other hand, many exploits are attributed to Sesostris of which no parallels can be found in the history of Rameses II, and we are compelled to come to the conclusion that the Sesostris of Greek legend is a hero round whose name the legends and traditions of many great kings and warriors have gathered, and he must be put in the category of such popular characters as Gilgamesh, the narrative of whose exploits delighted the Sumerians and Babylonians for thousands of years, and Nimrod, and Alexander the Great, to whom tradition has ascribed the wisdom and power and conquests of dozens of historical heroes, and whose history, having been translated into many languages, has charmed men of every nationality from Malaysia in the East to England in the West.

The fullest account of the hero Sesostris is given by Diodorus Siculus, who not only repeats some of the matters which are related by Herodotus concerning him, but, what is far more interesting, adds a number of others which well-illustrate the growth of the legends concerning his life and exploits after the death of Herodotus. The expedition of Rameses II down the Red Sea was, of course, nothing but an expedition to the country of Punt, and though it may have been larger than usual, it must not be regarded as a great expedition of conquest. There is no record of conquests of Rameses II in Bactria and other remote Asiatic countries, but yet it seems that his name must have penetrated as far as those distant lands, for the prince of Bekhten sent to ask him first to send a physician, and the next time to send a god to heal his daughter; and as we are told that Bekhten was 17 months' journey from Egypt it must have been far away. The facts of the reign of Rameses II have been given above, but in order that the reader may be enabled easily to compare legend with fact extracts concerning Sesostris from the works of Herodotus and Diodorus are here appended. Herodotus says:

> '.... the worthy Prynce Sesostris. Him the pryestes recounte firste
> of all the kings of Aegypt to have passed the narrow Seas of Arabia
> in longe Ships or Gallyes, and brought in subiection to the Crowne
> all those People that marche a longe the redde Sea. From whence

retyringe backe againe the same way, hee came and gathered a greate power of men, and tooke his passage over the waters into the mayne lande, conquering and subduing all Countreyes whether so ever hee went. Such as he found valiaunte and hardye not refusinge to ieoparde their safety in the defence and maynetenaunce of their liberty, after the victory obtayned, hee fixed in theyr countrey certayne pyllers or Crosses of Stone, wherein were ingrauen the names of the kinge and the countrey, and how by his owne proper force and puissaunce he had made them yelde. Contrarywyse, such as without controuersie gave themselves into his handes, or with litle stryfe and lesse bloudshed were brought to relent: with them also, and in their region he planted Pillers and builte up litle crosses, as before, wherein were earned and importrayed the secret partes of women, to signifie to the posterity the base and effeminate courage of the people there abyding. In this sorte he trauayled with his army by and downe the mayne, passing out of Asia into Europe, where he made conquest of the Scythians and Thracians, which seemeth to have bene the farthest poynt of his voyage; for so much as in their land also his titles and marks are apparantly seene and not beyonde. Herefro hee began to measure his steps back agayne incamping his powre at the ryuer Phasis: where, I am not able to discusse, whether king Sesostris himselfe planted any parte of his army in that place ever after to possesse yt countrey: or whether some of his souldiers wearyed with continuall peregrination and trauayle, toke up their mansion place and rested there…. This noble and victorious prince Sesostris making his return to Aegypt came (by report of ye priests) to a place named Daphnae pelusiae, with an infinite trayne of forraine-people out of al Nations by him subdued; where being very curteously met and welcomed by his brother, whom in his absence he had left for Viceroy and protectour of the countrey, he was also by ye same inuited to a princely banquet, himselfe, his wife, and his children. The house whereinto they were entered, being compassed about with dry matter, was suddaynely by the treachery of his brother set on fire, which he perceiving toke counsayle with his wife then present, how to escape and auoide the danger. The woman either of a readier wit or

riper cruelty, advised him to cast two of his sixe children into the fire,
to make way for himselfe and the rest to passe: time not suffering him
to make any long stay, he put his wyues counsayle in speedy practise,
and made a bridge through the fire of two of his children, to preserve
the rest aliue. Sesostris in this sorte delivered from the cruell treason
and malicious devise of his brother, first of all tooke reuenge of his
trecherous villany and diuelish intent: in the next place bethinking
himselfe in what affayres to bestowe the multitude which he had
brought with him, whome afterwards he diuersely employed: for by
these captures were certayne huge and monstrous stones rolled and
drawne to the Temple of Vulcane. Likewise, were many trenches cut
out and deriued from the riuer into most places of the countrey,
whereby the land being aforetime passable by cart and horse, was
thencefoorth bereaved of that commodity: for in all the time ensuing,
the countrey of Aegypt being for the most parte playne and equall,
is through the creekes and windings of the ditches brought to that
passe, that neyther horsse nor wayne can have any course or
passage from one place to another. Howbeit, Sesostris inuented this
for the greater benefite and commodity of the lande, to the ende that
such townes and cities as were farre remooued from the riuer, might
not at the fall of the floud be pinched with the penury and want of
water, which at all times they haue deriued and brought to them in
trenches. The same King made an equall distribution of the whole
countrey to all his subjects, allotting to euery man the lyke portion
and quantitie of ground, drawne out and limited by a fouresquare
fourme. Heereof the king himselfe helde yeerely reuenewes, every
one being rated at a certayne rent and pension, which annually he
payd to the crowne, and if at the rising of the floud it fortuned any
man's portion to be ouergone by the waters, the king thereof was
aduertised, who forthwyth sent certayne to survey ye ground, and to
measure ye harmes which the flood had done him, and to leavy out
the crowne rent according to the residue of the land that remayned.
Heereof sprang the noble science of Geometry, and from thence was
translated into Greece. For as touching the Pole and Gnomon (which
is to say) the rule, and the twelue partes of the day, the Graecians

tooke them of the Babylonians. This King Sesostris held the Empyre alone, leauing in Aethiopia before the temple of Vulcane certayne monuments to the posteritie, to wit, certayne images of stone, one for hymselfe, another for his wife, beeyng eache of them thirtie cubites: the foure images also of hys foure sonnes, beeyng each of them twentie cubites apeece. In processe of time when the image of King Darius that gouerned Persia should have bene placed before the picture of Sesostris, the priest of Vulcane which serued in the temple woulde in no wise permit it to bee done, denying that Darius had euer achieued the like exploits that Sesostris had done. Who, besides the conquering of sundrie other nations (not inferiour in number to those which had been overcome by Darius) had also brought in subiection the most couragious and valiaunt people of Scythia: for whyche cause, it were agaynst reason to preferre hymselfe in place before him unto whome he was inferiour in chiualry, whiche bold annswere of the priest, King Darius tooke in good parte and brooked welynough. Sesostris dying, the seate imperiall came to his son Pheco.'

The history of Sesostris according to Diodorus is as follows:

'Seven descents after (they say), Sesostris reigned, who excelled all his ancestors in great and famous actions. But not only the Greek writers differ among themselves about the king, but likewise the Egyptian priests and poets relate various and different stories concerning him. We shall relate such as are most probable and agreeable to those signs and marks that are yet remaining in Egypt to confirm them. After his birth his father performed a noble act, and becoming a king, he caused all throughout Egypt, that were born the same day with his son, to be brought together; and together with his son to be bred up with the same education, and instructed in the same discipline and exercises, conceiving that, by being thus familiarly brought up together, and conversing with one another, they would be always loving and most faithful friends, and the best fellow soldiers in all the wars. Providing, therefore, everything for

the purpose, he caused the boys to be exercised daily in the schools with hard and difficult labours; as that none should eat until he had run a hundred and four-score furlongs; and by this means, when they came to be at men's estate, they were fit either to be commanders, or to undertake any brave or noble action, both in respect of the vigour and strength of their bodies, and the excellent endowments of their minds. Sesostris in the first place being sent with an army into Arabia, by his father (with whom went his companions that were bred up with him), toiled and troubled himself with the hunting and killing of wild beasts; and then having at last overmastered all his fatigues and wants of water and provision, he conquered all that barbarous nation, which was never before that time subdued. Afterwards, being sent into the western parts, he conquered the greatest part of Libya, being as yet but a youth. Coming to the crown after the death of his father, encouraged by his former successes, he designed to subdue and conquer the whole world. Some report that he was stirred up by his daughter Athyrte to undertake the gaining of the empire of the world; for being a woman of an extraordinary understanding, she made it out to her father, that the conquest was easy; others encouraged him by their divinations, foretelling his successes by the entrails of the sacrifices, by their dreams in the temples, and prodigies seen in the air. There are some also that write, that when Sesostris was born, Vulcan appeared to his father in his sleep, and told him that the child then born should be conqueror of the universe; and that that was the reason why his father assembled all of the like age, and bred them up together with his son, to make way for him with more ease to rise to that height of imperial dignity, and that when he was grown to man's estate, fully believing what the god had foretold, he undertook at length this expedition. To this purpose he first made it his chief concern to gain the love and goodwill of all the Egyptians, judging it necessary in order to effect what he designed so far to engage his soldiers, as they should willingly and readily venture, nay, lose their lives for their generals, and that those whom he should leave behind him, should not contrive any rebellion in his absence; to this end, therefore, he obliged everyone, to the utmost of his power, working upon some by money, others, by giving them lands, and many by free pardons, and upon all by fair words, and affable and courteous behaviour. He pardoned those that were condemned for high treason, and freed all that were in prison for debt, by paying what they owed, of whom there was a vast multitude in the gaols. He divided the whole country into thirty-six parts, which the Egyptians call Nomi, over every one of which he appointed a governor, who should take care of the king's revenue, and manage all other affairs relating to their several and respective provinces. Out of these he chose the strongest and ablest men, and raised an army answerable to the greatness of his design, to the number of six hundred thousand foot, and twenty-four thousand horse, and twenty-seven thousand chariots of war; and over all the several regiments and battalions, he made those who had been brought up with him commanders, being such as had 'been used to martial exercises, and from their childhood hot and zealous after that which was brave and virtuous, and who were knit together as brothers in love and affection, both to the king, and one to another, the number of whom were about seventeen hundred. Upon these companions of his he bestowed large estates in lands, in the richest parts of Egypt, that they might not be in the least want of anything, reserving only their attendance upon him in the war. Having therefore rendezvoused his army, he marched first against the Ethiopians inhabiting the south, and having conquered them, forced them to pay him tribute of ebony, gold, and elephants' teeth. Then he sent forth a navy of four hundred sail into the Red Sea, and was the first Egyptian that built long ships. By the help of this fleet, he gained all the islands of this Sea, and subdued the bordering nations as far as to India. But he himself marching forward with his land army, conquered all Asia, for he not only invaded those nations which Alexander the Macedonian afterwards subdued, but likewise those which he never set foot upon. For he both passed over the river Ganges, and likewise passed through all India to the main ocean. Then he subdued the Scythians as far as to the Tanais, which divides

Europe from Asia; where they say he left some of his Egyptians at the lake Moeotis, and gave origin to the nations of Colchis; and, to prove that they were originally Egyptians, they bring this argument, that they are circumcised after the manner of the Egyptians, which custom continued in this colony as it did amongst the Jews. In the same manner he brought into his subjection all the rest of Asia, and most of the islands of Cyclades. Thence passing over into Europe he was in danger of losing his whole army, through the difficulty of the passages, and want of provisions. And, therefore, putting a stop to his expedition in Thrace, up and down in all his conquests, he erected pillars, whereon were inscribed, in Egyptian letters, called hieroglyphics, these words: "Sesostris, king of kings, and lord of lords, subdued this country by his arms." Among those nations that were stout and warlike, he carved upon those pillars the privy members of a man: amongst them that were cowardly and faint-hearted the secret parts of a woman; conceiving that the chief and principal member of a man would be a clear evidence to posterity of the courage of every one of them. In some places he set up his own statue, carved in stone, (armed with a bow and a lance), above four cubits and four hands in height, of which stature he himself was. Having now spent nine years in this expedition, (carrying himself courteously and familiarly towards all his subjects in the meantime), he ordered the nations he had conquered, to bring their presents and tributes every year into Egypt, every one proportionable to their several abilities and he himself, with the captives and the rest of the spoils, (of which there were a vast quantity), returned into Egypt, far surpassing all the kings before him in the greatness of his actions and achievements. He adorned all the temples of Egypt with rich presents, and the spoils of his enemies. Then he rewarded his soldiers that had served him in the war, everyone according to their desert. It is most certain that the army not only returned loaded with riches, and received the glory and honour of their approved valour, but the whole country of Egypt reaped many advantages by this expedition. Sesostris having now disbanded his army, gave leave to his companions in arms, and fellow victors to take their ease, and enjoy the fruits of their conquest. But he himself, fired with an earnest desire of glory, and ambitious to leave behind him eternal monuments of his memory, made many fair and stately work admirable both for their cost and contrivance, by which he both advanced his own immortal praise, and procured unspeakable advantages to the Egyptians, with perfect peace and security for the time to come. For, beginning first with what concerned the gods, he built a temple in all the cities of Egypt, to that god whom every particular place most adored; and he employed none of the Egyptians in his works, but finished all by the labours of the captives; and therefore he caused an inscription to be made upon all the temples thus: "None of the natives were put to labour here." It is reported that some of the Babylonian captives, because they were not able to bear the fatigue of the work, rebelled against the king; and having possessed themselves of a fort near the river, they took up arms against the Egyptians, and wasted the country thereabouts: but at length having got a pardon, they chose a place for their habitation, and called it after the name of that in their own country, Babylon. Upon the like occasion, they say, that Troy, situated near the river Nile was so called; for Menelaus, when he returned from Ilium with many prisoners, arrived in Egypt, where the Trojans deserting the king, seized upon a certain strong place, and took up arms against the Greeks, till they had gained their liberty, and then built a famous city after the name of their own. But I am not ignorant how Ctesias the Cretan gives a far different account of these cities, when he says, that some of those that come with Semiramis into Egypt, called the cities which they built after the names of those in their own country. But it is no easy matter to know the certain truth of these things: yet it is necessary to observe the different opinions concerning them, that the judicious reader may have an occasion to inquire, in order to pick out the real truth. Sesostris moreover raised many mounds and banks of earth, to which he removed all the cities that lay low in the plain, that both man and beast might be safe and secure at the time of the inundation of the river. He cut likewise many deep dykes from the river, all along as far as from Memphis to the sea, for the ready and quick conveying of corn and other provisions and merchandize, by short cuts thither, both for the support of trade and commerce, and maintenance of peace and plenty all over the country; and that which was of greatest moment and concern of all, was, that he fortified all parts of the country against incursions of enemies, and made it difficult of access; whereas, before, the greatest part of Egypt lay open. and exposed either for chariots or horsemen to enter. But now, by reason of the multitude of canals drawn all along from the river the entrance was very difficult, and the country not so easily to be invaded. He defended, likewise, the east side of Egypt against the irruptions of the Syrians and Arabians, with a wall drawn from Pelusium through the deserts, as far as to Heliopolis, for the space of a thousand and five hundred furlongs. He caused likewise a ship to be made of cedar two hundred and fourscore cubits in length, gilded over with gold on the outside, and with silver within; and this he dedicated to the god that was most adored by the Thebans. He erected likewise two obelisks of polished marble, a hundred and twenty cubits high, on which were inscribed a description of the large extent of his empire, the great value of his revenue, and the number of the nations by him conquered. He placed likewise at Memphis, in the temple of Vulcan his and his wife's statues, each of one entire stone, thirty cubits in height, and those of his sons, twenty cubits high, on this occasion. After his return from his great expedition into Egypt, being at Pelusium, his brother at a feast having invited him, together with his wife and children, plotted against his life; for being all overcome by wine, and gone to rest, he caused a great quantity of dry reeds (long before prepared for the purpose), to be placed round the king's pavilion in the night, and set them all on fire; upon which the flame suddenly mounted aloft; and little assistance the king had either from his servants or lifeguard, who were all still overloaded with wine; upon which Sesostris with his hands lift up to heaven, calling upon the gods for help for his wife and children, rushed through the flames and escaped; and being thus unexpectedly preserved, he made oblations as to other of the gods, (as is before said), so especially to Vulcan, as he by whose favour he was so remarkably delivered. Although Sesostris was eminent in many great and worthy actions, yet the most stately and magnificent of all, was that relating to the princes in his progresses. For those kings of the conquered nations, who, through his favour still held their kingdoms, and such as had received large principalities of his free gift and donation, came with their presents and tributes into Egypt, at the times appointed, whom he received with all the marks of honour and respect; save that when he went into the temple or the city, his custom was to cause the horses to be unharnessed out of his chariot and in their room four kings, and other princes to draw it; hereby thinking to make it evident to all, that there was none comparable to him for valour, who had conquered the most potent and famous princes in the world. This king seems to have excelled all others, that ever were eminent for power and greatness, both as to his warlike achievements, the number of his gifts and oblations, and his wonderful works in Egypt. After he had reigned three-and-thirty years, he fell blind, and wilfully put an end to his own life; for which he was admired not only by priests, but by all the rest of the Egyptians; for that as he had before manifested the greatness of his mind by his actions, so now his end was agreeable (by a voluntary death), to the glory of his life.'

It is interesting to note that Diodorus does not seem to have realized that the tomb of Osymandyas was the funeral temple of Rameses II, many of whose wars and exploits he attributed to Sesostris in accordance with the form of the legend of Sesostris, which was current in his time.

Of the tomb of Osymandyas, i.e., User-Maat-Ra, or Rameses II, Diodorus says:

'There [i.e., Thebes], they say, are the wonderful sepulchres of the ancient kings, which for state and grandeur, far exceed all that posterity can attain unto at this day. The Egyptian priests say that, in their sacred registers, there are entered seven and forty of these sepulchres; but in the reign of Ptolemy Lagus, there remained

only seventeen, many of which were ruined and destroyed when I myself came into these parts, which was in the 108th Olympiad. And these things are not only reported by the Egyptian priests, out of their sacred records, but many of the Grecians who travelled to Thebes in the time of Ptolemy Lagus, and wrote histories of Egypt, (among whom was Hecateus) agree with what we have related. Of the first sepulchres, (wherein they say the women of Jupiter were buried), that of king Osymandyas was ten furlongs in circuit; at the entrance of which they say, was a portico of various-coloured marble, in length 60 metres (200 feet); and in height five and forty cubits; thence going forward, you come into a four-square stone gallery, every square being 121 metres (400 feet), supported, instead of pillars, with beasts, each of one entire stone, 16 cubits high, carved after the antique manner. The roof was entirely of stone; each stone eight cubits broad, with an azure sky, bespangled with stars. Passing out of this peristylion, you enter into another portico, much like the former, but more curiously carved, and with more variety. At the entrance stand three statues, each of one entire stone, the workmanship of Memnon of Sienitas. One of these, made in a sitting posture, is the greatest in all Egypt, the measure of his foot exceeding seven cubits; the other two, much less than the former, reaching but to his knees; the one standing on the right, and the other on the left, being his daughter and mother. This piece is not only commendable for its greatness, but admirable for its cut and workmanship, and excellency of the stone. In so great a work there is not to be discerned the least flaw, or any other blemish. Upon it there is this inscription: "I am Osymandyas, king of kings; if any would know how great I am, and where I lie, let him excel me in any of my works." There was likewise at this second gate, another statue of his mother, by herself, of one stone, twenty cubits in height; upon her head were placed three crowns, to denote she was both the daughter, wife, and mother of a king. Near to this portico, they say there was another gallery or Piazzo, more remarkable than the former, in which were various sculptures, representing his wars with the Bactrians, who had revolted from him, against whom (it is said) he marched with

400,000 foot, and 20,000 horse; which army he divided into four bodies, and appointed his sons generals of the whole. In the first wall might be seen the king assaulting a bulwark, environed with the river, and fighting at the head of his men against some that make up against him, assisted by a lion, in a terrible manner; which some affirm, is to be taken for a true and real lion, which the king bred up tame, which went along with him in all his wars, and by his great strength ever put the enemy to flight. Others make this construction of it, that the king being a man of extraordinary courage and strength, he was willing to trumpet forth his own praises, setting forth the bravery of his own spirit, by the representation of a lion. In the second wall, was carved the captives dragged after the king, represented without hands and privy members; which was to signify, that they were of effeminate spirits, and had no hands when they came to fight. The third wall represented all sorts of sculptures, and curious images, in which were set forth the king's sacrificing of oxen, and his triumphs in that war. In the middle of the peristylion, open to the air at the top, was reared an altar of shining marble, of excellent workmanship, and for largeness to be admired. In the last wall were two statues, each of one entire stone, 27 cubits high; near to which three passages opened out at the peristylion, into a stately room supported with pillars like to a theatre for music; every side of the theatre was 60 metres (200 feet) square. In this, there were many statues of wood, representing the pleaders and spectators, looking upon the judges that gave judgment. Of these, there were thirty carved upon one of the walls. In the middle sat the chief justice, with the image of truth hanging about his neck, with his eyes closed, having many books lying before him. This signified that a judge ought not to take any bribes, but ought only to regard the truth and merits of the cause. Next adjoining, was a gallery full of divers apartments, in which were all sorts of delicate meats, ready dressed up. Near hereunto, is represented the king himself, curiously carved, and painted in glorious colours, offering gold and silver to the gods; as much as he yearly received out of the gold and silver mines. The sum was there inscribed (according to the rate of silver) to amount unto 32,000,000 of minas. Next hereunto was the sacred library, whereon was inscribed these words, viz.: "The cure of the mind." Adjoining to this, were the images of all the gods of Egypt, to every one of whom the king was making offerings, peculiarly belonging to each of them, that Osiris, and all his associates, who were placed at his feet, might understand his piety towards the gods, and his righteousness towards men. Next to the library, was a stately room, wherein were twenty beds to eat upon, richly adorned; in this house were the images of Jupiter and Juno, together with the kings; and here it is supposed, the king's body lies interred. Round the room are many apartments, wherein are to be seen in curious painting, all the beasts that are accounted sacred in Egypt. Thence are the ascents to the top of the whole monument of the sepulchre, which being mounted, appears a border of gold round the tomb, 365 cubits in compass, and a cubit thick; within the division of every cubit, were the several days of the year engraven, with the natural rising and setting of the stars, and their significations, according to the observations of the Egyptian astrologers. This border, they say, was carried away by Cambyses and the Persians, when he conquered Egypt. In this manner they describe the sepulchre of king Osymandyas, which seems far to exceed all others, both for magnificence and curiosity of workmanship.'

Menephthah
Ba-Ra-Mer-En-Amen, son of the Sun, Mer-En-Ptah Hetep-Her-Maat

Mer-En-Ptah or Menephthah, was the 13th son of Rameses II, and his mother was Queen Ast-nefert; he had been associated with his father in the rule of the kingdom for several years before he became the sole king of Egypt, and it is clear that he was a man well past middle age when he ascended the throne. Besides the Horus name, 'Mighty Bull, rejoicing in Maat,' he styled himself the 'Soul of Ra, beloved of Amen, he who resteth on Maat, lord of the shrines of Nekhebet and Uatchet, the Horus of gold, the lord of risings,' and he adopted titles which refer to his adoration of the Sun-god Ra, and to his establishing of good laws throughout the world. The principal event in the reign of Mer-en-Ptah, or Menephthah, was the Libyan war, concerning which a considerable amount of information is furnished by a long inscription at Karnak.

In the fifth year of his reign, as we learn from two inscriptions published by Maspero, Menephthah heard that a revolt had broken out among the Libyans, who had gathered together a large number of allies from among the Mediterranean peoples, and that their king intended to invade Egypt. He was in Memphis at the time, and soon after the report of the revolt had reached him he heard that the Libyan king had attacked all the outlying Egyptian and other cities to the east of the Delta and conquered thein, and that he had crossed the frontier and was actually in Egypt and was master of all the territory through which he had passed. Menephthah at once began to fortify 'Annu, the town of Tem', i.e., Heliopolis, and the 'fortress city of the god Tanen', i.e., Memphis, and the city of Per-Baire-Ast, probably the modern Belbes, which was situated on the canal Shakana. In due course the 'wretched king of Libya', called Mareiui, the son of Tit, invaded the country of the Thehennu, with his bowmen and his allies the Shaireten, and the Shakelesha, and the Qauasha, and the Reku, and the Turisha, and then made his way with his wife and children across the western frontier into the fields of the city of Pa-art, or Per-iut, which must not, according to Brugsch, be identified with Prosopis, but with some place to the east of the Delta.

When Menephthah saw his foe 'he roared like a lion', and made a long speech to his generals and officers, in which he reminded them that he was their king, and would be responsible for their safety, and then went on to upbraid them for being timid as birds, and for their inactivity and helplessness. He pointed out that their lands were being laid waste, that those who chose passed over the frontier whensoever they pleased, that the invaders robbed the people and seized their lands, that the Oasis of Ta-ahet, (i.e., Farafra), had been occupied, that the enemy were swarming into Egypt like worms, and their sole aim in life, he declared, was to fight and to plunder, and that once in Egypt, to which they had come for food to eat, they would settle down and dwell there. As for their king he was like a dog, and was a cringing, fawning, senseless being, and he should never more sit upon his throne. Then the king ordered his army to make ready to attack the enemy, telling them that Amen would be to them a shield, and he promised to lead them in person to battle on the 14th day of the month.

Before the fateful day, however, the king dreamed a dream, and in it a colossal figure of the god Ptah appeared to him and, bidding him to stay where he was, reached out to him a divine scimitar, and ordered him to lay aside all faint-heartedness and to be strong, and to send forward large numbers of soldiers and chariots to the city of Pa-art. Mareiui, the king of Libya, had arranged to fight the battle on the first day of the month Epiphi at daybreak, but he was not able to do so until two days later, when the Egyptian troops attacked with such vigour that the enemy was driven hither and thither, and by the help of the gods Amen-Ra and Nubti, they were overthrown in thousands by the chariot charges of the Egyptians, and the dying and dead lay drenched with their own blood. For six hours the battle raged, and the Egyptians gave no quarter; finally the king of the Libyans, seeing that the field was covered with the corpses of his soldiers, took to flight, and in order to make good his escape, he threw away his bow and quiver, and sandals, and when he found he was being pursued he cast away even his clothes, and succeeded in saving nothing but his skin. His followers were not so fortunate, and hundreds of them were cut down by pharaoh's horsemen. The wife and children of Mareiui, and his silver, and gold, and vessels of iron, and bows, and even the ornaments and apparel of his wife were captured by Menephthah, as well as large numbers of prisoners. The spoil was loaded upon asses, and the king ordered it to be driven to Egypt, together with the hands and other portions of the dead Libyans which they had cut off. Among then slain were six of the brothers and children of the Libyan king and 6,350 officers and soldiers; all these were mutilated in the manner in which the Egyptians treated their uncircumcised foes. Of the Shakaresha 250 were killed, of the Turisha 790, but the numbers of the other allies who were killed are unknown; 9,376 prisoners, including 12 women, were taken, and the loot consisted of 9,111 swords of the Masha tribe, 120,314 weapons of various kinds which had been found with the Libyans, 126 horses, etc. Thus, fortunately for Egypt, ended the Libyan war, and Menephthah was, no doubt, very thankful that he was the victor, for Egypt was never so nearly being conquered from one end to the other as she was at this time.

When we consider that two generations of Egyptians had never seen or heard of war in their own time, it is little short of marvellous that this mighty confederation of Libyans and their allies was vanquished by Menephthah's army; his soldiers fought well because they realized that they were fighting a battle on the result of which depended their freedom, as the loss of it would entail a life of slavery with peoples whom they held to be abominable and unclean. There is small wonder that the whole land rejoiced madly, or that the Delta was filled with songs of gladness and thankfulness from east to west. Fortunately for Menephthah the Palestinian tribes were quiet, and from the Kheta he had nought to fear, because during the famine which had broken out in Northern Syria in the early years of his reign he had sent corn to his father's ally, the prince of Kheta. To commemorate his victory in the Libyan war, Menephthah caused a 'hymn of triumph' to be inscribed on the back of a huge granite stele of the time of Amenhetep III, which was found in the Ramesseum at Thebes in 1896, and in this text we find the principal events of the war treated in a highly poetical manner. The king of Libya is heartily abused, and the gift of the divine scimitar to Menephthah is mentioned, and after a few remarks on the happy times which have once more returned to Egypt through the victory of the mighty king of Egypt, we find the following passage: 'The princes are cast down upon the ground, and utter words of homage, and no one of the people of the Nine Bows lifteth up his head. Thehennu is laid waste. Kheta hath been pacified, Canaan hath been seized upon by calamity of every kind, Ascalon hath been carried away, Qatchare, (Gezer), hath been captured, Innuamam, (Yamnia), hath been reduced to a state of not being the Isiraare, or Isiriaale, have been ravaged and their seed destroyed, Syria, hath become the widow of Egypt, and all the lands together are at peace.'

Judging from this passage it would seem that Menephthah had conducted some campaign in Palestine or Southern Syria, and that as a result the whole of the country of Libya had been laid waste, and several districts of Palestine reduced to want and misery, but there is no reference to any such campaign in the inscriptions except this. In the time of Rameses II, the treaty which he made with the king of Kheta allowed him to have full authority over Palestine as far north as the Dog River, and all the land which lay to the south of it was the property of Egypt. Why then boast of having reduced to misery towns like Ascalon, and Gezer, and Yamnia, etc.? M. Naville has discussed the passage in a careful article, and translates the last part of it thus: 'Kanaan est done reduit a l'impuissance, parce qu' Askalon et Ghezer se font la guerre: Iamnia est comme n'existant plus; Israel est detruit, il n'a plus de posterite, et la Syrie'est comme les veuves d'Egypte.' The passage which M. Naville renders, 'Israel is destroyed, and hath no posterity', is translated 'Israel ist verwustet und seine Saaten vernichtet', by Prof. Spiegelberg, and 'Israel ist verwustet, ohne Feldfrucht', by Prof. Krall. Thus all three scholars are certain that in the inscription of Menephthah under consideration the Israel of the Bible is mentioned, but they differ in the meaning which they assign to the word *peru*, which M. Naville translates by 'postérité', and Spiegelberg by 'Saaten', i.e., 'crops', and Krall by 'Feldfrucht', or 'fruit of the field'.

Some writers have seen in the Egyptian text a reference to the passage in Exodus i. 16, where we are told that the king of Egypt ordered the Hebrew midwives to destroy the male children of the Hebrews, and to keep alive the female children; but we are also told in the following verse that 'the midwives feared God, and did not as the king of Egypt commanded them, but saved the men children alive.' So that if we accept the Bible narrative we must believe that the male children were not destroyed after all, and therefore the passage in the Egyptian text of Menephthah cannot refer to a destruction of the seed of Israel which never took place. There is no doubt that the word *peru* does sometimes mean 'progeny', 'offspring', and the like, but on the other hand the proofs adduced by Prof. Spiegelberg make it tolerably certain that his rendering 'Israel hath been ravaged and his crops destroyed' is the correct one.

We must now consider the name Isiraare, or Isiraale, which is rendered 'Israel'. It is clear from the determinatives at the end of the word that we have to deal with the name of a people of foreign race ... The fact that all the other places mentioned with Isiraale have the determinative of foreign country placed after each of them emphasizes its omission in the case of Isiraare or Isiraale, which has a group of determinatives meaning 'foreign people' placed after it only; this may indicate that the Isiraare or Isiraale people had no country, and were nomads, but in that case how did they come to have crops which could be destroyed?

The question of the identification of this people with the children of Israel seems to depend on what view is taken as to the period in which the Exodus happened. If the Exodus took place in the reign of Amenhetep III, a matter which will be referred to later on, the Children of Israel would by the time Menephthah began to reign have obtained some position among the tribes of Palestine and Canaan, and they may even have acquired land in sufficient quantity to justify the king of Egypt in mentioning their name with the names of countries like Thehennu, Kheta, etc. But if the Exodus took place in the reign of Menephthah the Isiraare, or Isiraale, cannot be, in the writer's opinion, identified with the children of Israel, because according to the Hebrew tradition as preserved in the Bible the latter wandered about in the desert for 40 years, i.e., for a period which was longer than the whole of the reign of Menephthah, and they did not effect a settlement in Palestine until some time later. Moreover, to assign to the fugitives from Egypt a position among the nations which would make them to be worthy of mention side by side with those like the Kheta and the Thehennu is to give them an importance which they would never possess in the eyes even of the writer of a high-flown composition, such as that which appears on the stele usurped by Menephthah. The composition has no real historical importance, as we may see from the fact that the writer of the text, after declaring that the Libyans were destroyed, goes on to say that the 'Kheta have been brought to a state of peace'; the reader of this statement who was ignorant of the true history of the period would imagine that Menephthah had reduced the Kheta, but we know that he did not, and that the peoples of the Kheta country had forced Rameses II to be at peace with them. Among the last words on the stele we read, 'Syria hath become as the widows of Egypt', by which we should expect the writer to mean us to understand that Syria had been reduced to a state of misery of the most abject character, but when we notice that he is making a pun on the words *Khar*, 'Syria', and *khart,* 'widows', it is natural to doubt if the words have really that meaning at all. The pun is probably an old one, and dates from the early part of the Eighteenth Dynasty, and the writer was clearly more anxious to use it than to report a mere historical fact. Finally, all that can be said for the identification of the Isiraare, or Isiraale, with the children of Israel is the resemblance between the two names, and if it be accepted we must admit that the Israelites left Egypt *before* the reign of Menephthah, and were settled in Palestine at the time his inscription was written.

The building operations of Menephthah appear to have been considerable, especially in the Delta, where he repaired the old frontier fortresses and built new ones, no doubt with the idea of keeping strict watch upon the various peoples who went in and out from Egypt. He built largely at Tanis, where he usurped a number of Twelfth Dynasty statues, and two so-called Hyksos sphinxes, etc., and he carried on repairs at Heliopolis, Memphis and Abydos, and his name is found upon many buildings on both banks of the Nile at Thebes, where many works were carried out by his commands. He usurped some of the granite sphinxes, an obelisk, etc., which had been set up by Amenhetep III and Thothmes III, and as far as can be made out his own buildings were few and of no great importance. Stelae, in which he is represented adoring the gods, are found at Gebel Silsila, and his name appears at Pselchis in Nubia, and in the old quarry works in the Sinaitic Peninsula. Menephthah built himself a tomb in the Valley of the Tombs of the kings at Thebes, which is known today as 'No. 8'. It consists of three chambers and three corridors, the walls of which are decorated with extracts from the *Book of Praising Ra* and the *Book of the Underworld*, or as Dr. Birch read the title some 50 years ago, *The Book of the Gate*, and with scenes in which the deceased is represented in the act of adoring Harmachis and other gods, and that of the passage of the sun through certain hours of the night. The king's sarcophagus stands in the second room from the end of the corridors, but there is no mummy in it.

Some years ago it was the fashion to explain the absence of the king's mummy by a reference to the Bible narrative (Exodus, chapters xiv and xv), and to assume that Menephthah was drowned, together with his captains, during his pursuit of the children of Israel through the waters of the Red Sea. But the tradition as given in Exodus only tells us, 'Moses stretched forth his hand over the sea, and the sea returned to his strength when the morning appeared; and the Egyptians fled against it; and the Lord overthrew the Egyptians in the midst of the sea. And the water returned, and covered the chariots, and the horsemen, and all the host of Pharaoh that came into the sea after them; there remained not so much as one of them'. There is nothing in this passage to indicate that Pharaoh was pursuing the Israelites in person, or that he was drowned as a result.

When the great haul of Royal mummies was made at Der al-Bahari in 1881, and the mummy of Menephthah was found not to be among them, the belief that he had been drowned with his 600 chosen captains of chariots was confirmed in the opinion of many. It will be remembered that early in 1898 M. Loret reported the discovery of the tombs of Amenhetep II and Thothmes III at Thebes, and that in the tomb of the former king a number of royal mummies were found. Later in the year M. Loret read a paper in Cairo at the Institut Egyptien on his discovery, and dealt with the identifications of the mummies which he had found; the mummies were declared by him to be those of Thothmes IV, Amenhetep III, Seti II, Amenhetep IV, Sa-Ptah, Rameses IV, Rameses V and Rameses VI. The discovery was an important one, but it was a remarkable thing to find the mummy of the heretic king Khu-en-Aten carefully stowed away with the mummies of his orthodox father and grandfather and descendants, all of whom worshipped and adored the god Amen, whom he scoffed at and abominated; in fact it was hardly credible that the priests of Amen should have taken the pains to save the body of their old enemy from the wreckers of mummies and the robbers of tombs.

Soon after the reading of the paper an examination of the hieratic characters which were supposed to represent the name of Khu-en-Aten was made by Mr. W. Groff, and he became convinced that they had been misread by M. Loret.... In other words, he had, according to Mr. Groff, read Khu-en-Aten instead of Ba-en-Ra, and had identified as the mummy of Amenhetep IV, or Khu-en-Aten, the mummy of Menephthah. The views of Mr. Groff provoked discussion, and on February 10, 1900, M. Maspero, Daressy and Brugsch Bey specially examined the writing on the wrappings of the mummy with the view of deciding so important a matter; later they were joined by MM. Lieblein, von Bissing, Lange and others, and these savants came to the conclusion that the mummy was not that of Khu-en-Aten but of Ba-en-Ra, i.e., Menephthah, the son of Rameses II, and brother of the famous magician Kha-em-Uast, in fact, the king of Egypt who has been styled generally the 'Pharaoh of the Exodus'. Thanks to the courtesy of Brugsch Bey the writer also was allowed in January 1900, to examine the writing on the wrappings of the mummy, and he has no doubt that Mr. Groff is right and that M. Loret is wrong.

The Exodus of the Israelites from Egypt

☥

IN CONNECTION WITH THE REIGN of Menephthah must be
mentioned the great Exodus of Israel from Egypt, because many
of the greatest Egyptologists think that this remarkable event in
the history of the Hebrews took place at this period. Of the Israelites
and their Exodus from Egypt we have, besides the narrative in the
Bible, several short accounts by various writers, and a longer, more
detailed statement on the subject by Josephus.

According to this last writer, a king of Egypt called Amenophis was
desirous of beholding the gods, as Orus, one of his predecessors in the
kingdom, had seen them. And be communicated his desire to a priest of
the same name as himself, Amenophis, the son of Papis, who seemed to
partake of the divine nature, both in his wisdom and knowledge of futurity;
and Amenophis returned him answer, that it was in his power to behold
the gods, if he would cleanse the whole country of the lepers and other
unclean persons that abounded in it. Well pleased with this information,
the king gathered together out of Egypt all that laboured under any defect
in body, to the amount of 80,000 and sent them to the quarries which are
situated on the east side of the Nile, that they might work in them and
be separated from the rest of the Egyptians. And there were among them
some learned priests who were affected with leprosy. And Amenophis, the
wise man and prophet, fearful lest the vengeance of the gods should fall
both on himself and on the king, if it should appear that violence had
been offered them, added this also in a prophetic spirit: that certain people
would come to the assistance of these unclean persons, and would subdue
Egypt, and hold it in possession for 13 years. These tidings, however, he
dared not to communicate to the king, but left in writing an account of
what should come to pass, and destroyed himself, at which the king was
greatly distressed.

When those that were sent to work in the quarries had continued for some
time in that miserable state, the king was petitioned to set apart for their

habitation and protection the city Avaris, which had been left vacant by the Shepherds; and he granted them their desire; now this city, according to the theology above, is a Typhonian city. But when they had taken possession of the city and found it well adapted for a revolt, they appointed for themselves a ruler from among the priests of Heliopolis, one whose name was Osarsiph, and they bound themselves by oath that they would be obedient. Osarsiph then, in the first place, enacted this law, that they should neither worship the gods, nor abstain from any of those sacred animals which the Egyptians hold in veneration, but sacrifice and slay them all; and that they should connect themselves with none but such as were of that confederacy.

When he had made such laws as these, and many others of a tendency directly in opposition to the custom of the Egyptians, he gave orders that they should employ the multitudes of hands in rebuilding the walls about the city, and hold themselves in readiness for war with Amenophis the king. He then took into his counsels some others of the priests and unclean persons; and sent ambassadors to the city called Jerusalem, to those Shepherds who had been expelled by Tethmosis; and he informed them of the position of their affairs, and requested them to come up unanimously to his assistance in this war against Egypt. He also promised in the first place to reinstate them in their ancient city and country Avaris, and to provide a plentiful maintenance for their host, and fight for them as occasion might require, and assured them that he would easily reduce the country under their dominion. The Shepherds received this message with the greatest joy, and quickly mustered to the number of 200,000 men, and came up to Avaris.

Now Amenophis the king of Egypt, when he was informed of their invasion, was in great consternation, remembering the prophecy of Amenophis, the son of Papis. And he assembled the armies of the Egyptians, and having consulted with the leaders, he commanded the sacred animals to be brought to him, especially those which were held in more particular veneration in the temples, and he forthwith charged the priests to conceal the images of their gods with the utmost care. Moreover, he placed his son Sethos, who was also called Ramesses from his father Rampses, being then but five years old, under the protection of a faithful adherent; and marched with the rest of the Egyptians, being 300,000 warriors, against the enemy who advanced to meet him; but he did not attack them, thinking it would be to wage war against the gods, but returned, and came again to Memphis, where he took Apis and the other sacred animals he had sent for, and retreated immediately into Ethiopia with all his army, and all the multitude of the Egyptians; for the king of Ethiopia was under obligations to him. He was therefore kindly received by the king, who took care of all the multitude that was with him while the country supplied what was necessary for their subsistence. He also allotted to him cities and villages during his exile, which was to continue from its beginning during the predestined 13 years. Moreover, he pitched a camp for an Ethiopian army upon the borders of Egypt as a protection to king Amenophis.

In the meantime, while such was the state of things in Ethiopia, the people of Jerusalem, who had come down with the unclean folk of the Egyptians, treated the inhabitants with such barbarity, that those who witnessed their impieties believed that their joint sway was more execrable than that which the Shepherds had formerly exercised alone. For they not only set fire to the cities and villages, but committed every kind of sacrilege, and destroyed the images of the gods, and roasted and fed upon those sacred animals that were worshipped; and having compelled the priests and prophets to kill and sacrifice them, they cast them naked out of the country. It is said also that the priest, who ordained their polity and laws, was by birth of Heliopolis, and his name Osarsiph was derived from Osiris, the god of Heliopolis; but that when he went over to these people his name was changed, and he was called Moyses.

The above story reported by Josephus has no historical value, for it is based upon an imperfect knowledge of the facts of Egyptian history. It represents that the famous architect and sage Amenhetep, who is a historical personage, and who flourished in the reign of Amenhetep III, told the king that if he wished to see the gods he must expel the 'lepers' from the country; whether these men were actually lepers, or whether the word is employed to describe them as a term of abuse, cannot be said. The king collected these 'lepers', 80,000 in number, and sent them to work in the quarries [of Tura?], but later he gave them the city of Avaris to dwell in, for it had been evacuated by the Shepherds. There they made a priest of Heliopolis, who changed his name from Osarsiph to Moses, their ruler, and they next sent and invited the Shepherds who were living in Jerusalem to come and help them, promising to give them in return the city Avaris which they had formerly occupied. The Shepherds came, 200,000 in number, and though Amenophis collected an army of 300,000 men to fight them, he did not do so, but taking his gods from Memphis he retreated to Ethiopia, where he remained for 13 years, whilst strangers ruled the country according to the words of the Egyptian sage.

Now we know enough of the history of the reign of Amenhetep III to be able to assert that no invasion of Egypt by the Shepherds, 200,000 strong, ever took place in his reign, and that this king did not retreat to Ethiopia for 13 years, and that the city of Avaris had been in the hands of the Egyptians since the beginning of the Eighteenth Dynasty. A copyist of Manetho, from whom Josephus says he takes the story, having very possibly access to some Egyptian tradition of the Exodus of the Israelites, which ascribed it to the reign of Menephthah, erroneously confused his name (A)menephthes with the better-known Amenhetep III. Thus the theory which would place the Exodus in the time of Amenhetep III falls to the ground. Moreover, the details of the story reported by Josephus do not agree with the details of the Bible narrative, and it is clear that Manetho is describing one event, while the writer of the Book of Exodus is describing another. Elsewhere Josephus himself connects the expulsion of the Hyksos by the Egyptians with the Exodus of the Israelites, but here also his remarks are equally without historical value, for he assumes that the Hyksos were the ancestors of the Hebrews, and with characteristic boastfulness attempts to make his readers believe that among the ancestors of the Hebrews were the Hyksos kings of Egypt who, according to the passage which he professes to quote verbatim from Manetho's history, reigned over that country for about 511 years.

An examination of the facts derived from the Egyptian monuments shows that a vast number of people, probably Semites, were expelled from the Delta at the close of the Seventeenth Dynasty, and that the process of the expulsion went on vigorously under the reigns of the first three or four kings of the Eighteenth Dynasty; thus there must have been on several occasions an exodus of Semites, or at least of Canaanites, from Egypt. Of this great series of forced emigrations traditions no doubt remained among the Canaanitish tribes of Palestine and, when the Hebrews had occupied the country, were very possibly, in the process of time, incorporated by the Hebrew annalists in their account of the emigration of their own ancestors from Egypt. Of this earlier stratum of the Biblical narrative traces may yet be identified. This theory is rendered more probable by the fact that the Egyptians undoubtedly identified the Israelitish Exodus with the expulsion of the Hyksos; the Egyptian history of Manetho, when appealed to by Josephus for information from Egyptian sources concerning the Exodus of the Israelites, can only tell him of the Exodus of the Hyksos, confused with a later story of an exodus of foreigners which took place in the reign of Menephthah, who is identified with Amenhetep III, under whom lived the great magician Amenhetep, the son of Pa-Hapu, who appears in the story. We thus see that the Egyptians, according to the version of Manetho as quoted by Josephus, confused the traditions of two distinct events; the Expulsion of the Hyksos, for which they had historical documents as proof, and which therefore seemed more important to them, and the Exodus of the Israelites, which was not mentioned on their monuments, and of which they, if we may trust the narrative of Josephus, possessed a confused legend. It is, therefore, very probable that similarly in the Exodus legend of the Hebrews we have a faint reminiscence of the expulsion of the Hyksos as well as a strange tradition of the events which accompanied their own emigration from the land of Goshen.

The Egyptian version of the name of the legendary king, i.e., Amenhetep III, whom Osarsiph drove into Ethiopia, under whom no such event as the Exodus can have taken place, renders it very probable, as has been seen above, that the Israelitish emigration really took place under Menephthah, whose name was easily confused with Amenhetep. The existence of an obscure Egyptian tradition that the Exodus took place under Menephthah is thus indicated. This supposition agrees with the views of the greater number of the Egyptologists who have discussed the subject, and Menephthah is very commonly considered to have been the pharaoh of the Exodus, which will thus have taken place about 1270 BCE, about 400 years after the expulsion of the Hyksos.

This view is entirely supported by the narrative of the Book of Exodus, as we shall see. From this we gather that the Israelites were pressed into the *corvée*, i.e., they were compelled to perform a certain amount of physical labour in connexion with the public works which the king of Egypt had ordered to be carried out. Curiously enough the work was not in connection with the maintenance of the banks of the Nile during the period of the inundation of the river, but with the erection of some wall or building, for the gangs of Israelites were compelled to make so many bricks per day.

The Egyptians made the lives of the Israelites 'bitter with hard bondage, in mortar, and in brick, and in all manner of service in the field: all their service wherein they made them serve, was with rigour. Therefore they did set over them taskmasters to afflict them with their burdens. And they built for Pharaoh treasure cities, Pithom and Raamses' (Exod. i. 11). Finally, 'Pharaoh commanded the taskmasters of the people, and their officers, saying, Ye shall no more give the people straw to make brick, as heretofore: let them go and gather straw for themselves. And the tale of the bricks, which they did make heretofore, ye shall lay upon them; ye shall not diminish ought thereof: for they be idle; therefore they cry, saying, Let us go, and sacrifice to our God. Let there more work be laid upon the men, that they may labour therein: and let them not regard vain words.... So the people were scattered abroad throughout all the land of Egypt to gather stubble instead of straw. And the taskmasters hasted them, saying, Fulfil your works, your daily tasks, as when there was straw. And the officers of the children of Israel, which Pharaoh's taskmasters had set over them, were beaten, and demanded, Wherefore have ye not fulfilled your task in making brick both 'yesterday and today, as heretofore?' (Exod. v. 6-14).

We may note in passing that the only name by which the Hebrew writer calls the king who oppressed his countrymen so cruelly is 'Pharaoh', which is, of course, the Egyptian Per-aa, i.e., 'Great House'; but this was a title which was borne by every king of Egypt, and it therefore does not enable us to identify the oppressor king. The custom of employing foreign captives or aliens was inaugurated by Thothmes III, who employed them largely on the works connected with the great temple of Amen-Ra at Thebes; the example which he set was followed by his successors, so we cannot identify the oppressor king by his employment of captive or alien labour. We touch firm ground in the statement that the Israelites built 'for Pharaoh treasure cities, Pithom and Raamses', for the names of these cities are well known from the hieroglyphic inscriptions, and their sites have been identified by M. Naville with considerable success.

The name of Pithom is, of course, the Egyptian Pa- (or Per-) Atemt, i.e., the 'house of the god Tem'; this was situated in the district called in the inscriptions

Thuku or Thukut, which lay at the eastern end of the Wadi Tumilat, and is marked by the ruins called by the Arabs, 'Tell al-Maskhuta'. Here M. Naville found a number of strong chambers, well built of mud bricks, which he considers to have been used for storing grain and provisions for those who were about to make a journey into the Arabian desert, or as a stronghold wherein to keep the tribute which was brought from Syria and Palestine into Egypt until such time as it could be disposed of in the ordinary manner.

As nothing older than the time of Rameses II has been found at Pithom we may reasonably assume that he was the builder of the city; it is, of course, possible that there was an older city on the site before his time, but even so it was Rameses II who built the strong city which has been made known to us by its ruins. Thus, as we are told in the Bible that the Israelites built Pithom for the pharaoh of the oppression, and as we know from the monuments discovered by M. Naville that Rameses built Pithom at the 'mouth of the East', i.e., the frontier city on the east of Goshen in which the Israelites had their abode, we get a tolerably clear idea that the pharaoh who had the Israelites forced into the *corvée* was none other than Rameses II.

But the Bible also tells us that the Israelites built the treasure city of 'Raamses', and this city can be no other than Tanis, the Zoan of the Bible, the San of Arabic writers, and the Sekhet Tcha, or Sekhet Tchant, or Tchart of the hieroglyphic inscriptions. We may note in passing that the words 'field of Zoan' in Psalm lxxviii 12, 43, are the exact equivalent of the Egyptian name Sekhet Tchanet, i.e., 'Field of Tchanet'. That the Hebrews regarded Zoan as a very old city is proved by the fact that it is noted in Numbers xiii 22, that 'Hebron was built seven years before Zoan in Egypt'. The city of Tanis was an exceedingly old one, and the monuments of Pepi I which have been found there prove that it was of considerable size and great importance in the Sixth Dynasty, about 3233 BCE. The history of Tanis is a chequered one, but the great kings of the Twelfth and Thirteenth Dynasties built largely there, and many of them set up colossal statues of themselves in the famous temple; the Hyksos kings established themselves there, and usurped the sphinxes and other monuments of their predecessors which they found in the place.

Seti I was the first of the kings of the New Empire who seems to have perceived the great strategic importance of the city to the Egyptians if they wished to maintain their hold upon Palestine, and it was he who brought it into a state of comparative prosperity after a long period of neglect by the kings of the Eighteenth Dynasty, who, associating it with the Hyksos kings, would do nothing whatsoever for it. Rameses II, following the example of his father Seti I, thought highly of the importance of Tanis, and did a great deal to restore the city. He repaired the old temples and rebuilt parts of them, he fortified the walls, and made every part of its defences strong, and he laid out gardens, and either founded or re-founded a temple there in honour of the gods. Amen, Ptah, Harmachis and Sutekh and, in fact, made it his capital city. He usurped large numbers of statues and other monuments which had been set up by his predecessors, and by adding new ones of his own here, there and everywhere, he made the city almost a rival of Thebes.

A certain Panbasa who had visited Tanis, which he calls the 'city of Ramessu-meri-Amen', i.e., the city of Rameses II, in writing home to a friend says that 'there is nothing in the Thebaid which can be compared with it'. As Rameses II was the great restorer of the city his name became attached to it, and when the Egyptian spoke of 'Pa-Ramessu', i.e., the palace or temple of Rameses, he as often referred to the whole city as to the king's private residence. It will be remembered that Rameses II was at Tanis when he agreed to the treaty which the king of the Kheta proposed, and it was from this place that he watched the development of events in Palestine and Syria, and decided to rule his country. The 'Treasure city Raamses' is, then, almost beyond doubt, none other than Tanis, or Pa-Ramessu. Rameses II was the builder king of Egypt *par excellence,* and the state of misery to which the Israelites were reduced, and which is so vividly described in the Bible, is exactly the condition to which an alien people in the Delta would be brought when turned into gangs for the *corvée* of the day.

It was Rameses II who built the wall from Memphis to Pelusium to keep out of Egypt the hordes of nomad Semites, and he certainly carried out some works either of lengthening or deepening the canal which was intended to run eventually from the middle of the Delta to the Red Sea. In both these undertakings a vast amount of human labour would be required, and it would be of that kind which made the lot of the Israelites unbearable. Thus there seems to be no doubt that the period of greatest oppression described in the Book of Exodus fell in the reign of Rameses II, and that the works wherein the Israelites toiled were in connection with the rebuilding of the city of Tanis and the founding of the frontier fortress of Pa-Temu, or Pithom. We may see, however, that although the Biblical account points to the period of the Nineteenth Dynasty as the time when the Exodus took place, there are difficulties in it which cannot altogether be explained away. In the opening verses of the first chapter of Exodus we are told that Joseph died, and all his brethren, and all his generation, and that a new king arose who knew not Joseph and who oppressed Israel; we are clearly intended to understand that the oppression and the Exodus took place after Joseph's death. But we learn from Genesis xli. 45, that the pharaoh who raised Joseph to a high position of trust in his kingdom called him Zaphnath-paaneah, and gave him to wife Asenath, the daughter of Potipherah, priest of On. Now the name Zaphnath-Paaneah is, undoubtedly, the equivalent of the Egyptian Tchet-pa-neter-auf-ankh, i.e., 'The god spake, and he (i.e., Joseph) came into life', which, owing to the dropping of the letters t and r in quick pronunciation Tche-pa-nete-auf-ankf. This name, however, is not found in the Egyptian inscriptions, though it is clearly imitated from names which are composed in this manner, e.g., Tchet-Ptah-auf-ankh, 'Ptah spake and he came into life', Tchet-Amen-auf-ankh, 'Amen spake and he came into life', etc. The name Asenath is probably the Egyptian 'Nes-Net', i.e., 'belonging to Neith', and Potipherah is undoubtedly Pe-ta-pa-Ra, i.e., 'the gift of Ra'. But all these names belong to classes of names of the Twenty-Second and Twenty-Sixth Dynasties, and are not found earlier in the inscriptions, and we must therefore assign the first few verses of the Book of Exodus and Genesis xii. 45 to a much later period than the story of the Exodus given in the Bible.

The date of Exodus and the line of the route which was followed by the children of Israel on their departure from Egypt have given rise to endless discussions and theories, none of which, however, explain away the difficulties of the Bible narrative. We have already said that the Exodus took place about 1270 BCE, but other dates which have been proposed for it are 1314 BCE and 1335 BCE, the former by Lepsius, and the latter by Dr. Mahler, who declares that it took place on Thursday the 27th of March, 1335 BCE. Of Dr. Mahler's date, Prof. Marti says, 'Mahler assigns the Exodus to the 27th March, 1335 BCE, which was a Thursday, because fourteen days before that day there occurred a central solar eclipse. This calculation rests on Talmudic data that assign the darkness mentioned in Ex. 10. 21, to the 1st of Nisan, and explain that that day, and therefore also the 15th of Nisan, was a Thursday. In Ex. 10. 22, indeed, we read of a darkness of three days; but Mahler argues that this note of duration really belongs not to *v.* 22, but to *v.* 23: and is meant simply to explain how intense and terrifying was the impression which the darkness produced on the inhabitants of Egypt.... so that no one dared for three days to leave his house. It is just as arbitrary to assume in Gen. 15. 5 ff. an eclipse enabling Abraham to count the stars before sunset, and then to use the eclipse for fixing the date of the covenant.'

The Israelites, we know, were living in Goshen, i.e., in a portion of the Delta and of the Wadi Tumilat which lies between Zakazik on the north, Belbes, probably the ancient Pharbaethus, on the south, and the modern Tell al-Kebir on the east, and we know that they set out on their way eastwards along the Wadi Tumilat. Two ways were open to them, one went by way of Tanis and then led to the Mediterranean and thence to Syria, and the other going eastwards passed through the district of Rameses, and so reached the northern end of the Red Sea, which it is supposed then extended nearly as far as the modern town of Isma'iliya.

Many Egyptologists and theologians think that having reached Succoth, which district has been by some identified with the Thukut of the hieroglyphic texts, and its capital city Pa-Temu, or Pithom, they went on into the desert of Etham, and then turned towards the south, whilst others are convinced that they must have gone to the north. The former view agrees with the Bible narrative which records the divine command given to Moses that the Children of Israel should 'turn and encamp before Pi-hahiroth, between Migdol and the sea, over against Baal-zephon' (Exod. xiv. 2). It is, however, impossible to identify the sites of these three places with certainty, although there is no doubt that at the time when the Bible narrative was written these frontier towns or fortresses were well known. Assuming that the Israelites turned towards the south they might have crossed over into the desert at a place to the south of the Bitter Lakes, or at a place more to the north and between the Bitter Lakes and Lake Timsah; another view is that they crossed the Red Sea a little to the north of the modern town of Suwez or Suez.

The boldest theory ever put forward on the route of the Exodus is that of Brugsch who, making the Israelites start from Goshen, leads them by way of Tanis through the 'field of Zoan' to a fortress, called in Egyptian Khetem, which he identifies with Etham; they then journey past 'Migdol', i.e., the Migdol near Pelusium, and make their way by some road near the great Sirbonian Bog past Pi-hahiroth, which Brugsch here regards as the equivalent of the 'gulfs' or, 'pits' of the Sirbonian Bog. The route here sketched is pretty well that which was in common use by travellers from Egypt to Syria and *vice versa,* but the Israelites were specially commanded not to use that road, the obvious reason being that the fugitives would have marched straight into the line of fortresses which the Egyptians maintained along their eastern and north-eastern frontiers, which it was their object to avoid. Moreover, it does not follow that Etham is the equivalent of the Egyptian word 'fortress', and even if it did, we do not know *which* 'fortress' is referred to; and in like manner with 'Migdol', which also means 'fortress' or 'strong place', and which is the equivalent of the Egyptian *makthare*, we know not which 'Migdol' is indicated, for there was more than one Migdol both in Egypt and in Syria. Taken together, the known facts about the land of Goshen and the land of Rameses indicate that the passage of the 'Red Sea' was not made either as far north as any portion of Lake Menzaleh or as far south as Suez, and that whatever water was crossed by them, be it lake or be it sea, was situated at no great distance from the eastern part of the Wadi Tumilat.

There is no evidence to show that the Red Sea and the Mediterranean Sea were connected by means of a series of lakes, or swamps or lagoons when the Exodus took place, and it is far more reasonable to believe that the Israelites crossed over into the desert by means of a passage through some part of Lake Timsah, which is relatively quite close to the eastern end of the Wadi Tumilat, than by a passage through the Red Sea itself. The narrative of the Book of Exodus calls the water which the Israelites crossed 'Yam Suph', i.e., the 'sea of reeds', a name which they would never have given to the sea in general; and there is no doubt that they called the water by that name because it was of great extent, and because it contained reeds. This fact points to Lake Timsah as the 'sea of reeds', because being fed from the Nile reeds would grow in it in abundance. The application of the name 'sea of reeds' to the Red Sea was a blunder made by later writers who, knowing nothing about the geography of the Isthmus of Suez, as soon as they heard or read that the Israelites had passed over a vast stretch of water, assumed that that water was the Red Sea because they knew not of the existence of any other in that part of the world.

Of the theories put forward in recent years on the Exodus a few are new, but many are either modifications of old ones, or the old ones themselves resuscitated both new and old are, however, usually put forward by men who have no competent knowledge either of the district which they are attempting to discuss or describe, or of the conditions under which the events related took place. It is also futile to argue that the Misraim out of which Israel came is not Egypt, but some country to the east or north-east of it, for all the evidence of an archaeological character which has been collected during the last few years points to the fact that Misraim in the Exodus narrative means Egypt and Egypt only. The views on the subject of Goshen and the route of the Exodus which M. Naville has enunciated during the last few years are worthy of careful attention, for they are based on the first-hand knowledge derived from the results of the excavations which he made in the Wadi Tumilat, where he was so fortunate as to discover the store-city of Pithom. He has treated the subject of the Exodus and the identifications of the cities mentioned in the Bible narrative with common sense and moderation, and he has not overstated the facts from which he has drawn his deductions. In the present state of Egyptological knowledge it is impossible to 'settle' the difficulties which beset the Exodus question, but the present writer, who has gone over the routes proposed both by M. Naville and Sir William Dawson, thinks that, if the matter is to be considered from a practical standpoint, the only possible way for the Israelites to escape quickly into the Etham desert was by a passage across Lake Timsah; on their route after they had crossed he offers no opinion.

Seti II
Ra-Usr-Kheperu-Meri-Amen, son of the Sun, Seti-Mer-En-Ptah

The immediate successor of Menephthah appears to have been Seti II, Mer-en-Ptah, and he is regarded as such by the greater number of Egyptologists, though definite proofs of it are not forthcoming; M.E. de Rouge considered that Amenmeses and Sa-Ptah preceded Seti II in the rule of the kingdom.

Seti II adopted as his Horus name 'Mighty Bull, beloved of Ra', and the inscriptions apply to him several of the titles which had been borne by his predecessors; he appears to have lived usually at Tanis, and to have kept watch over the unruly tribes on the north-east frontier, but although he kept the Egyptian border fortresses in a state of efficiency, he does not seem to have engaged in any wars with the peoples whom they were intended to keep out of Egypt.

As a builder, however, he exhibited considerable activity. He carried on certain works at Heliopolis, for his prenomen, wherein, by the way, he is called 'beloved of Set', is inscribed on a large granite block, which was found near Matariyehy; he also usurped the two granite obelisks which stood in that city, and are commonly called 'Cleopatra's Needles'. At Karnak he built a small sandstone temple in the north-east angle of the court between the First and Second Pylons; it contained three sanctuaries, which were dedicated to Amen-Ra, Mut and Khensu respectively. On the walls are scenes in which the king is represented worshipping these gods. He appears to have made some of the sphinxes which were placed before the great temple of Amenhetep III at Luxor, but it is very doubtful if he built or repaired all the temple buildings on which he caused his name to be inscribed. His name occurs on monuments as far south as Abu Simbel, where it is found on one of the four colossal statues in front of the temple of Rameses II.

Seti II built for himself a tomb in the Valley of the Tombs of the Kings of Thebes, wherein, presumably, he was buried, but as his mummy was found in the tomb of Amenhetep II in 1898, it must have been removed there for safety in the troubled times which came upon Egypt at the end of the Twentieth Dynasty. The tomb consists of three long corridors, two rectangular chambers, the second having in it four square pillars, and a sanctuary. The walls of the corridors and chambers are decorated with scenes and texts from the *Book of the Praises of Ra*, and the *Book of the Tuat*, and with scenes representing the king worshipping the gods and holding converse with them. At the end of the tomb are two large fragments of the sarcophagus of Seti II; the cover was in the form of a cartouche.

In the reign of Seti II the scribe Anna or Annana, either made a copy or composed the famous 'Tale of the Two Brothers', which has formed the subject of many discussions and comments. The first part of the story deals with two brothers, the one married, and the other not, who live in the same house, and are engaged in the same occupation, i.e., farming. The wife of the elder brother attempts to seduce the younger brother when he returns alone one day to the homestead to obtain a fresh supply of corn, but he resists her and goes back to his work. Meanwhile the wife makes herself ill, and when her husband comes home in the evening he finds no fire lit, no supper ready and his wife lying sick and prostrate. The husband rushes out to slay his brother, who has been accused by the wife of making a violent attack upon her, but the younger brother, being warned of his brother's coming by one of the cows, takes to flight, and is pursued by the furious husband who wishes to slay him. When the younger brother is almost caught the Sun-god causes a river to come into being between the pursuer and the pursued, and the younger man succeeds in making the elder believe that he is innocent, and mutilates himself. The elder brother now becomes furious with his wife, and having gone back to his house seizes her and cuts her in pieces, which he throws to the dogs.

The second part of the story is in reality quite independent of the first, and we need not concern ourselves about it here. It has often been stated that the story of the younger brother Batau and the wicked wife is nothing more than the story of Joseph and the wicked wife of Potiphar, but beyond the fact that the two women appear to have made use of much the same words, there is probably no more connection between the narrative of the Book of Genesis and the Egyptian story in a late Twenty-Ninth Dynasty papyrus than there is between it and the stories of the dozens of unfaithful women which could be collected from the various literatures of the world. If, however, there was any borrowing at all it was on the part of the Hebrew writer or copyist, for, as we have already seen, part of the Biblical narrative of Joseph is not older than the Twenty-Second, or even Twenty-Sixth Dynasty.

Amenmeses
Ra-Men-Ma-Ra-Setep-En-Ra, son of the Sun, Amen-Meses-Heq-Uast

Of the circumstances which led to the occupation of the throne of Egypt by Amenmeses nothing is known, and the details of his life and reign that have come down to us are very few. He adopted as his Horus name, 'Lord of festivals, like Amen', or 'Mighty bull, great one of two-fold strength, stablished like [Ra]', and he gave himself the titles 'Mighty Bull, beloved of Maat, stablisher of the two lands, lord of the shrines of Nekhebet and Uatchet, mighty one of wonders in the Apts' (i.e., in Karnak and Luxor).

His mother's name was Ta-khat, who is described as 'divine mother, royal mother, great lady', and his wife, 'the royal spouse, the great one, the lady of the two lands', was called Baket-ur-nu-re; but whether he obtained any claim to the throne through his mother or wife seems very doubtful. He probably usurped the throne in the troubled times which followed the reign of Menephthah, when, as we shall see later, there was no central government to control affairs. In an inscription of Amenmeses, published by Lepsius, he is called 'beautiful god, son of Amen, divine essence coming forth from his (i.e. Amen's) members, august child of Hera (?), set apart for fair sovereignty in the North land', and the story adds that 'Isis nursed him in the city of Khebit to be prince'.

And relying on this statement, M. E. de Rouge decided that the king was born in Khebit, a city situated in the nome of Aphroditopolis. But M. Maspero holds a different view, which is probably the correct one, that these words are not intended to be taken in a literal but in a mythological sense, and that they indicate that the king was not intended from his birth to ascend the throne, in other words, that he was not of royal descent. A somewhat similar thing is said of Thothmes III, who in an inscription relates the great gifts which the gods had bestowed upon him, and goes on to say that he was 'emanation of An-mut-f, and as like the child Horus in Khebit'; Dr. Brugsch argued from these words that the king 'had been banished to the marshy country, difficult of access, so as to remove him from the sight of his faithful subjects and to destroy all remembrance of him'. But they meant nothing of the kind, and were merely intended to convey to the reader the fact that the king identified himself with Horus, whose powers and attributes he assumed in consequence.

Amenmeses carried out some repairs on the temple at Medinet Habu, where his name is found with those of Seti I and Heru-em-heb as a 'restorer of monuments'; in some places at Thebes he seems to have usurped buildings, and his name appears where it has no right to be. He built a tomb at Thebes in the valley of the Tombs of the Kings (No. 10), and he and his mother and wife were buried in it; the tomb consists of three corridors, the first of which has a small chamber opening out of it, and two chambers, the second having in it four square pillars. The first chamber contains scenes in which his mother is making offerings to the gods, and the second scenes in which his wife is making adoration to various deities. Some of the pictures on the walls are also found among the series of vignettes which illustrate the text of the 17th chapter of the Theban Recension of the *Book of the Dead*.

Sa-Ptah
Ri-Khu-En-Setep-En-Ra, son of the Sun, Sa-Ptah-Mer-En-Ptah

Sa-Ptah, who was undoubtedly the successor of Amenmeses, appears to have owed his claim to the throne of Egypt to the fact of his marriage with the lady Ta-user, or Ta-usert. In an inscription at Sahal dated in the first year of the king's reign we see the Prince of Kush called Seti, kneeling in adoration before cartouches of the king, and a scene at Aswan represents the king seated upon his throne with this same Seti, who is described as a 'royal scribe, fanbearer on the right hand of the king, steward of the palace', etc., standing before him. Behind him is the chancellor Ra-meses-kha-em-neteru-Bai, who declares that he 'set the king upon the throne of his father', and from this statement some have argued that this official was the chief instrument that raised Sa-Ptah to the throne of Egypt.

The Horus name of Sa-Ptah is of interest, and we must read it 'Horus rising in Khebit', i.e., the north land, which proves that the allusion is to the god Horus whom his mother Isis reared among the papyrus swamps round the city of Per-Uatchet, or Buto, in the Delta, and not to the actual birthplace of the king. We thus see that Sa-Ptah reproduces as his Horus name the words which Thothmes III applied to himself some hundreds of years before.

The exact length of the reign of Sa-Ptah is unknown. An inscription, found by Major Lyons in the temple of Thothmes III at Wadi Halfa in 1893, mentions his sixth year, and another in the same place mentions a 'royal envoy' or 'king's messenger' to Syria and Nubia, from which we may perhaps assume that some communication was kept up between the kings of Syria, and the shekhs of Nubia, but that Sa-Ptah assumed any right of rule over these countries is extremely doubtful. The 'royal son of Kush' as a permanent official in Nubia could make the Nubian tribes bring gifts, but that is all.

Sa-Ptah seems to have added nothing to the great temples of Egypt, and though he is depicted in reliefs at Silsila and at other places adoring the gods Amen, Ptah, Sekhet and Nefer-Temu, such scenes are probably only commemorative of small repairs which he carried out. The king does not seem to have built a tomb for himself in the Valley of the Tombs of the Kings at Thebes, and we must assume that his mummy was buried in the tomb of his wife Ta-usert; but it was removed during the disturbed times of the Twentieth Dynasty for safety to the tomb of Amenhetep II, for it was found there early in 1898.

The tomb of Queen Ta-usert (No. 14) was made on the plan usually adopted by royal personages, and consisted of three or four corridors and a number of rectangular chambers, the largest of which contained eight square pillars. The walls of the chambers were decorated with scenes representing the queen in adoration before various gods, and with texts from Chapters cxlv, clvi, clvii, clviii, etc., of the *Book of the Dead*. The tomb was usurped by Set-nekht, who plastered over most of the portraits of the queen which were on the walls, and who caused his own portrait to be drawn on the new plaster, together with his cartouches, titles, etc. The remains of the funeral temples of Ta-usert and Sa-Ptah were excavated by Professor Petrie in 1890, and the evidence which he obtained by deduction from the foundation deposits apparently supports that which had been long ago obtained from the inscription of Ra-meses-kha-em-neteru-Bai at Aswan.

The temple of Ta-usert was situated between those of Mer-en-Ptah and Thothmes IV; the temple of Sa-Ptah lies to the north of the temple of Amenhetep II. Many of the foundation deposits and sandstone blocks are inscribed with the names and titles of the king, and many with those of the great chancellor who 'put an end to iniquity', and raised Sa-Ptah to the throne of Egypt. With the death of Sa-Ptah the Nineteenth Dynasty came to an end, and there seemed to be no man who had the power to take in his hands the sceptre of Egypt, which was once more falling into a state of lawlessness and anarchy. About this time a Syrian called Arsu, of whom more will be said later, succeeded in making himself master of a portion of Syria and Egypt, and he compelled several local chieftains to acknowledge his authority and to pay him tribute; but for how long he continued to exercise his illegal authority cannot be said.

The Twentieth Dynasty

☥

Set-nekht
Ra-Usr-Khau-Ra-Setep-En-Amen-Meri, son of the Sun, Set-Nekht-Merer-Ra-Merer-Amen

SA-PTAH WAS SUCCEEDED BY A KING called Set-nekht, or Nekht-Set, who seems to have been a relative, or connection by marriage, of Rameses II, but we have no evidence which will show how close that relationship or connection was. His reign must have been very short, and it is probable that Set-nekht was obliged to spend several years in conflict with the Syrian usurper Arsu and with his own relatives who, like himself, were descended from the great kings of the Ninth Dynasty, before he could consider himself the actual ruler of Egypt. We find that he adopted a Horus name, but on account of the absence of inscriptions dating from his period we are unable to say what other titles he bestowed upon himself.

Our knowledge of the condition of the country when he ascended the throne is derived from the great papyrus written by order of Rameses III, wherein we read:

> 'The land of Qemt (i.e., Egypt) had fallen into a state of ruin, and every man did that which it seemed right for him to do, and for very many years the people had no chief governor (literally, 'upper mouth') who was able to maintain dominion over the others. The land of Egypt was in the hands of the governors of the nomes, and among the nobles and lords of the land one killed the other [as he pleased]. There came a period after that of years of want and great misery, and Arsu the

Syrian made himself prince over them. He placed the whole country under tribute to him, and each man gathered whatsoever he could for himself, and plundered the property of others, and they treated the gods in this manner likewise as well as men, and the sacrifices which ought to have been made to the gods in the temples according to law were never offered up at all. Then the gods overthrew these men and brought peace into the country, and they made the country to be what it ought to be, and fashioned it according to what was right. And they stablished their son who had proceeded from their members to be the Prince (Life, Strength, Health!) of every land which was under their throne, Ra-usr-khau-setep-en-Ra-meri-Amen, son of the Sun, Set-nekht-merer-Ra-merer-Amen. And he became like Khepera-Set when he burneth with wrath and rageth, and he provided with all things the land which was in a condition of revolt and misery, he slew all those who were disloyal in the Land of the Inundation (i.e., Egypt), and he purified the great throne of Egypt. He became the sovereign Prince of the two lands upon the throne of the god Tem. He gave himself to the reconstruction of the things which had fallen into a state of decay, and at length every man regarded as his brethren those who had been divided from him as by a wall. He stablished the temples, and provided them with divine offerings, and men made the offerings which they ought to make unto the company of the gods according to their ordinances.'

As soon as Set-nekht, or Nekht-Set, had established himself on the throne he appears to have associated his son Rameses III with him in the rule of the country. A proof of this is supplied by a scene at Medinet Habu, where over a door are seen figures of two kings kneeling, one on each side of the sun's disk resting on the horizon; the cartouches on one side are those of Set-nekht, and the cartouches on the other are those of Rameses III. Of the building operations of Set-nekht we know nothing, but it is probable that he carried out a few pressing repairs, for his name has been found at Memphis and Karnak. The king was mummified, and was probably buried in the tomb of the queen Ta-usert, which he usurped, but if M. Loret is to be relied upon, his mummy must have been removed from it in the unsettled times of the

Twentieth Dynasty to the tomb of Amenhetep II, which was found by him early in 1898.

Some think that the tomb of Rameses III in the Valley of the Tombs of the Kings at Thebes was begun by Set-nekht, for the name of this king can be distinctly traced in several places in the first three chambers. When Set-nekht died his own tomb was not finished, and his relatives seized the tomb of Ta-usert, and enlarged it by adding a corridor, and a large chamber with eight square pillars, and four small side chambers, and a sanctuary or niche for his statue at the end of it. The portraits of the queen in the entrance rooms were plastered over and the king's portrait put in their places, but the whole work was so hastily executed that those who carried it out had not the time to make the necessary alterations in the grammatical construction, etc., in the hieroglyphic texts which were rendered imperative by making them apply to a man instead of a woman. We may note, before passing to the consideration of the reign of Set-nekht's great son Rameses III, that Prof. Wiedemann thinks the Exodus of the Israelites from Egypt is far more likely to have taken place in the period which followed the rule of Seti II than under Menephthah, because the condition of the country, with its lack of a central government and with uprisings on every side, was far more favourable to the flight of the children of Israel immediately after the death of Seti II than earlier.

Rameses III
Ra-Usr-Maat-Mer-Amen, son of the Sun, Ra-Meses-Heq-An

Ra-Messu III or Rameses III, the Rhampsinitus of Herodotus, was the son of Set-nekht, with whom, for a short period, he had been associated in the government of the country. His Horus names were, 'Mighty Bull, great one of kings', and 'Mighty Bull, beloved of Maat, stablisher of the lands'; and he styled himself, 'Lord of the shrines of Nekhebet and Uatchet, mighty one of festivals, like Ta-Thenen, the Horus of gold, mighty one of years, prince, protector of Egypt, vanquisher of foreign lands, victor over the Sati (Asiatics), subduer of the Libyans, enlarger of Egypt', etc.

The youth of Rameses III must have been passed amid scenes of revolt and bloodshed, for in the summary of his reign given by him in the great Harris

Papyrus, the few lines of text which describe his accession are followed at once by a summary of two or three of his great wars which he waged against the Libyan tribes and their allies.

Of himself he says, 'He (i.e., his father Set-nekht) appointed me to be the *erpat* (or, hereditary chief) on the throne of Seb, and I became the great chief mouth of the lands of Qemt, and ruler of the whole country, everywhere alike.... Father Amen, the lord of the gods, and Ra and Tem, and Ptah of the Beautiful Face made me to rise up as lord of the two lands upon the seat of my begetter, and I received the rank of my father with cries of joy, and the whole country was content thereat, and it was pleased, and rejoiced and was glad to see me the Ruler of the two lands even as Horus ruleth the two lands from the throne of Osiris. I was crowned with the Atef crown and the uraei. I fastened upon myself the crown with the double plumes like Ta-tenen, and I seated myself upon the throne of Heru-khuti, being arrayed in the decorated apparel of royalty like Tem.'

In the line which follow these words among hostile peoples are enumerated: Shairetana; the Qehaqu; the Taanaunau from their islands; the Tchakireu; the Puirsathau; the Uasheshu of the sea; the Sasaireu; the Shasu; the Rebu, or Lebumer; the Mashuaashan; the Sabatau; the Qaiqashau; the Shaiu; the Hasan; the Bakanau and other Libyan tribes. The tribes here mentioned and their allies seem to have been preparing for war for some years before they ventured to make a great attack upon Egypt, and it appears that Rameses III made no attempt to check their preparations, whilst he was himself making ready an army of sufficient size and strength to make the victory of the Egyptians certain. The enemy, however, was strong, and had the practical sympathy not only of the tribes which were akin to him, but also of the dwellers in the Delta, and in the land which lay between Egypt and Syria.

In the fifth year of Rameses III the allied forces attacked Egypt under the leadership of Tit, Mashaken, Mareaiu and Tchamare, but their hosts were defeated, and they had the mortification of seeing about 12,000 of their dead warriors mutilated. Large numbers of prisoners were taken, and Rameses III tells us that he made many of them enter his service, and that when he had done so he garrisoned some of the larger cities of Egypt with them.

Three years later, i.e., in the eighth year of his reign, an invasion of Egypt on its north-east frontier was threatened by the allied armies of a number of nations and tribes, among whom were the Puirsatha or Philistines, and peoples from Crete and Cyprus and from the northern shores of the Mediterranean, who arranged their plan of attack in such a way that the invaders of Egyptian territory by sea might be assisted by their allies on land. Among the allies on land were many nations which had formerly been numbered with the Kheta, but which, owing either to the weakness of the central government in Northern Syria or to its entire overthrow, had been drawn into the league of the Mediterranean sea robbers, and so once again appeared as the foes of Egypt.

Rameses III collected his ships and his soldiers, and when all was ready he left Egypt, and passing through the famous frontier fortress of Tchar, made his way into Palestine; we may assume that his soldiers who were in the ships were never very far from his soldiers on land, and that their movements were always carefully regulated. At length the combatants met, and a fierce fight took place between them; the site of the battlefield is unknown, but it cannot have been situated many days' march from the fortress Tchar, and it is most probable that the battle was actually fought in Palestine. The Egyptians, thanks to the mercenaries, were victorious, and though the enemy appear to have fought with great bravery, they yielded by degrees and at length took to flight, and tried to reach their vessels, which seem to have been drawn up on the seashore. They were followed by the Egyptians, who pursued them with vigour, and when the foe arrived at the coast and attempted to escape in their ships they found their course blocked by the ships of the Egyptian navy, and they were thus caught between two fires; the allies dwelling on the Mediterranean coasts and the robbers on the high seas were completely defeated, and large numbers of them were killed or taken prisoners.

The Egyptian annalist naturally magnifies this sea fight in which his countrymen were so signally victorious, and rightly so, because the victory was all-important to the Egyptians; had the enemy escaped in the ships of their allies they would have been free to repeat the exploits of their predecessors in the reign of Amenhetep IV, which resulted in the downfall of the Egyptian power in Syria. Rameses III having thus disposed of the enemy in Palestine marched up into Syria, and passing through the provinces which had once been in the possession of Egypt, attempted to make the people acknowledge his sovereignty, and also to pay him tribute as their ancestors had paid tribute to the kings of Egypt in the days of old. His attempt was not, apparently, very successful, if we may judge by the destruction which he wrought in the country, for he cut down the fruit trees, and set fire to the standing corn, and laid waste whole villages, and looted and plundered in true Oriental fashion.

When Rameses III returned to Egypt laden with spoil, the people probably thought that there was to be a revival of the annual campaigns which had formed such a prominent feature of the reigns of the great kings of the Twenty-Eighth Dynasty, but if they did they were mistaken, for both in the sea fight and in the raid which followed it, the Egyptians knew well that they had only saved themselves by the greatest good fortune, and that henceforth Egypt would have to guard herself with the utmost diligence if she intended to keep even the line of frontier fortresses in her own possession.

Rameses III, having returned to Egypt, devoted himself to the work of building a palace and other edifices at Thebes, but before they were finished the peace of Egypt was again disturbed by the Libyans, who made a second attack upon the country under the leadership of Kapur and his son Mashashare, chiefs of the Mashauasha tribe. Rameses III marched out to meet his foes, who had assembled in very large numbers, and if we may believe the Egyptian annalist it was the individual acts of bravery on the part of the king which won him the day. The gods Bar and Menthu seemed to have taken up their abode in the body of the king – for he was as terrible as they in battle, and the enemy believed that they had a supernatural being to contend with.

The Libyans 'were surrounded by fire and their bones were burned to powder in their flesh; they marched on the land as if they had been marching to the place of slaughter; their hosts were massacred where they were, their mouths were shut forever, and they fell down at a blow. Their captains who marched in front of them were tied together like birds before the hawk which darts upon them from his hiding place within the wood. The soul of the enemy said for the second time that they would pass their lives on the frontiers of Egypt, and that they would till the valleys and plains thereof as their own possessions. But death came upon them in Egypt, and on their own feet they entered into the furnace which burneth up filth, and into the fire of the bravery of the king who raged at them like Bar from the heights of heaven. All his limbs were endowed with the might of victory; with his right hand he seized the multitudes, and his left stretched itself out over those who were in front of him and was like arrows against them to destroy them; his sword cut like that of his father Menthu. Kapure, who had come to receive the adoration [of the king], was like a blind man, and cast his weapons down upon the ground, and his army did likewise; he uttered a cry for mercy which went up to the heights of heaven, and his son stopped his foot and his hand.... His Majesty fell upon their heads like a granite mountain, and he crushed them utterly, and mixed the earth with their blood which ran down like water. The soldiers were slaughtered, and their warriors slain; [others] were captured and beaten, and their arms were tied together like the wings of geese on a boat beneath the feet of his Majesty. The king was like unto the god Menthu, and his victorious feet rested upon the head of the enemy, whose chiefs were smitten and held fast within his hand. The enemy fell at the feet of his Majesty, and his captains, and his allies, and his soldiers were lost. His eyes were smitten as if he had looked upon the form of the Sun, and his warriors came quickly leading their children and carrying gifts in their hands to make themselves the prisoners of his Majesty.... The lord of Egypt was [as] the fire of the goddess Sekhet among them, and he destroyed their hearts, and their bones were burned to powder in their bodies. All the country rejoiced to see the valour of Rameses [III]. The enemy said, "We have heard of the plans of the fathers of our fathers, and the breaking of our backs by Egypt hath arisen through them; we put ourselves in revolt, and we imagined that we could do what we pleased, and we ran at our own instigation to seek the flame. The Libyans have troubled us even as they troubled themselves; we have listened to their thoughts and the fire hath burned us up; we have sinned, and we have been punished for all eternity. Their offence was to see the frontiers of Egypt, and Menthu with the victorious arms who delighteth in battle, Rameses [III] hath made them to enter into the underworld." The country of the Mashauasha hath been smitten down at a blow, and their friends the Libyans have been slaughtered, and they shall never reap again.'

Setting aside all these high-flown descriptions of the prowess of Rameses III, it is clear that the Egyptians gained what they well believed to be a great victory, and that they took great booty from the vanquished. They captured 342 women, 65 young women, 151 girls, the commander-in-chief of the Mashauasha, five generals, 1,205 men, 152 petty officers and 131 young men; and 2,175 of the Mashauasha were slain by his Majesty. Among the spoil carried off by the Egyptians were 115 swords five cubits long, 124 swords three cubits long, 603 bows, 93 chariots, 2,310 quivers, 92 spearheads, 183 horses and asses, and large numbers of cattle.

Rameses III was now master of the countries on both sides of the Delta, and he was able to resume his building operations, and to carry out at his leisure various schemes in connection with the development of trade between Egypt and the neighbouring nations, for the only other expedition which he undertook after the defeat of the Libyans was directed against the people called Saaire. The Saaire are described as belonging to the 'tribes of the Shasu', and are thought to have lived on and about Mount Seir, and ... they may well have been Edomites.

Some have thought that, because Rameses III included the names of certain Nubian countries in the lists of conquered lands which were inscribed upon his temples, he waged wars in Nubia, but this does not follow, for many of his lists are palpable copies of those of his ancestors, and there is very good reason for doubting the historical character of many parts of them. If it be remembered that, according to the Egyptian evidence, fewer than 2,500 Libyans were killed in the great battle of Rameses III against the Libyans and their allies, and that fewer than 2,500 were taken prisoners, we shall be able to estimate at their true worth the boastful rejoicings, which, when translated into words, he allowed to be inscribed on the walls of his temples. The punishment which Mer-en-Ptah inflicted upon the Libyans was much more severe, and there is little doubt that Rameses III wished fervently that his predecessor had followed up his advantage and pursued the Libyan king until he had caught him and killed him.

The last few pages of the great Papyrus of Rameses III supply us with some valuable information concerning the works which were carried on by the king, both architectural and mining, and we find that for purposes of trade he built a large well, in the country of Aaina, i.e., a district between Mount

Casius and Raphia on the road from Egypt to Syria, which he surrounded with a strong building 20 cubits square (?) and 30 cubits high. The object of this fortified well was, of course, that the royal caravans which passed that way from Syria into Egypt might be certain of always finding water for their camels there. Rameses III next built a fleet of large boats, which he provided with crews, among whom were numbers of bowmen, and he directed them to trade on the Phoenician coast; it seems, too, that the same fleet, or at any rate a part of it, went to the land of Punt, to the south of the Red Sea, for the king declares that his ships returned laden with all the marvellous products of the country or region called Neter-taui, and that they unloaded at the mountain of Qebti, or Coptos, i.e., at some port near Kuser. We may then conclude that one fleet was kept in Mediterranean waters and another in the Red Sea.

The copper industry of the Sinaitic Peninsula was, apparently, re-started by Rameses III, and envoys were sent from Egypt to work the copper mines of Aathaka, i.e., the Gebel Ataka of the Arab authors, and the metal in ingots was brought in ships to the port for Egypt in the Red Sea, and then loaded on asses and so carried by way of the Wadi Hammamat into Upper Egypt. Other officers were sent to work the turquoise mines in the Sinaitic Peninsula, *Mafek,* and large numbers of fine genuine stones were carried to the king in Egypt. The greatest efforts were made by Rameses III to ensure the success of his trading expeditions, and all his care seems to have been devoted to the development of new markets and the maintenance of the old ones. The mercenaries who were scattered throughout Egypt maintained peace, and as long as their wages were paid, and they were allowed to lead a life of comparative ease they were faithful enough; their presence was now all-important to the Egyptians because it prevented the Shasu and the Rebu, or Libyans, from renewing their attacks on the country.

The latter part of the reign of Rameses III was an era of peace and plenty, and of great mercantile success, and the merchant princes of Punt and Syria feared not to come to Egypt with their wares because they knew that Egypt was no longer a sovereign country bent on conquest, but a land ruled by a king whose aim was the prosecution of successful commercial enterprise. The king says, 'I made the whole country to be covered with blossom-bearing trees, and I made all the people to sit down (or, dwell) beneath their shade.

I made it possible for an Egyptian woman to walk with a bold and free step whithersoever she pleased, and no man or woman among the people of the land would molest her. In my time I made the cavalry and the bowmen of the Shairetana and Qehaq to dwell in their towns, and to lie down stretched out at full length on their backs, and they were not afraid, because there was no fighting with Kush, nor with the Syrian foes. Their bows and their weapons or war were laid up inside their guard-houses, and they were filled with meat and drink which they partook of with rejoicings, and their wives and their children were with them, and they looked not behind them because their hearts were glad.' And in conclusion the king says that he gave entire freedom to gentle and simple, and to rich and poor, that he pardoned the malefactor and relieved the oppressed, and that he did that which was good both to gods and to men. The facts of the history of the reign of Rameses III bear out the general accuracy of the above description of the state of the country, and it is easy to understand the rapidity with which Egypt lost her position of power among the nations after the death of Rameses III.

Among the numerous buildings of Rameses III must be specially mentioned the so-called 'Pavilion of Rameses III' and the Great Temple which he erected at Medinet Habu. The pavilion represents an attempt to reproduce in Egypt a small fort or strong city similar to the forts in use among the people of Northern Syria. It consisted of two rectangular towers about 22 metres (72 feet) high and eight metres (26 feet) wide; the walls behind them open out and form a small court, but they soon contract, and come close together until finally the two wings of the building unite. On the south tower are sculptures in which the king is represented clubbing his enemies, i.e., the Ethiopians and the Libyans who live on the west bank of the Nile, and the chiefs of the Tulsha, or Tursha, and Mashauasha. Some of the chiefs here represented have the features of negroes, but the chief of the Mashauasha somewhat resembles a Semite. On the north tower are represented the chiefs of Asiatic and Mediterranean peoples, among them being the 'vile prince of Kheta, the vile prince of Amare', or Amaur, and the chiefs of the tribes of the Tchakaire, of the Shairetana of the sea, of the Shakalasha, of the Thuirsha of the sea, and of the Pulastha, or Philistines. In the space between the two towers are scenes in which the king is depicted in the act of worshipping the gods Anher-Shu, Tefnut, Temu, Iusaaset, Ptah,

Sekhet, Thoth and other gods. The walls of the upper rooms, which are entered by a staircase in the south tower, are decorated with reliefs in which the king is surrounded by a number of women who fan him or play the tambourine, and who bring him flowers and fruit and drink, etc.; in some reliefs the king is seated and is playing draughts with a naked woman who stands on the other side of the table which supports the draught board.

The meaning of these scenes has been much discussed, and many writers have thought it proved by them that this portion of the building was used as a palace by the king, but as M. Daressy has said, the rooms are far too small ever to have been employed as a dwelling place by Rameses III and his train. The palace of Amenhetep III at Birket Habu and of his son Amenhetep IV at Khut-Aten, or Tell el-'Amarna, prove that the palaces of Egyptian kings consisted of large one-storied buildings, made of unbaked brick, which contained a great number of rooms wherein the only luxury apparent was in the decorations which adorned the walls. As there are no inscriptions with the reliefs we cannot say who the ladies with the king are, but some of them appear to be of royal rank, although the queen is not among them. M. Daressy is inclined to think that this portion of the building was used as a place where the king's daughters were educated under the care of priestesses, but, on the other hand, it may have been the abode of the servants of the god Amen, to which the king only, as the incarnation of the god Amen on earth, had access.

The Great Temple of Rameses III was built by the king to commemorate himself, and it is, perhaps, the most interesting of all the funerary chapels on the Nile at Thebes; it measures 152 metres (500 feet) by 48 metres (160 feet), and its walls were ornamented with scenes, reliefs and texts illustrating the campaigns of the king. On the lower parts of the towers of the first pylon the reliefs represent the king clubbing a number of representatives of vanquished peoples, and near these are 86 captives, arranged in two rows, with their names enclosed within ovals on their bodies. The types of features of these captives are Semitic, Northern Syrian and Negro, but it is clear that the arrangement of the faces is an artificial one and it does not follow that the features of any captive necessarily represent those which are suggested by the name on his body. The list of names is made up of portions of the lists of nations conquered by Thothmes III, Seti I, and Rameses II, and is of little value for purely historical purposes. The peoples represented are from Syria, Phoenicia, Cyprus, Libya, Kush, etc., and the accompanying text describes in boastful language the king's victory over the Libyans.

In the first court are reliefs which describe his battle with the Libyans in the 11th year of his reign, and texts which describe the chief events in it and give the amount of spoil taken; in this court are seven rectangular pillars, in the front of each of which was a statue of the god Osiris, about six metres (20 feet) high. In the second court are reliefs which depict the defeat of the Mediterranean peoples and of their allies from Northern Syria. A great deal of damage was done to the temple by the earthquake which took place 27 BCE, and this is not to be wondered at when we remember that the foundations of the temple are only 2 metres (six feet) deep, and that they rest upon a bed of sand. At Karnak Rameses III built a temple in honour of the god Khensu, the third member of the Theban triad, but the greater part of its decoration was completed by Rameses IV and by others of his successors; he also built a small temple near the great temple of the goddess Mut.

At Tell el-Yahudiyeh, i.e., the Mound of the Jewess, Rameses III built a small palace which contained a chamber lined with beautifully glazed tiles ornamented with floral designs, and figures of birds, and animals and representatives of foreign conquered tribes and nations; a large number of the finest examples of these tiles were acquired by the British Museum through the exertions of the late Rev. Greville J. Chester, B.A., and they form one of the most interesting groups of the objects in faience exhibited in that institution. That Tell el-Yahudihey represents the site of the temple which Onias, the high-priest of the Jews, built at Onion in the reign of Ptolemy Philometor I seems clear enough, but it is not so evident what ancient Egyptian city once stood there. Some have thought that the site is that of the city of Heliopolis, but this seems hardly possible; there may, however, have been a northern and a southern part of the city which were called 'Annu Meht' and 'Annu Resu' respectively, especially as we learn from the great Papyrus of Rameses III that he built 'the palace of Rameses [III], prince of Annu, in the House of the Sun to the north of Aunu,' and that he called this palace 'the palace of millions of years of Rameses [III], prince of Annu'. The 'palace of millions of years' was dedicated to Ra-Harmachis, and this suggests at least that the site of the palace of Rameses III was in or near Heliopolis.

Many of the ancient temples of Egypt were either rebuilt or repaired by Rameses III, and his name is found upon their remains in many places between the Mediterranean Sea and Wadi Halfa. The temples, however, which he most favoured were those of Amen-Ra at Thebes, Temu at Heliopolis, and Ptah at Memphis, and the enumeration of the offerings which he made to the gods and of the gifts of gold, silver, copper, scented woods, precious stones, linen, perfumes, oil, incense, wine, bread, cakes, oxen, sheep, feathered fowl, fish, fruit, flowers, garden herbs, statues, etc., fills dozens of large sheets of papyrus.

An idea of the magnitude of his gifts may be gathered from the following figures: To the three gods he gave, besides other things, 2,756 images, 113,433 men, 490,386 oxen and cattle of various kinds, 1,071,780 *aruras* of land, 514 vineyards and orchards, 88 boats, 160 towns of Egypt, nine towns of Syria, 324,750 bundles of fodder, 71,000 bundles of flax, 426,965 water fowl, 1,075,635 rings, scarabs, etc., 2,382,650 sacks of fruit, 353,919 fat geese, 355,084 blocks of salt and natron, 6,272,431 loaves of bread, 490,000 fish, 19,130,032 measures of vegetables, 1,933,766 jars of honey, oil, etc., 48,236 images of Hapi, and 5,279,552 bushels of corn, etc. In Syria, Rameses III built a 'hidden temple, like unto the horizon of the heaven above' in the region called Pa-Karnina, which some identify with a city in Galilee, and others with the country of Canaan. This temple was dedicated to the Sun-god, and the Asiatics of Retennu, hastened to bring their offerings to it.

Rameses III built a magnificent tomb for himself in the Valley of the Tombs of the Kings, and though not as fine a piece of work as the tomb of Rameses II, it is certainly one of the largest and most interesting of all the royal tombs at Thebes. It is commonly known as the 'Tomb of the Harper', or, 'Bruce's Tomb'; the first name is given to it because it contains two famous scenes in which harpers are depicted playing harps before the gods An-her, Shu and Temu, and the second because it was discovered by the great traveller James Bruce (born December 14th, 1780; died 1794).

The tomb was begun by Set-nekht, the father of Rameses III, who hewed out the first three chambers, and in places where the plaster has fallen away his name may yet be read. It is about 122 metres (400 feet) in length and is remarkable for the side chambers which open off the corridors, two from the first and eight from the second. The walls of the chambers, etc., are ornamented with scenes in which the king is represented worshipping the gods, and with texts extracted from the *Book of praising Ra*, and from the *Book of that which is in the Underworld*, etc. The red granite monolithic sarcophagus of the king was found in the large hall with eight square pillars at the end of the tomb … it is covered inside and outside with scenes and inscriptions from the *Book of that which is in the Underworld*, and is now preserved in the museum of the Louvre at Paris. Its cover was brought to England by G. Belzoni (died at Gato in Benin, December 3rd, 1823), and was presented to the University of Cambridge in 1823; it was for many years allowed to lie exposed to the ill effects of the weather on the top of the steps of the Fitzwilliam Museum, Cambridge, but it is now inside the building itself.

The mummy of the king was found among the royal mummies brought from Der al-Bahari, and is now in the Egyptian Museum at Cairo. It had, in ancient times, been deposited in the coffin of Queen Nefertari, and was for some time regarded as her mummy; but when it was unrolled on June 1st, 1886, it was seen from the hieratic writing on the bandages that it was certainly the mummy of Rameses III, and that new linen bandages had been provided for it in the ninth year of the high-priest of Amen-Ra, Painetchem I, about 1100 BCE. According to M. Maspero, the features of Rameses III resemble those of his great ancestor Rameses II, but are somewhat softer, and finer and more intelligent; his figure, however, is less straight, the shoulders are narrower, and there is less vigour in it.

If Rameses III did not become one of the most powerful of the Theban heroes of Egypt, it was not due to any want of energy or ability on his part, but to the feebleness of the century in which he was born which prevented him from giving full play to his genius. To him, however, some credit is due, for when he ascended the throne of Egypt the country was impoverished, and was without soldiers and ships and money; on the west the Libyans had seized some of her possessions, and on the north-east her allied enemies were threatening an attack by sea. During the 32 years of his reign he built a fleet of war and merchant ships, and formed an army of natives and mercenaries, and re-established the commerce of Egypt on broad lines.

Towards the close of his reign a conspiracy was hatched by a number of the ladies of the court, who were helped by certain high officials, the object of which was to kill or depose the king and set in his place upon the throne of Egypt one Pen-ta-urt., the son of the royal concubine (?) Thi, who wished that her son should reign instead of one of the sons of the 'royal wife, the great lady, the lady of the two lands, Ast', whom she probably hated. Thi was joined by several ladies of the court, and she and they succeeded in corrupting Paibakakamen the steward, Mest-su-Ra the chancellor, Paanank the inspector, Pen-tuauu the scribe, and the officials Panifuemta-Amen, Karpusa, Kha-em-Apt, Kha-em-maa-en-re, Seti-em-pa-Tehuti, Seti-em-pa-Amen, Uarma, Ash-hebs-heb, Paka-Ra and Rebu-inini; beside these a number of other officials were also implicated in the conspiracy.

The lady Thi and her friends selected Paibakakamen the steward for their chief confidant, because his high position at court made him practically above suspicion, and he was free to go where he pleased and do what he liked without question. It was he who carried the details of the plot from Thi to the mothers and brothers of her sympathizers, and it was he who advised the officials who were his subordinates how to act. The downfall or death of the king was to be brought about by inciting the Egyptian troops stationed in Nubia to revolt and to attack Egypt, and by stirring up the people of Egypt themselves to rise at the moment of revolt, and to join the rebels in working the ruin of the existing government. The commander of the troops in Nubia was favourable to the plot, for his sister was one of the court malcontents, and she had won him over to the cause of Thi and her son Pen-ta-urt.

Not content with the means here described, the conspirators took into their service a certain cattle inspector called Hui, who had the reputation of being a great magician, and having obtained for him from the Royal Library at Thebes a book of magic, they directed him to do such things as would result in the death of the king and his friends. Hui made figures of men in wax and amulets which were inscribed with words of magical power, and these he introduced into the palace by means of a man whom he bewitched by his magic. The amulets were intended for the ladies in the conspiracy, who by means of them hoped to make themselves irresistible to the officials whom they wanted to win over to their side, but the wax figures seem to have been designed to work evil on the king. But in an evil hour for the conspirators the plot was revealed to the king, with the result that the ringleaders were at once arrested. Rameses appointed a commission of inquiry, and having told the members thereof to investigate the matter quickly and thoroughly, he ordered that those who were found guilty of death should commit suicide, and that those who were condemned to suffer punishments of a less serious nature should undergo them without his knowing anything about it. The king would give the members of the commission none of the information which had been communicated to him by the man who revealed the plot to him, for he wished the matter to be threshed out by the usual legal or illegal means employed in such cases.

The commission consisted of 11 judges, six of whom tried the officials who were connected with the court or *harim*, and whose offences were not considered to be sufficiently grave to warrant the sentence of death being passed upon them; the punishments inflicted by the court of six judges were probably beating with sticks on the back or feet, and slitting of the nose and ears. The court of five judges tried Pen-ta-tut, the son of Thi, and his friends the general of the bowmen in Ethiopia, certain scribes of the 'Double House of Life', a high-priest of the goddess Sekhet, Paibakakamen the steward, and others, and found them guilty of carrying out the plans of the lady Thi, and of inciting the soldiery and people to rebellion, and of having full knowledge of the conspiracy and of making no report on the same to the king. The commander-in-chief of Nubia seems to have escaped death, probably because his sister was a lady in the *harim*, but all the ringleaders were sentenced to death, which they were compelled to suffer by their own hands; and 40 men and six women seem to have been executed.

Concerning the would-be king, Pen-ta-urt, it is said, 'Pen-ta-urt, who is also known by another name, was brought before the court and charged with complicity in the conspiracy which his mother Thi made with the women of the *harim*, and with acting in a manner hostile to his lord the king; having been examined by the officers of the court the judges found him guilty, and they sent him away to his house where he took his own life.' Towards the end of the case against the ordinary officials of the *harim*, it was found that three of the six judges who were trying them had been concerned in the plot, and they were degraded and tried forthwith and eventually sentenced to death. It is interesting to note that certain of the criminals who were of high rank, and who were probably nearly related to the king, were allowed to commit suicide, or at least choose their own manner of death, in their own houses, in order that their families might be spared the disgrace which would necessarily attach itself to death at the hands of the common executioner.

By what manner of death Pen-ta-urt died cannot be said, but it was probably by poison. Among the mummies which M. Maspero found at Der al-Bahari was one which may well be that of Pen-ta-urt; it was enclosed in a simple, uninscribed coffin painted white, and it is evident that the body was not prepared in any way before it was turned into a mummy, for it was laid in a thick layer of linen and then swathed. The hands and the feet are tied together with strong bandages, the hands being clenched and the feet drawn up as if under the influence of some terrible pain; the abdomen has collapsed, the chest and stomach are thrust forward, the head is thrown back, and the lips are drawn tightly away from the teeth. M. Maspero is of opinion that the deceased was bandaged alive, but the appearance of the body rather suggests that he died in great agony from the result of some strong irritant poison, and that the bandaging was done after *rigor mortis* had set in. But whatever the cause of death, the man must have been of royal rank, otherwise he would not have been found with the other royal mummies at Der al-Bahari.

From the great papyrus of Rameses III we learn that this king assembled the nobles of his kingdom in solemn conclave in the 32nd year of his reign, and associated his son with him in the rule of the kingdom; it seems that the joint rule of father and son lasted for four years. The chief wife of Rameses III was called Ast, but it appears that she had also another name; her father's name was Hu-bunu-re-tchanth. The sons of Rameses III were called after the names of the sons of Rameses II, e.g., Pa-Ra-her-unami-f, Menthu-her-khepesh-f, Meri-Tem, Kha-em-Uast, Amen-her-khepesh-f, Ra-meses-meri-Amen, etc. As might be expected, tradition as preserved by Greek writers busied itself with the name and deeds of Rameses III, and it is interesting to note how the common facts of his history became distorted in the hands of authors who repeated popular accounts of him, and who added to or altered them to suit their individual views and fancies.

According to Herodotus, Rameses III, or as he calls him Rhampsinitus, was the son of Proteus, the successor of Pheron, the successor of Sesostris, and of him he relates the following:

> 'After the deceasse of Protheus, Rampsinitus tooke uppon hym
> the rule of the countrey, who in memorie of hirnselfe, lefte behynde

hym certayne porches of stone, planted westward agaynst the temple of Vulcane right ouer agaynst the whych, stoode two images fyue and twentye cubites in length. One of the which standyng northerly, they call sommer, and the other lying to the west, they tearme winter, contrary to all reason and order. This King in aboundance of wealth, and plenty of coyne so farre excelled all those that came after hym, that none coulde go beyonde him, no not approch neere unto hym in that kynde: wherefore desirous to possesse hys goodes in safetie, hee builte hym a treasurie or jewell-house of stone, one of the walles whereof bounded upon the outsyde of hys courte. In framing whereof, the workeman had wrought thys subtile conueyance, one stone in the wall hee layde in that forte, that a man might easily at pleasure plucke it in or out, which notwithstanding serued so fittingly to place, that nothing coulde be discerned. When the building was finished, the King caused his treasure to be brought into it, minding henceforth to be secure and to lay aside all feare of misfortune. In processe of time, this cunning artificer lying at the poynt to dye, called unto him his two sonnes, and disclosed unto them in what manner he had prouided for theyr good estate, in leauing a secret and most priuy passage into the King's treasurie, whereby theyr whole lyfe might be lead in most happy and blessed condition. In briefe, he shewed them all that was done by hym, delyuering them the just measures of the stone, that they mighte not bee deceyued in laying it agayne, whych the two young youthes well marking, thought from that tyme forwarde to be of the Kings counsayle, if not of hys court, and to become the priuy surueyers of hys jewell-house. Theyr father beeing dead, they made no long delay to put in execution theyr determinate purpose, but repayring to the court by night, they found the stone, which with small force reinoouing it from the place, they sped themselues wyth plentie of coyne, and so departed. In shorte space after the King entering hys treasurie, and fyndyng the vessels wherein hys money lay to be somewhat decreased, was exceedingly amazed, not knowing whome to accuse, seeyng both hys seales whyche he had set on the dore, untouched, and the dore fast locked at hys commyng thyther. Howbeit, repayring sundrie tymes to beholde hys wealth, and euermore perceyuing that it grewe lesse and

*lesse, deuised with hymselfe to beset the place where hys money lay
with certayne greens or snares to entrappe the theefe in. These subtile
merchaunts accordying to theyr former wont approching the spring
head where they had dronke so oft before, one of them went in, and
groaping for the money, was so fast intangled in a snare, that for hys
lyfe hee wist not how to shifte, but seeyng hymselfe in these braakes,
hee called hys brother, to whome he disclosed his euill happe, willing
hym in any wise to cut off hys head, least beeyng knowne who hee
was, they both myght bee serued with the same sauce. His brother
hearing hys counsayle to be good, did as he bade hym, and fitly
placing the stone as hee founde it, departed home, bearyng with hym
the head of hys slayne brother. The nexte day the King opening hys
jewell-house, and espying an headlesse theefe surprized in a ginne,
was wonderfully astonied, seeing euery place safe, and no way in the
world to come in or out at. In this quandary, uncertaine what to
thynke of so straunge an euent, he deuised yet to go another way to the
wood, causing the body of the theefe to be hanged out uppon the walles
in open view to all that passed by, appoynting certayne to attend in
that place, with straight charge, that if they hearde any making moane
or lamentation at the sighte thereof, they shoulde foorthwyth attache
them, and bryng them to the Kyng. The Mother of these two Brethren
not able wyth patiente eyes to beholde the wretched carkasse of her
pitifull sonne, called the other brother unto her, aduising him by some
meanes or other, to take awaye his brothers body and burie it,
threatening moreouer, that in case he neglected to accomplishe it
wyth speede, shee woulde open all hys thefte and treacherie to the
Kyng. Whome her sonne endeuouring wyth many woordes to
persuade, and nought auayling (so tender was her affection towardes
her childe) hee set hys wittes abroache to the framing of some subtyle
concepte, to beguyle and inueigle the Kyngs watchemen. Pannelling
sertayne Asses whyche hee loaded wyth bottels of sweete wyne, hee
proceeded forwarde wyth hys carryage, tyll suche tyme as hee came
agaynste the place where the watche laye, where priuily unstopping
one or two of hys bottles, the wyne flowed out in greate aboundance,
whereat, fayning as though hee had beene besydes hymselfe, hee*

piteously cryed out, tearing hys hayre add (sic) stainpyng as one bitterlye ignoraunte whyche to remedye fyrste. The keepers seeyng the wyne gushe out so fast, ranne hastely wyth pottes and cannes to receyue it least all should bee lost, but the dryuer (who had alreadye cast hys plotte) seemed heereat muche more inraged than before, tauntyng and raylyng at them wyth most bitter and reuiling woordes. Contraryly, the watchmen geuing him very fayre and gentle language, hee seemed better contented, leadyng asyde hys Asses out of the way to newe girde them, and place his carriage in better order. Manye woordes grewe betweene thein whyles he was addressing hys Asses to proceede on theyr waye, till that one of them bolting foorth a merry iest, caused hym to laugh hartily, so that lyke a good fellowe, he bestowed amongst them a bottle of wyne, which courtesie they all tooke in very good parte, requesting hym to sitte wyth them for companye, and drinke parte of hys owne cost. Whereto bee willingly consenting, they dranke a carouse, every man hys cannikin, tyll the wyne began to runne of the lyes, whyche thys coapesmate perceyuing, set abroach another bottle, and began to quaffe afreshe, whyche set my keepers in such a tantarra, that beeyng well wetted, they set more by three drainmes of sleepe, than syxe ounces of witte. When all was hushe, and the watchmen fast asleepe, hee tooke the bodye of hys brother, and in mockage, shauing off the hayre of theyr right cheekes, he returned home, beyng right gladly enterteyned of hys mother. The Kyng seeyng hys deuises no better to proceede, but for ought he coulde imagine the theefe still beguyled hym, waxed woonderous wrath: howbeit, determining to leave nothing unattempted, rather then to let such a villayne escape scot free, he built yet another trappe to catch the foxe in. He had at that time abiding in hys courte a goodly gentlewoman, his onely daughter, whome he tenderly loued from her childhood. This Lady he made of his counsayle, willing her by the duety of a chylde, to abandon chastity for the time, making hirselfe a common stalant for all that would come, on condition they shoulde sweare to tell her the subtilest and the sinfullest prancke that ever they had played in all theyr lyfe tyme, and who so confessed the facts lately atchieued in imbesileing the Kings treasure, and stealing away the theefe, him to lay hold on, and not suffer to depart. The gentlewoman obeying her fathers will, kepte open house, having a greate repayre unto her out of all partes of the countrey. Now the theefe whyche knewe full well to what intente the Kyng had done thys, desirous to bee at oast wyth hys daughter for a nighte, and fearing the daunger that myghte ensue, beeyng of a verie pregnaunt and readie witte, deuised yet another shifte wherewythall to delude the Kyng: he strake off the hande of hys brother that was dead, and closely carying it under his cloake, he repayred to the place where the Kings daughter lay, who demaunding hym the question as she had done the rest, receyued of him this aunswere, that the sinfullest acte that ever he committed, was to cut off his brothers head, being inueigled in a snare in the Kings treasurie, but the subtilest in that he had deceyued a fort of dronken asses, whome the King had appoynted to watch the body. The Lady that had listned to his tale, hearing the newes she longed for, stretched out her hand to lay hold on him, who subtilly presenting her with the hand of his brother (which beeing darke, she fast gripped instead of his owne), he conueyed himselfe from her and was no more seene. The King heereof aduertised, was stricken with so great admiration as well of his wit in deuisiug, as his boldnesse in aduenturing, that forthwith he caused notice to be geuen throughout all partes of his gouernement, that in case the party whiche had done these thinges woulde disclose himselfe, and stand to his mercy, he woulde not only yeeld him free pardon, but also indue and honour him with so princely rewards as were fit for a person of such excellent wisedome. My yonker yeelding credite to the Kings promise, came foorth in presence, and described himselfe, with whome Rampsinitus ioyning his daughter in marriage, did him the greatest honour he could deuise, esteeming him for the wisest man that liued upon the earth, holding it for certayne, that the Egyptians excelled all others in wisedom, amongst whome he judged none comparable to hym. The same King (say they) whiles he was yet liuing, trauelled so far under the ground, till he came to the place which the Graecians call the seates infernall, where he played at dyce with the goddesse Ceres, and sometimes winning, sometimes losing, he returned againe at length, being rewarded by her 'with a mantle of gold. In the meane space while Rampsinitus undertooke this voyage to hell, the Aegyptians kept holyday, prolonging the celebration till such time as he retyred backe againe, which solemne obseruance, since our memory hath been duely celebrated. But whether this be the cause of that sacred festiuall, I dare not anowe, howbeit, the priests shewed me a certayne cloake, wouen in the space of one daye, wherewith once a yeare they attyre some one of theyr petie vicares, blinding moreouer hys eyes wyth a myter. Beeing in thys sorte attyred, they conduct hym to the hyghway that leadeth to the temple of the goddesse Ceres, whereafter they haue placed hym, they leaue hym grabling in that place, and departe their waye. To whome incontinently resorte two wolues, conducting the priest to the temple aforesayde, whyche is distaunte from the city twentie furlongs, where hauing accomplished certayne rytes, the wolues leade hym backe agayne to the same place. All these thyngs they doubt not to reporte for certayne true, which we leaue to euery mans lyking to iudge of them as they deserue. For myne owne parte I haue thought it meete to make relation of such things as I heard amongst them, going no farther in many thyngs than hearesay.'

According to Diodorus when Proteus died, 'his son Remphis succeeded him, 'who spent all his time in filling his coffers, and heaping up wealth. The poorness of his spirit, and his sordid covetousness was such, that they would not suffer him to part with anything, either for the worship of the gods, or the good of mankind; and therefore, more like a good steward than a king, instead of a name for valour and noble acts he left vast heaps of treasure behind him, greater than any of the kings that ever were before him: for it is said he had a treasure of four hundred thousand talents of gold and silver.'

In confirmation of this statement may be mentioned the words of Herodotus, who says that in the reign of Rhampsinitus there was a perfect distribution of justice, and that all Egypt was in a high state of prosperity. This prosperity was the result of the successful trading which Rameses III carried on by means of his ships in the Mediterranean and Red Sea, and of the freedom which every merchant enjoyed in managing his own business in his own way.

Rameses IV
Ra-Usr-Maat-Setep-En-Amen, son of the Sun,
Ra-Meses-Meri-Amen-Ra-Heq-Maat

Ra-Meses IV, 'the prince of Maat, the beloved of Amen-Ra', was the son of Rameses III, and he was associated in the rule of the kingdom during the last four years of his father's life. His Horus name appears to have been, 'Mighty Bull, living in Maat, the lord of festivals, like [his] father Ptah-Tanen', and he styled himself 'Lord of the shrines of Nekhebet and Uatchet, protector of Egypt, smiter of the Nine Bows, the Horus of gold, mighty of years, great of strength, prince, child of the gods, who maketh the two lands to exist.' Rameses IV reckoned the years of his reign from the time when he became co-regent, but his reign as sole king of Egypt only lasted six or seven years.

On a stele published by Lepsius, it is stated that the Retennu, or people of Northern Syria, brought much tribute to him, but this must be the statement of a scribe who was also a courtier and who, perhaps unconsciously, exaggerated an affair of trade and barter into the payment of tribute. Rameses IV continued to work the mines in the Sinaitic Peninsula, hoping, no doubt, to draw therefrom as great revenues as those which his father obtained from them. The great event of his reign was an expedition into the Valley of Hammamat, i.e., Ant Rehennu, which seems to have been undertaken in the first instance for the purpose either of crushing a revolt among the quarrymen who worked at Bekhen, where the quarries were situated, or of driving out some nomad peoples from the valley. He could not have wished to work the quarries there, for not being engaged in great building operations he had no use for large quantities of stone.

An inscription at Hammamat dated in his third year, states that he ordered a road to be built through the valley from the Nile to the Red Sea, so that caravans might make their way through it with greater speed and safety; he also commanded that a temple to the goddess Isis should be built in a suitable part of it. The expedition consisted of a number of skilled mining engineers, with 130 quarrymen and masons, 5,000 soldiers with their officers, 2,000 of Pharaoh's workmen, 50 Matchaiu or police, a large number of scribes and other officials, and 800 of the Aperiu, who belonged to the tribes of the neighbourhood. The total number of men engaged in the expedition was 8,368, and 900 men died of hard work, disease or wounds between the time of its leaving Egypt and the time of its return. Provisions for the expedition were taken from Egypt in 10 carts or waggons, each of which was drawn by 12 oxen, and by large numbers of men who brought loads of bread, fish and garden produce; the work which the expedition was sent to perform was inaugurated or finished by a solemn feast, at which oxen and calves were sacrificed, incense burned, libations of wine poured out and songs of praise sung.

Rameses IV carried out certain small repairs at Memphis, Tell el-Yahudiyeh, Abydos and Karnak, his name being found on several buildings at this last-named place; as his prenomen was so much like that of Rameses II he was able to usurp the buildings of his great ancestor without much trouble. Rameses IV built a large tomb for himself in the Valley of the Tombs of the Kings at Thebes on a somewhat unusual plan. It is entered by a staircase with an inclined plane in the centre, made, probably, to enable the stone sarcophagus to be lowered easily into the tomb, and consists of three main corridors, six side chambers and the large hall which contains the granite sarcophagus. The walls are, for the most part, ornamented with scenes and texts of chapters from the Book of the Gates, and with large figures of various gods who are occupied in preventing the king from being hindered by the fiends and demons who would obstruct his passage in the underworld; on some of the walls are scenes and extracts relating to the passage of the sun through the hours of the night in the underworld.

The mummy of the king was, presumably, buried in this tomb, but as it was found in the tomb of Amenhetep II in 1898, it must have been removed from its original resting place to that tomb during the period towards the close of the Twentieth Dynasty, when so many of the royal sepulchres in that neighbourhood were broken into and plundered by professional robbers of tombs.

Rameses V
Ra-Usr-Maat-Sekheper-En-Ra, son of the Sun, Ra-Mes-F-Su-Amen-Meri-Amen

Rameses V is thought to have been the brother of Rameses III by some, and the son of Rameses III by others; he reigned about four years, and adopted as his Horus name 'Mighty Bull, Maat Amen'. He built a tomb for himself in the Valley of the Tombs of the Kings at Thebes, but it was afterwards usurped by his successor Rameses VI; his mummy was, presumably, buried in it, though it was found in the tomb of Amenhetep II in 1898, where it had been removed for safety during the troubled times at the close of the Twentieth Dynasty. His building operations and repairs were insignificant.

Rameses VI
Ra-Amen-Maat-Meri-Neb, son of the Sun, Ra-Meses-Amen-Neter-Heq-Annu

Rameses VI was the son of Rameses III, but some think that he never ascended the throne of Egypt. His Horus name was 'Mighty Bull, great one of might, vivifier of the two lands', and he styled himself 'Lord of the shrines of Nekhebet and Uatchet, strong in valour, subduer of hundreds of thousands, the Horus of gold, mighty of years like Ta-thenen, prince, lord of festivals, protector of Egypt, filling the land with great monuments to his name'.

The name of his mother and of his daughter was Ast, or Isis. From the scenes and inscriptions ornamenting the walls of a rock-hewn tomb near the village of Anibeh, which is situated near Ibrim in Nubia, we learn that the 'Royal son of Kesh', called Pennut, dedicated the revenues from a piece of land for ever to the maintenance of the service which was connected with the worship of the statue of the king. The inscriptions give the length and breadth and superficies of this parcel of land, which contained an area of 320,000 square cubits. Pennut was a trusted official of the king, and was overseer of the districts in Nubia, and Uauat and Akita, wherein the gold mines were situated, and he was governor of the neighbouring town. The tomb proves that the office of 'Royal son of Kesh' was still in existence, but it is doubtful if it indicates that Rameses VI possessed any real authority in Nubia, as some would have us believe.

The occurrence of his name on buildings at Karnak seems to show that he carried out certain small repairs in Thebes, but it is certain that he did not undertake building operations on any large scale. The greatest of all the buildings of his time was the tomb which he usurped and added to in the Valley of the Tombs of the Kings at Thebes. It was made originally for Rameses V, but it is clear from the various inscriptions which were placed there by visitors in the Greek and Roman Periods that it was believed to be the Tomb of Memnon; it seems that this belief arose because a portion of the prenomen of the king, Neb-Maat-Ra, is identical with the whole of the prenomen of Amenhetep III. The tomb was originally known as the 'Tomb of the Metempsychosis', and Lepsius called it 'No. 9'; it consists of three corridors which lead into two rectangular chambers of unequal size, and from these two further corridors lead into two rectangular chambers of unequal size, one of which held the sarcophagus, which is now broken. The first three corridors and the two chambers into which they lead probably represent the tomb of Rameses V, for it is clear that the second chamber, which contains four rectangular pillars, was intended to receive the sarcophagus of that king.

When Rameses VI usurped the tomb he penetrated further into the mountain and added the last two corridors and the two chambers into which they lead. The scenes and the inscriptions which relate to them are of interest, and consist for the most part of extracts from the religious works which were popular at that period, i.e.; the *Book of the Gates of the Underworld*, and the *Book of what is in the Underworld*, etc. The most valuable of all are the astronomical representations which are found on the vaulted ceiling of the sarcophagus chamber; the tables of stars which are found on the walls were declared by M. Biot to have been drawn up about 1240 BCE, but later investigators make them about 46 years later. Near the star tables is a scene in which the Boat of the Sun is passing over the back of the double human-headed god Aker, who was the personification of the passage through or under the earth into which the sun entered in the evening, and from which he emerged in the morning. From a papyrus preserved at Liverpool it appears that the tomb of Rameses VI was broken into and robbed in the reign of Rameses IX, and it was probably at this period that the king's sarcophagus was smashed to pieces; the mummy of Rameses VI was removed for safety to the tomb of Amenhetep II, wherein it was found early in 1898.

Rameses VII
Ra-Usr-Maat-Amen-Meri-Setep-En-Ra, son of the Sun, Ra-Meses-Ta-Amen-Neter-Heq-Annu

Rameses VII, 'the emanation of Amen, the divine prince of Annu', was probably the son of Rameses III, and his reign, like the reigns of most of his brothers, was very short, probably not exceeding five or six years. Of the events of his reign nothing is known, and it seems that he neither built temples nor repaired them; the few buildings upon which his name occurs appear to have been usurped by him.

The Horus name of the king was 'Mighty Bull, the gracious (?) king', and we find that this insignificant monarch styled himself 'Lord of the shrines of Nekhebet and Uatchet, protector of Egypt, subduer of the Nine Boys, the Horus of gold, mighty of years like Ra, prince, mighty one of festivals like unto Amen-Ra, the king of the gods.' These facts prove that the titles, which under the Eighteenth Dynasty represented valour and deeds of prowess on the part of the king, were adopted by the successors of Rameses III as a matter of form.

Rameses VII built himself a tomb in the Valley of the Tombs of the Kings at Thebes, but it was not as large as many of those of his predecessors and successors. It consisted of a hall and a corridor, the walls of the latter being ornamented with texts from the religious books of the period, and scenes in which the king is burning incense and pouring out a libation before the god Ptah-Seker-Asar, and the king, dressed in a garb of Osiris, is undergoing the ceremony of purification, which is performed by the priestly official whose title is *am-khent*. On the walls of the hall are figures of the goddesses Urt-hekau and Sekhet-Bast-urt-hekau, and on the ceiling are tables of the risings of stars, and scenes in which are a number of celestial personages and animals, e.g., lion, crocodile, hippopotamus, rain (or cow), etc. The sarcophagus is ornamented with a double line of inscription and with figures of Isis, Nephthys, winged uraei, etc. In the small chamber behind the hall are scenes in which the king is offering to Osiris, and representations of the Boat of the Sun, of the Tet with the attributes of Osiris, etc.

Rameses VIII
Ra-Usr-Maat-Khu-En-Amen, son of the Sun, Ra-Meses-Amen-Meri-Amen

Rameses VIII, the 'spirit of Amen, beloved of Amen', was probably a son of Rameses III; he must have reigned but a very short time, and of the events of his reign we know nothing. It seems that he was unable to build a tomb for himself in the Valley of the Tombs of the Kings, and as his name is not found on any of the buildings at Thebes we may assume that he neither usurped nor repaired them.

Rameses IX
Lord of the land, Sekha-En-Ra-Meri-Amen,
lord of risings, Ra-Meses-Sa-Ptah

Rameses IX was probably a son of Rameses III, and he reigned 18 years alone; as the 19th year of his reign was the first of that of his successor it is clear that Rameses X must have been associated with him in the rule of the kingdom before his death.

Rameses IX was neither a warrior nor a builder, but his name will be always remembered in connection with the great prosecution of the robbers of tombs which was carried out by the government of his day; our knowledge of the prosecution is derived from the Abbott Papyrus in the British Museum, and from papyri in the collections of Lord Amherst and in the Museum at Liverpool. From these documents we may gather that there existed at Thebes, and no doubt in other parts of the country also, a well-organized gang of expert thieves who lived by breaking into the tombs and carrying off the small and valuable objects which they found in them, as well as the ornaments and jewellery with which the mummies of well-to-do people were always decked.

A certain amount of plundering of tombs must always have gone on in Egypt, for the large quantities of funeral furniture which was invariably deposited in fine tombs must have proved an irresistible temptation to many a poverty-stricken thief, whether professional or not. We know that Rameses III was a wealthy man, for otherwise it would have been impossible for him to have made such great gifts to the temples of Heliopolis, Memphis and Thebes, and that he must have left behind him great wealth which his sons inherited. These sons devoted themselves to leading lives of pleasure or indolence, for they neither led their soldiers to war nor built temples in honour of the gods like their ancestors; on the other hand, most of them built large and costly tombs for themselves, and it is pretty certain that they were buried with great pomp and ceremony, and that many costly ornaments and much valuable jewellery were buried with them.

Under the lax rule of Rameses IV, Rameses V, Rameses VI, Rameses VII and Rameses VIII, the power of the government had become weak, and the work of the state was carried out in a very perfunctory manner; the overseers and inspectors neglected their duties, and the subordinate officials took advantage of their remissness and neglected theirs also, and as a result the workmen who were under them scamped their work. We know that the royal tombs were at one time well cared for, and that the priests and officials in charge of them kept them in good order; offerings were offered up at the appointed seasons, and sacrifices were made, and when any portion of the tombs needed repair it was carried out at once. But under the late Rameses the robbers of tombs, seeing the weakness of the central government, turned their attention from the tombs of high officials and wealthy commoners to the sepulchres of the kings, which formed one of the principal features of interest at Thebes. Little by little they corrupted the master masons and workmen who were attached to the great royal Theban necropolis, and eventually a number of scribes and other officials who performed certain duties in connection with it joined them, and the plundering of the tombs of the kings then began on a large scale.

As to the manner in which the thieves worked we obtain a very good idea from the confession of one of the thieves which is preserved in one of Lord Amherst [of Hackney]'s papyri; he says that he and his companions effected an entry into the tomb of Sebek-ein-sa-f where the mummies of the king and queen Nub-kha-s were buried, and that the tomb itself was protected by masonry, and that its entrance was filled up with broken stones, which were covered over with slabs of stones. 'These we demolished entirely, and we found the [queen] lying there., We opened their coffins and their inner cases which were in them, and we found the venerable mummy of the king. There were two daggers (or, swords) there, and many amulets and necklaces of gold on his neck; his head was covered with gold, and the venerable mummy of the king was decorated with gold throughout. The inner case [of his coffin] was decorated with gold and with silver, both within and without, and was covered with precious stones of every kind. We tore off the gold which we found on the venerable mummy of the god, and the amulets and the necklaces which were on his neck, and the materials on which they rested. And having found the royal wife also we tore off all that we found on it likewise and then we burnt their swathings. We carried off the funeral furniture which we found with the mummies, and which [consisted of] gold, and silver, and copper vases, and we divided the gold which we found upon the venerable mummies of these two gods, and the amulets, and the necklaces, and the cases into eight parts.'

The names of some of the eight thieves were Hapu, Aaru-en-Amen, Nesi-Amen, Amen-em-heb, Ka-em-Uast, and Nefer; the eight thieves were beaten with a stick upon their feet and hands, and it was by these means that the man who turned 'king's evidence' was made to speak and say what he and his friends had done. It is quite clear that the thieves could not have broken into the tomb of Sebek-em-sa-f if a proper watch had been kept, and that some of the officials of the necropolis must have helped them to dispose of the stolen property. The priests who took over the stolen goods could sell the funeral furniture to the relatives of people who had died recently, and thus it was to the interest of both priest and thief to plunder the tombs of the wealthy; many an object made under one dynasty has been re-used under another, and as the space in the mountains and elsewhere in Egypt available for sepulchres has always been very limited, many a tomb was used over and over again. This fact has not been sufficiently taken into consideration in dating Egyptian antiquities, and it has given rise to considerable discussion among archaeologists concerning the age of many objects of an important character. A tomb was maintained in good order as long as the relatives and descendants of the deceased provided an endowment sufficient for the purpose; when this came to an end the tomb was abandoned, and it was either plundered by the professional robber, or its occupier was quietly removed by the priest of the necropolis and his furniture used for a new burial.

The prosecution of the thieves undertaken by Rameses IX began on the 18th day of the third month of the season Shat, in the 14th year of his reign, and the court of inquiry was formed by Kha-em-Uast, the governor of Thebes, the trustee of the property of the priestesses of Amen-Ra called Nes-Amen, and the herald of Pharaoh called Nefer-ka-Ra-em-pa-Amen, and these officials employed to help them in their investigations the head of the police; Pa-ser-aa, the governor of the Necropolis; some officers of police; Paibauk, the scribe of the governor of the city; Paia-neferu, the chief scribe of the governor of the treasury; and two priests called Pa-an-khau, and Ur-Amen. This body of high officials went through the Valley of the Tombs of the Kings at Thebes and inspected the tombs there; the first tomb which they examined, that of Amenhetep I, which had been reported to the governor Kha-em-Uast by the sub-governor Pa-ser, possibly on untrustworthy evidence, to have been broken into, was found to be uninjured. They examined the tomb of Antef, and though the building itself was in ruins, they found that the stele which represented the king with his dog Behuka between his legs, was still standing; and when they came to the tomb of Sebek-em-sa-f they found that the thieves had got into the chamber and had wrecked the mummies of the king and queen.

Of 10 tombs which the commission examined they only found one which had really been broken into, though they discovered among the other nine damage made by the attempts which the thieves had made to break through the walls. A number of tombs of private persons had been entered by the thieves, who had torn to pieces the mummies of several priestesses of Amen in their search for gold ornaments, jewellery, etc.; it seems as if the men who had committed this act of sacrilege were well known, for they were at once arrested.

We have already seen that the eight men who plundered the tomb of Sebek-em-sa-f were brought before the commission and that one of them confessed, but we are not told what punishment was inflicted upon them eventually. While the commission was still inquiring into the robberies a certain man called Pai-kharei, the son of Khareui and of the woman called 'Little Cat', who had declared three years before that he had been in the tomb of Queen Ast, the wife of Rameses III, and had stolen some things therefrom and had destroyed them, was arrested by order of the court, and having been blindfolded was taken to the necropolis. When he had arrived there his eyes were uncovered and he was ordered to make his way to the tomb from which he said he had stolen certain things, but he went into the tomb of one of the children of Rameses II and to the house of one of the officials of the necropoli, and declared that these were the places to which he referred in his evidence. The commission, of course, disbelieved him, but though they beat him upon his hands and feet they could not make him admit that he knew of any other place, and he told them that even if they were to cut off his nose and ears, or to flay him alive, they could obtain no further information from him.

The commission had been appointed as the result of the information concerning the robbery of royal tombs which had been supplied by Pa-ser, the sub-governor of Thebes, to the governor Kha-em-Uast, but it seemed as if the court of inquiry which the commission had appointed had been treated with contempt, for the tomb of Amenhetep had not been broken into, as Pa-ser had declared, and Pai-kharei had himself proved that the evidence which he had given three years before was false. Either Pa-ser had himself been deceived, or he had made a serious accusation against Pa-ser-aa, the governor of the royal necropolis, with the view of doing him a grievous injury in the eyes of the governor Kha-em-Uast. There is every reason to believe that Pa-ser was correct, but that the court of inquiry made its exaimination of the royal tombs in a very perfunctory manner, and that it did not, in consequence, examine into matters so closely as it should have done.

It is interesting to note that the tomb of Nub-kheper-Ra Antuf, which the court of inquiry pronounced to be in 'sound condition', is stated by its own report to have had a hole in it two and a half cubits long, which had been made by the thieves, who could have made their way through it into the tomb whenever they had an opportunity of returning to their nefarious work. The fact that the court of inquiry could regard a tomb which had suffered such damage to be in 'sound condition' proves that they took a very optimistic view of the matter.

Pa-ser was extremely dissatisfied with the result of the work of the commission, and he told the governor Kha-em-Uast so in an angry letter, wherein he threatened to write and report the whole matter to the king. How the affair ended we know not, but it seems that the governor found some means of shutting the mouth of Pa-ser, and that the matter was never brought before the king at all. What happened was what has happened always, and what always will happen in a purely oriental court of inquiry; the man who brings the charge is proved by the false-swearing of hired witnesses to be either misinformed or a liar, a number of people are wrongfully accused and punished, and the guilty man pours into the bosoms of the judges and other officials the gifts which blind the eyes.

The chief building operations which were undertaken in the reign of Rameses IX were carried on by Amenhetep, the high priest of Amen-Ra, who under this king enjoyed such influence and power as were never possessed by any of his predecessors. This official says, in an inscription which is dated in the 10th year of the king's reign, that he took in hand the restoration of certain buildings which were first set up in the time of Usertsen I, and that he rebuilt the walls, and repaired the columns, and provided new doors of acacia wood, and made the whole edifice beautiful to look upon. It is curious enough to find the high priest of Amen recording the restoration of the building by himself, instead of by the king, but it is more remarkable still to find him going on to say that he built himself a new house with fine wooden doors furnished with copper bolts, and that he made and set up a statue in honour of each of the high priests of Amen in a courtyard which he planted with trees. Hitherto it had been the proud boast of every great king that he had repaired, or beautified, or added to the great temple of Amen-Ra, the king of the gods, and that he had made such and such gifts towards the maintenance of the service of the god and of the exalted position of his priests.

It was a fatal day for Egypt when the high priest of Amen was allowed by Rameses IX to usurp the proper functions of the king, but, on the other hand, small blame must be attached to the high priest for usurping royal powers, for unless he and his immediate predecessors had done so the brotherhood of the priests of Amen would have been ruined. None of the sons of Rameses III had contributed by foreign conquests to the coffers of the priesthood, and this fact in itself was sufficient to make the priests of Amen anxious about ways and means, for without the tribute of vassal nations or the money derived from successful trading, the buildings and service of the great god of Thebes could not be maintained.

In another place in the inscription already mentioned we are told that Rameses IX, with the gods Menthu, Amen-Ra, Harmachis, Ptah and Thoth as witnesses, and in the presence of Nes-Amen, a high official in the priesthood of Amen, and Nefer-ka-Ra-em-pa-Amen, the royal herald, solemnly gave to the high priest of Amen, Amenhetep, the son of Ramessu-nekht, the power to levy taxes on the people for the support of the temple and priesthood of Amen-Ra. Thus Rameses IX by solemn decree gave the greatest power which the king of Egypt possessed, i.e., the right to levy taxes on the people and to raise money, into the hands of the high priest, who built a house of a most royal magnificence for himself, and dedicated statues of his predecessors in the courtyard thereof.

Four years after this decree was promulgated the prosecution of the robbers of the royal tombs began; whether it was due to the initiative of the high-priest Amenhetep or to that of the governor of the city cannot be said, but we may assign the abortive nature of the results obtained by the court of inquiry to the influence of the high priest of Amen, who had discovered that a large number of scribes and subordinate members of the priesthood of Amen were implicated in the robberies.

Rameses IX built himself a large tomb in the Valley of the Tombs of the Kings, wherein presumably he was buried. It consists of a staircase and three corridors, the first having four side chambers, and three large rectangular chambers which are joined by two short corridors; the last chamber held the sarcophagus. The walls are ornamented with scenes from the religious works which were popular at that period, and with texts from the *Book of praising Re* and from the Theban Recension of the *Book of the* Dead; of the last-named work a text of Chapter 125 appears on a wall in the third corridor. In the sarcophagus chamber are some extremely interesting astronomical texts and scenes.

Rameses X
Ra-Nefer-Kau-Setep-En-Ra, son of the Sun, Ra-Meses-Merer-Amen-Kha-[Em]-Uast

Rameses X, 'beloved of Amen, rising like Ra in Thebes', was probably a son of Rameses III, and the length of his reign did not exceed six or eight years; a few papyri dated in his reign exist, and from these and a small number of miscellaneous objects which are inscribed with his names and titles, we know that the Horus name of Rameses X was 'Mighty Bull, rising [like Ra] in Thebes'. He adopted as a matter of form the old title 'Lord of the shrines of Nekhebet and Uatchet', and also styled himself, 'mighty of valour, vivifier of the two lands, the Horus of gold, mighty of years like Ptah-Tanen, mighty prince of kings, destroyer of the Nine Bows'.

Rameses X built himself a tomb in the Valley of the Tombs of the Kings at Thebes, but it is relatively small and it seems not to have been completed; the scenes and inscriptions are of little interest, and the workmanship is poor. In many ways the tomb indicates the increasing poverty of the kings of Egypt, and it seems as though the priests of Amen either would not or could not afford to provide a large and richly ornamented tomb like the sepulchres of his predecessors; moreover, both priests and king probably felt that it was useless to provide expensive funeral furniture, etc., which the thieves might steal and burn, or the subordinate officials of the necropolis carry off and sell for other burials. The prosecutions of the tomb robbers which had taken place in the 14th and 16th years of the reign of Rameses IX had resulted in the beating with sticks of a number of the robbers who belonged to the lower classes, but they did not stop the plundering of the tombs.

In the first year of the reign of Rameses X about 60 people were arrested, presumably by order of 'the high priest of Amen-Ra, the king of the gods, Amenhetep, the son of the high priest of Amen in the Apts (i.e., Karnak and Luxor), B.Rameses-nekht', and were charged with plundering the royal tombs. The tombs of the kings of the Middle Empire had been probably cleared out by the thieves by this time, for we learn that the tombs of Seti I and Rameses II were now attacked by them. The ringleaders appear to have been priests and scribes who were attached to the service of the temples of Amen and other gods, and they succeeded in stealing and selling large quantities of the funeral furniture which had been deposited in the chambers near the entrances of the tombs of Seti I and Rameses II; a number of women were implicated in the thefts, and it is probable that these disposed in the daytime of the objects which their husbands and brothers had stolen during the night. In fact the more the document which records the arrest of the 60 suspected persons is considered, the more clear it becomes that large numbers of the officials and others who lived on the western bank at Thebes were connected with and interested in the robberies.

The thieves must have been introduced into the tombs by the masons and workmen who had helped to construct them, and they were told what to seek and where to look by those who had planned the tombs and who had probably assisted at the burial ceremonies. All who remember how some 30 years ago, whole villages on the western bank of the Nile at Thebes lived ostensibly by farming, but actually by plundering ancient tombs and selling what they found to travellers and others, will understand exactly the condition of things which must have existed in the days of the later Rameses kings. The modern thieves ransacked the tombs by night, often with the knowledge and help of the government officials who were paid to prevent them from doing so, and those men were the most successful who were lucky enough to find the shafts and tunnels which the thieves had sunk and driven in ancient days into the rock-hewn tombs of the great Theban necropolis. The thieves of old cared chiefly for amulets made of gold and precious stones and for jewellery in general, and when they had stripped the mummies of such things they left the papyri and articles of funeral furniture strewn on the floors of the tombs; some of the greatest treasures of European Museums consist of objects which were tossed aside by them as worthless.

Rameses XI
Neb ta Ra-Kheper-Maat-Setep-En-Ra, son of the Sun, Ra-Messu[-Meri]-Amen

Rameses XI adopted as his Horus name the title 'Mighty Bull, whom Ra hath made to rise', of his reign, which must have been a very short one, nothing is known. Whether this king built a tomb for himself cannot be said, but neither a tomb nor mummy inscribed with his name has yet been discovered.

Formerly in Egyptological books which dealt with history and chronology it was customary to insert after Rameses XI a king whose prenomen was Usr-Maat-Ra-setep-nu- (or, en) Ra and whose nomen was Ra-meses meri Amen, and he was usually called Rameses XII. This king is made known to us by the famous stele which records the story of the 'Possessed Princess of Bekhten', of which the following brief summary must be given.

The king Rameses, beloved of Amen, was according to his wont in Western Mesopotamia, and the chiefs of all the lands came to pay homage to him and to offer him gifts; each chief brought according to his power, some gold, others lapis lazuli, and others turquoise, but the prince of Bekhten added to his gifts his eldest daughter, who was a beautiful girl. Rameses was pleased with her, and when she came to Egypt with him he made her a royal wife.

In the 15th year of the reign of Rameses an envoy came from the prince of Bekhten and asked the king of Egypt to send a skilled physician to his country to heal the prince's daughter Bent-reshet, the younger sister of the royal wife to whom the name of Ra-neferu had been given in Egypt. Thereupon Rameses summoned all the sages of his court to his presence, and asked them to choose from among themselves a skilled physician to go to Bekhten, and their choice fell upon the royal scribe Tehuti-em-heb.

When the Egyptian physician arrived in Bekhten he found that Bent-reshet was possessed of a devil which he could not cast out, therefore the prince of Bekhten sent a second time to Egypt for help, and besought the king to send a god to heal his daughter. Rameses then went into the temple and asked the god Khensu-nefer-hetep if he would go to Bekhten to deliver the princess from the power of the demon, and the god agreed to do so. The figure of the god was placed in a boat, and escorted by a large number of horses and chariots arrived in Bekhten after a journey of 17 months.

The prince of Bekhten welcomed the god with great ceremony, and as soon as his daughter was brought into the presence of the god his saving power healed her straightway. The devil who was driven out of the princess said to Khensu, 'Grateful and welcome is thy coming unto us, O great god, the vanquisher of the hosts of darkness; Bekhten is thy city, the inhabitants thereof are thy slaves, and I am thy servant; and I will depart unto the place whence I come that I may gratify thee, for unto this end hast thou come hither.' At the devil's request the prince of Bekhten made a feast in his honour, and when it was over Khensu gave the command, and the devil departed to the country which he loved.

As soon as the devil was gone the prince of Bekhten determined to keep the Egyptian god in his city always, but at the end of three years, four months, and five days Khensu left the country in the form of a hawk of gold and flew away to Egypt. When the prince of Bekhten knew that the god had departed to Egypt he sent back his image with many gifts and with a large escort of soldiers and horses to Egypt, wherein it arrived in the 33rd year of the reign of Rameses.

Now there are several points in the narrative, to say nothing of the peculiarities of grammar and spelling, which prove that we are dealing with a version of a piece of legendary history, and not with a record of actual facts. In the first place Rameses XII, as he was styled, was never in Western Mesopotamia, and he neither received gifts from the chiefs of that country nor married the daughter of one of them; but Rameses II did all these things, and the titles of 'Mighty Bull, the form of risings', the 'stablished one [among] kings like Temu', etc., in reality apply to him and to no other Rameses. We must therefore regard the story as having reference to Rameses II, and this 'Rameses XII' must disappear from the list of the kings of the Twentieth Dynasty.

The text of the story which has come down to us belongs to a very late date, as Prof. Erman has proved, and it is clearly the work of the priests of

Khensu-nefer-hetep, who wished to spread abroad the fame of their god, and to make known the great favour with which he was regarded by Rameses II. Finally, we must not forget that the journey to Bekhten is said to have occupied a period of 17 months, and if this be true Bekhten must have been situated away in Central or Eastern Asia. It is possible that the fame of Rameses II, or of some greater Egyptian king, may have been carried to the far East by some nomad tribe, but it is quite certain that the renown of any of the sons of Rameses III was never spread abroad in this fashion.

Rameses XII
Ra-Men-Maat-Setep-En-Ptah, son of the Sun, Ra-Meses-Merer-Amen-Kha-[Em] Uast-Neter-Heq-Annu

Rameses XII, who was formerly known as Rameses XIII, chose for his Horus name the title 'Mighty Bull, beloved of (or, loving) Ra', and he styled himself, 'Lord of the shrines of Nekhebet and Uatchet, subduer of hundreds of thousands, the Horus of gold, mighty one of strength, vivifier of the two lands, Prince, life, strength, and health! resting upon Maat, making to be at peace the two lands'. He reigned 27 years, a fact which is made known to us by the stele of the scribe Heru-a ... but so far as is known he did not undertake any war or military expedition, and was, to all appearances, content to lead the indolent life of his brothers or kinsmen.

In the temple of Khensu at Thebes he decorated the walls of the larger outer chambers which had been left unornamented by Rameses III, and he added a number of decorative scenes on the walls and columns with cup-shaped capitals, in the hypostyle hall of the same building, wherein he is represented making offerings to various gods. The name of Rameses XII appears in a few places in the great temple of Amen-Ra at Karnak, but it is doubtful if he carried out there any restorations or repairs. A few objects inscribed with his name have been found at Abydos, and it has been argued that he carried on certain works there, but if he did, all traces of them have disappeared. He built a tomb for himself in the Valley of the Tombs of the Kings at Thebes, but the decoration of the walls and ceilings of its two corridors and three rectangular chambers was never finished; in the last chamber is a shaft which seems to indicate that the tomb builders of that time resorted to the old form of the tomb with a deep pit leading to the mummy chamber as a means of preventing thieves from plundering the tomb.

We have already seen how Amenhetep, the high priest of Amen, had obtained from Rameses IX the right to levy taxes from the people, and how he succeeded not only in preserving the privileges and power which his father Ra-meses-nekht had acquired, but also in adding to them, and we have now to notice that Her-Heru, the high priest of Amen who succeeded him, was able to make himself at least the equal of the king in power. On some of the reliefs found on the walls of the temple of Khensu at Karnak we see Her-Heru with the uraeus, the symbol of royalty, on his brow, and we learn from the texts which accompany the scenes that he styled himself the commander-in-chief of the army, and the 'governor of the South and North'; these reliefs were sculptured whilst Rameses XII was still alive, and so we must understand that before his death there were living in Thebes two kings of Egypt, the one *de jure* and the other *de facto*.

Her-Heru was astute enough to make himself chief of the army, and, as his predecessor had obtained the mastery over the treasury of the country, his authority over the material and spiritual resources of the country was complete. Of the circumstances which attended the death of Rameses XII we know nothing, and whether Her-Heru waited for him to die before he ascended the throne of Egypt as the first king of the Twenty-First (Theban) Dynasty, or whether he compelled him to abdicate and retire and eat the 'bread of banishment' in the Great Oasis, as Brugsch thought, cannot be said. But whilst the high priest of Amen was devoting all his energies to the attainment of the crown and throne of Egypt and of the office of 'royal prince of Kesh', he steadily neglected the affairs of the Delta, and took no steps to protect it from invasion or to safeguard its interests.

If he had been doing his best to break up the union between the kingdoms of the South and North, which had cost the kings of the Eighteenth Dynasty so much trouble to make, he could hardly have acted otherwise. There may, of course, have been good reasons for his acting as he did in the matter, especially when we remember that there must have existed in all parts of Egypt at that time many male descendants of Rameses II and Rameses III, each of whom would consider that he had more right to the throne of Egypt than the high priest of Amen. In Upper Egypt, however, no claimant of this kind to the throne would have had the smallest chance of success, because during the period of the rule of Rameses IV to that of Rameses XII the high priests of Amen had succeeded in winning over to their side the principal member of the official class which had sprung into being in Egypt, and in laying their hands upon the endowments, both private and public, of the principal sanctuaries of the country of the South and of Nubia.

As the god Amen had been made to usurp the attributes of all the older gods of Egypt, and had even been forced into the position of Osiris as god and judge of the dead, so his priests had made themselves the representatives of all the old nobility of Egypt, and the equal of the king. Their influence over the priests and people of Memphis, Heliopolis, Tanis and other large cities of the North was not so great, and thus it became possible for a man whose name was Nes-su-Ba-neb-Tet, who was possibly a descendant of Rameses II, to proclaim himself king of Egypt and to establish himself king at Tanis, the city of his great ancestor and the 'House of Rameses' *par excellence*. But the high priest of Amen, Her-Heru, who called himself Sa-Amen, 'Son of Amen', was, we know, lord of the South, and Thebes was his capital: it follows then that Egypt was once more divided into two kingdoms, the one ruled by a descendant of the legitimate line of kings, and the other by the high priest of Amen, who attempted to legalize the power which he had usurped by means of his marriage with the lady Netchemet.

Her-Heru was the founder of the dynasty of priest-kings at Thebes, while at Tanis a rival dynasty was founded by Nessu-Ba-neb-Tet, whose name was Graecized by Manetho under the form of Smendes; we must therefore divide the Twenty-First Dynasty of the kings of Egypt into two parts – I. Kings of Thebes, and II. King of Tanis.

FLAME TREE PUBLISHING